"The rain," Schalberg barked. "The rain! The airstrip is mud!" He looked at his watch and shrieked out the order for the men at either end of the strip to douse the bonfires that had been lit, by prearrangement, at the cessation of the firing. From overhead they heard the sound of the Condor, its four big engines feathering back for its landing . . .

The engines reversed with a throat-rattling roar, and the plane skidded onward, not slowing down, even gaining momentum, tail slewing, white muck flying off its landing gear. It plummeted ahead with a sudden, horrible lurching swoop up the far rim, over it, and into the outcrop called the Giant's Chair with a metal-crushing crash that split the night asunder. The crash left a momentary, gaping silence. Then flames erupted from amidships, followed by a thunderous roar and two more explosions as the wing-tip gas fuel pods erupted. Columns of flames ascended furiously into the night, and the desert was lit for miles around in a ghastly orange light . . .

By Jake Page
*Published by Ballantine Books:*

*Del Rey® science fiction*
OPERATION SHATTERHAND

*Mo Bowdre mysteries*
THE DEADLY CANNON
THE STOLEN GODS
THE KNOTTED STRINGS
THE LETHAL PARTNER

# OPERATION SHATTERHAND

## Jake Page

A Del Rey® Book
BALLANTINE BOOKS • NEW YORK

A Del Rey® Book
Published by Ballantine Books
Copyright © 1996 by Jake Page
Map copyright © 1996 by Random House, Inc.

All rights reserved under International and Pan-American Copyright Conventions. Published in the United States by Ballantine Books, a division of Random House, Inc., New York, and simultaneously in Canada by Random House of Canada Limited, Toronto.

http://www.randomhouse.com

Library of Congress Catalog Card Number: 96-96367

ISBN 0-345-39721-5

Manufactured in the United States of America

First Edition: November 1996

10   9   8   7   6   5   4   3   2   1

Dedicated to
Edward T. Hall
and my wife Susanne
and our Navajo and Hopi friends

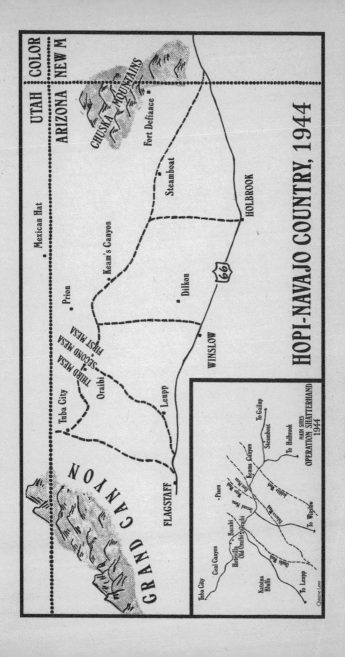

HOPI-NAVAJO COUNTRY, 1944

MAIN SITES
OPERATION SHATTERHAND
1944

# Author's Note

After a considerable amount of debate in the offices of the Oberkommando des Heeres, the German Army High Command in World War II, what came to be called Operation Shatterhand was launched. Shatterhand is a reference familiar to virtually any German in the 1930s and 1940s who had learned to read, and a testimony to the romantic fantasies that ever palpitate in the Teutonic breast, especially in the clangorous times of war and iron. Shatterhand was a frontiersman known to generations of German boyhood for his unrivaled skills and canny wisdom. He was a Leatherstocking Siegfried of the wild American West invented by Karl May, one of the best-selling authors of all time. No feat of manly action lay beyond Old Shatterhand's talents, or beyond those of his friend and partner in the great days of the American frontier, Winnetou, mighty chief of the Apaches, the very paragon of savage nobility: a warrior-philosopher in elk-skins who spoke in the heroic rhythms of Longfellow's *Hiawatha*. German boys feasted on the perils these two noble partners faced everywhere they rode in the vast stretches of the desert West of America, and these same boys surely imagined themselves pricking their wrists and sharing sacred blood with them, and riding too— blood brothers all—to the next escapade, and the next.

# THE GATHERING STORM

The beginning of all war may be discerned
not only by the first act of hostility,
but by the counsels and preparations foregoing.
—JOHN MILTON

# 1937: Jeddito

Ben Cameron was sure he was being watched.

Not by the four Navajos who patiently troweled dirt away from the now visible tops of geometric rock walls, sifting for the crude remnants of earlier human lives. Each Navajo worked within a four-by-four-foot square Cameron had marked off with stakes and string that morning. Their faces in deep shadow under broad-brimmed and high-crowned black hats, the Navajos knelt prayerfully in their separate quadrants, long black hair tied up in buns behind their heads, peering at the ground with the unbreakable concentration of monks deciphering the texts of an old and slightly puzzling wisdom.

Overhead, a molten white sun bleached the world around them. The crumbling yellow sandstone behind them was colorless, the gray-green sage that stretched out before them for miles also colorless. Low mesas fifteen miles away on the horizon seemed insubstantial in the mid-afternoon glare. The nape of Ben Cameron's neck prickled.

There was no one else within miles, no one but Cameron and the four Navajos who were absorbed by their attention to the sandy earth which, on billowing winds, had filled in these old walls, silencing forever their real meaning and the meaning of the pots and whisks and other artifacts made in a time that had passed without the notice of the world. For the Navajos, this was a home of the Old Ones, the enemy. Here on the high ground overlooking Jeddito Wash under the blue-black core of the sky, the Navajos scraped, and murmured parts of old songs that could make the world right even as they, with their trowels, interfered in a place of the dead.

After nearly two months in this part of the vast reservation lands of the Navajos and the Hopis, Ben Cameron had absorbed enough to feel that he was being watched. He turned and looked at the colorless mesa behind him. Nothing. He peered into a purple shadow under an overhanging slab of sandstone—had he seen a lizard whip into the purple? If so, it had now certainly paused, motionless, staring into the stillness. What did a lizard see? Motion? If so, its world was for the moment mostly empty. Such short lives, lived so urgently in a world without time. But it was not the lizard who watched in the heat, nor the Navajos, scraping away dirt, spurred to such a strange task by cash money paid out to satisfy the white man's inexplicable curiosity about a past that made no difference to them: the Anasazi. The others.

Here in this high desertland of scrub and piñon pine, sand and rock, the young archeologist had begun to wonder if the locals were not right in perceiving that the landscape was presided over by other sensibilities, what the Navajos called the Holy People, inherent in the rocks, the wind, even the lizard. Idiotically, a song fragment came to his mind, a new one he had heard on the radio a week earlier during a logistical trip to Winslow, the border town to the south of the reservation: "Poor Johnny One Note . . ." Here there was only one note of importance. Rain. It had not rained now for two months.

"Poor Johnny One Note . . ." The rest of the lyrics escaped him. "Ta-dah-da, ta-dah-da, ta-*dah*-da, ta-DAAA . . ." he hummed to himself in the silence of the day.

Ben Cameron had been schooled in the outdoors, at an expensive but rustic boarding school in the mountains outside Santa Fe that was both a school and a ranch. Without his having much of a say in it, his father had sent him off to the Southwest at age fourteen, thus fulfilling what he took to be his paternal duties, and also completing an estrangement that had begun years before, a silence of the heart. After graduating three years later, an expert wrangler and horseman, a competent mechanic, and a fair student, Ben Cameron drifted around the Southwest for a year, assuaging an appetite he had never felt or imagined during his boyhood in the East—a yen to explore each new vista of stark land that lay before him, to be alone in the almost melancholy clarity of the air, the towering indifference of mountains. Then, almost by accident, he found himself enrolled in the University of New Mexico, sifting through the course lists, again almost by accident focusing on the field of archeology. In the spring of 1937, in his junior year, he had received a letter from the Office of the Commissioner, Bureau of Indian Affairs, United States Department of the Interior. Suspicious, he opened the envelope and discovered that none other than John Collier himself, the commissioner, was inviting him to be part of a team that would undertake several archeological digs on the Hopi-Navajo reservation that coming summer. He would be assisted on his digs by Navajo workers, part of an effort to create employment on the reservation as well as produce useful knowledge of the native past.

He wrote back by return mail, eagerly accepting this posting into the unknown, and was informed by mail a few weeks later that he should report to the Keams Canyon Indian Agency on June 1 or before. He would be paid ten dollars a week, good pay for a college kid in the seventh year of the Great Depression.

Four years earlier, embarked on his urgent if aimless quest, he had driven through the Navajo reservation in a Model A Ford, finding a roadless wasteland with dry arroyos to navigate, wagon tracks in the sand to follow and then lose sight of, with—every now and then, far off in the distance tucked up against an outcrop of rock or just over the lip of some higher scrubland—a lonely Navajo camp. Each seemed improbable in its remoteness, and each seemed much the same as its remote neighbors: a low octagonal house he would learn was called a hogan, an open shade house made of branches, a ragged corral or two, a herd of sheep tended by a woman or a kid. His trip had taken him past the three high mesas in the middle of Navajo country that almost imperceptibly were topped by the ancient Hopi villages—villages with names like Walpi, Shongopavi, Oraibi, brooding hundreds of feet above the Painted Desert. On the horizon, almost any horizon, were improbable shapes, needles, buttes, mesas like motionless battleships in a frozen brown sea. It had taken him five days to cross these Indian lands—wordless days, stopping for the night wherever he was at day's end, sleeping under familiar stars—and he took his first welcome bath in the San Juan River, which sent its chilled snow-melt waters hastening toward the grander gorges of the Colorado.

He was haunted by the land he discovered. Rattling along on the dirt tracks with only the rarest signs of life—a part of a wire fence, perhaps, or the occasional abandoned wagon sagging into the earth, a golden eagle spiraling far overhead, the glimpse of pronghorns far off—Ben Cameron had easily imagined himself as the first white man to see this countryside, and thus in a way it became his.

So he had looked forward to his government job in the desert with a combination of avid delight and uneasiness bordering at times on terror. He knew something about doing archeology, but what did he know about running a dig, even a small one? He had never run anything. And running a dig with Navajos? He didn't know much about Navajos, or Hopis, except what he had read in a survey anthropology course on North American Indians, and the pressure of course work prohibited much by way of further study of these two tribes. He learned that it was one of his professors who had suggested his name to Commissioner Collier, and he shared some of his doubts with the man.

"Don't worry," the professor had told him. "Just talk quietly and don't look a Navajo in the eye. You'll do fine."

One of his Navajo crew, the one called Slink and the only one who spoke English, stood up in his quadrant and twisted his head back and forth on his neck. He was a big man—broad-chested, narrow-hipped, taller by a few inches than the others and taller too than Cameron. Slink turned toward him and said, "Smoke?"

"Yeah, time for a break."

Slink said some quiet thing in Navajo, and the other men put down their trowels and stood up. Cameron thought again about these quiet Navajo voices. Like a breeze in a piñon tree. Like a courtesy to ... to whomever presided over the land, maybe. He fished a green and red pack of Lucky Strikes from his shirt pocket as the men approached, their eyes averted, and tapped out a cigarette for each, then one for himself. He lit all five with a wooden match struck on the seat of his jeans, a trick that, he had noticed, amused the Navajos in some mysterious way. They stood smoking, looking south, relaxed and comfortable. Cameron was surprised to find how comfortable he felt with these men, these strange, self-confident men with their Mongolian bearing, after only two months among them. He had been told a few days earlier by the trader at Keams Canyon that the local Navajos had their own name for him. Since Navajos never call anyone by their name, the trader said, he would never hear it unless the trader told him. And of course the trader was expected to pass it along in the odd minuet of reservation communications. It was a Navajo

word meaning "digger of holes." Not very grand,
Cameron had thought, not "warrior for truth," say, but he
was extremely proud to have what seemed like a real
identity among these people.

Slink exhaled some smoke and gestured to the east
with puckered lips and a lift of the jaw, the Navajo way
of pointing. *"Chitti,"* he said. Far off, about six miles,
a small cloud of dust was visible in the glare, slowly
making its way west through the sagebrush scrubland.
Cameron wondered who it might be. Maybe the trader
from Keams, coming back from Holbrook. The Navajos
flipped their cigarette butts into the sand and went back
to work.

Fifteen minutes later Cameron made out that the *chitti*
was a black truck, crawling toward Jeddito Wash below
them. Not the trader's. Not any vehicle he had seen on
the reservation. There were only a handful, mostly GM
flatbed trucks like the one parked a few yards away, and
Model A Fords, these mostly the property of the Indian
Agency, and this was not one of them. Tourists, he
thought, and he looked forward to seeing how they fared
when they reached the dry wash below and had to cross
it. There was only one way to do this: find the right place
and gun it screaming down to the sandy bottom, praying
all the while to any and all gods, and hope the momentum was enough to carry you up the other side. No driver
Cameron knew of on the reservation had been blessed
with a perfect record. Distantly, the truck's engine could
be heard groaning unevenly.

A few more minutes and Cameron knew they were
greenhorns. As the truck approached the wash about a
quarter of a mile away and two hundred feet below them,
he could see that its bed had been covered over like a
little house and painted black. It must be an inferno in
there, he thought. The truck paused at the edge of the
wash like an uncertain steer, and presently a man got out
of the passenger's side. He peered down into the wash

and walked a few paces east, then a few paces west. He got back into the truck and it went gingerly over the side, reaching the bottom, where it came to a halt, engine screaming, narrow back wheels spinning helplessly, sinking into the sand. The Navajos were all on their feet, watching, smiling.

*"Billegannas,"* Slink said, using the Navajo word for white men, and again Cameron felt a twinge of warmth. As if, in the Navajos' minds, he was in a slightly different category than the normal run of incompetent white aliens who turned up from time to time for incomprehensible reasons on Navajo lands.

The engine in the wash stopped screaming, the truck shuddered and died, and two men leapt out of it in a state of high agitation. They waved their arms at the truck, at each other, and bent over to peer at the back wheels. They argued. The driver got back in the truck, the engine roared to life, the passenger put his shoulder to the back of the truck and heaved as the engine screamed again, its wheels spewing dust over the man. The truck slewed, wiggled, and the back end sank farther into the sand.

Without a word the Navajos and Cameron got aboard their flatbed, Cameron driving, and headed down into the wash, watching as the two men below came to the realization that they were, miraculously, saved. On the edge of the wash the archeology team stopped and got out, and Cameron wondered what they must look like to the greenhorns, these four big men with slit eyes and big black hats, a scouting party sent forth by Genghis Khan maybe. He squatted down on his heels, pushed his straw cowboy hat back with a thumb and called out: "Where you coming from?"

One of the men in the wash said, "We're stuck."

"Yeah, I can see that. Where you coming from?"

"We come from Holbrook. We're stuck."

Cameron looked at their truck, canted backward in the dust. It was covered with dents. There was something

odd about it. It looked as if the dents had been inflicted
. . . all at once? It looked like a new truck, with more
dents than even a greenhorn could inflict on a truck driving it across the desert. And that housing on the back?

"Where you headed?" Cameron asked, taking a curious pleasure in prolonging their agony.

The man below shrugged, and pointed up at Cameron.

"We can get her out for you," Cameron said.

"We'll pay," the man said.

"My friends here would appreciate that."

Slink said something in Navajo and the others were
silent.

"What do you think?" Cameron said, and the Navajos
went back to their truck, selecting two shovels from the
tools there. A half hour later, after a lot of digging, fetching of old driftwood to put under the wheels, and a sus-
tained heaving, along with subtle pressure on the gas
pedal by Cameron, the black truck stood on high ground.

"What brings you out here?" Cameron said sociably
after the driver of the black truck, squinting in the sun
and bowing slightly, handed him a five dollar bill, which
he in turn handed to Slink.

"Fish," the man said. "We are hoping to find new markets for fish."

*"Fish?"* Cameron laughed. "Fish? In the desert?" He
turned to Slink. "You got a word for fish?"

"Yeah," the big Navajo said. "But we don't eat things
that grow in water."

Cameron looked back at the man. He was wearing
new jeans, stiff as cardboard. His shirt looked new. The
other man was dressed the same. Both were blue-eyed—
supplicant eyes, the eyes of the lost—and both had light
brown hair, matted with sweat.

"I don't think you're gonna sell much fish out here,"
Cameron said. Nobody who came out here was normal,
he thought, but this was . . . fishmongers in the desert?

"My name is Carl Mandel," the man said tentatively.

"This is interesting country. So isolated. So remote. You can see such long distances."

"And there aren't any fish to speak of," Cameron said, unable to keep from smiling. "Not much interest in fish. Maybe a coupla mackerel snappers at the agency, the Indian Agency in Keams, you know, they'd eat fish on Fridays, but chicken's what they get. I don't see—"

"Excuse me," Mandel said, "but I have never seen a place like this. Are there springs? Flat places here where you can see farther all around? I would like to see such a place."

Cameron was puzzled even further. Flat places. Who cared about flat places? More craziness, he thought proprietarily.

"Well, you drive through Keams Canyon and over to the Hopi mesas, the land south of them is sure as hell flat. If that's what you want to see."

"The Hopi mesas?"

"Yeah," Cameron said, and gave the man directions, drawing in the dirt with a stick. Presently, the black truck beetled its way north along a wagon track headed for Keams Canyon and, Cameron thought sardonically to himself, the fish-eating capital of the world. He looked at his crew as they stood expressionlessly watching the truck disappear over a rise, and shrugged by way of suggesting that those *billeganna* fishmongers were nothing he was responsible for. The Navajos smiled minimally and walked over to the flatbed, murmuring among themselves.

Later that afternoon, Cameron negotiated his way down the precipitous switchbacks into Keams Canyon, the engine whining against the low gear. Below, cottonwood trees were dry green over the tin roofs and military-looking rows of yellow stone buildings laid out along a dirt road: the Keams Canyon Indian Agency, a brave and slightly silly attempt to impose order in the canyon, with its tumbled slabs of yellow rock lying around like some sort of junkyard. At the bottom of the road Cameron stopped and the crew slipped off the flatbed and began walking east toward the commissary, a tent with tables where crews and crew leaders were fed great quantities of boiled potatoes, overcooked meat, and gray vegetables under a thick gray gravy. The thought of it made Cameron's stomach knot up, hungry as he was, and he turned west, bumping along the dirt track toward the Hopi mesas. Maybe something was up at Raphael's, he thought. There usually was. It would take more than an hour to get there, if he was lucky, but he had nothing else to do.

Raphael Luna owned the trading post at a relatively new Hopi village called Oraibi. It had somehow inherited this name from the village above it on the yellow sandstone mesa, the oldest continuously inhabited spot, it was said, in all of North America: Old Oraibi, now in melancholy disarray. Hopis had been living on that mesa in that village since the eleventh century, as far as anyone could tell, and in the near millennium that ensued, Old Oraibi had witnessed—indeed been the center of—most of the mysterious disputes that always evidently plagued Hopi life. It had been a teeming place at the turn of the century, with houses of two and three stories ranged around several plazas, each with its own underground chambers called kivas, with ladders striking upward through their roofs, the plazas ringing in the summer with ancient chants, drums, and dancers. But, partly in response to intrusions by the white officials of the U.S. government and partly in response to some mysterious interior tribal dialectic, the village of Oraibi had suffered one of the most disastrous splits in Hopi history and the population had fallen apart, some going off to found three new villages elsewhere on the mesa, while much of the old village fell into disuse. Those who stayed there seemed to have taken to looking inward and backward, brooding over old memories, old traditions, old and bitter prophecies. Once a proud ceremonial center, Old Oraibi was becoming a living ruin. On the southern end of its mesa, separated from the crumbling village by a quarter of a mile of empty rimrock, sat the decaying ruin of an old mission, established by Franciscans in the Hopis' uncooperative midst in the early 1600s, sacked by the Hopis in a region-wide uprising in 1680, and left to decay—a reminder of some sort . . . to someone.

Below the mesa and a hundred yards or so from the clutter of newish, one-story buildings of yellow stone that comprised the new village of Oraibi, Raphael Luna's trading post consisted of two unprepossessing, boxlike buildings joined together into an L in a hard-packed clearing. One of the boxes housed the store itself, the other Luna's office, two bedrooms, and a primitive but comfortable kitchen. Out beyond the open area surrounding the trading post was a wooden privy with an open doorway facing the slabs of sandstone that lay about below the cliff. Some pretty fancy people had used that privy over the years, staring nervously at the slabs of rock. Raphael Luna had an extraordinarily wide circle of aquaintances: writers, both foreign and American, government officials, artists, and various swells turned up every now and then at the post to sit around the dinner table in the kitchen and spend the night—women in the bedrooms, men rolled up in Navajo blankets on the porch.

A few times since coming to the reservation, Cameron had been invited to stay and have dinner, and on one of these occasions he had sat next to Mabel Dodge Luhan, a dumpy, quiet little woman who lived in Taos and evidently some sort of self-appointed queen of its art colony. Also present had been a composer with a Russian name who was visiting Mabel, one of Raphael's truck drivers, an unexplained Frenchman, and an old Hopi. Raphael, from a prominent New Mexican Hispanic family, had grown up a trader's son on the reservation, though well to the east of the Hopi mesas, and was fluent in Spanish, Navajo, Hopi, and English. He presided over these chance salons of his with a raspy voice and innumerable stories whenever the conversation flagged, stories that typically illustrated some subtlety of Hopi or Navajo culture for the benefit of his white listeners. Ben Cameron's employer, Commissioner Collier, had visited Raphael on several occasions, seeking advice, as had the wife of Collier's boss, Secretary of the Interior Harold Ickes. Raphael's influence was rumored to extend much further than one would expect from an Indian trader in the middle of nowhere, and such rumors received ever greater impetus whenever Raphael, as was his wont, vanished for weeks at a time, leaving his business in the hands of a clerk and telling no one where he was going, when he was coming back, or, once returned after a few weeks, what he had done.

Whatever he accomplished on his mysterious trips, Raphael's reputation on the reservation was that of chief diplomat and, in some sense few understood, power broker in the vast wilderness of the reservation. His trading post, established decades earlier in the midst of the ancient Hopi villages, also attracted Navajos from their camps in the surround, especially those who lived off to the west in the Painted Desert and in the shadows of the buttes to the south, through which a dirt track ran to Winslow eighty miles away. The Navajos, having arrived in these parts only some four or five hundred years ago, nomads, now pastoralists, always unreliable from the Hopi standpoint, given to raiding and stealing the stores of Hopi corn whenever things went bad for them, interlopers ... Navajos were not admired by Hopis. Since the arrival of the Anglos into the lives of the Hopi sixty years ago, some of these problems—the raiding in particular—had ceased for the most part. But in the dry lands resentments, though bleached by the sun like bones, could linger on, adding their dead weight to each new dispute that arose, magnifying each minor trespass into an invasion. Now living in the same land, in what was never more amicable than an uneasy truce, people from both tribes often looked to Raphael to mediate disputes between them. And both tribes also looked to Raphael to explain, or change altogether, the dictates—incomprehensible in their senselessness—that from time to time, like lightning, crackled into their lives from the stiff-necked agents of the U.S. government at Keams Canyon.

When Cameron pulled up at Luna's Trading Post, the sun was sitting low on the horizon, and the empty lot contained an unfamiliar Ford, along with one of Raphael's trucks. Cameron sat quietly in his own truck for a moment, letting the dust settle, and got out. He opened the wooden door to the store and entered quickly and quietly, closing the door behind him, letting his eyes adjust to the gloom. Beside the door, the wall was festooned with turquoise and silver jewelry—pawned in some moment of more than the usual need, and waiting here where its Navajo owner could see it until he or she was able one day to return with something of value to trade, or more rarely, cash. Shelves on the walls were full of dry goods mostly, and horse tack hung from the beams called vigas that supported the roof. A glimmer of light entered through two small windows placed near the ceiling. An old Navajo woman stood before one of the high counters with her back to him. Broad of beam and bow-legged, she wore a gathered velvet skirt that came down to her calves, and a purple velvet blouse. She spoke at length to the tall clerk who, standing on a raised floor behind the counter, peered down at her, listening attentively. Cameron waited patiently as he had learned to do, and eventually the clerk looked at him. Cameron motioned with his head toward the door that led to Raphael

Luna's office, and the clerk nodded, again attending to the Navajo woman.

Cameron knocked on the door and heard the now familiar rasping voice.

"Yes?"

He entered, smiling at Raphael, who sat behind his plain wooden desk, a large man, nearly obese, in his early fifties, with a large face and heavy lips. Raphael did not look up, but instead continued to listen intently to a small Navajo man seated opposite him. Unlike the cheerful clutter of the dark store, the office was simply furnished and bright—light from a window glowing from whitewashed walls.

The Navajo man finished, or at least his voice trailed off, and Raphael leaned over to spit into a spittoon next to his desk. He leaned back, smiled at the Navajo, revealing crooked yellow teeth, and spoke in Navajo, the sounds reminding Cameron of both a stream splashing over rocks and the gagging of someone with asthma. In another chair another Navajo man, older and much bigger than the other, sat quietly.

The small Navajo nodded, stood up, and left.

"Ya-ta-hey, Ben," Lorenzo rasped. "This is Hosteen Yazzie. From Pinon. This is Benjamin Cameron, my young archeologist friend. Digging up the past out near Jeddito. What brings you here today, Ben? Boredom?"

Cameron smiled.

"It must be tedious," Raphael said, "rooting around in the dirt like that all day. But it is your calling, eh?" The large man's eyes gleamed.

"Some days it's boring," Cameron admitted. "But today we had a couple of visitors. Got stuck in the wash."

Raphael's eyebrows rose a quarter of an inch.

"They said they were looking for markets for fish."

"Fish?" Raphael said, and the man beside Cameron chortled.

"Can you believe that? Slink told 'em Navajos don't eat things that grow in the water."

"And you pulled them out of the wash?"

Cameron nodded.

"Did they pay for the tow?"

"Five dollars."

"Excellent," Raphael said, and heaved himself to his feet. He said something in Navajo, and the old man nodded. "Come with me, please," Raphael said.

Cameron followed him out of the office, across a narrow hall into a spartan bedroom. Raphael sat heavily on the bed.

"Tell me more."

Cameron gave the trader a full account, including their strange curiosity about "flat" places. "So I sent 'em over to the land out there, south of Second Mesa. That's pretty darned flat. But I didn't see 'em when I went by this afternoon."

Raphael was silent for a moment. "Were they Oriental, these men?" he asked at last.

"Oriental?"

"Japanese, for example."

"No, no, why?"

"There's a great deal of unrest in the world beyond us here. The Japanese are at war. China. The Pacific. There are fears they will attack the United States. And a man named Hitler in Germany is making the blustering noises of someone about to start a war. Were these fishmongers German?"

"They didn't have an accent. Just sounded—uh, well— formal."

Raphael sighed, staring into the distance. "Did you ever hear of a man named Homer Lea?"

"No."

"Strange little man. A hunchback. Took an interest in geopolitics, back around the turn of the century. Mostly self-taught and evidently a genius. He went to China and became a general of the army, Sun Yat-sen's army. Then, I don't know when, around 1910, he wrote a book called *The Valor of Ignorance*. It predicted that the Japanese would one day declare war on the United States, attack Hawaii for starters, then invade America."

"Aren't they going in the wrong direction if they're fighting in China?" Cameron asked.

Raphael looked up at him without expression. "Shall we join the others?" he asked. "You'll stay for dinner, I hope."

∽ ∾

# 1937: Berlin

Two months had passed since Heinrich Schalberg had attained the rank of *sturmbahnfuhrer*, or major, and received his assignment to the Oberkommando des Heeres, the German Army High Command, assigned to the office of General Franz Halder. The top secret assignment to the Department of Strategic Planning was an attractive one, and the promotion excellent for an officer only twenty-seven years old, and an officer who was, though an ardent member of the Nazi party, foreign-born.

Schalberg had been born in Guatemala as Heinrich Schalberg Raminoz in the department of Alta Verapaz, where a German colony had arisen in the late nineteenth century and was granted land by the government in the highlands of the Sierra de Chama for growing coffee for export to the fatherland. At the age of nineteen, Heinrich's mother, Frieda Schalberg, had done the unusual thing, in this cliquish group, of marrying a Guatemalan. Senor Raminoz was not only a Guatemalan but thirty years her senior, and, as it turned out, not only extremely rich, but extremely frail. He died two years after Heinrich was born. Tainted among her own xenophobic countrymen in Guatemala by her choice to marry "out," impatient with their provinciality and pathetic slandering, she decided in the early 1920s to move. In 1922 she took her sizable inheritance and her young son to Mexico, where she established herself as proprietress of a 16,000 hectare cattle ranch in the sparsely vegetated and even more sparsely inhabited northern state of Sonora. In contact with the large though dispersed German community in Mexico, she dropped Raminoz from both her and her son's names, and Heinrich grew to adolescence steeped in things Teutonic, proud to possess his mother's name.

It was, for Heinrich, an idyllic youth, riding day in and day out on his own Arabian horse, selected for him by his mother from her large herd. She had taken to raising horses, showing the best in Mexico City, and selling some at high prices. By six, Heinrich knew all about the nearly sacred lineage of these horses, some tracing back to a stallion owned by Napoléon. By eight, he also knew a great deal about his mother's lineage, tracing itself back into times of near myth. By fourteen, he knew life on the range in the company of Mexican brazeros, life in the drawing room where visiting Germans spoke of grand things in store for the fatherland, and life in the bedroom where, at his mother's quiet bidding, a warm-hearted mestizo maid in her twenties introduced the lad to the manly pleasures of the body. Heinrich, of course, worshiped his mother, who was his best and only true friend.

As the ranch prospered, Frieda told her son that Germany would rise, while the gringos to the north would remain mired in their Depression. When Heinrich was fifteen, Frieda took her son to Berlin and enrolled him in the gymnasium, returning to Mexico with her heart filled with the promising things going on amid the fatherland's economic and social turmoil—most notably, the rise of the dynamic man, Adolf Hitler. At home, she wrote weekly to her son, explaining her pride that he would soon become part of the grand rise of order from the chaos inspired by communists, Jews, and foolish old men in Europe. Heinrich became an early member of Hitler's youth corps, and mother and son together took pride in their membership in the Nazi party, each active in his own sphere. At home, Frieda extended her German contacts to the leaders of the fascist movement in Mexico and helped these ultraconservative Mexicans found the Union Nacional Sinarquista, whose ideology rested on God, Church, and total adherence to authority. Under Frieda's patient diplomacy, the authority in question became the word from the Fuhrer—the word from God becoming so much window dressing, lest deep-seated Catholic superstitions be offended—and the Sinarquistas quickly grew from a collection of rich fools posturing in public to a trained and silent underground, ready for whatever actions a greater duty would summon them to.

In Germany, Heinrich went on to attend the university and study geopolitics, but a year later quit and joined the German Army, where he was schooled as an officer. Now, only five years later, he bore on his arm the insignia of *sturmbahnfuhrer* and sat in an office of his own in the low-ceilinged and carefully cordoned underground section of the German Army High Command. His office was small and spare, to be sure, a desk, two chairs, a table covered with a clutter of books, charts, typed directives and reports bound in gray-green cardboard stamped Top Secret. On the gray-green walls was a large printed portrait of the Fuhrer, as stern and inspiring as the German eagle, and a large pull-down map of North and South America, yellowed around its oilcloth edges.

On his first day at the High Command, he had been briefed by General Halder himself. Heinrich sat erect as a post in a Chippendale chair before Halder's shining, empty desk, awed to be meeting with this renowned man, a general who, it was rumored, would eventually rise as high as army general chief of staff, perhaps higher. Halder, a sharp-featured, acid man, had leaned back comfortably, smoking a cigarette plucked from a gold case, and outlined the future to the young officer as it had been set forth by the Fuhrer himself.

First, Germany would take dominion over Central Europe, and with those vital resources under control, establish a continental empire, embracing all of Europe including the eastern, or European, part of the Soviet Union, along with the unruly places south, down to the Middle East, with its inexhaustible oil reserves. Then, by acquiring colonies in Africa with bases on the Atlantic for an overpowering fleet, this German empire, the Third Reich, would be far more than on a par with the remaining great powers—Britain, the United States, and Japan. Those former great powers—France and the USSR— would, of course, no longer exist, and soon enough Britain would fall under German sway, an island province of the fatherland, and in due course join the Germans in a decisive victory over the United States. All perhaps, the general said with an odd smirk, within the lifetime of a young *sturmbahnfuhrer*.

Heinrich's heart had leapt in his chest, leaving him breathless at the glory of the idea. World dominion!

With German thoroughness and confidence, the High Command had instructed the Department of Strategic Planning four years earlier to produce the detailed strategies and even, as needed, tactics for each stage of this grand vision, this Master Plan by which the Master Race would dominate the planet. For the more immediate goals—Europe and the Soviet Union—many officers had already been assigned, and plans were in hand and being field tested quietly, in places where the British and French did not notice. Now it was time to begin even the longest-range planning. Thus, Heinrich Schalberg, who as a boy had grown up within a hundred miles of the American border with Mexico and shared with his fellow if negligible Mexican countrymen an extreme distaste for the gringos, was to begin plotting out the demise of the United States. With his top-secret clearance, he would have access to all but the most sensitive reports developed from information supplied by an extensive espionage network strung throughout the Western Hemisphere from Argentina to Alaska, operated by General Canaris's Abwehr.

Schalberg realized that his part of the Master Plan was perhaps the least important, being so distant in the future, but it was exhilarating work, being ordered and paid to dream—no, not merely to dream—to *plan* the domination of the world by the fatherland. When the unimaginably potent spirit of the Teutonic race was arrayed against the mongrel Americans—sometime within his lifetime too—the invading German forces might well be following what would be called the Schalberg Plan.

It was exhilarating too to work with the brilliant, self-confident officers, to join in the camaraderie at the officers' mess, to laugh about the ease with which a technically superior Germany would roll over Europe imminently, and then . . .

Exhilarating, as well, to stride the streets of Berlin in his proud, eye-catching uniform, aware of the admiring and hopeful looks bestowed on him by the Aryan populace, while members of the inferior races scuttled out of his path. Oh, it was a heady time, and he, striding to and from work, his leather belt and boots gleaming, was one of the heroes, one of the strong, chiseled young men who would deliver Germany to her destiny. And the girls—how easy was it for them to love, to open themselves to such a hero. How anyone in Berlin these days not clad in the uniform of a warrior ever got any tail, Heinrich could not imagine.

Heinrich Schalberg was confident too that he would in due course rise up through the ranks of the High Command in the promising wake of General Franz Halder. Perhaps, he even allowed himself to imagine, it would be Heinrich Schalberg who would one day execute the Schalberg Plan.

The thought made him smile as he turned now to an Abwehr report documenting a buildup of military facilities at Fort Bliss in El Paso, Texas, just across the

Mexican border from the state of Chihuahua. An armored division in training. And another report—this one excerpts from a recent speech in New York City by Charles Lindbergh, the great aviator and American idol, urging his countrymen toward a deeper appreciation of the German race and the Third Reich.

The mongrel Americans, he thought. Always in chaos, always about to split apart. Had not one of their beloved presidents said that a house divided cannot stand?

Divide and conquer.

There was a way to do just that. He, Heinrich Schalberg, had already perceived the outlines of such a plan.

# 1938: Old Oraibi

Banyongye was tired all the way through to the bone, and it was bone that protested the most shrilly to him as he turned and took his first step down the ladder into the underground kiva below. The other elders and priests awaited him around the fire at the base of the ladder, and he smelled rich piñon smoke drifting upward past him into the night sky like a prayer. Banyongye's old head was filled with new things, new meanings to illuminate the oldest Hopi meanings, and he was impatient with his protesting bones.

Returning from his trip, he'd had to wait a day and a night in Winslow, sitting in front of the hotel there, waiting for his nephews to come for him in the old wagon with its two old horses. He had watched the white people come and go, so confident but so abrupt, like nervous birds. Old Banyongye watched the white man's world carefully whenever he had such a chance, seeking to make sense out of it, testing it against the ever-present history of his people. If there was sense to it, besides the sheer weight of numbers, the sense of it eluded him. Sitting on the wooden bench in front of the hotel, he had dwelled in his mind yet again on the day of shame when the agents from Keams Canyon had brought the soldiers to Oraibi and rounded up the children, taking them off screaming from out of their homes, away from their parents, their uncles and aunts. A much younger man then, Banyongye had stood there watching, powerless, as the children, his little clan uncles and aunts, had been wrenched away to go to the white man's school. Later he had watched as the Hostiles left Oraibi, gone away to start another village, while the Friendlies stayed behind. Banyongye, comfortable with neither position, had remained behind, and was ridiculed for his indecisiveness, shamed. But he had remained in Oraibi, not wishing to break the priestly chain that had come down since before memory, linking him to this kiva where the prophecies were kept, the true prophecies and not those false ones that some Hopis still held.

Banyongye took another step down the ladder, the round pine crossbar familiar to his feet, and breathed in the piñon smoke.

The noisy train had stopped in Winslow, and he had stepped down from the carriage onto the pavement, followed by three other members of the kiva, younger men now sitting below, waiting for him along with the others who had stayed behind. Banyongye and the others had found their way to the hotel, with its large room inside the front door with many chairs, but after a while they found it too noisy, like the train, so they went outside to wait for Banyongye's nephews.

New images had flickered through the old man's mind as he waited there in Winslow, images from New York City, images of ear-shattering and noisy automobiles, more than he could count, in the deep stone canyons. New York City. Jostled and shoved by the people on the concrete sidewalks, all streaming like ants, but huge ants. Banyongye had followed the woman as best he could, the big woman from the Indian rights people, keeping his eye on her feathered hat while the crowds surged around him.

He thought now of the huge red flag hanging in the silent hall they had been taken to, with the black sign on it in a circle of white, the Hopi sign but backward, a complementary image for the sign his ancestors had etched into the yellow rock of Hopi. Sacred. Images in the silence of the great hall, recalled now in a pleasing confusion, sleek silver things, black metal things, great engines, sleek vehicles unlike anything Banyongye had ever seen even in Albuquerque during his one trip there. The courteous hosts, the German people talking about some World Fair, so glad to see Banyongye and his "compatriots." Banyongye's mind had spun with excitement.

Back on less unfamiliar ground, in Winslow, on the bench outside the hotel, he had tried to relate these images spinning now in his mind with what he knew. It was important to be certain about such things. He rehearsed again the chief events of the Hopi—in particular, those surrounding the time they had emerged from the Third World in an earlier time into this, the Fourth World, from the *sipapu*, the providential hole between the Third World and this one, with the giant reed through which the people had climbed, leaving the two-hearts, the witches, behind, along with those who were for them.

The history said that the Elder White Brother, the Pahana, had emerged with the people at this time and, in spite of their invitation to stay with them, had gone eastward into the sun, promising to return one day with the things the people would need. And when he came, the prophecies said, it would be the time of the last purification. For somehow some two-hearts had managed to sneak up the reed into this Fourth World, and the cycle of bad things had continued to plague the Hopi during their long migrations around the world, migrations that had finally led them to their present homes on the mesas. How many times, during those long migrations, had the Hopi had to purge themselves and seek again the humble path?

Yes, the many paths had led the different clans to the Hopi mesas, where they were commanded to stop and practice humility and harmony and respect, their hard but good life. Upon emergence, after Mockingbird had awarded the different people their languages, they had all been offered ears of corn, different colored ears. And the

Hopi had chosen the blue corn, the short blue corn. The meaning of this was that they had chosen the hard way, the long and difficult way, but the way that would endure. And some of the Hopi would endure even the great purification.

Banyongye took another step down into the kiva, the roof now at his eye level.

Some of the Hopi would live on after the great purification. Even following the path of the blue corn, Banyongye thought again in a kind of incantation, the harmony of the Hopi had been breached again in this Fourth World, as it had been before. Two-hearts, witches, had made their presence known, and harmony was replaced by ambition, new things, a wrongful abundance. People were driven by greed. The villages were rancorous with gossip, argument, divisiveness. This was the prophecy so carefully guarded below him in this kiva by the men assembled there, the prophecy also etched into the rock beyond the village.

He took another step, and below him could see the heads of his brothers. His bones ached.

And before the great purification, the end of this world gone awry, the Pahana would return. He would arrive from the east, and single out those of the Hopi who had never lost sight of the prophecies and the Hopi ideals. It was these Hopis who, with the Pahana, would survive the purification and begin a different world somewhere else, one that would last forever. So it said in the prophecies.

Banyongye now felt the packed earthen floor under his foot. He paused below the ladder, and took cornmeal from the leather pouch that hung at his belt. He turned to the right and stepped around the fire in the floor, making a circle, sprinkling cornmeal within it, and when he reached the other side, he subsided onto the banco that lined the three sides of the kiva. He sat quietly, listening to the pains in his bones stop their complaints, part of his mind filled with the blurring images of shiny steel and the vast black sign the German hosts called a "swastika."

Eventually, Banyongye lifted his eyes and looked, one after the other, at the men assembled there with him. Then he let his eyes follow the blue smoke upward, out of the kiva, to become a prayer in the night sky.

"I have met him," he said. "I have met the Pahana."

# 1939: Berlin

On September 1, 1939, one and a half million German warriors struck at the 1,750-mile border of Poland to the east. The annexation of Czechoslovakia having been acceded to by the weakling *great* powers of Europe, symbolized by the foppish Neville Chamberlain and his tightly furled umbrella, the Fuhrer's troops thrust fast and deep in the soft lands of Poland, surprising the world with the lightning potency of Germany's armored divisions and its Luftwaffe, which almost immediately eliminated the entire Polish air force, obsolete in any event. From then on it was child's play. The panzer attack was born, the blitzkrieg, a word coined in fact by an admiring American, Henry Luce. The world was new, the atmosphere of Europe redolent with cordite, just as the air smells metallically of ozone after an electrical storm. The last Polish resistance ended on October 5, when that old and ambiguous nation was partitioned by the grinning forces of both Germany and the USSR, who met just west of the Bug River. Germany's beloved eastern lands were hers again. By then all the proper international protocols had been completed and Europe was officially at war.

With his comrades in the Army High Command, Heinrich Schalberg had been among the first to see the black-and-white motion pictures clatter through the projector, images of the victory, advancing tanks, planes screaming overhead like hornets, the great explosions of smoke and fire. Most striking to Schalberg had been the images of white-gloved Polish horsemen, their Arabian horses rearing up in terror in the clamorous onslaught of tanks and artillery, wheeling and falling in the fire. He and his colleagues had laughed at the fecklessness of the Poles.

The day after the Polish surrender, Sturmbahnfuhrer Heinrich Schalberg received new orders. He was to report to Kiel, from where he would be deployed as part of the force poised to subjugate Denmark, a strategically important peninsula for maintaining supply lines to the soon-to-come invasion of Norway, as well as holding control of the Baltic Sea where, to the east, lurked the Great Bear. Despite Soviet-German pacts and promises, no one in the fatherland, least of all the Fuhrer himself, trusted the empire of Joseph Stalin and his red legions.

Schalberg was of two minds when he received his orders. He had always yearned for combat, as any soldier does, wanting to establish himself as a man of action and courage, not just a deskbound strategist, however glorious an end the strategy pointed to. But he still had some details to work out on his plan, the Schalberg Plan, as he now routinely thought of it.

He went to the hotel where his mother was staying on one of her frequent visits to Berlin. These days she split her time between the ranch in Mexico and the heady excitement of Berlin as Hitler rose to greater heights of power and now conquest. On this trip, Heinrich had suddenly noticed, she looked old. He had never thought of his mother as old, or even older in any significant way. She was only different, more like a wise sister than a member of another generation. On horseback, patrolling her Sonoran ranch with him in tow, her blond hair streaming out behind her, urging her horse to a pounding gallop with young Heinrich gamely racing her, the two of them hurtling across the scrubby land, she had seemed, what? A girl. A princess. Perpetually youthful. Now, here in Berlin, determined to be part of the glorious rise of the Third Reich, she had somehow lost her youth. She smoked a bit too much, Heinrich thought, and lines were beginning to appear around her mouth and in the corners of her pale blue eyes. Firm flesh had begun to soften. It had shocked Heinrich when he first noticed it; the notion of her mortality had struck him for the first time in his life, as his own was yet to do, and he felt a profound sadness. He decided this day to break the rules and tell her exactly what he had given birth to at the High Command.

She was loyal, after all, fanatically so, and would say nothing of it to anyone, if so bidden. Indeed, she would one day have to know the entire plan. Why not, then, let her see its outline now? It would be their secret, a secret that would sustain this beautiful woman whenever she was at home, so far from the glorious affairs of the Reich. His mother, the stunning horsewoman, the fierce patriot, could be trusted to hear the outlines of the Schalberg Plan. The plan that had, in a true enough sense, sprung from her loins.

In an elegant sitting room furnished with deep brown, nearly black, heavily varnished turn-of-the-century settees and chairs, she had listened intently to her son's recital, her blue eyes filling with tears. She had wept at the beauty of his plan. When he had finished, and smiled at her, she lunged across the room with its teacups and teapot on a small table between them, sending the chinaware clattering around them. She had clutched him in her arms, tears streaming down her face, mingling now with his own tears. She had choked and in a broken voice said: "My son. My son! My God! It is so beautiful!" She had stood back, her hands on his shoulders, and looked up at his face with a joy he had never seen. She had buried her face in his shoulder, pulled him to her breast, and hung onto him.

When, two days later, he stepped off the sooty train into the steam-filled railroad station at Kiel, now to be tested in the iron realities of war, he kept in his mind his mother's joyous, radiant face, tears of elation on her cheeks, and he was proud. This image, and that too of the Polish horses reeling and falling before the German armor, would remain somewhere in his mind throughout the years of war, until its very end.

## 1940: Santa Fe

Ben Cameron reread the letter he had just written on a tablet now struck by the sun beaming through the one window in the thick adobe wall of his two-room house. In the back of his mind were a few nagging questions, most notably how he would sell the car. The hell with the car. Give it away. What difference would it make? The words before him were the first he had written to his father in two years.

June 5, 1940
Dear Dad:

I've been long out of touch, for which I am sorry, but so have you. Here I go getting argumentative again. When will we ever stop? Well, anyway, I suppose the news has penetrated even your fortress and the disaster in Europe is clear. Dunkirk! Imagine all those boats! I've made some decisions. One of them is easy. I'm enlisting today. U.S. Army. Try to be an officer. It's coming. The world in flames. And I'll be there, I guess. Pray for me, if you do that sort of thing now.

I also decided I'm not going to be an archeologist. If of course I get back. I think I'm more interested in the living than in the dead, tho I guess I'll get even more involved in that aspect of things now.

I've got 200 bucks in the bank here in Santa Fe. If I don't come out of this ok, please take the time to get it and give it to a guy named Slink on the Navajo reser-

34

vation. You can find him through the Luna Trading Post in Oraibi. That's in Arizona. I just thought of this or otherwise I would have asked someone else to take care of it.

Anyway, I'm off—to fame, glory, whatever. I'll let you know where I wind up.

Your son,
Ben

He folded up the letter and slipped it into the envelope he had already addressed. Oliver Cameron, Lawrence Farms, Mount Kisco, New York. A white house with green shutters and a big ash tree outside which, as a little boy, he had counted as his home, swinging up into it and shinnying up a thick branch to a special sitting place where he would stay for hours looking up in the higher branches. Watch squirrels dart around above him, and wonder what it would be like to be a squirrel instead of a kid. He remembered when they had let him wear long pants for the first time and he had put a tear in them that first day, climbing his ash tree.

He put the envelope in his pocket and went out into the morning sun, looking yearningly into the shadows cast by the adobe wall surrounding his little front yard. He sniffed the lilacs, now at the end of their run, and wondered what he faced. Not lilacs, he guessed. He closed the gate behind him and set off down the winding dirt road toward the center of town, the plaza where the recruitment office had been set up. The sleepy little town of Santa Fe, where nothing happened. An art colony in the middle of nowhere, but home, now that he had left the ash tree behind long ago. Santa Fe, lit every day by a burnishing sun, where most people still spoke Spanish and talked quietly and did whatever they did to subsist. Maybe he would see Paris. That would be swell.

And when this was all over, he would start again, as an anthropologist this time. Maybe back with the Navajos.

And the Hopis, he added, though he wondered if he could ever understand the Hopis. So focused on the past, lugging it around like an enormous suitcase, full of what? He had begun losing interest in the past, in digging up the past, even though it had brought him a spot of fame in his narrow field. The summer before, up near Gobernador's Knob in northwestern New Mexico, he had been part of the team that found an early, crude version of a hogan, the earliest one so far found, that dated to about A.D. 1400. Its discovery had put to rest part of the argument about when the Navajos had arrived in these parts, part of migration of Athabascans from the far north. So they'd arrived five hundred years ago. So what? Cameron now thought. They were here, transformed, a new people, a new and living culture amid older ones. And that was what interested him, Cameron now knew. The patterns and currents that underlay the behavior of living, breathing, eating, working, laughing, praying, quarreling, fornicating cultures. Maybe he'd come back, work on the reservation. Maybe he'd work somewhere else. Who knew? Maybe Africa. Maybe Arabia, live with the bedouins in the desert, find out what lay behind those dark hawk-faced nomads. If he came back at all.

From a Spanish kid, what was his name? Raoul. From Raoul he bought a copy of *The Santa Fe New Mexican* for five cents and paused in the cool shade of a tree to look at the front page—the front page of the newspaper on the very day he would join the army. There was a photograph of a row of men standing downcast before the camera, with two guys in business suits, one at each end. A headline:

GERMAN SPIES NABBED!
FBI handcuffs eight Nazi snoopers in Santa Fe

He stared at the picture in a kind of dream. A sheepish man on the left looked familiar. He looked again at the eight faces. The man third from the left also looked familiar.

It was the fishmongers. The nuts with the formal voices and the newly beat-up black truck. Up to its ass in Jeddito Wash. The greenhorns.

Spies?

What was it they were looking for out in that desert?

Hun bastards. At least they caught 'em.

Ben Cameron walked on toward the plaza and the enlistment office, wondering what on earth the Nazis could possibly need to know about a place so far removed from the rest of the world, so backward, so unimportant as the sleepy, empty, otherworldly reservation of the Indians. Maybe, he thought, the Germans were as stupid as people said they were. Thick.

Five minutes later, reporting his desire to serve in the United States Army, Benjamin Cameron of Santa Fe found himself gathered up into a whirlwind new world, soon to be propelled into the exotica of military intelligence in places like El Paso, Washington, D.C., Athens, the island of Malta, and Cairo. It would be almost four years before he thought again about the two blue-eyed, brown-haired fishmongers who had turned up, stuck up to their axle in the old sands of Jeddito Wash.

~ ~ ~

# MAY 1944:
# OPERATION
# SHATTERHAND

# Part One
# THE TWILIGHT WAR

Those who do not use local guides
are unable to obtain the advantages
of the ground.
—SUN TZU,
*The Art of War*

∽ ∾

# One

On May 7, 1944, at one o'clock in the morning, the power went out in a vast area of the American Southwest. The outage coincided with the onslaught of near-gale winds that pounded the region, accompanied by rank after rank of violent thunderstorms and record rainfall. Flash floods filled dry arroyos with torrents. Most people were awakened by the storms that plummeted through but did not notice until morning—when they found that appliances such as refrigerators and radios were not working—that electrical power was out. Blackouts of the grievously strained power systems had occurred often enough in this technologically fragile and even backward part of the United States that its citizens had no reason to believe it was anything to worry about, and had no way to learn of its extent. In fact, electrical power was cut off in a region extending east to west from Lordsburg, New Mexico, to Casa Grande, Arizona, and south to north from the Mexican border to Flagstaff, Arizona.

Marana Air Base in Tucson, always on alert, turned on its emergency generators, as did the other military installations and some medical facilities in the region, and as a routine precaution sent a wing of reconnaissance aircraft into the predawn skies. No one in the military still believed that a Japanese attack on the nation's West Coast was a possibility, but such worries were still abroad in

43

the public mind, and it was policy to send reassuring missions into the sky in such moments.

The extent of the power outage—greater than any other to date—soon began to dawn on the military around the region, and the utilities and civil defense people were alerted and re-alerted, indeed bombarded with altogether redundant demands that repairs be made immediately. It was not until May 10, four days after this large area of the Southwest went dark, that power was restored to all its important municipalities. Of these, Winslow, Arizona (pop. 3,912), was the last to resume life as usual, the power coming back on at 5:02 in the morning, just as the sun's light had caused the merest glow on the eastern horizon.

Two miles east of the city limits of Winslow, and about the length of a football field back from the tracks of the Santa Fe railway at a railroad crossing called Hobson, a weathered two-room house stood among the sagebrush and creosote bush of the high desert. In a corral behind the house a very old range horse pricked up its ears and turned to face south, just as a screen door slammed shut with a thunk and bounced twice against the doorjamb. Edgar L. Flynn, a retired employee of the Santa Fe railroad and a sometime ranch hand, now seventy-four years old and clad in a pair of cowhide gloves and a worn-out set of gray cotton long underwear, stood on the porch, bending from side to side to limber up his lower back, and scratching his bottom. He glanced at his horse, its attentions focused southward, and his eyes looked in that direction as well, seeing nothing but familiar scrublands stretching monotonously away to the horizon.

Edgar Flynn stood on the porch, idly staring, his mind elsewhere, until the sky brightened with the sun's imminent arrival. In the glow, he could now make out what had piqued the curiosity of his old horse earlier. Out in the middle of the scrubland, a cloud of dust was moving his way. It was not the time of year for a cattle drive to be headed toward Winslow. Indeed, those days were about over, Edgar reckoned, what with the war and all, and the changes that had already come to the West. Winslow, he guessed, didn't have much of a future ahead of it. He went back inside, where a blue metal coffeepot was gaily simmering on the woodstove, and poured the thick liquid into two metal cups. He took one of these into the small bedroom attached to the house and put it down on the floor next to a cot where his father, now ninety-three years old as far as anyone could tell, lay snoring. Steam rose from the metal cup on the floor, drifting up past the old man's nearly hairless skull. Edgar Flynn watched as the old head stirred, sniffed, and said, "Goddammit." The eyelids fluttered, opened, stared blankly at the steam rising past them, and again the older man said, "Goddammit." He smiled thinly. "I fooled that sonofabitch again." The old man's voice was a papery wheeze.

Edgar Flynn knew he was referring to Death, a figure well-known and at large in these precincts and against whom Edgar's father imagined himself to be engaged in a titanic war of attrition.

"Yup," Edgar said. "You did. Looks like we got somethin' comin' across the desert at us."

"What?"

"Damned if I know."

Edgar left the old man and went out on the porch again, the screen door thunking behind him. The cloud to the south was larger now, still headed in his direction, and lit gold by the first direct rays of the sun. He glanced up as a raven flew by, arrowing off on some dawn mission. Edgar's old mare, a bay, had taken to snuffling around the wire perimeter of the corral, ever hopeful that something green had emerged during the night into her dusty plot of ground. Edgar sipped his coffee on the porch and watched the world fill with sunlight and the dust cloud grow as it came nearer. Presently, he made out what looked like a small convoy of military vehicles, half-track trucks, some larger troop trucks, followed—by God!—by some tanks. How many he couldn't see, what with all the dust the convoy was throwing up into the morning. Looked like they were going to pass by about three or four hundred yards west of his house.

"What the hell is that out there?" his father said, now standing beside him on the porch, squinting through pallid, cloudy blue eyes.

"Armored detail," Edgar said. "Headed right by us if they stay on that course."

"Some boys out of Fort Bliss, huh?" the old man wheezed. "One of them recruiting drives like they used to do."

"Must be," Edgar said, puzzled. He watched as the convoy came more clearly into view three hundred yards west of his house. A man—an officer, it looked like—was standing in the lead half-track looking ahead. From the high front fender, the flag of the United States fluttered in the wind stream. Edgar saw the sun light the officer's face as he turned in their direction and whipped his arm up and to the side in a smart salute. Edgar saluted in return and looked at his father. The old man, head erect on his thin neck, his backbone curled by age almost into a C, stood stock-still, staring blindly at the convoy and holding his hand to his forehead in salute.

"God bless you, boys," the old man said. "God bless you." The last action the old bird had seen was as one of the white officers of the Tenth Cavalry, a black cavalry unit known as the Buffalo Soldiers, who had made a hell of a reputation running the last of the Apaches out of western Texas and southern New Mexico in the 1880s.

"God bless you, boys," the old cavalry officer said again, and Edgar watched them slow down, crawl over the railroad crossing and then heave and creep over Route 66, headed north.

"They're goin' up the Second Mesa Road," Edgar said. "Gonna tear hell out of it." He watched the convoy, forming into a single file, proceed up the long ungraded dirt track, kicking up plume after plume of dust that formed a great cloud in the early sunlight.

"Nothin' up there but Indyinns," the old man wheezed. "Maybe they on the warpath again." He cackled himself into a coughing fit. When he caught his breath, he said, "You make terrible coffee, Edgar. Terrible." He poured out his dregs into the sand.

Major General Heinrich Schalberg glanced down at his map as the half-track lurched off the pavement and onto the dirt road leading north by northwest. The track showed on his map as a thin dashed line, an unnumbered roadway that would soon turn due north. Except for a track leading from the city of Flagstaff some sixty miles to the west, and another leading north from the city of Holbrook about thirty miles east, there were no other north-heading roads into the vast empty place on his map. He grinned with exhilaration and leaned forward to shout into the ear of the driver, Corporal Hans Schwabe, a thickset man without an apparent neck: "That was it. Route 66. We have done it. Another three hours."

Schwabe glanced up, grinned, and made a thumbs-up sign.

They had been three days under way, pushing north through the heat and the storms of day and the blackness and storms of the night, only once coming into contact with American troops—this a convoy of trucks full of bored and incurious enlisted personnel on Route 80 just north of the Arizona–New Mexico border. Schalberg, in his U.S. captain's uniform, had offered them a smart salute as they roared across his path, headed east, and he had breathed a deep sigh of relief when his salute was returned in the shabby, casual manner of the Americans. Perhaps it was all that was expected of men in this situation, he thought, and made a point to mimic the gringo slovenliness if they met up with other patrols. He had watched the trucks disappear, one by one, over a distant rise, and allowed a look of contempt to cross his face, matching his opinion.

They had pushed on, stopping from time to time only to refuel from the supply trucks, their milch cows on wheels, drivers alternating every four hours, pressing across the American landscape for fifty-six exhausting hours, miraculously reaching and crossing Route 66, the last east-west roadway in their path, the last evident sign of civilization before they reached their destination. Dressed in American uniforms, driving American trucks and tanks all captured on European battlefields, showing the red, white, and blue colors of the United States, they fell, of course, into the category of spies, not soldiers. Were they to be caught, according to the conventions of war, they risked execution rather than prison camp.

Careful planning, excellent reconnaissance and sabotage by the Sinarquistas, and luck in the form of the weather front that had stalled storms over the entire region during the blackout, pummeling it with rain and lightning, had all conspired to preclude such a drastic eventuality. For all intents and purposes, now that they were north of Route 66 and had nothing but a few kilometers of scrubland between them and the Indian reservation, they had arrived.

Once they breasted the rise before them, Schalberg decided, a distance he guessed to be about twelve kilometers, they would halt to allow the men a brief rest. Schalberg himself was dizzy with sleeplessness, having spent most of the preceding fifty-six hours standing Rommel-like in the half-track. Over the years, he had learned to grab catnaps on his feet, but these could hardly sustain a man for long. He shook himself to alertness. Later, when they had split in two and reached their two destinations—one in Keams Canyon and the other in Oraibi—they could also exchange the American uniforms, captured in Italy, for the proud uniforms and insignia of the Wehrmacht, throw down the cluttered asymmetrical flags of the United States and unfurl the standards of the German Reich, and carry out their mission with the pride of a proper invading force. Schalberg allowed himself the thought that Operation Shatterhand was triumphantly under way.

How many months had they been in training? Four? Nearly four. Crack troops assembled from the Russian front, formerly under Rommel's command in North Africa. Desert troops, forged by the greatest tactician in the history of mobile armored warfare, tempered in Saharan sun, wind, and sand, survivors of the awful final defeat in the desert and of months in the awful, frozen killing fields of the Soviet Union. Brought together in the lowlands of Holland for training that included learning enough American English, enough soldier slang, to be taken as Yanks, memorizing the names of baseball players and baseball teams, listening to the trivial, tinny music of Glenn Miller and Artie Shaw until they hummed it in their sleep. And treacly songs like: "Don't sit under the apple tree with anyone else but me . . ." Equipment and men brought by milch-cow submarine to the remote sandy coastline of Mexico, to be spirited by friendly hands across its desertlands to the great Sonoran holdings of his mother Frieda Schalberg, assembling there under two square miles of camouflaged canvas over a period of two weeks before the final and perilous push onto American soil.

Schalberg could see in his mind's eye the face of his mother, joyous then as she had been years earlier in Berlin when he had outlined to her the Schalberg Plan, now come to an early fruition, and come, in a stunning reality of weapons, ammunition, men and armor, to her very hearth. No greater honor, she had said repeatedly, could come to any daughter of the Reich. Heinrich had been astonished at how effective a fifth column Frieda had forged in the Sinarquistas, a group he had

remembered as a youth as presumptuous mestizo roost-
ers. But Frieda had assured him otherwise, and she was
of course correct.

As Schalberg's half-track breasted the rise in the
desert, the track swept down through an ocean of colorless scrubland and then upward, leading to yet another
rise many kilometers distant. Off to the right, the ground
swept upward to the rocky base of an enormous outcrop
of rock, a vast castlelike thumb of reddish-brown rock,
vertical striations lining its rounded sides like the fluting
of Grecian columns. It surged up out of greenish, almost
emerald land, perhaps some kind of desert grass that had
responded to the torrential rains, if indeed it had rained
this far north. Perhaps not, he thought; there seemed not
the slightest moisture in the air. The pinnacle's lofty
blunt tip reached some two hundred meters in the blue
sky, he estimated, casting a long, dark shadow all the
way across the land to the dirt track and beyond. His
glance returned to the shadows at the huge column's
base, and there, nestled between two of its vertical striations, he made out a tiny dwelling, a round-looking one-
story house of some kind, and a ragged wooden fence,
perhaps a corral. No doubt the dwelling of one of the Indians, perhaps a Navajo. No one in sight. His eyes swept
up the column again and, with the rude little dwelling as
a point of reference, he reestimated the column's height
at six hundred meters.

Distances, heights, the measures of this land would be
deceptive, Schalberg thought, until he got the hang of
them. It must have something to do with the nearly
painful clarity of the dry air. He decided to press on
down the gentle slope and up the next inviting rise before
he halted the column. Standing in the half-track, the air
hot on his face, his head ringing with the exultation of a
command proceeding according to plan, he turned and
waved his force on.

He glanced at his watch. They had crossed Route 66

within an hour of their schedule. Within another hour, according to plan, Mexican-American members of the Sinarquistas established in the towns ringing the reservation—Flagstaff, Winslow, Holbrook, Gallup in New Mexico—would see to it that the few dainty threads of telephone lines linking the reservation with the world would be severed. And once repaired, severed again. Except for those at the Indian Agency in Keams Canyon. There, before the end of the day, the phones would be repaired and manned reassuringly by an American puppet. The work of God, Schalberg said to himself, lies in the details.

They had called her Agnes in the *billeganna* school in Leupp, but that was not how she was known. Not to her people, the Dineh, not even to the trader at Oraibi. Her people, her family, called her by her honorific title, except of course her three sons-in-law who never called her anything and, properly, never looked at her directly. They were good sons-in-law—except for the one they called Black Legs, off somewhere again, probably drunk in Winslow. When he came back, if he came back, she would have to call the family together, maybe make them all go over to Dilkon, have a public talk about Black Legs. There was no other way, she thought.

Earlier, with these things on her mind, she had left the hogan and prayed to the east as the sun came up, placing a pinch of corn pollen on the branches of the piñon tree that grew near the entrance. Afterward, she had stood for a time idly watching the family's sheep in their corral and watching the world fill up with light. Now she walked around to the other side of the hogan and looked at the butte's shadow stretching across the land to the dirt track from Winslow. A long row of military vehicles was making its way north along the track, raising a vast cloud of sunlit dust above them, clinging to them. She had never seen so many military vehicles, and the only ones she had seen were in Gallup, a few trucks and tanks parked along the highway, with a band playing. They were encouraging young men to join the army. That had been years ago, at the beginning of the war that had taken her son and killed him someplace in the Pacific Ocean. It would not do to think of her son, remember him, even that far away. Fleetingly, she wished his spirit to be at rest, and shuddered. Changing thoughts by an act of will, she puzzled about the long line of military vehicles—some of them tanks. What were they doing here? Where were they going? Her grandfather had told her when she was a girl about when the military came to the reservation—never any good comes of it, he said. She went into the hogan and peered across its earthen floor. Her husband was sitting against the wall on a blanket, eating *naneskadi*, Indian bread she had made the day before. She motioned for him to come, pointing to the door of the hogan with her lips and a lifted chin.

Outside, her husband looked at the armored column passing north about a half mile away on the Winslow road. He squinted under the brim of his large black hat, but said nothing, simply chewing his mouthful of bread. A light breeze was blowing from behind them, and they could not hear the sound of engines or metal tracks grinding along the road. Only the tinkle of the bellwether sheep behind them in the corral, signaling an eagerness among the sheep to forage in the fresh grass of the desert.

Without a word, her husband disappeared behind the hogan, and presently she heard the gate of a corral open, wire creaking against wood. He came around the hogan on his horse, the narrow-hipped black one he had won from a Hopi man last year in the horse races over at Bird Springs. His saddle was old, cracked, and it sat on three blankets she had woven for him.

"Luna," he said, pointing northward with his lips, and set off at a lope due west. He would cross the Winslow road, she knew, well behind the convoy, and keep west halfway to Bird Springs, then head straight north to the trader in Oraibi. Perhaps tomorrow he would return and tell her what these *billegannas* were up to. As for her, she would spend the day out with the sheep and think about Black Legs, her son-in-law, and what they would say to him when everyone had gathered. Yes, in Dilkon. Where some of his own people lived too.

Slink had been awake and about for some two hours when he saw them coming, steaming along the Winslow road at what he guessed was fifteen, maybe twenty miles an hour, each vehicle keeping barely ahead of the cloud of dust it spun billowing into the air, like rabbits about to be seized and consumed by pursuing eagles. There was an unspeakable violence to the procession of armor across the land.

He had arrived late at his mother's camp the night before and, lest he disturb anyone—even the feral dogs that lurked around the camp—he had stolen quietly into the shade house, where he'd slept curled in a blanket. It was something of a game for Slink, this stealth, and something of a birthright. His grandfather had received the name Slink from those who both admired and deplored his ability to sneak into a corral and make off with a horse or two without anyone waking up. His father too had been named Slink, and for the same reason.

It was a matter of family honor, this "old Apache trick," as his grandfather had explained it to him when he was a boy. The old man had been a rover in his youth and had spent some time, he said, with Geronimo and the Chiricahua Apaches way down south before they were caught and sent off to prison camp in Florida. He told stories of how an Apache could be standing next to you in the desert one minute, with nothing around but bunch grass and sage, and you look away for a minute, then look back and he's gone, vanished. Hiding behind a bit of grass not big enough to hide a jackrabbit—but somehow invisible.

The old man could not master that trick, he confessed, but he knew how to get into an enemy camp without anyone—even the horses—hearing him, and that's what he had taught his son, and what *he* had taught *his son*, and it had come in handy in the green jungles in the Pacific. And after so many successful sorties behind the shifting murk of enemy lines in those jungles, slipping up on Jap snipers and sending them silently off into whatever realm they believed awaited us all, it had been a chance event—a stray mortar shell in a bivouac distant from the Japanese, that sent the metal—the shrapnel—screaming into Slink's right leg, causing him to collapse in agony, knowing even as he first smelled the rotting earth below his face that he would never again walk as he once had.

Three months later he had limped out of the military hospital in San Diego, his right leg stiff as a log, and was mustered out of the United States Marine Corps, his warrior days over, with a heavy purple and gold medal, the Purple Heart, in a box in his duffel bag, another ribbon to add to the collection of those he had worn on his chest, a permanently ruined right knee, and a train ticket to Winslow, Arizona. Two days after he arrived there, his people had brought in a medicine man from Teas Toh, a man they called Lucky, and in his mother's hogan in the shadow of Nipple Butte, he performed a four-day Enemyway ceremony to cleanse the returned veteran of whatever evil still clung to him from the jungles and the killing in the Pacific.

For several months now—the Enemyway had been performed in January—Slink had busied himself around his mother's camp, doing long-neglected chores like repairing fences and outbuildings, along with restorative hours herding sheep, trying but unable to forget about the war he had fought and which still went on so far away. From time to time he would hitch up the wagon, apparently eager to run errands for his mother in Winslow, but secretly wanting to hear war news, wondering if his buddies were alive or dead. Of them, he would hear nothing, of course, those *billegannas* he had fought with from places like Brooklyn, New York, and Portland, Oregon, and Ocala, Florida, but he did hear enough from radio programs and newspapers on these visits to know that the tide seemed to be turning now. In the Pacific, U.S. forces had begun climbing the long chain of islands that would lead to Japan itself—Eniwetok, Truk, the Mariannas. In Europe, Allied forces had landed in Italy at a place called Anzio, and bombs were falling from vast armadas of Flying Fortresses on the Germans in Austria, Czechoslovakia, even in Germany itself.

And there were other signs, even in Winslow, that the war was being won.

Waking up that morning in the shade house, Slink had found his mother at her loom in the hogan. He sat down across the dirt floor with a cup of coffee from the pot simmering on the old oil drum that served as a stove and watched her until, with a slight gesture of her head, she signaled that the pattern in her mind would not be interrupted by him speaking.

"We must be winning the war," he said. "People in Winslow, they're all excited."

His mother said nothing, but patted the edge of the rug she was weaving with a stick toothed like a narrow comb.

*"Billegannas,"* Slink resumed, "in Washington, they got this Office of Price Administration. They do the rationing. You know, tires, gas, sugar, meat. They just told everyone that meat isn't rationed anymore. So we must be winning the war."

The old woman smiled, laughed quietly. Except for severe shortages in gasoline that concerned only a few people on the reservation, traders mostly, rationing had not reached the Navajo in any significant way during the past three years, while others in the country, clutching their coupons, had measured out the necessities and luxuries of life. On Indian lands there were no luxuries, and necessities had always been hard to come by—except sheep in the case of the Navajos, whose herds had remained largely intact throughout the war years. Government agents, busybodies who had always been coming to hector the Navajo about reducing their herds, and sometimes simply taking matters into their own hands, slaughtering sheep and leaving them to rot, had had other things to do for the war effort.

"Lucky for us," Slink's mother said, "those white people don't like mutton." She went on to explain to her son that her comb—she held it up—was missing some teeth and she needed him to make her another. So, having finished his coffee, Slink pulled himself painfully to his feet and exited the hogan, bent on finding the right scrap of wood down where the few scraggly piñon trees eked out a living near Nipple Butte. It was then that he saw the convoy.

"What the hell . . . ?" he said to himself in English. What the hell was an armored battalion, or whatever, doing out here? He watched as the convoy came to a halt, the dust rising up and gradually moving west, carried by the breeze, leaving half-tracks, trucks, and tanks to bake in the sun. He watched the officer who had been standing in the lead half-track get down and walk back and forth beside his vehicle while another officer from one of the trucks behind got out and approached him. The two men talked for a while, then they saluted each other and climbed back into their vehicles.

Then it struck him. The salute.

Those weren't Americans.

That was the German salute.

Germans? In American vehicles? What the hell . . . ?

Slink continued to watch as the convoy moved out. The lead half-track continued north on the Winslow road, followed by most of the convoy. But one of the half-tracks and three tanks along with a truck split off, lurching off the dirt track into the desert, heading northeast. Heading for Keams Canyon, where the Indian Agency was, Slink figured, if they continued in that direction. What was going on?

Swinging his right leg painfully forward with each step, he returned to his mother's hogan, spoke to her with unusual rapidity, and limped out to the corral. He had not been on a horse since leaving for boot camp on Parris Island years before, and he wasn't sure if he could ride now at all, what with his knee. But he had to. Minutes later, as two columns and two clouds of dust made their separate ways northward across the desert, he set off down the incline from Nipple Butte, his horse at a gentle lope. He would cross the Winslow road where it crossed this end of Jeddito Wash, head westward for a few miles through the desert, and then turn straight for Oraibi. He guessed that he would make better time in the desertlands on his horse than the column of trucks and tanks would on the Winslow road. Ahead of the column, Slink knew, were several treacherous places where the flash floods of spring had rendered parts of the road nearly impassable.

An hour later, his knee shooting pains from foot to hip, he pulled up on a slight rise, expecting to see before him the few cottonwoods and willows that lined the dry bed of Polacca Wash, which, like Oraibi Wash and Jeddito Wash north and south of it, took the occasional waters of winter to a combined entry into the wider bed of the Little Colorado River. Now they were all dry—even the Little Colorado was nothing more than a trickle appearing here and there on the surface—but they all had enough year-round moisture in the sands below to support the pale greenery of cottonwoods and willows.

Sure enough, Polacca Wash was visible two miles ahead. Slink reached down and squeezed his knee, grimacing with the added pain. He let up and that pain subsided, giving him a sense of relief, and he set out again, his eye on the lone rider up ahead near the wash, a Navajo. As he approached, he recognized him—Yellow Tooth Yazzie from down near Castle Butte, a member of the Bitter Water clan. Yellow Tooth had spotted him and was waiting on the edge of the wash.

They exchanged greetings, Yellow Tooth asking about Slink's leg, nodding when Slink shrugged.

"You should lengthen that stirrup," Yellow Tooth said. "Take the pressure off your knee."

"That's as far as it goes," Slink said.

"I seen some tanks," Yellow Tooth said. "Trucks, a big bunch going north on the Winslow road. You seen them?" Yellow Tooth said this in a combination of Navajo and English. Slink nodded, and Yellow Tooth continued, excitement audible in his quiet voice: "Said to myself I better let Raphael Luna know about them. Maybe find out what's going on. Tanks don't come up here. Not even years ago when they were out recruiting." Yellow Tooth was a man in his forties, too old to have joined up for this war, too young when the last one had broken out. Never a warrior.

Slink said nothing.

"Nothing good happens when them guys come out here like that," Yellow Tooth said, referring to old events. "My uncles told me that."

Around them was only silence.

"I don't mean you, warriors like you," Yellow Tooth said, remembering his manners. "But them guys aren't bringing any Dineh heroes home."

"I saw them too," Slink said. "Those American tanks and trucks?"

"Yeah."

"Well, it's more than you think," Slink said.

"What do you mean?"

"One bunch is going off toward Keams. Most of them are going north."

Yellow Tooth considered this for a moment. He smiled, revealing the reason for his name, four yellow upper teeth with black toothless spaces at either side. "Maybe the government's going to surround the Hopis, take 'em away somewhere. Give us that land."

Slink reached down and squeezed his knee again.

"I saw the officers," he said. "I was over near Nipple Butte and I watched the officers. They got out and talked, then they split up. Two columns. Those officers saluted like Germans. You know, like this?" He raised his arm stiffly at an angle from his shoulder. "Heil Hitler."

"Shit," Yellow Tooth said. Between the wars, he had worked in some of the copper mines to the south, Morenci Bisbee, a couple of others, where he had picked up the non-Navajo habit of cussing, along with a lifetime supply of turquoise that he traded cannily to his people, gaining enough wealth in his egalitarian society that some thought he might be a witch.

"So we better get goin'," Slink said. "That road's not too good now. Maybe we can get to the trading post ahead of them. Talk to Big Mexican." Big Mexican was the name by which Navajos for miles around knew Raphael Luna, but of course they never said it in front of him.

The two men eased their horses down into the wash and across its sandy bottom, past the remains of an old buckboard, silvered with age, that had been excavated from the sand by the spring runoff. Seconds later the two horsemen emerged on the other bank, headed due north at a ground-eating lope.

Victor Talaswaima had finished his chores in his father's cornfield down below Second Mesa in the dry wash near the mission church—hoeing the early weeds, seeing to the windbreaks behind each tiny corn plant, saying the proper prayers. The sun had turned to afternoon, and Victor made his way up the steep rocky trail to his village, Shipaulovi on Second Mesa. He could have ridden the burro, now burdened only with a few tools, but he preferred to strengthen his legs, to feel the spring in his muscles. Victor was seventeen years old, a member of the Hopi Corn clan, and he was in love.

The girl lived in the neighboring village of Mishongnovi, watched over by her eagle-eyed mother, the Bear clan matriarch of the village, who regarded her daughter as too young and maybe too good for the attentions of Victor. He pictured his love now, her hair done up into the twin whorls of maidenhood, imagined the swell of breasts under her black manta, jiggling ever so slightly as she rhythmically moved back and forth on her knees, hands clutching the dark round . . . aagh. Clutching the round rock, the grinding stone, dutifully grinding blue corn on the metate, grinding corn beside her mother, who watched her like an eagle even as she herself worked, spreading watery gray dough from blue corn on the hot black rock to make piki bread. If only, Victor thought, if only . . . He would be patient, courteous, make his presence known each day.

Before the rocky trail up the mesa turned precipitously back on itself in the direction of Shipaulovi, it passed by three immense sandstone columns jutting out of the ground and rising some forty feet in the air. These were known as Corn Rocks to the Hopi, and all Hopis looked upon these columns with reverence since they were believed to bring, by their very presence, a blessing to the fields below. There, in the desert, the Hopis had for untold generations planted their particular strains of corn, and of melons, all of which—with the help of numerous ceremonies in the plazas above, ceremonies joined in the late spring and through the summer by the katsina spirits—come to bear fruit in late summer and early autumn. If, that is, all the prayers and ceremonies were done properly and a few timely rains came. And if Corn Rocks, by its very presence, brought its particular blessings.

It was where the trail passes Corn Rocks that Victor Talaswaima paused, not for breath or rest, but with the idleness of a youth in love, there to imagine again the tender growing fruits of his beloved in the village of Mishongnovi, now almost directly above him.

In his daydreaming, he looked south out across the tawny dry lands that stretched away far below him to the Hopi Buttes, blue on the horizon. His eye singled out one butte, the one they called Nipple Butte, seeing in it every lover's dream, as had those who had named it. And then a light, and another, flashed into his eye, dazzling from the direction of the Winslow road. Again the lights flashed, several lights, on, off, how many? Maybe twenty. Maybe more. Victor had never seen anything like this. Many times he had seen a lone vehicle, the trader's truck or a tourist's car or some other vehicle, making its way up the Winslow road in the early afternoon, the sun glancing from its windshield, signaling its oncoming presence. But this many! And these days there was so little gas. Few trucks, even fewer cars, made the trip these days.

Squinting into the glare, Victor made out the dust rising above the lights. It was like his uncles had told him, the old stories handed down in the kivas at night, the story about how centuries ago Hopi men on the mesas had looked out on the desert and seen light flashing. It had been sunlight reflecting from the breastplates and shields of the Spaniards, the conquistadors, come from the south and looking for gold—those old Hopi had mistaken some of them for huge men with four legs. There had been little but trouble ever since those times long ago, the old men said in the kivas—one kind of people or another turning up on the desert below the mesas, interrupting the Hopi way.

Victor wondered what this interruption could be. The reflected glare had by now resolved itself into a column of what appeared to be military vehicles headed north. He took one last look and turned, breaking into a trot that would carry him swiftly up the side of the mesa to his village, where he would look for his uncles and let them know that an army of some kind was coming their way.

At four-seventeen on the afternoon of May 11, 1944, the first military action of Operation Shatterhand took place in Keams Canyon, Arizona. It lasted, in all, eight minutes and claimed one casualty. At its completion, all the employees of the United States government within ninety miles in all directions were suffering the humiliation of surrender and incarceration in a small cramped jailhouse that some of them—without ever thinking that anyone but the occasional drunken Indian would inhabit it—had designed themselves.

At four-seventeen a half-track, a troop truck, and three tanks, followed by a huge truck that was clearly a tanker of some sort, clattered down the narrow dirt road and came to a halt before the row of yellow sandstone buildings that comprised the Keams Canyon Indian Agency. Besides the agency office itself, there was a school, a small hospital building, a stable and garage, and the jail—all neat and rectangular—carefully laid out in a formal style along a single dirt road and towered over by the steep sandstone walls of the narrow canyon, a canyon named for Thomas Keams, one of the pioneering Indian traders of the late nineteenth century. The military vehicles turned everything in the canyon small. This was especially true of the three tanks, a huge and unprecedented presence like great beasts from some awful earlier geological era, dwarfing the buildings around them, narrowing the canyon itself, huge bodies on vast clanking tracks, cannons pointed like enormous eye stalks this way and that in an appalling metallic swagger.

Within seconds of this awesome arrival, armed men swarmed out of the half-track and the troop carrier, and the few dogs that had not already run off, tails between their legs, scuttled out of sight. With the precision of the well-trained, soldiers simultaneously thrust open the doors of the buildings of Keams Canyon and marched inside.

In the agency office, a young clerk at his desk behind a wooden balustrade looked up, amazed to see two soldiers and an officer heavily armed and wearing what were clearly the uniforms of the German Army glowering at him. Immediately, he thrust his hands skyward, at the same time managing to duck his head, thus becoming the first American official to surrender to an enemy force on American soil since the War of 1812. He stood up, managing to knock the telephone off his desk, and it clattered to the floor.

"Leave it," the officer said. "Stand still." He motioned to the wooden door behind the clerk, and a soldier approached it just as it opened. A tall, even reedy man, spectacles on his beaklike nose and black hair pulled sideways across his pate—no doubt to cover a bald spot—stepped through the door and stopped, his mouth a black round hole of shock. This was the superintendent of the Keams Canyon Indian Agency, a man whose parents had probably contributed at the very beginning of his life to his general mean-spiritedness by giving him the name of Luther Orange Lemon. Nothing in Luther Orange Lemon's career as a government bureaucrat—the years in Wyoming and Montana with the Bureau of Land Reclamation, the years in the Bureau of Indian Affairs here and there around the West on various sorry reservations, dealing with what he considered to be the dregs of the dregs—had prepared him for a confrontation with enemy soldiers festooned with ugly weapons, glowering at him in his own office. Luther Orange Lemon peed the pants of his black suit. The German soldiers and his clerk all looked down at his feet when they heard urine drip onto the floor.

The officer sneered. "You are captives of the Third Reich. I am Captain Wilhelm Muller of the German

Army, 108th Panzer Battalion, and you are our prisoners. What is your name?"

The agent coughed, stammered. "Luther Lemon," he finally said. "I'm superintendent of this agency." Just as he said this, a man flew into the room from the superintendent's office, a young man wearing a cowboy hat, his face and hands black with grease, and carrying a large monkey wrench.

"What's this?" he demanded, brandishing his wrench. "Who are you bastards?"

The corporal near the door swung the butt of his weapon upward, catching the young man with the wrench directly under his jaw and breaking it, and he sagged to the ground, eyes immediately glazed, the wrench clattering on the floor.

"Take these people to the jail," Captain Muller commanded. "Except for Mister . . . Lemon, is it? You will come with me."

Outside in the dusty street, Captain Muller and Luther Orange Lemon stood while soldiers of the 108th Panzer Battalion hauled twelve people out of the buildings—all of them men except for two nurses from the hospital, and all of them in a state of shock from this violent change in their lives—and led them to the jailhouse. None of the prisoners spoke as they were pushed along. Overhead, gray clouds had formed over the canyon, cutting off the late afternoon sun and adding to the utter gloom of the occasion.

"The jail," Superintendent Lemon said. "It wasn't built for . . . for so many."

Captain Muller merely stared at the man, marveling that someone of such height—probably six feet four—could be so thin, probably no more than 120 pounds.

"And, uh," Lemon resumed, "there's only one cell, a holding cell. The nurses. There's no place for . . ."

Captain Muller's smile was taut across his jaw. "Men

and women in the same cell. Too crowded. No privacy. Is that right, Mr. Lemon?"

"Er, yes."

"So what is good enough for the Indians in your charge," the officer said with a sneer, "is not good enough for you. Is that what you are saying?" They watched as a corporal emerged from the jail with a short copper-skinned man in tow and approached them.

"Sir," the corporal said, standing at attention, in direct contrast to the Indian, whose body might well have been stuffed with straw or cotton. The Indian was mumbling through a lopsided grin. "This man was in the cell."

"Release him," Captain Muller ordered. "With our blessing." The corporal let go of the Indian, whose legs began to crumple. But he regained them and stood swaying in the road. "Have him rest on that bench over there," the captain said, pointing to a wooden bench on the narrow porch in front of the agency office. "Get him some coffee. Find out his name. Now, you, Superintendent Lemon. At five o'clock the telephone will be restored. I want you to get on the telephone and call your superiors. Where are they, in Holbrook?"

"In Gallup."

"Good. Good. It is wise you tell the truth. And I want you to give them a routine report that everything is in order here, the phones are working again. Do you understand?"

"Yes."

"Yes *sir*."

"Yes sir."

"If you make a mistake, you will be shot. Yes, you will be shot immediately along with all the others. Except the two nurses. They will be reserved for a more prolonged agony before being shot. Do I need to explain this in more detail?"

"No sir."

"Good. Come along."

And with that, the capture of Keams Canyon was complete, its communication with the outside world securely in German hands. Operation Shatterhand's first engagement with the enemy was a resounding success. Before disappearing into the agency office with a shaken Luther Lemon, Captain Wilhelm Muller dispatched an enlisted man on a motorcycle to carry the news to Herr Major General Heinrich Schalberg in Oraibi.

Most of the twelve Hopi villages clustered on three southern prongs of a huge formation called Black Mesa look out to the southwest where, some ninety miles away on the horizon, the old volcano now called San Francisco Peaks sits, usually one or another shade of blue and even in May capped with white snow. Called Dok'osliid by the Navajos, whose lonely camps dotted the land surrounding the Hopi mesas, San Francisco Peaks is one of the four sacred mountains that delineate the extent of their world, and a place where medicine men go to gather herbs for use in their healing ceremonies. Called Nuvateekia-ovi by the Hopis, San Francisco Peaks is also the home of the katsinas, spirits that arrive in the Hopi plazas from winter to summer solstice and dance, dressed in masks, turtle shells, foxtails, and other sacred paraphernalia. When the katsinas are not dancing in the Hopi villages, they are on the peaks, rehearsing the important business of bringing moisture to the Hopi cornfields and peach orchards, and the clouds that often build up over the old volcano are reassuring signs that these important practice sessions are taking place.

Such a cloud loomed distantly over San Francisco Peaks in the late afternoon of May 10 when the main force of the 108th Panzer Battalion, led by Major General Heinrich Schalberg, arrived outside the relatively new town of Oraibi down below the mesa upon which the tattered remains of Old Oraibi lurked in gloomy solitude. Before the war years, enough tourists showed up in Oraibi each year to witness the katsina dances that the people there had seen fit to put cautionary signs up at each entrance, reminding visitors that no photographs were to be taken in the village, no sketches made. Earlier, at the turn of the century, it had taken some time for the Hopis to put two and two together—that a person with a camera might well lead to unauthorized photographs of Hopi life appearing in books and museums—but they had done just this and rigorously enforced their caveat ever since, often taking a camera away from a bewildered tourist or an outraged anthropologist and dumping the film in the dust.

Approaching Oraibi from the southwest, Heinrich Schalberg in the lead half-track had stopped to read the sign, not surprisingly seeing *Oraibi* in the crude hand lettering and believing he had arrived at the older Oraibi, which was where Banyongye lived, a man whom Schalberg's compatriots had made contact with before the war and who, they said with assurance, would welcome the Germans as mythical brothers into their midst.

Leaving the tanks and trucks on the outskirts of the ramshackle village of yellow stone houses, wooden corrals, disheveled wagons, and other matériel, Schalberg proceeded into the town, seeing no signs of life but a few feral dogs skulking in the shadows. Thoroughly depressed, he continued on until he came upon a trimmer and more promising structure—two rectangular buildings joined together under a tin roof, with a sign that said LUNA TRADING POST. In the dusty clearing around the trading post were a Ford truck that had seen much use and had a flat rear tire, and two horses—also showing signs of much use—hitched to a wooden railing and evidently asleep. As the half-track stopped in the clearing, the door to the trading post opened and Schalberg thought he glimpsed a face with dark eyes peering out. Then the door shut again without making a sound. All around him, but for the creaking of metal as his half-track's engine began to cool, was silence. He could smell some pungent smoke but, surveying the village, could not see any rising from any of the houses.

Presently, the trading post door opened again and a man of great girth and medium height emerged, wearing a black hat and black pants with suspenders over a white shirt. He stood outside the door looking over the half-track with eyes that dazzled behind droopy lids. He smiled, and Schalberg climbed down from the half-track and saluted. From somewhere near the trading post the silence was broken by what sounded to Schalberg like the croak of a giant frog. He realized that this sound had come from the man, presumably Luna, the trader, perhaps clearing his throat. Then the man spoke.

"No *sprechenzie deutsch*."

"We speak your language," Schalberg said, and noticed a smile creep over the trader's face. He had thick lips and yellow teeth and an odd air of authority.

"Which one?" the trader croaked. He raised a hand and gestured around him inclusively.

"Only English," Schalberg said, reciprocating the man's smile. "I am Major General Heinrich Schalberg, 108th Panzer Battalion of the German Army. This reservation is now under my command."

The trader Luna nodded. "You have been expected here," he said. "I am Raphael Luna. I am the Indian trader here. I am one of the few links that exist between the outside world and these Indians, and my allegiance lies with them. I and my family before me have cast our lot with these people. Perhaps you can understand that."

Schalberg nodded and the trader resumed.

"You have come to a strange world here, Major General. A world apart. Life goes on here much as it did a century ago. From time to time the government of the United States makes its presence felt, its powers known, and this has usually not been to the benefit of these people. They merely wish to be left alone, to carry out their ancient ways in peace. If your intentions here are to make that possible, to lift the yoke of oppression from their backs, I can assure you of their cooperation."

Schalberg nodded again. "That is precisely our intention. The German people have long sympathized with the plight of the Indian. We are here, among other things, to liberate the Indian and return his lands to him."

The trader smiled, revealing a row of yellow teeth. He raised his right hand from the elbow up, his palm outward, in a gesture between a salute and a preacher's blessing. "In that case," Luna said, "you are assured of my complete cooperation. When you appeared out there on the desert"—he pointed behind him with his head—"I took the liberty of sending a boy up there"—he pointed again with his head, this time to the mesa above them—"to find a man called Banyongye. He will be with us shortly, I think. He was very impressed by you people and your displays in New York City some years ago. I am sure he will make you properly welcome."

By this time two Indians had slipped through the trading post door, along with a lanky white man, and they stood in the shade next to the building, watching the proceedings without expression. So far, Schalberg thought, so good. He motioned the driver Schwabe to rest easy in the half-track. The trader turned to the men by the wall and said something in a voice that sounded a bit like he was choking. Among the outlandish words, Schalberg heard his own name. The three men on the porch nodded.

"You are in the land of the Hopis," the trader said, facing Schalberg again. "Banyongye is a respected Hopi elder. Beyond the Hopi land is Navajo country. But the two tribes intermingle here, Hopi and Navajo, especially at this trading post. These men here—one is my clerk, Jenkins. He is a mute. He cannot speak. The other two are Navajos. The Navajos are a soft-spoken race. None of us here, I am sure"—again he gestured as if to include all the land in sight—"mean you any harm."

"Yes," Schalberg said. "I will count on your cooperation." His eye caught movement on the edge of the dusty ground around the trading post and he turned to see three men and a boy approaching, clambering down a trail from the mesa above, picking their way among the yellow boulders and rock slabs that had tumbled down its edge. In the lead was a short man with gray hair cut off across his forehead, and, on the sides, at chin level rather like a woman. He had a red bandanna folded up and wrapped around his head and wore a white shirt, faded and baggy gray trousers, and brown leather moccasins. A necklace of turquoise beads hung around his neck and a chunk of turquoise hung by string from each fleshy earlobe. The two men walking behind him, younger by a decade perhaps, were similarly dressed, and the boy, barefoot, wore only a pair of ragged blue pants.

"Here is Banyongye now," the trader said in his raspy voice.

Surely, Schalberg thought, this was all a far cry from Winnetou and his noble kinsmen conjured by the books of Karl May. It was a far cry even from the actual photographs of mounted warriors with warbonnets and lances he had seen in German texts about the great warriors of the plains. The seedy, impoverished look of the village, cluttered with junk and sad one-story stone buildings, no more than a room or two each, and these frail little men with red bandannas around their heads and cheap homespun clothes—none of this was what Schalberg had expected. How short a time it had taken the hated Americans to turn the West, the frontier, into a rural slum, and its original inhabitants into such a degraded lot.

But neither had Schalberg imagined that his entry into these Indian lands, his occupation of this vast portion of the United States of America, could have gone any

smoother than it so far had. Operation Shatterhand—
based as it was on the original Schalberg Plan formulated
years ago in the basement offices of the Oberkommando
des Heeres in Berlin—was taking shape on the ground as
if watched over by a smiling, magical star of its own.

# Two

The old man called Banyongye, flanked by his two lieutenants, approached the natty gray-uniformed German officer, Heinrich Schalberg, from the west and stood before him, their shoulders pulled back and their heads up, as if in a childish imitation of a soldier at attention, or posing for a photograph. The late afternoon sun shone directly into Schalberg's face over the heads of the little Hopis, and he began to sweat under the heavy cloth of his uniform, the weight of his high-peaked military hat, the leather belts, the high leather boots. Banyongye's face was deeply lined, and he looked up at Schalberg from dark brown eyes sunk like knots in an old tree.

After what seemed several minutes but was only a few seconds of silence, Banyongye cleared his throat and launched into a speech, his voice rising and falling in formal liquid flourishes as strange vowel sounds poured forth from his narrow lips. Glancing to his left, Schalberg noticed that several more men were now under the porch roof of the trading post, short men like Banyongye and therefore, he reckoned, Hopis too. They had materialized as if out of nothing.

Here and there during Banyongye's address, Schalberg heard the word *pahana* and also *German*. He stood bemused until the old man had finished. Then he turned toward the heavyset trader and raised his eyebrows questioningly.

"Let me translate," Luna said. "Banyongye has said

many things in a highly formal version of the Hopi language. You might think of his use of the formal, or ceremonial, mode as a kind of certification of his words. To be brief, he welcomes you here as a representative? Yes, a representative of the White Brother, the Pahana. That is a figure from the deep Hopi past, and I will be happy to explain it all to you later. Suffice it to say that Banyongye is pleased you have come. He says that he speaks for all when he welcomes you here on your mission. He has arranged a place for you, sir, to stay in Old Oraibi—up there—but was unaware that you'd be accompanied by so many. He regrets that he has not made room for all of your men but will see what can be done. He invites you—and of course all your men—to attend the long-haired katsina dance that will take place in the plaza—this one, down here—tomorrow." Luna finished and rolled back on the heels of his black, narrow-toed boots. They were cowboy boots, Schalberg realized, and they looked very expensive.

Schalberg nodded his head in a slight bow to the old man before him, turned to Luna and said: "Please tell him that I accept his welcome in behalf of all my men. Tell him that his hospitality is deeply appreciated, but we will make our own arrangements rather than inconvenience him and his people in their village. I will stay with the men, of course. Tell him that we will appreciate his cooperation, and that of all the Indian people here, in the completion of our mission. Part of that mission, tell him, is to free his people from the yoke the Americans have placed upon them, and to restore to them the lands that are rightfully theirs."

Luna's eyebrows danced briefly over his eyes, and he nodded.

"Tell him also," Schalberg went on, "that our schedule will not permit me or my men to accept his kind invitation to the festivities tomorrow. Indeed, we will require the work of many of his people for our preparations. I presume that he, as chief, will be able to assign his men, his braves, to these details."

Out of the corner of his eye Schalberg detected some motion among the Indians on the porch, and glancing over, saw one Indian, one of the Navajos, bent over in a violent coughing fit. Schalberg hoped it wasn't tuberculosis or some other communicable disease to which this wretched place was probably subject.

The heavyset trader emitted a froglike croak. "A word of advice, Herr Major General, if I may."

"Yes?"

"Several things. First of all, you can speak directly to Banyongye in English. He spoke in Hopi at the outset only by way of making his welcome—how shall we say it?—as lofty as possible." At this, Banyongye grinned and nodded. "Second, it is customary, and a very important custom, to accept his hospitality, for you to stay at the house he has arranged for you personally. Perhaps you can assign another officer to be with your troops down below. Also, you or someone from your command should attend the katsina dance. It is more than a courtesy, you see. A katsina dance is a highly sacred ceremony, and your attendance is a matter of"—Luna searched for a word—"solidarity."

"I see," Schalberg said, frowning.

He turned to Banyongye, clicked his heels, and said: "I accept with gratitude your kind offer of a house, and I look forward to the dance tomorrow. Perhaps, now, you would like to accompany me while I inspect my men. And we can talk further."

The old man beamed, all the wrinkles in his face deepening. Together the three Hopis and the German officer turned and began walking to the village outskirts, beyond which the men and armor rested in the sun, casting shadows on the ground. Schalberg stopped abruptly and turned back to the trader.

"You, Luna. I will need to talk with you later. About

the availability here of certain supplies. Food. Fuel. Oh yes, I am expecting a messenger from your Keams Canyon. Please send him to me if he comes here first."

"But of course," Raphael Luna said, bowing his head in salute, and watched the odd little phalanx of the German officer followed closely by the Hopis, three abreast, move off. On the porch, two of the Hopi men were smiling. As the German and Banyongye's party disappeared, one of them put his hand to his open mouth and patted it, emitting a quiet but high-pitched whooping sound while ducking his head and lightly stomping his feet in an exaggerated Indian dance.

"Big Chief Banyongye," chanted the other. "Big Chief Banyongye. Son of Great Chief Hiawatha. Banyongye Big Chief of all the Hopis and all the Navajos. He makum Big Medicine."

At the far end of the porch the two Navajos and Luna's clerk watched these antics expressionlessly.

"All right," Luna said. "All right. Let's go inside. We have some work to do here."

Raphael Luna sat stolidly behind his plain wooden desk in the bare office with whitewashed walls and one window. Before him, seated on a long wooden bench and two chairs, were Jenkins, the clerk, the two Navajos— Yellow Tooth and Slink from the south—and two Hopis, Secakuku, and Quavehema. Both of the latter lived on Second Mesa, twelve miles away from Oraibi, and had recently finished high school in the public school at Winslow, where, two days earlier, they had signed up at the recruiting office to join the United States Army.

"Jenkins," Luna said. "I trust you have no quarrel with my sudden maiming of you." Jenkins, a preternaturally thin man with a skull-like face, grinned and pointed to his open mouth. Luna turned to the Hopis. "When are you two supposed to report to the army?" he asked.

"A week," Secakuku said. Of the two Hopi youths,

Secakuku was a bit taller, perhaps five-six. Both were lean and, under their cotton shirts, stringy with sinew. The two were letting their hair, cut short for the white man's school, grow out, even though it would soon be shorn again by army barbers.

Luna nodded. "Let's hope you can. But in the meantime, there's plenty to do here. We have been invaded by a panzer battalion of the German Army. The 108th." Luna spat into the brass spittoon on the floor beside his desk and leaned back in the chair. "It seems impossible. It seems absurd," he said, as if to himself. "But it has happened. My telephone is out," he resumed. "I imagine all the others on the reservation are. I'm sure they've seen to that. And who in the wider world will notice? But we need to get word out. Have you two been running, keeping in shape?"

The two Hopi youths nodded.

"Mexican Hat, Utah," the trader said. "There is a man in Mexican Hat. His name is Fenwick. He's a ham."

The Indians looked puzzled. "A ham?" Secakuku asked.

"He has a shortwave radio setup. How long will it take you to get there? Two days?"

"Tomorrow night, maybe before," Secakuku said. He smirked. "If all those Big Mountain Navajos on Black Mesa don't catch us."

The other Hopi, Quavehema, grinned. "Tomorrow afternoon," he said. "I been there once. Go through Kayenta, maybe a hundred miles. My grandfather ran all the way to Fort Wingate and back in two days."

"Ah, yes," Luna said, again as if to himself. The feats of Hopi runners were well-known, and occasionally exaggerated. "The legendary Hopi runners. Are you ready to go?"

The two Hopis nodded. Luna opened a drawer before him with a squeak and took out some plain white paper and an ornate black Waterman fountain pen. He began to scratch out a message while the Indians and his clerk sat motionlessly and the late sun began to fade in the room. As Luna's fine, spidery script filled the page, he looked up at the two Hopis.

"You'll take whatever you need for the trip from the store." They nodded, and Luna went back to his writing. Finished with the one sheet, he took the other and wrote:

Fenwick: Get this message exactly as written to Harry Hopkins. I hardly need tell you it is urgent. Do not, repeat not, tell another soul. These boys will wait for the reply. Expect more runners. RL

The trader folded the sheets of paper together into thirds, then in half, and wrote *Oscar Fenwick* and an address on the front. He handed them to Secakuku, whom he knew was the older of the two by two months, and said something in Hopi, a standard blessing.

"If there's any trouble, any likelihood you'll be caught, swallow these."

Secakuku took the papers, slipped them in his belt. Without a word, the two Hopi youths left the office.

"The major general," Luna said into the room. "The major general needs to remain confident of our loyalty. Confident for the next few days that he has hundreds of Hopis and Navajos, able-bodied men, to call on for whatever plan he has in mind. He would seem to be the sort who is easily reassured. Surely, Banyongye is now exaggerating to him the respect with which the Hopis regard him. The German should also be given the idea that the Navajos regard Banyongye with similar respect"—He paused elaborately—"during this time of great opportunity for the Indian people as a whole. The return of their ancestral lands, and all that. Does that sound about right?" Luna leaned back again. "But I doubt Herr Schalberg is anyone's fool. We'll have to be very careful. Slink, what would your great-grandfather do?"

"Manuelito?"

The trader nodded. One of Slink's maternal great-grandfathers, Manuelito, was deeply revered as a great Navajo warrior of the modern era, having been one of the leaders of the Navajo charge of two thousand against the soldiers at Fort Defiance in 1860. The largest Navajo force ever assembled, it poured into the canyon and nearly succeeded in overrunning the fort until the troops rolled out artillery and drove the Navajos off. After this, Manuelito and others went back to the traditional form of warfare, small raiding parties with less ambitious goals—a little retaliation here, a little there.

Slink said, "I don't know. You been to Fort Defiance, back there in that canyon. All those Navajos went in there, just the one entrance. I don't think it was my grandfather's idea. It didn't work real good. I guess he'd say let's wait, take a look, see what these guys are doing."

"How long can we do that?" Luna asked. "You were in the military. What do you suppose their plan is?"

Slink shrugged. "I don't know. Whatever it is, I guess they're gonna take a day or two to get organized, get us Indians organized to help 'em." Slink shrugged again. "Probably take longer than two days to get us Indians organized." He smiled. " 'Specially those Hopis."

Raphael Luna permitted himself a rare laugh out loud.

On the barren flat land west of the village of Oraibi, Heinrich Schalberg led his Hopis among the armor of the 108th Panzer Battalion. German soldiers, in fatigues, and many of them stripped down to the waist in the heat, were tinkering with engines and equipment. Others were off-loading cartons of rations from the personnel carrier trucks and busying themselves erecting a small, orderly town of four-man tents and netting on poles with brush added to conceal the vehicles from any possible flyovers by U.S. reconnaissance planes. Here and there, on the periphery of this activity, small clusters of Indians appeared, watching silently.

"Those are your people, eh?" Schalberg inquired, gesturing to the observing Indians.

"Some Hopi," Banyongye said. "Some Navajo. Navajos used to steal a lot. You gotta watch 'em."

"So?" Schalberg said.

"They don't do that no more too much," Banyongye added.

"Do they have a chief? Like you?"

Banyongye shrugged. "Old Hopi knowledge. A Navajo comes up on a horse to fight, you're gonna lose. You get him off his horse, you can win."

"Ah," Schalberg said. "I understand." He called out to the driver of one of the half-tracks now parked under a tarpaulin and waved it toward him. The engine rumbled, roared, and the vehicle slowly inched its way forward into the open. Schalberg stepped over to the open rear section of the vehicle where, above its tanklike tracks and armored sides, a .50 caliber machine gun protruded ominously. He spoke briefly in German to the gun crew, and pointed off to the west where, about half a mile away, three rock pinnacles stood like hunchbacked men with broad-brimmed hats against the horizon. Schalberg noted that all the Indians nearby turned to look where he was pointing.

One of the half-track crew placed what looked like a steel pipe at an angle on a shelf in the half-track's open rear. He reached down and fiddled with some dials, finally nodding. Then he reached down and lifted a heavy bomblike object up, holding the mortar shell out for all to see. Suddenly, he let it fall down the pipe and it spun away. A vicious thunk of fire and smoke sent the projectile off to the west, and within seconds the middle one of the three pinnacles shattered in a burst of smoke and a spray of yellow rock. The sound of an explosion then arrived, followed by a long silence and then a low bass sound, like a moan, arising from the clusters of Indians.

"Excellent," Schalberg said. He leaned down to speak to Banyongye. "Perhaps the Navajos will understand that they have been unhorsed, yes?"

Banyongye, his brown face now underlain by a gray pallor, nodded bravely, smiled, and nodded again. Banyongye, of course, as well as the other Indians watching, and the Hopis and Navajos who would soon hear about this feat and see its results, were aware that the Wehrmacht had just destroyed one-third of a natural shrine and praying place sacred to the Hopi, and therefore regarded with a certain awe by the Navajos as well.

"You can tell them all," Schalberg said, "that you speak for me."

Banyongye swallowed, nodded again, and looked nervously over his shoulder at two Indians approaching on horseback. Both wore black hats with high crowns and wide, flat brims. They pulled up about fifteen yards from where Schalberg and the three Hopis stood, and one of them, a man with huge, round shoulders, dismounted awkwardly.

"Navajos," Banyongye said. "This one is named Slink. The other"—he pointed with his lips to the one still on his horse—"he's Yellow Tooth. They're from down at Castle Rock." He gestured with his head to the south.

Schalberg watched the big Navajo limp toward him, his eyes apparently focused on something behind the officer and to his left. He stood before the German officer, and said "Ya-ta-hey."

Banyongye said, "Navajo hello."

"You injured your leg?" Schalberg said.

"Fell off my horse a while back," Slink said. "Broke my knee. Name is Slink."

"Slink," Schalberg repeated.

"Come to see what you need. Navajos, lot of Navajos, good with engines."

Schalberg looked at Banyongye, who seemed to be dreaming. The old man looked up and nodded.

"Banyongye here will let you know what we need. How many are you?" The Navajo was still looking somewhere past him, and Schalberg thought that the name Slink probably fit the man well, a shifty Indian.

Slink shrugged. "A lot." His eyes now swept the horizon from south through the west to the north, and he gestured behind him with his head. "All around."

Banyongye cleared his throat. "You and Yellow Tooth, you can bring them here to help the Germans?"

Slink nodded, and the man called Yellow Tooth, leaning on the horn of his saddle, spat, smiled and nodded. "Lot of Navajos," he said. "Here." He pointed at the ground and made a circle. "Tomorrow morning." He grinned again, revealing four ugly yellowed teeth flanked by black spaces.

Schalberg turned to the Hopi leader. "When does the ceremony begin tomorrow?"

Banyongye looked up at the sky and turned to face the east. He pointed about midway up from the horizon. "When the sun gets there."

"Good. Now, Slink, can you have your Navajos report to Banyongye here when the sun is there?" He pointed to a spot lower in the sky, just above a ragged-looking mesa to the east, lit gold in the late sun and sitting mute like a mothballed battleship in a frozen sea of rock.

Slink glanced in that direction, then down at his feet. He nodded, turned and began to limp toward his horse. Off in the distance a whining sound broke the silence, and presently a cloud of dust appeared over the flat rooftops of the village of Oraibi, moving in their direction. A motorcycle appeared around one of the houses and made its way slowly over the bumpy ground. A helmeted soldier with goggles covered with dust, as was the rest of him, cut the engine, climbed off, saluted, and stood at attention.

"Report," Schalberg said.

"Keams Canyon is secure, Herr Major General," the soldier said, as if reciting. "Twelve prisoners in the jailhouse. One slightly injured. Two of them women. Nurses. The chief, the—uh—superintendent . . . Lemon has spoken to his superiors in Gallup, reporting all is normal. Captain Muller is in charge, of course. A thirteenth person was found in one of the residences, a woman. Frau Lemon. She is also in custody. Radio contact is now open to Arabian Nights. The first flight is scheduled to arrive at 0200, twelve May."

Schalberg nodded. "Very good, Corporal. Dismissed. But stand by for further orders." The man snapped his arm out in salute.

"Heil Hitler," he said, and Schalberg touched the visor of his cap.

Major General Heinrich Schalberg spent the rest of the afternoon and early evening overseeing the deployment of his men and armor, and to their care and feeding, making a point of personally congratulating each unit for the smooth and glorious arrival of troops of the Third Reich on the soil of the hated Americans. At each stop, he presented Banyongye, the Hopi leader and chief who held the allegiance of both Hopi and Navajo tribes, whose members would join the Germans tomorrow for orientation and training. Schalberg understood the benefit of personal contact between a commander and his men— something he had witnessed many times serving under Rommel, the legendary Desert Fox. It had been Schalberg's habit, for instance, to be seen sharing the men's rations rather than partaking of the slightly more palatable food provided in the officers' mess.

Leaning in the shade against one of the Sherman tanks under its camouflage, Schalberg listened to the crew's banter as they happily loitered in his presence. An officer had escorted the three Hopis to the mess tent, where they could watch a crew doling out rations. In their absence, the tank crews' conversation turned to these new German allies.

"Whatever happened to these people? Where's Winnetou when we need him?"

"The Americans must have bred them all down."

"Yes, down and out."

(Laughter.)

"I heard these Indians were one of the lost tribes of Israel, got blown off course and wound up here."

"You mean they were Jews once?"

"Yeah."

"All right, but what *happened* to them?"

(Prolonged laughter.)

"Where are the women? God knows what *they* look like."

"Maybe there aren't any. Maybe they breed some other way."

"God, Willie, what a disgusting thought."

(Laughter.)

"Gentlemen, maybe we should wait before forming an opinion. These people are our allies now."

"Yes, sir."

"And we will find ways of making them useful. They know the terrain, for one thing."

"Yes, sir."


As the sun went down and a deep, cloudless dark began to descend over the buttes and mesas, Schalberg accompanied the three Hopi elders up the rocky trail to Old Oraibi. His driver, Corporal Schwabe, had asked to go along, ever protective, but Schalberg had waved off his concern. "Come, come, Hans," Schalberg had said. "These people mean me no harm. They'll appreciate my show of faith in their good intentions." Corporal Schwabe had grumbled but complied. Similarly, Schalberg had reasoned, having his second in command, Colonel Franz Liepzichte, prepare the landing strip for

the arrival of the first troop plane at 0200 hours the following night was a morale-building show of confidence
by the leader. Tomorrow night the great Condor, painted
black and stripped down to little more than engines and a
cargo-holding shell, would leave his mother's ranch in
Sonora, code-named Arabian Nights, fly four hours, land,
unload, and be back on the Mexican side of the border
before dawn. According to plan. Three such nightly shipments, and stage two of Operation Shatterhand would be
complete. There were many details to be seen to in the
interval, Schalberg thought. Nearly an impossible number of details. But his subordinates knew their orders, and
he needed to sleep. God, how he needed to sleep.

The Hopis led Schalberg silently past the ruin of the
old mission church, looming against the now dazzling
stars like a vengeful angel at rest, wings folded, and proceeded across a wide stretch of rimrock into the alley-
ways of the village. Here and there, a dim orange light
showed through a curtained window, and the sounds of
chanting and drumming haunted the night as if a wind
had arisen from a distant cave.

"The men are preparing for the katsinas," Banyongye
said. "In the kivas."

"Kivas."

"Over there. See that ladder coming out there? That's
a kiva. It's like your church, but under the ground. Inside
Mother Earth."

"I see," said Schalberg, who, though no churchman—
indeed far from it—found the idea utterly barbaric.

Minutes later Schalberg stood in a small, low-
ceilinged room with walls of rough whitewashed plaster
over rocks. A woodstove in one corner heated a huge
metal pot where something resembling stew bubbled.
Next to it was an oil drum filled nearly to the brim with
water, and around the walls were cots covered with
cheap rugs. An old woman stood by the stove, idly stirring her pot, bent over like a fairy-tale witch, clad in a

black dress and a multicolored apron. Seated on the cots
was an assortment of children ranging from infants to
what appeared to be a teenage girl. Her shiny black hair
had been wound up into two flat whorls, one on either
side of her head, and she looked vaguely Oriental. Like
the old woman, she wore a black robe that hung from one
shoulder. They all giggled when Banyongye presented
Schalberg to them, first in Hopi, then in English.

"Seet down, seet down," said the old crone—
Banyongye's wife—in a reedy, high voice. "Eat, eat."
She gestured toward a rickety table beyond the oil drum
and flanked by two wooden chairs with straight backs.

"Sit down," Banyongye reiterated, and pulled out a
chair for the German officer.

The two men sat, and Schalberg watched as the old
woman put a bowl of the stew in front of him, dropping a
battered spoon beside it. She put another bowl down for
Banyongye, who began to spoon some gray meat into his
mouth along with white puffy matter. He looked up at
Schalberg.

*"Noquivi,"* he said. "Hopi stew. Mutton. Hominy. It's
real good. Real good." He took another mouthful, and
Schalberg followed suit. It had a smoky, salty taste—
rich—and it felt wonderfully warm in his mouth. Schalberg hadn't tasted salt for three days. All the Hopis
smiled as he spooned in the stew with obvious relish. The
girl seemed especially fascinated, and several times he
looked up to catch her averting her nearly black eyes and
then giggling at the child next to her, a younger girl, perhaps ten or eleven years of age.

The old woman put a loaf of bread on the table. It was
baked into a strange bifurcated shape that reminded
Schalberg of the twin whorls of hair on the teenager
across the room. Banyongye broke a piece off and used it
to soak up the juice left in the bottom of his bowl. Schalberg again followed suit, finding the bread excellent—
not unlike some heavy German breads—and Banyongye

summoned more stew for their bowls and watched appreciatively as the old crone ladled it. They ate again, the children all watching, and then Banyongye stood up.

"I go to the kiva now. Help out with the singing. I'll show you where you can sleep."

The heat of the room along with the comfortable weight of the Hopi stew and the bread in his stomach had made Schalberg pleasantly drowsy, and he welcomed the idea, the luxury, of a bed. Even a cot like those against the wall. He thanked the woman for the food, nodded to the rest of the family, and followed Banyongye into the night, now chilly with a steady breeze blowing through the alleyway. In what seemed to be the next house, nothing more than a separate room with a separate entrance, Banyongye lit an old oil lamp. Clearly it was a storeroom of some sort, small, perhaps three meters square. Among stacks of cardboard cartons and fifty-pound sacks of flour was a narrow cot covered with a brown blanket and a pillow.

"This is your place," Banyongye said. "You want to get up with the sun? Before it?"

"Before. A little before."

"I wake you."

Schalberg, almost asleep before he had undressed, stretched out on the cot and pulled the blanket over his chest. The thought occurred to him before he sank into slumber that this Hopi hospitality surely did not include anything like a shower or a bath. He must stink like a pig, he thought as he drifted happily off.

As with many military men, Schalberg's dreams tended to be about organizing, often nearly impossible jobs of organizing complex affairs against an unpredictable kaleidoscope of interferences and challenges, none of which make the slightest sense when recalled upon awakening. This night, Schalberg was engaged in bringing together the many elements—both human and mechanical—required for building a huge boat, something like a tanker, before an enormous, slow-moving tidal wave swept him and the entire operation out to sea. He was successfully supervising twenty men lowering a diesel engine into the hull when he found himself being pestered by hands tugging at him. He waved them off, swearing, but they persisted, and he awoke in the pitch-black to someone breathing on his face, hands plucking at the blanket.

"Ach!" he said, starting violently.

"Sshhh," said a whisper, and he felt soft lips on his chin, hands peeling the blanket down, the warmth of a body pressed against his side. However, he could see nothing. Shaking off the cobwebs of sleep, his eyes becoming somewhat accustomed to the dark, it became apparent to the major general what was taking place in the storeroom full of cartons and sacks of flour, and his senses began to respond while his mind raced, even careened, wildly. He reached out in the dark and touched a velvety shoulder, thinking, My God, is this traditional Hopi hospitality? Indian hospitality? Like Eskimo men I read about somewhere? Giving a visitor a wife. Not Banyongye's wife, God forbid. No.

Karl May said nothing of this. No soft, anonymous body like this ever joined the noble Winnetou or the mountain man Shatterhand in the dark of the night. Schalberg laughed inwardly.

The touches in the dark moved on while Schalberg thought, *Are* these people descended from a lost tribe of Israel? Will I be doing it with one of *them*? Can I? Aren't they subhuman? Well, that part surely isn't. Nor is that part. Can I bring myself to do this? Heh, it's not a matter anymore of bringing myself, is it? Who is this? That girl with the whorls. The whorls are gone, long silky hair. Handfuls of it. I wish I could see. No, maybe it's better that I don't. Lips on my neck, nice, nice . . . Ow! What's *that*? Christ, like a vampire, a leech on my neck. This is *savage* ... This *is* a savage ... oh, savagely, barbarously, yes ...

Major General Schalberg turned off his mind and gave himself over to the tempestuous, anonymous lover in his cot, and when he felt Banyongye's hesitant touch on his shoulder about a half hour before the sun rose over the mesa to the east, she had of course disappeared. As he sat groggily on the edge of the cot, reaching around in the dark for his clothes, he wondered if the entire sweet, heaving, enveloping thing had been nothing more than a lonely soldier's dream.

A predawn glow began to fill the room, and he noticed that the old Hopi had left a bowl of water for him on one of the cartons. From his kit, he took a small hand mirror, propped it beside the bowl and washed his face. The room grew lighter. The sun, he thought, must come up very fast here. But how could that be?

He disliked shaving with cold water, but he had gotten used to it. As he began to prepare himself for that, he noticed something, a dark place, on his neck. He looked more closely. It was oval-shaped, and in the dim light it appeared to be a dark purplish-red. It had been no dream last night.

He reached for his jacket, hastily put it on over his bare chest and buttoned it up. The collar covered only half of the oval mark. He stared at the bruiselike half oval peering back at him from his collar near his jugular vein. He shrugged. Savagery. He would have to find out that girl's name, give her a present of some sort, some trinket. He smiled.

In return for this fine badge.

Rank, Major General Schalberg thought, has its privileges. He looked again at his image in the dull little mirror. His hair needed cutting. It was especially ragged over his left ear, and he tried to smooth it down.

Once shaved and properly dressed, he stepped out into the thin sun streaming over the mesa to the east, and looked up and down the alleyway. Yellow stone houses on both sides looked like they were soon to fall down of their own weight. Dusty ground. Yellow sky overhead turning to blue. He smelled a particularly pungent wood smoke, a delightful smell, and followed his nose toward it, losing it in the chill morning but finding himself soon enough on the edge of the village where the rocky ground fell precipitously away, strewn with boulders and slabs of what he guessed was sandstone. From where he stood, he could see down to the desert below where his troops and armor were. There were the usual early morning signs of activity. His men looked like ants out there, the vehicles like toys.

Closer to him, about ten meters down a narrow trail between two immense boulders, he spotted a wooden shack, an outhouse. He needed it, wondered if it were in use. Clambering down to it, his nose was assaulted, and he peered around its side. No door. No one in it. A two-seater. How revolting. He used it hastily, wondering what kinds of spiders and other grotesque forms of desert life might dwell there under the wooden planks, eyeing his tenderest parts, and went back into the village, to Banyongye's house and the rich smell of Hopi stew— what was its name? *Noquivi.* That was it.

Inside the little house the old woman greeted him with a toothless grin, then served him a metal cup of thin coffee and a bowl of steaming stew at the rickety table. He learned that Banyongye had gone to the kiva to welcome the long-hair katsinas. While he ate, the girl entered the house, her hair done up in twin whorls. Her little sister, or whatever, followed her. The girl with the whorls glanced at him, turned to her little companion and put her hand briefly to her mouth, as if suppressing a smile, and began sweeping the floor with a broom made of stiff grass. The old woman said: "Eat, eat," and put a loaf of the oddly shaped bread before him.

Feeling strangely at home in this outlandish and alien

place, Heinrich Schalberg smiled, nodded, said: "This is all very good, very good, I thank you," and finished his breakfast, his mind now running smoothly through a list of military details, chiefly logistical. The airstrip needed building, a fuel inventory was essential, the surrounding land needed reconnaisance, and the Indians . . . he needed to discover how much they could be used, and for what.

Banyongye was not in the kiva where the long-haired katsinas were preparing for their long day of dancing in the heat and dust of the plaza of the new village down below. He was in the kiva of the One-Horn Society, responding to the ornately phrased questions raised by other elders, men who had assembled there at dawn from several of the Hopi villages to find out about these new people, these Germans, now in their midst with all their weapons of war and destruction.

The old men were seated on bancos on both sides of the kiva near where the ladder rested, rising up through the square hole in the roof. Below the ladder, in a shallow pit in the dirt floor, a small fire smoldered, smoke rising languidly upward to disappear in the sky outside.

Banyongye's mind was working as fast as it could, having been confronted with a difficult question: If, it had been asked, the Germans represented the Pahana, the White Brother who was one day to return to assist the Hopi people, then why had they used their pipe gun on the truck tank and blown up the middle figure of Powatemaskewa, the sacred Eagle clan shrine? The place from which the Eagle clan priests could look out and measure with their eye the eagle-gathering lands that were ancestrally theirs?

Banyongye looked from his interlocutor, a man several years older than he from Second Mesa, to the others, eight in all, everyone now looking politely down at the fire in the ground while the question hung there in the kiva with the weight of a lightning-bearing cloud.

"According to the prophecies," Banyongye began, and some of the men shifted their weight with what appeared to be impatience, "the Pahana will have come at the time of the purification. Our history is one of purifications, of returning time and time again to the simple things, to humble ways. Of casting away the ways that have been corrupted and have grown away from the meaning of Hopi. My uncles told me that many of our ways have been corrupted and that it is time coming again that we cast off some of those things."

"And Powatemaskewa is one of those?" asked the priest from Second Mesa with a hint of sarcasm in his voice. He was the leader of the Bluebird clan, whose sacred responsibilities included knowing and interpreting the history of the people. Banyongye, whose clan had less exalted duties, knew he was on shaky ground here.

"My uncles," Banyongye replied, "said us Hopis would again put too much meaning in things that don't mean anything, and those things would have to be destroyed."

"And my uncles told me that your uncles didn't know nothing," the Bluebird man said.

A silence fell over the kiva and an early shaft of sunlight appeared through the roof, slanting across the angle of the ladder in a complex geometry of light, shadow, and wood.

"I do not say that these Germans are the Pahana. Only his representatives. How could they know everything? Even the Pahana has been gone from here a long time. Since the beginning. Things change."

Two of the old men in the kiva nodded, seeking peace and finding something of value in Banyongye's nearly sacrilegious suggestion that the Pahana's wisdom could be imperfect. "This is true," one of them said. "Things change."

"Aren't these the same people we are at war with across that other ocean?"

"The government, yes," Banyongye said. "The government is at war with them. In Europe. They are different than the Japanese people where some of our Hopi men have gone. But these Germans, they have come to liberate us Hopi people, give us back our land. That is what the man Schalberg has said."

"What land? The land the Navajos have taken? That's the only land we have lost."

"No, all our land, our *chuska*," Banyongye said. "All the land within the eight shrines." Banyongye referred to a vast territory stretching north as far as Utah, south almost to Phoenix, where Hopis had ancestrally roamed alone, communing with ancient spirits, gathering ceremonial materials. Some of the Hopis—only certain select priests—were authorized to make pilgrimages to the eight shrines, to pray for the land and the people within it, people who now included the Anglo citizens of such places as Flagstaff, Winslow, Holbrook, and a host of smaller towns, ranches, along with Indian settlements of Apaches, Walapais, Havasupais, a few Utes, and a large number of intrusive Navajos. Such was the complexity of the Hopi worldview that they felt in some way spiritually responsible for even their most distrusted neighbors.

"What do you know about the *chuska*, the eight shrines?" the Bluebird man asked. "Only what you have heard."

"Neither have you visited all the shrines," Banyongye retorted.

At the far end of the row of men on the western side of the kiva, a very old man raised his head and stared in the direction of the fire through eyes opaque with cataracts.

"This is not good," he said in a near whisper. "We cannot have anger here with the katsinas. It must stop." The men in the kiva all nodded. "We need a sign, Banyongye," the old man went on presently. "We need a sign that these men, these Germans, are from the Pahana. You shall find such a sign and show it to us. And we shall investigate it to see if it is a true sign after all. Tomorrow. Bring us the sign before the sun goes down."

The meeting was over. Slowly, one by one, the old priests stood, walked counterclockwise around the still smoldering fire and climbed the ladder into the morning sun. Last to leave, the Bluebird clan leader stared into the fire before he climbed the ladder, and shook his head. One of his grandsons had joined the navy and died on a ship somewhere in the ocean, that Pacific, two years ago. They had never been able to find his body in the ocean so it had not come back to the Hopi to be buried, even long after the prescribed four days from death-to-burial that assured the deceased's spirit passage. The old man wondered where his grandson's spirit was now, restless, lost. Things were confusing in this world now. The trader, Luna, he had told the old man that Pacific was an English word meaning peaceful. Nothing made any sense anymore. Maybe it *was* time for the purification. He pulled his old body up the ladder and, with a sense of relief, let his mind turn to the blessed katsinas, now nearly ready to dance in the plaza below.

Mary Beth Lemon's life had been going steadily downhill, she reflected, ever since she got that first job as a clerk in the Bureau of Land Management office in godforsaken Enid, Oklahoma, far from her green family farm in rural Illinois, but a job was a job in those hard times— God knows they were still hard times—and she'd been able to send some money home to her mother the first few years. But the work had been boring, the hours long, and the whole place filled with jerks who wanted to grab her fanny all the time, and leered, and told stupid off-color stories on the dumb theory, she guessed, that stupid stories about cows doing it or whatever were the sort of thing to get a woman excited. Mary Beth—her name was

Ogden then, her maiden name—was no prude, and she was no maiden either, she'd seen to that back in Illinois, but she wasn't about to let any one of those BLM creeps get anywhere near her private parts. Not on their life.

But it was lonely and she'd tried to find some proper society in Enid, which was about as easy as growing hay on a lake. There were a couple of seedy dance halls full of true champion idiots and women that had to be selling it to them for cheap, and so it was with relief that she learned in the fall of 1936 that the government had transferred her to Indian Affairs and would ship her to the White Mountain Apache reservation in Arizona. She liked the idea of Indians, having never met any in southern Illinois when she was growing up, and hadn't been disappointed when she got to Arizona. The mountains were green and beautiful most of the year, and covered with gorgeous pure white snow in winter, and the Apaches fascinated her, what with the sour look they always wore, and their gentle voices and, she learned after a while, their peculiar sense of humor.

Even so, it was desperately lonely for a young white woman there in the middle of nowhere, a woman who wasn't about to mess around with any Indian men, no matter how strong they looked or how good they could shoot deer or elk or whatever, and eventually she had let herself get involved with old sourpuss, as she now called him, the lanky, buttoned-up Luther Orange Lemon, then an assistant superintendent and eleven years her senior. He was boring even then, but kind enough and devoted, and so they had gotten married by the minister, who was otherwise always out trying to persuade Apaches to be Christians, which they weren't suited for, even Mary Beth knew that. The couple had settled down to a sorry life in a government-issue, three-room house where Mary Beth had nothing whatsoever to do but wish she was even back in Enid where you could at least dance with a drunken jerk if you wanted to and have a couple of beers before you had to slap his hands away from your tits and go home.

And then old sourpuss had gotten transferred to Keams Canyon here, and made superintendent of all these Hopis and Navajos, and even less went on out here than on the Apache reservation if you didn't include the Hopi dances which made her uncomfortable, as did the animosity between the Hopis and Navajos that Luther talked about whenever he did talk, which was less and less often, especially after he had helped the government people shoot down half the Navajo and Hopi sheep as part of that stupid livestock reduction program and no one would talk to him. And the men in the agency office were even more depressing than the ones back in Enid in the BLM, losers going nowhere, nothing but boring empty routine ahead of them all, world without end. And all this yellow stone falling down around them—well, it wasn't falling, but it had fallen—and the place looked like a junkyard, Keams Canyon did, and Luther had gotten stranger and stranger, his face getting all tight whenever anyone asked for something, and the other men in the office obviously hated him, and those nurses—well, Mary Beth wondered if they weren't what they called queers—and Luther wouldn't talk none about any of this, only walked around, getting more and more stooped like an old heron. Mary Beth had begun to wonder if he wasn't getting himself ready to commit suicide and was a bit alarmed when she realized she couldn't care less. He paced around at night, an insomniac, and when he did get in bed, it was with his back to her, his scrawny back with all the bones showing under the skin, and she was pretty disgusted by the whole thing, her whole life and her prospects, which is why she had been pretty quick to latch onto the young mechanic, Ollie Beatty, when he had arrived earlier this year, and they'd found plenty of time to make love here and there up on the edge of the canyon in the piñon trees, or right in her own house when old sourpuss went off to Gallup once a month. But it was mostly a lot of athletic thrashing, not anything loving or nice the way it was supposed to be. Ollie was what they called wooden-head dumb back in Illinois, and about as gentle as a diesel engine. If only she'd had a kid maybe, back there on the Apache reservation when Luther was sort of alive . . . but they hadn't, had they? She figured maybe she was barren.

Barren.

That was the word for it, wasn't it? Her whole adult life. Barren.

And now big dumb Ollie Beatty was in jail with the others, Luther was tied up in his office with some enormous pig of a German soldier farting and watching him—they'd taken her there to see him for a minute last night after they found her hiding in her bathroom—and she was here tied by the wrist to her brass bedstead with this Captain Muller, the little runt, in the kitchen making coffee, she guessed from the clattering going on in there, and probably after that getting ready to rape her, the Hun bastard. He'd spent the night snoring in the other room after they'd found her and tied her up here, and talked German to all those other men until they'd left, belching and haw-hawing like a bunch of gangsters, and he'd surely been thinking about raping her the whole night, and here he came now.

She tightened all her muscles and got ready to scream like a banshee, not that it would do any good whatsoever in this godforsaken dump with everybody in jail. She looked up at the white walls of her bedroom, and they seemed to have closed in on her, making the room smaller even than it was. Above the bed was a chromo of a mountain lake with a deer standing in the water, poised to flee. She'd had that picture in her bedroom in Illinois.

The kraut came into the room in his uniform with the gray tunic unbuttoned at the neck, clonking on the wood floor with his shiny black boots, a big black holster attached to his belt, and holding two mugs of coffee. He had pink ears, sunburned almost to a crisp, and they stuck out from his close-cropped blond temples like some kind of junior elephant. He smiled, a thin line on his sun-pink fair skin. But the smile didn't reach as far as his eyes, blue eyes as pale as the morning sky, the eyes of a maniac rapist-killer, and she figured he was mentally licking his lips. He sat down on a wooden chair next to the bed and held out one of the mugs.

"For you," he said. She guessed he was about twenty-eight, twenty-nine, from the few little lines in the corners of his eyes. About the same age as Ollie the mechanic.

She reached out with her free hand and took the mug. "Oh, so I get to drink this coffee before you rape me, right? You fucking Hun bastard sonofabitch shithead kraut."

Mary Beth was far more surprised at the string of invective that came from her mouth than at the pure, molten anger that had suddenly welled up inside her and propelled the words.

"Ah, a woman of spirit," Muller said.

"Look, you, I am a patriotic American citizen, I work for the government of the United States of America, and you're a slimy little pile of criminal German shit." Again Mary Beth was astonished by what she had said.

"I mean you no harm," the German officer said. "Here, let me untie your wrist so you can sit up. Otherwise your coffee might spill, eh?"

"You touch anything but my wrist, I'll scratch your eyes out of your head," Mary Beth hissed. "You fucking—"

"Now now, calm down, Mrs. Lemon. That's right, isn't it? Mrs. Lemon. Mary Beth Lemon. I found your name in the family Bible in the other room. Mary Beth Ogden, daughter of Lucian and Anne Ogden, herself née Jorgenson. Norwegian, I suppose. We mean you no particular harm here, Mary Beth Ogden Lemon with a drop or two of good Aryan blood in your veins. It's just that you must remain in custody for a few days."

"What then? Do we get executed?"

Muller smirked. "No, no. *Nein.*"

"You mean I'm going to be tied up to this bed for *days*? How long? When do I get to take a bath?"

Muller took a sip from his mug and smiled his thin smile again. "A few days before we move on. And you will spend them in jail with the others, not here. But first, if you wish, you can bathe."

"And you're going to watch, right? You German pig."

He shrugged. "A necessary precaution."

Mary Beth suddenly realized that she knew something that might be valuable: a few days, he had said. A few days before they moved on. Maybe she could pin it down a little better. Find out when. Maybe where. Let someone know. Who? Luther? What the hell would he do, the pathetic old stork? So who, then? Well, she'd think about that later. She stood up from the bed and looked down at the officer, then into the bathroom where the tub stood on its metal animal feet.

"Suppose I close the door. Couldn't you wait out here?"

"I could, of course," Muller said. "But what if you escaped through the window?"

Mary Beth sighed, like a mother may at a child's pestering. "Okay, I'll leave the door open for you, kraut. You can see the whole show from here."

She crossed the floor to the bathroom, unhitching her belt buckle, and threw the German officer a smile over her shoulder. Suddenly she felt free. A prisoner in all respects, but free. Free to cuss out this kraut with his stupid-looking sticking-out pink ears. Free to cuss him with words she'd heard plenty of times but never used until this very day. Free to trick the little German shit into revealing important information. She'd damn well think of something to keep her out of that jail. Yes, free. Free to serve her country. Free of a barren life that she could hardly remember now. Maybe she'd get a medal.

# Three

Having made his way down the rocky trail that led off the mesa from Old Oraibi to Oraibi, Heinrich Schalberg found his driver, Corporal Hans Schwabe, he of virtually no neck at all, slouching against the wall on the porch of the trading post, smoking a cigarette.

"Good morning, Herr Major General." He saluted casually.

"Good morning, Corporal. A beautiful morning." Schalberg saluted in return.

Schwabe looked carefully at the officer from his piglike eyes, immediately spotting the reddish-purple bruise almost but not quite concealed by the tunic's collar.

"You know," Schwabe said, expelling a long column of blue smoke into the air, "I heard once that Chinese women, Japanese women are built sideways. You know? The slits? Indian women like that?"

"Hold your tongue," Schalberg said, smiling.

"I just can't imagine for the life of me how it would work," Schwabe went on. "Sir."

"What is that you're smoking?"

Schwabe turned the cigarette in his thick red hand and looked at it as if for the first time.

"It's called a Lucky Strike, sir. American. Damn good. It's from the trading post."

"Let me have one, Corporal, if you don't mind."

Schwabe took the white pack with its red circle from his tunic pocket, shook out a cigarette, and handed it to

**100**

the officer. "Looks to me like you already had a pretty lucky strike. Sir."

"*Schwabe!* Just light this cigarette."

"Yes sir," he said, holding out a lit match. "But really, sir, how does it work, with it sideways and all?"

Schalberg took a deep drag and exhaled the potent smoke in a long column. "Let's go, you Bavarian hog. I need to talk to Colonel Liepzichte. There's a war on, or didn't you notice? We have radio communication with Muller, yes? In Keams Canyon where the Americans are jailed."

The two men strolled through Oraibi's narrow dirt streets, Schalberg speaking in German to his driver, whose personal loyalty to the major general was absolute and had been since Schalberg pulled him from a burning tank near El Alamein in the last, disastrous days of the Africa campaign. Schalberg's gait was naturally erect, while the bulkier driver walked with an oddly graceful roll under thick shoulders.

It was a fine day, cloudless, the air like crystal. Schalberg was feeling optimistic, and was mildly irritated to notice the cloudy expression that had descended on Schwabe's large, round face.

"What is it now, Hans? Out with it."

"It's nothing."

"Hans, I mention Captain Muller and your face clouds over. What is it about Captain Muller? And don't give me one of those country maxims that nobody but you Bavarian peasants understand. Out with it."

"He is not a soldier first," Schwabe said.

"Who is a soldier first, Hans? We're all born innocent babes. Goddammit, what are you talking about?"

"When you and I were in the desert in Africa, where was he?"

"He was in Berlin. In the office of the High Command. And then in Russia, where he was a casualty. He acquitted himself admirably. You know all that."

Schwabe shrugged. "I don't trust him on a mission like this." He spat in the dust.

"Because he's a city boy, right?"

Schwabe spat again, and was silent. On the outskirts of the village now, the two men walked past a last yellow stone building and paused to look out across the brown land beyond where the 108th Panzer Battalion rested. On the far horizon, a large blue mountain with a white cap rose like a gigantic frozen wave. Closer to them were the two pinnacles of rock which yesterday had been three. North of the pinnacles was a lone windmill, too far away for Schalberg to tell if it was turning in the breeze that blew in from the west. The windmill struck Schalberg as odd, so far off from the village—a sign of hope, to be sure, but also, in so dry and sunbaked and empty a land, an emblem of futility. Schalberg was abruptly taken with something akin to doubt—doubt that he could bend this strange and ugly place to his will—but it passed over him as quickly as a cloud on a windy day. A few hundred meters off, Colonel Liepzichte had separated himself from a group of men and was approaching.

"Hans," Schalberg said.

"Sir?"

"If you are determined to play Sancho Panza during the remainder of this mission, then you will keep it strictly between us, yes?"

"Who the fuck is Sancho Panza?" Schwabe said. "Sir."

Colonel Franz Liepzichte approached and saluted the major general with elaborate precision. Though only thirty years old, he was a seasoned veteran of the Afrika Korps, in whose service he had risen quickly to the rank of major. Severely wounded in the last days of that ill-fated campaign, he had not been called to the eastern front and the deadly killing fields of Russia, as had so many of Rommel's soldiers who escaped capture by the British. Instead he had languished for months in a hospital in Weisbaden while surgeons put his right leg and abdomen back together, and when his name came up late in 1943 for a special and top secret assignment with the 108th Panzer Battalion, a unit he had never heard of, he nevertheless eagerly leapt at the assignment, longing as he did to be again embroiled in the smoke and stink of combat.

The son of a Hanover fisherman, Liepzichte had discovered he was a born warrior; life had no other meaning for him. Like all other officers in the German Wehrmacht, he had sworn an oath of personal loyalty to Adolf Hitler, and like many younger officers of the Wehrmacht who had known no other leader since they were young adults, he made no distinction in his mind between Adolf Hitler and the German state, the Third Reich. And, to such a mind, there was no distinction to be made between absolute loyalty to the Reich and to one's commanding officer in the field. The minds of such men were never troubled with questions of purpose—there was but one—or with strategy, which came down from the state. Such a mind dwelled instead only on technique, on the practical matters involved in carrying out orders. Yet even though Colonel Franz Liepzichte possessed such an unquestioning mind, he was clearly troubled on this crystalline morning on the scrubby desertlands that lay outside the ramshackle Indian village of Oraibi. His face—long and narrow, with a prominent beak of a nose and a mouth that consisted of two nearly invisible lips—was set like granite, and his normally smooth forehead was pinched into a frown over his dark glasses.

Heinrich Schalberg thought he knew what was making his second in command uncomfortable. He himself had been uncomfortable since the 108th Panzer Battalion began to assemble on his mother's ranch, weeks ago in the Sonoran desert in Mexico, bits and pieces of armor arriving on each successive night like ants following a trail. For the 108th was unlike any battalion Liepzichte had known, unlike any that appeared in any book of regulations he had seen. It was not that it consisted chiefly of captured American equipment—Sherman tanks, American half-tracks. He knew that nothing resembling German tanks—the superior Panthers or Tigers—could be spirited across the border into the United States. He had seen to it that his crews mastered the American machinery and learned to make the most of their characteristics, including—he had to admit it—superior maneuverability and greater range.

What bothered Liepzichte was that the 108th was smaller than a battalion. Its size was more like a company—even a Stab, the armored reconnaissance units that had lent communication support to the panzer units of the Afrika Korps. Yes, there were indeed tanks, unlike a Stab, which consisted almost entirely of light and medium half-tracks and other smaller, more mobile vehicles. But there were only twenty tanks. And there were only four half-tracks. Assembled now in the scrubland under camouflage nets strung with uprooted sagebrush—all, that is, but the three tanks, the truck, and the half-track that Muller had taken to Keams Canyon—they seemed wholly inadequate, as did the 106 enlisted men and the 12 noncommissioned officers that made up their crews. Yes, he knew that other light armored vehicles were to be transported in by Condor beginning that very night, including some American jeeps, and yes, he knew that another hundred men would arrive in the air shipments over the next three nights as well, along with light arms, ammunition, and other supplies. But the bizarre configuration of this *company*-called-a-battalion made Colonel Liepzichte extremely uncomfortable.

Schalberg knew Liepzichte's concerns well, and the thought now crossed his mind that an uncomfortable Liepzichte looked for all the world like a man at an elegant and formal dinner party who had just gotten a whiff of the unmistakable aroma of a fart.

"It's a very large country we're in, Colonel, is it not?"

Schalberg said. "And we seem very few, do we not? Very unorthodox. Well, Colonel, again let me assure you that a great deal of thought has gone into the configuration of this force. It's new country, not like the African desert, a different place altogether. It will be full of surprises if nothing else. How do you design a force to take advantage of unknown surprises, eh, Colonel? Let me ask you that."

"Flexibility, sir," Liepzichte said.

"Precisely. Flexibility. Mobility. Speed. Speed, Colonel. The ability to take advantage of surprises with surprises of our own."

"Yes, Major General, as you have said before. I understand."

Schalberg was himself surprised. "Then what is troubling you this morning, Colonel?"

Liepzichte cleared his throat. "It's our allies here. These Indians."

Schalberg looked over the colonel's shoulder to where the tank and half-track crews were engaged in the endless tasks of repair drills and actual repairs. Indians, mostly wearing broad-brimmed black hats, were standing in circles around some of the vehicles, watching German crews work.

"What about them?" Schalberg asked.

"What am I supposed to do with them? They just stand around, watching, talking among themselves. It's making the men nervous."

"Put them to work, Colonel. Don't you have an airstrip to build? Come with me." Schalberg strode toward his battalion, followed by Liepzichte and, at a distance, Corporal Schwabe, whose normally expressionless features were brightened with a lopsided smile.

As he approached one of the half-tracks, Schalberg greeted its crew and nodded to the small ring of Indians who were watching. Two of the crew returned to their tinkering under the raised hood. Schalberg stood, hands behind his back, watching the crew and glancing sideways at the Indians. In all, there were seven, faces of copper, eyes shadowed under the brims of their hats. Some of the Indians looked at the ground, a few looked past Schalberg—all were silent. Aside from the clank of metal on metal, of a wrench grinding on a metal bolt, there was no sound.

"Is Banyongye here this morning?" Schalberg said into the silence, and was greeted by yet more silence. He turned to face the Indians.

"Who's in charge here this morning?" Schalberg asked affably. The Indians shifted, looked briefly at each other, and looked away. Schalberg cleared his throat, and spoke again.

"Is there anyone here among you men who is the chief?"

Feet shifted in the dust. An Indian looked over his shoulder and back at the ground. Another murmured.

"Yes?" Schalberg said softly, but the Indian who had murmured something simply looked away. Schalberg swallowed the rage growing in his throat, and smiled.

"Come come," he said. "Let us talk."

He heard footsteps and turned to see Corporal Schwabe approaching. Limping beside him was a big round-shouldered Indian who seemed familiar. Like the others, this one also looked beyond him, over Schalberg's shoulder, as if he weren't there. It was, he realized, the man called Slink, whom he had met the day before. Under the brim of the Indian's black hat, the Mongol visage was expressionless.

In German, Schwabe said, "Sir? I think you want to talk to this one."

"Why, Corporal? Is he the leader here?"

"He is someone you can talk to," Schwabe said, a glint of a smile in his pale eyes.

The Indian Slink put out his hand, eyes still averted, and said: "Ya-ta-hey."

Schalberg took the man's hand, feeling no pressure from its fingers before it was hastily withdrawn. "You are . . . ?"

"Slink," the Indian said.

"You are the leader here."

"Navajos don't have no leaders, sir. Not like you. But we want to work. I can talk to them."

Schalberg didn't understand. No leaders? He shrugged.

"Hopis have leaders," Slink said. "Hopis have lots of leaders. Banyongye, other guys. Talk a lot."

"Where are these Hopi leaders?" Schalberg asked, and wondered if he hadn't made a mistake in asking.

"They're all goin' to the dance," Slink said, pointing toward the village of Oraibi with his lips.

Schalberg decided to pay a visit to the trader. He needed some clarification. He turned to Liepzichte. "This is Colonel Liepzichte. He will explain what work needs to be done. And you will explain to your men? To your people?"

Slink nodded. Schalberg turned to his driver with relief and said: "Let's go." The corporal's lips were pursed tightly and his eyes gleamed. They headed for a tent that had been set up as the communications center. "I must speak to Muller, and then to that trader. Tell me, Schwabe, why did you choose that man from among all those slouching Indians?"

Schwabe walked along in silence. Overhead a shadow coursed by, and Schalberg looked up to see a black bird, a raven, sweep across the sky and disappear beyond a rise. He looked at his watch: it was 0810 hours, and the sun, though still low in the sky, had disposed of the crisp chill of morning. Schalberg felt its heat prying into his body. Ahead of them the Hopi village had begun to bustle with activity. Sparsely clad children ran back and forth between the houses haphazardly sprinkled here and there around the outskirts. Short, round women—most of them old—were issuing forth from the houses, walking purposefully past piles of gnarled firewood toward the interior of the village, where the houses were closer together. Here and there a spavined dog slunk out of the way. Schalberg noted to himself that he had not seen any men in the village. He had almost forgotten the question he had asked Schwabe—about turning up the man Slink—when the corporal spat and said, "It's one of those peasant things, sir."

Schalberg closed the door of the trading post behind him and stood still, waiting for his eyes to adjust to the dark. In the gloom he could make out shelves on the walls sparsely filled with canned goods, in the corner, bags of what he guessed was flour. As his eyes accustomed themselves, he saw that beside him to his right the wall was festooned with heavy silver jewelry studded with turquoise. To his left was a row of saddles on wooden racks, and above, from the logs of the ceiling, hung tack of every description. Across the room, the white man, the mute, stood behind a high counter of dark brown polished wood. He was listening to a woman in a purple velvet shirt with a long blue skirt whose back was turned to him. The woman's black hair was done up in a knot behind her head, secured by a silver and turquoise barrette.

The mute looked up at him, and Schalberg said: "Where is Luna? I must talk to him." His voice was loud in the cluttered room. The woman turned her head and glanced at him. He saw the curve of a high cheekbone, the flash of a dark eye, and thought he had glimpsed the corner of her mouth pulled back in a smile. She was of indeterminate age—not a girl, not old. Perhaps thirty? No way of telling, but now she had turned back to the mute behind the counter, who gestured with his head to a door set between ranks of shelves.

"In there?" Schalberg said.

The mute nodded, and Schalberg strode to the door,

knocked twice, and opened it. He glanced back to see the Indian woman looking at him—he had the sense he was being measured, carefully if appreciatively—but she looked away, and Schalberg went through the door.

"Ah," Raphael Luna croaked, pushing himself to his feet behind a bare wooden desk. A long wooden bench and two uncomfortable-looking chairs with slatted backs were in front of the desk. "Herr Major General. You had a restful night? Please come in." In the sparsely furnished room with bare whitewashed walls and one window, it was bright, and Schalberg blinked.

"Everything must seem a bit strange, I imagine," Luna said. "I'm sure you have many questions in your mind." The trader's smile seemed genuine enough. In his office, the man seemed less overweight, less incongruous, than he had appeared the afternoon before, standing outside the trading post in the late afternoon sun.

"Please sit down," Luna said, his voice a raspy whisper, and let himself down into his chair. Schalberg chose one of the slat-back chairs. "So you have a Navajo workforce now to assist you. You will find that they are very good workers. Steady, efficient. The Hopis, they are also excellent workers, but you have none with you today. All the Hopi men are involved with the katsinas, with the dance. Everything, of course, stops when there is a dance. You will accompany me to the dance"—he glanced at a watch on his thick wrist—"in an hour or so, I hope? You are expected there."

"Of course."

"You may have seen the Hopi cornfields out there," Luna said. "It's a form of dry-farming, an ancient practice. It seems miraculous these people can grow such a plenitude of corn, melons and beans as well, but corn is the central crop—it seems a miracle, doesn't it? The land appears so poor."

"Extraordinary," Schalberg agreed, recalling the sorry-looking plots he had seen, dusty fields here and there on the desert with a few pathetic plants struggling in the sun.

"They've been at it for nearly a thousand years," Luna went on, "and of course they've developed special strains that need only the slightest help from an occasional rain. You might say that Hopis are excellent agricultural engineers, having adapted their crops to the local conditions. But of course, the main kind of engineering they employ is what you would think of as magical. They appeal to the katsina spirits in the dances—like the one you will witness this morning—to provide the few needed sprinkles of rain." The trader paused, and smiled. "The katsina spirits are, you might say, Hopi ancestors. They can appear in the form of the katsina spirits, or as clouds. It's rather sweet, isn't it, to imagine oneself returning to this mortal plane as a cloud capable of raining on your descendants' fields?" He cleared his throat, a loud, phlegmy croak.

"This all may seem quaint to someone such as yourself, educated in a world of science and technology," he said, "but it has worked all these years, all these centuries. And of course the katsina dances are merely an outward tip of a far more elaborate spiritual, ritual life of the Hopis. It's very complex, very complex indeed. For someone like me who has grown up among all these people, it doesn't seem—well, shall we say wise—to dismiss the very real power of spiritual things in this desert."

Schalberg crossed his legs and folded his arms across his chest. "You make it sound almost like a warning."

"A warning?" The trader croaked in what Schalberg took as laughter. "No, not a warning. I merely want you to understand. The engine that drives these societies is a spiritual one. Let me put it this way. The Germans, if I may say so, are known to possess a mystical streak in their national ethos. Yes? It's all the more so here, you see, far more a matter of daily life, of everyday expression, of utter reality. The land is alive with spirits here, alive. It breathes. For the Hopis—and for the Navajos.

"You must understand that the two tribes don't see the same spirits, don't see the world the same way, but both . . . well." He paused, leaned back in his chair and closed his eyes. For a moment Schalberg thought he had fallen asleep. There were, he knew, people who did that, fell asleep in mid-sentence. One of his professors at gymnasium had had that habit, and the boys all thought it quite marvelous. But with his eyes still closed, the trader resumed in his raspy whisper.

"The Navajos arrived here after the Hopis, long afterward. They were nomadic, lived in small bands, hunted, planted a few crops. About the time they arrived, so did the Spanish, and the Navajos soon became sheepherders, pastoralists. Excellent horsemen too. Superior horsemen. Very adaptable people, quick to learn, to take on new things, to create new traditions. They borrowed ideas from the people they found here already, and of course they raided too. Corn, women, all that sort of thing. It's all stopped now, but it's a source of continuing uneasiness among the two tribes here. A little problem of what you might call lebensraum, yes?

"But I digress. One could say that some of the Navajo religious view of things is colored by their association with people like the Hopis, but it retains its ancient roots. A kind of shamanism brought here from the north, a need to intervene in the spirit world and to keep it in balance, to wrestle with the forces of good and of evil. This is also a kind of engineering.

"The Navajo world is filled with the forces of evil, and they occasionally erupt into the lives of the people. The world is haunted, a dangerous place. The night particularly."

Luna opened his eyes and blinked.

"This may not seem so far-fetched if you recall your own Teutonic gods, locked in continuous combat with monsters, demons rising from the fiery mouth of the serpent of Midgard. You see?" Schalberg started at the familiar pagan place name, and wondered how this Spanish trader in the middle of this wasteland knew of such things.

"In any event," Luna went on, "the night in particular is dangerous. It's full of witches that are in some ways even more fearsome than the ghosts of the dead who haunt the landscape. Navajo witchcraft is highly developed, Major General, a grievous force. You know you have been witched when you see a wolfman at night, following you, or lurking out in the dark near your encampment. This is someone who has witched you, taken a piece of your hair, or sputum, perhaps your feces, and used it for ritual purposes. Then you will take sick, perhaps die."

In spite of himself, Schalberg shuddered inwardly.

The trader blinked again, and smiled. "I say this not to suggest that you should fear witches, of course, but to explain something you will notice here. The night is the time of the witch, the wolfman. The Navajos avoid the night as rigorously as they avoid touching a corpse. You won't find them of any help to you at night. Those men you have, that Navajo workforce—it will disband with the setting of the sun. It's best you understand why, and make this part of your plans here."

The trader paused again and looked meaningfully at Schalberg. Presumably, Schalberg thought, Luna was hoping to hear something of those plans. Instead Schalberg laughed.

"I must say," he said, "one heard nothing of this in one's childhood reading about these people, these Indians."

"Ah yes, the noble red man, warrior of the plains, that sort of thing. I understand. You read all of Karl May, I suspect. Winnetou, the philosopher and warrior of justice. Yes." He chuckled. "The European races have placed much of their romantic ideals on these people. A great burden for mere human beings to carry, wouldn't you agree?" Schalberg heard the sound of footsteps and looked over at the door that led from Luna's office to a hallway. He caught a glimpse of a purple shirt, a blue skirt, a copper-colored face going by.

Catching the direction of Schalberg's look, Luna said: "That's Mary. Mary Yazzie. A Navajo. She works here as my housekeeper. I'll introduce you. Mary!" he called. The woman appeared in the doorway. It was the same woman that had been in the trading post. She stood quietly, with her shoulders straight and her head raised, but her eyes somewhere on the floor. Her hands hung down at her sides. Schalberg took in the high, flat cheekbones, the triangular shape of the dark eyes, the broad nose. She was not beautiful in the sense of a German kind of beauty, but she was handsome. There was a muted strength in her stance, what might even be pride—certainly not what he would expect in a housekeeper.

Luna spoke in what Schalberg took to be Navajo. He heard the words—"Major General Schalberg"—amid the alien sounds, and watched the woman's eyes flicker up to his face, then away. She nodded, and vanished into the hallway.

"She speaks no English," Luna said. "She's worked here for me several years now. She's from Pinon originally, north of here, but her people died tragically. An outbreak of smallpox in 1941. It took everyone but her young brother, and he—" Luna stopped and closed his eyes. "Such is the nature of life here, Major General, often so tragic . . . Only months later the younger brother was struck by lightning out herding his family's sheep. This was all taken to be the result of witchcraft, of course, someone wishing her evil, and Mary has had several ceremonies to dispel it, but . . ." The trader shrugged and sighed, a rattling sound in his throat.

"Such ceremonies are costly." He blinked again. "We

do our best." He looked at his watch. "Well, I've gone on here, haven't I? We should go take our places in the plaza. The ceremony will begin soon." He heaved himself up from his chair. "It's a good day for it. Clear. But you'll see. The clouds will come." He laughed. "I can explain other things about this strange place as we walk."

Schalberg rose. His watch said 0935. He shook his head, as if to get his bearings, and braced himself for he knew not what.

Slink dumped another shovelful of heavy white dirt into a slight depression on the edge of what was to be a German airstrip located about a half mile east of Oraibi Wash where a few cottonwood trees eked out a living from the unseen moisture in the ground. The Navajos and the Germans were some five miles out on the desert from the Hopi village of Oraibi. They had followed two ruts of a wagon track across the scrubland while the German officer, standing in the half-track, glanced back and forth from the land to his map. Slink, standing beside him as the vehicle lurched along the ruts, had eventually pointed with his thumb off to a slight rise. The officer had looked at Slink, then at the rise.

"Over there?"

"Real flat over past that rise," Slink had said, raising his voice above the whining engine. "Hardpan."

The officer had bent down to speak to the driver, and the convoy, two trucks full of men led by the half-track, had veered off cross-country toward the rise. Once over it, the German held up his hand for the driver to stop and they had been enveloped in dust from the trucks behind. As it cleared, the German officer smiled and nodded.

"Excellent," he said. "Excellent." The ground before them was a long, flat depression perhaps a half mile in length, surrounded by gradual rises of some two feet—a vast, shallow bowl. Nearly barren of any vegetation, it was a whitish clay, largely free of the occasional rocky outcrop that dotted the land they had driven through. Only the occasional rock studded the ground, easy enough to remove. At the far northern end of the depression was a single outcrop of rough blackish rock, perhaps some twenty feet high, that looked like a gigantic chair.

"Giant's Chair," Slink said. "Maybe a good landmark. Put a fire up there." He turned to the south and pointed with his lips at another outcrop that peered over the southern rim of the shallow bowl. "Put another fire right there."

"Excellent," the German officer had said again, and within minutes the work of clearing the few rocks and filling in minor depressions had begun, with some thirty Navajos working among an equal number of German enlisted men. The German officer had asked Slink to stay with him and a big sergeant, but Slink demurred, saying it was better if he worked too.

Now, he paused in his shoveling and looked out to the west. Over the rim and maybe two miles beyond the wash was a long escarpment of red rock lying on the horizon, what looked like another of the great mesas that marked these lands. But it was no ordinary mesa. Instead it was, at its western end, a series of narrow ridges—some merely a pace wide in some places—falling a hundred or so feet straight down to the desert floor, a kind of labyrinth of high rock walls the Hopis called Katsina Bluffs and claimed as part of their history, as they did every landmark as far as anyone could see. Slink was not sure exactly how those red rocks with their mysterious canyons and grottoes had figured in the Hopi past—there was so much history in these lands, both Hopi and Navajo, all layered on top of each other, intertwined. It was hard to keep every detail of his own history in mind, never mind all the meanings the Hopis put on the land. He did know that Hopi priests went there to those red bluffs each year to hunt for eagles.

And on the far side of the great red outcrop there had

been a Navajo camp he had taken to visiting before he joined the Marines. It was the camp of the Benalis, and he'd gone there to visit one of the Benali daughters, a girl named Irene with a smile that shined like the sun and eyes that danced and danced. He thought he was really getting somewhere with Irene, had gotten her off on a long walk herding their sheep one day, and she'd laughed at the things he said, silly things, and he figured that the next time he visited they would . . . But back in his mother's camp near Nipple Butte, he heard that Irene had gotten sick. Gotten real hot and then cold, hot and cold, and before the doctor had come from the Public Health Service over in Keams Canyon, and before the medicine man had been able to get there and sing over her . . . she died, and they had to abandon the hogan. He wondered where the Benali camp was now. It was when he'd been hanging around there that he saw this place, all white with hard clay, with the Giant's Chair at one end and the other outcrop—he didn't know its name—at the other, and he'd remembered it when they were coming out here with the Germans. He wondered what kind of planes they were going to fly in here at night. What was it they called that? Luftwaffe. He'd read about the Luftwaffe somewhere. His mind wandered.

It was too bad Irene had died. He recalled her sunny smile, dancing eyes, the way she walked, putting each foot out, toes down, like she was part of the land. He wasn't scared to think briefly of the dead anymore. Not since he'd been with the Marines. He'd thought about her several times out in the jungles on those awful islands.

The half-track clattered by, raising white dust that got in Slink's mouth. He spat it out and resumed digging. It was getting on to the rainy season, he thought, such as the rainy season ever is. One little rainy season in May, another in August. Never much rain to go on, even in the best of years. Maybe those Hopi dances would bring some rain. He looked to the southwest, out where San Francisco Peaks rose up about a hundred miles away. Clouds were building up on top of the mountain already. Soon they would break off in tatters, and some of them might head this way. He shrugged and went back to work.

Mary Beth Lemon deftly hooked the ends of her Sears Roebuck mail-order brassiere together behind her back and, in answer to the unspoken question that hung in the air, said, "I don't owe that old stork anything. And I know a winner when I see one."

She looked at the German officer's back, ripply with muscles, surprisingly so, and dead white in contrast to the deep tan of his neck and hands. Like a farmer. He was buttoning up his pants, back turned to her, and she felt a little sick at what she had done. But it had to be done, she thought, and tried to put it out of mind.

"You're not gonna throw me in that jail, are you? After . . ."

Captain Muller turned to face her as he put on his jacket. "Are all American women as direct as you?" He smiled, but again only with his lips. She stared into the ice-blue eyes. "No," he said. "You I will keep as . . . my interpreter. Yes, my interpreter."

He reached out and placed a hand proprietarily on her breast and she shuddered inwardly. "That was good," he said. "Very good, wasn't it? For a fucking kraut." He laughed. "Come along now, Frau Lemon. I have work to do, and there will be things for you to interpret." He laughed again, a high-pitched intake of air.

Moments later, the screen door having banged behind her, she followed Captain Muller off the porch and into the bright sun of morning, allowing the rage to well up, a raw torrent, an inward screaming, coloring the world before her crimson, and she measured with her eye the distance between the little kraut bastard's shoulder blades, seeing where she would jam the knife blade, if only she could . . . or, better, when she could . . .

"Your husband," Captain Muller said, striding ahead of her toward the agency office, "will have been taken ill. A touch of the flu, but nothing that won't pass in three or four days. The others are out on routine business—you will know what that might be, of course—and you have volunteered, yes? Volunteered to handle routine messages to and from the office in Gallup. Yes, that will be fine. Everything here, they will understand, is in order. Yes? You can handle all that."

They turned the corner into the road. A tank loomed hugely, grotesquely, between them and the agency office, absorbing the yellow morning light from the canyon. Two soldiers leaned against its dull rear end. They snapped to attention when they saw the German officer, saluted and, Mary Beth thought, leered. She averted her eyes and, chin high, followed Muller onto the porch and through the door into the office. Luther sick for three or four days, she thought. Three or four days.

Luther Lemon, his black suit wrinkled like laundry, sat behind his assistant's desk in the anteroom, arms and legs at awkward angles, his head down. Mary Beth thought maybe he was dead, but he looked up at the German and then at her. His eyes, never particularly bright, were now as dull as those of some of the old Indians around here who had cataracts, and the skin on his face was gray and drawn. His mouth opened and closed, and he stared up at her.

Across the room a soldier stood with his arms behind his back, legs spread. He came to attention, and Muller said, "At ease." Behind the desk, Luther Lemon sagged even farther. Through the open door to her husband's office, she could see that some equipment had been installed on his desk—a radio of some sort, she guessed, to communicate with the rest of the German force. She knew there were others, from the conversation she had overheard last night while tied to her bed, conversation that alternated between German and English. But she had no idea where the other Germans were—somewhere west probably.

Now, her husband sagging at the desk in front of her, Mary Beth didn't know where to let her eyes rest. She chose the wall behind her husband, where a tattered government map hung, and kept her eyes on it while the bile rose in her throat.

"This man is relieved of his duties," Muller said. "Take him to the jail." The soldier stepped quickly behind Luther's chair, snatched up a fistful of his jacket in one hand and lifted him to his feet. Mary Beth glanced at her husband as he gained his footing and walked toward her. She stepped to the side, unable to look at him, and he went through the door ahead of the soldier without a word.

Captain Muller moved to the desk and sat on it with one haunch, his booted leg swinging back and forth. "Sit down, Frau Lemon. We will rehearse your message to the people in Gallup. Once they are informed that all is normal here, except for your husband's unfortunate illness, we shall eat something." He patted the desk. "Come along. When we are on duty, by the way, you are Frau Lemon. There will be other times when you are Mary Beth." He grinned. "And when I am Captain Willie, your fucking kraut."

Mary Beth grinned back at him, she hoped with what he took to be a conspiratorial intimacy. "No, no. My fucking kraut *bastard*," she said, and the German emitted his high-pitched laugh.

In the sunlit plaza of Oraibi, a few small children darted here and there and a multihued dog with yellow eyes scuttled out of their way, disappearing into the shadow between two tawny stone houses. Thirty-odd women in shawls, some of them bent with age, some holding infants in their laps, sat in chairs and on low stone ledges outside the houses at one end of the plaza, patient and still. They had looked up briefly when the German officer and Luna the trader entered the plaza and sat down among them. On the rooftops along the eastern end of the plaza a few young people, boys and girls, stood waiting, shifting from foot to foot in the nearly palpable sense of expectation that bloomed in their midst.

Presently, from somewhere beyond, a drum sounded with a single sharp thud, followed by an eerie howl.

Like a distant baritone wind, voices chanted, the drum sounded again in a rhythmic beat, and between two houses the first of the black-bearded katsinas came, followed by other identical katsinas and a small band of men, one with the drum, the others singing. The katsinas formed a long, sinuous, swaying line, moccasined feet rhythmically treading the dust, legs adorned with clacking turtle shells and shiny round bells, hips enclosed in white kilts, foxtails jerking back and forth behind, copper-brown bodies painted with swatches of dull color, reds, yellows—arms bent, wrists enclosed with silver and evergreen, hands holding colored rattles, evergreen branches surrounding slit-eyed faces—large beaked faces of turquoise-green and geometric red and black, peering resolutely forward, held taut, black hair jutting out over their chests like straight beards . . . the long-haired katsinas treaded the dusty ground with purpose and as one, moving first one way and then back, singing their song, a nearly monotone lowing amid the motion and the noise and the firm thunder of the drum.

Again and again the serpentine line moved in one direction then back, while the sun gleamed overhead and the katsina father, an old man in baggy trousers and bare feet, sprinkled the katsinas with white cornmeal and called out to them over their song, encouraging them, welcoming them.

For an officer of the German army with a head full of

military details and logistical concerns, on a dangerous mission to be carried out with foreign equipment in an alien countryside so barren, so bizarre, and so forlorn, among a race of humans he had never properly imagined, the procession of the long-haired katsinas and their monotonous music seemed outlandish, without meaning, and both irritating and depressing. Beside him, the overweight trader sat stolidly, his eyes half closed, like a man at the philharmonic, no help at all, and Heinrich Schalberg felt trapped. He noted that the brown-faced women around him were all enrapt, and glancing upward, he saw that the young people on the roofs were still.

But with part of his brain he listened, with part of his vision he studied the repetitive motions of the katsinas, with part of his orderly mind he permitted himself to . . . what? Imagine? As time passed, minutes, perhaps more than minutes, he understood that time had somehow stopped amid all this medieval motion and color. Time, which he had so little of, was passing, yes, but also in this barbaric sea of dancers and noise, of sky and stone and dust, time was no longer a coefficient of the world. But what world? Mentally, he shook his head in the heat, unwilling to accept so strange a notion, but his body, he knew, had begun to relax, and Heinrich Schalberg sat with an increasing sense of wonder, wonder at himself, perched in two irreconcilable worlds in the passing morning while the dust swirled in little eddies and katsinas danced and their father encouraged them with cornmeal, and drums pounded with the very rhythm of the blood pulsing through his body.

On the arid land beyond the plaza and outside the random sprinkle of Oraibi's houses, the German encampment had arranged itself in a precise geometry of canvas and camouflage—rows of tents, an acre of netting adorned with brush wrenched from the desert floor, beneath which the iron predators lay poised amid the stink of sweat and fuel. Five miles west, an airstrip was taking form in the dry white clay. Far off to the southwest, out of the line of vision of those seated in the plaza at Oraibi, white clouds tore themselves away from the white-capped peaks and sailed above the barren lands, an armada of ghostly moist galleons in the dry air, heading toward the east and the Hopi mesas. And nearly a hundred miles to the north, Secakuku and Quavehema, with legs still elastic and strong, moved lightly across the earth, having reached the red sand that lies all around Monument Valley, its rose and crimson pinnacles jutting into the cloudless sky, motionless red rock glowing as if god-lit. Ahead of the two runners, perhaps a mere hour ahead of them, the waters of the San Juan River, cold with mountain snowmelt, rushed west between rocky cliff banks, and a few paces beyond the gorge lay the insignificant settlement of Mexican Hat.

It would not, then, be long before news of the German invasion reached beyond the huge inert stretches of the reservation, but the German presence was by now known throughout much of its vast extent. No one in the twelve villages of the Hopi was unaware of it, and no one was without an opinion. In Navajo camps as far east as the foothills of the Chuska Mountains and north to Teec Nos Pos, as far west as Leupp and north beyond Tuba City on the moonscape of the Painted Desert, women and old men consulted in lonely hogans and shade houses, opined in slow and quiet voices, and told relevant stories from the ancient past. Those on Black Mesa and all the way to Kayenta and beyond had noted the passing of the two Hopi messengers and, with the patience of pastoralists divining an imminent change in the weather, they waited.

## Four

Harry Hopkins did not like to bring up matters of any kind in the hours between six and seven, when his boss put aside the affairs of the globe and, usually with a few close friends but often joined by anyone who had been in the Oval Office at day's end, convivially mixed and passed out martinis to all from a silver tray. Today the group in the Oval Office consisted only, and most conveniently, of the President and his Secretary of War, the courtly Virginian, George C. Marshall.

The two men were apparently relaxing their worried minds with old stories of fox hunting and other equestrian pursuits when Hopkins tapped on the door and entered.

"Ah, Harry, just in time to listen to George here, extolling the hunt country of Loudoun County again!" The President immediately began to pour silvery liquid, pungent with gin, into a thin-stemmed glass. For all his enthusiasm and the famous smile, the President looked tired. More than tired: to so close a confidant and companion as Hopkins, the great man had begun to look like someone being gnawed away from the inside. Hopkins hated to add yet another care, particularly one so utterly bizarre but also potentially dangerous. Ignoring the proffered martini, he placed before the President a single sheet of white paper on which some twenty-five lines had been typed, double space, with an elite typewriter.

His glass in one hand, the President bent his big head

over the paper and took a sip, only to erupt in a gin-and-vermouth-spattering explosion.

"What?" he said. "What?" he repeated in a near bellow. "For God's sake, Harry, this isn't a prank, is it? George, come over here and look at this."

General Marshall, trim in his army greens, his chest bedecked with five rows of brightly colored campaign ribbons, stood beside the President, bent as if in a courtly bow, and read the words on the paper.

"It's unbelievable," he said. "It couldn't be . . ."

"Harry," the President said, "who is this man Luna? Sounds like a Spaniard."

"An Indian trader, sir, evidently the second generation of his family out there on the Indian reservation. I called Collier over at Indian Affairs. He knows him. So does Ickes. They're old friends. They both swear he's a man of impeccable honor, all that. Trustworthy."

"And what about this Cameron he mentions? Benjamin Cameron."

"One of George's," Hopkins said. "A captain in army intelligence, posted in London. He should be on his way here as we speak. He spent a few years with these Indians before the war. Some sort of archeologist. Highly rated by his military superiors."

The President leaned back in his wheelchair. "Good God almighty! Germans on American soil. I can't believe it. What on earth could they be doing? What does it say here? About twenty tanks, assorted armor, maybe a hundred men? Do we know anything about this officer Schalberg? George, see what you can find out. Good God! What's at risk? Isn't this the middle of absolute nowhere? How in hell did they get there? Hitler is mad as a hatter. Absolutely mad. We know that, of course. What do we do? What sort of a threat does this pose—I mean militarily, George?"

"I'll need to talk to—"

"George," the President interrupted. "I think for now we had better keep this—"

"But—"

"—between us, just us three," the President said. "For now at least. What about those scientist fellows out there? Los Alamos. Could the Germans be . . . ?"

"That's several hundred miles east of the German position," Hopkins said. "Security forces are on continuous alert there, and they outnumber the German force. I checked with General Grove."

The President leaned back again in his chair.

"What do we do, then?"

"In my opinion, sir," Hopkins said, and he bowed deferentially to General Marshall, "I suggest we take a wait-and-see attitude here. Keep it amongst ourselves. My feeling is that the political ramifications of this—morale and all—are more important than the military."

"Yes, our Republican friends would have a field day. So would some of our Democrats. And quite properly so. They'd be apoplectic."

"Communications with the reservation are basically nonexistent in the best of circumstances," Hopkins went on, "and the few phones appear to be out of commission. The nearest Indian Agency—a place called Keams Canyon—reports everything normal."

"The whole thing can be—ah, sealed off for now? Think of the panic. Germans on American soil."

"The trader," Hopkins said, "got this message out by using Indian runners, to a man on the Utah border . . ."

"I'd like to see a map of this place, Harry. It's a long time since I was out there."

"Yes sir, and he says—Luna says here that he'll keep word coming."

"Runners? Don't they even have horses?" the President asked. "What tribe are these Indians out there? How many are there?"

"Four or five thousand Hopi Indians all told, sir, and

about thirty thousand Navajos. I take it the Germans are concentrated near the Hopi lands, that's in the middle of the reservation approximately, and that is surrounded by Navajo lands. The whole place is about the size of West Virginia."

"Well, what about them?" the President asked.

"About the Indians? Collier at the Indian Department says they're astonishingly patriotic. Sent a lot of their men off to war. Mostly in the Pacific."

"Shocking, isn't it?" the President said.

"What's that, sir?"

"How little we in Washington know about our own people. All right, George? Harry? We'll wait and see. For another twelve hours. I don't want this to—"

"Yes sir," Hopkins said.

"And make sure I get a map of this place. God, I know every field of flax or whatever in Flanders, every damned hill in northern Italy, but I haven't the slightest idea what this—this reservation amounts to. Isn't this all we need now? Of all times. Harry, George here has just told me it's official. We've had to put D day off until early June. At some point I want to know how this happened, how they got there. A German regiment, or whatever it is, doesn't just materialize . . ."

Captain Ben Cameron had to drop everything, including the last cash he had in his wallet, onto the table, apologizing and asking the Englishwoman with long shiny black hair to handle the tab for their two rounds of sloe gin fizzes. They had been there an hour in the cave of a restaurant on the outskirts of London, and Cameron had just about convinced himself that this woman, so calm, so quiet, so beautiful, so—yes, even regal—was going to accompany him that night to his bed, if there wasn't another goddamned air raid . . . He had indeed persuaded himself that this would be a step, and an important one, along the road to matrimony and the making

of this luscious war bride, in due course, into a south-
westerner, once the goddamned war was done with. He
could see in his mind's eye how beautiful she would
look—slim-waisted and round-hipped—in a pair of
western-cut pants, her long black hair swept up under a
broad-brimmed Stetson, a silk bandanna around her neck
and some nice old turquoise mounted in Navajo silver on
her wrist—and he was regaling her at the tiny round table
with a single candle about the vast spaces of New
Mexico when the M.P.'s had appeared in the gloom beside the table and he had rushed off with them.

And now, seated uncomfortably in the even gloomier
confines of the transport plane, its four engines droning
outside and their vibrations penetrating his spine, he
thought of the woman, the beautiful Jenny, with a wrench-
ing sense of permanent loss. All he knew was that he had
been ordered to Washington, to appear in that new Pentagon building he'd heard about at some office with a complicated numerical address at 1030 hours. Who he was
reporting to, he had no idea. What was up? No idea. It was
not the first time during this man's war that he'd been
wrenched out of one billet and sent plummeting into
another.

He hadn't cared much those other times, sanguine
about his role as a cog in an incomprehensibly big set of
wheels that was inexorably grinding down the enemy in
Europe. Whatever anyone asked, he was happy to do.
Why fight fate and the generals? Just drop your cock and
grab your socks and get on with it.

For two months now in London he had been liaison officer with a British intelligence unit whose wizards had
been tracking the whereabouts of none other than Field
Marshal Erwin Rommel, the Desert Fox, who was patrolling the northern rim of Europe for the German High
Command. It was obvious the krauts had put the canny
field marshal in charge of the northern defenses against
the invasion they knew damn well was coming at some

point and from one place or another across the Channel.
The endgame. But for four days now the Allied operatives on the ground, known to Cameron only by regularly
changing code names, had lost track of the fox. Nobody
knew where he was. Cameron shrugged. He'd turn up.
Cameron didn't mind leaving that chase. Someone else
would fill his boots, already had.

But now it was different, being sent off, being torn
away from Jenny, and he had a nauseating feeling that
for one reason or another he wasn't going to get back,
wasn't going to see her again, smell the fresh smell of her
hair in his nose, feel her cheek against his . . .

For the first time in four years in the United States
Army, Ben Cameron felt sorry for himself, seated alone
on an uncomfortable bulkhead seat in this godforsaken
cargo plane in the dark, colder than a mackerel, somewhere out over the icy and uncaring waters of the North
Atlantic with his dream shot to hell.

Yellow Tooth Yazzie leaned on the pommel of his
saddle and looked down into the wash. He wore on his
face a wide grin, the four discolored front teeth showing
ugly and streaked. About twelve feet below him, the
front end of the half-track shuddered as the big engine
roared. Yellow Tooth caught the eye of the German behind the windshield and shook his head, still smiling. The
face behind the glass was taut with rage and frustration.

The half-track, with a crew of four and a leathery
sergeant, had been ordered out five hours earlier on a reconnaissance mission to learn something of the lay of the
land to the northwest of the German encampment. Yellow Tooth, picked as a guide, had insisted on accompanying the half-track on horseback, and it had come to a
tire-spinning stop in a shallow but, the Indian was pretty
sure, treacherous place on Dinnebito Wash, a few miles
beyond Howell Canyon and east of where the Moenkopi
Plateau haunts the horizon. To the north, Yellow Tooth

had explained, lay what the *billegannas* called Coal Canyon, a major canyon where the red-and-white stripes on the rock looked like war paint. There was no way to cross it, he assured the Germans; you had to go way around it. Behind them now was the wagon track to the outlying Hopi village of Moenkopi and beyond that to Tuba City, nothing but a few wooden buildings, a Navajo camp or two, and an aging, nearly senile trader and his wife, who was an old Ute with no teeth.

Behind Yellow Tooth the western half of the sky had turned a glowing pink that would soon darken toward red in the long process of setting. The few clouds on the far horizon were rimmed below with a violent gold, their cottony tops saffron and pink. Yellow Tooth shook his head again, and held out a hand palm down, gesturing to the German driver to stop. The man beside him, the sergeant, yelled, the engine's roar ended, and the heavy vehicle went still, smoke curling out from under its clumsy flat hood. The driver stepped out into the sand, swearing, and yelled at the men in the back who were draped around the protruding 50-millimeter cannon. They leapt out, armed with shovels, and peered from the metallic tracks now sunk a few inches in the sand to the big front wheels, both nearly a foot deep. In the reddening light their faces were lit mahogany.

Yellow Tooth nudged his horse's flank and it moved off a few feet down the edge of the wash. He pointed down.

"Maybe here," he said. "You got to go backward." He gestured to the other side of the wide bed of the wash. "Get a run on it. Come up here, maybe."

The Germans set to work with the shovels, while the driver, hands on hips, said something in rough German as he glared up at Yellow Tooth. The Indian smiled and shrugged.

Ten minutes later the half-track bucked up over the edge of the wash, the German soldiers below setting up a derisive cheer. The driver switched the engine off, and the sergeant stepped down, looking up at Yellow Tooth on his horse.

"It's gettin' late," the Indian said. "I gotta go."

"Go? Go where?"

Yellow Tooth turned and pointed north with his lips. "Over there. Up by Coal Canyon. My sister's havin' a sing. You know, a ceremony. You want to go that way." He swiveled in the saddle and pointed southeast. "It's okay. Real flat that way." The Indian nudged his horse and it broke into a gentle lope along the edge of the wash. Again Yellow Tooth grinned. It *was* real flat that way, to the southeast, all the way from Dinnebito Wash back to Oraibi. Except for that place that had gotten washed out down by Howell Mesa last winter. Now it was full of quicksand.

The trader had been right. By nightfall the Navajos had all disappeared. God knew where they went. Off to their ragged little camps dotted around the desert, Heinrich Schalberg supposed, safe from the witches—the wolfmen?—who plied the night. He would have to be on the alert out here for wolfmen, he thought sardonically. Overhead, the night was moonless, the only light—and a surprisingly great amount of it—coming from the stars. Not since he had been in North Africa had Schalberg seen so many stars. Different constellations here, mostly, but even the familiar ones eluded him, so thick was the sky with stars. He had made out Ursa Major, the Great Bear, but only by facing what he knew to be north and tracing back from the Pole Star.

It was chilly on the desert. Probably forty degrees cooler than the heat in the plaza of Oraibi earlier that day. Maybe fifty degrees. With the trader's approval, Schalberg had waited that morning through three separate dances—each the same—separated by breaks when, on some undetectable signal, the katsinas left the plaza, returning twenty minutes later.

Schalberg had been disoriented as he left the plaza and walked through the village toward the encampment, almost dizzy, and he had repaired immediately to the mess tent, where he had stood eating—he couldn't recall what—and hearing the barbaric noise still in his head. He had spent the afternoon on routine details. Liepzichte had reported toward the end of the day, describing the airstrip where he now stood in the starlight, shivering. The Navajos, Liepzichte had reported, were excellent workers. Even some of the men had been impressed. The airstrip was ready for the first flight.

Later that day, after the red had finally left the western sky, Liepzichte reported that Sergeant Schaeffer and four men were yet to return from their reconnaissance mission to the northwest. A half hour later they were still missing, and Liepzichte and Schalberg had discussed sending another squad out to look for them, deciding finally to wait. Two hours later Schaeffer returned in the half-track, cursing the Indian who had abandoned them at one point late in the afternoon, assuring them that the land between their position and Oraibi was flat. And it was, except for one more dry riverbed that they had attempted to cross. They had spent three hours haplessly trying to dig the half-track out of the soft sand, and thank God there had been an old stump that one of the men finally found in the dark when he was taking a leak, close enough to use with the winch, or they'd still be in the goddamned sand out on the goddamned desert . . . Sergeant Schaeffer had to be reminded that the Indians were for better or worse the Germans' allies, that calling them red nigger-Jew crossbreeds was going to accomplish nothing useful. Schaeffer finally had to be ordered to keep his mouth closed in their presence under pain of being stripped of his sergeant's stripes and relegated to latrine duty.

Earlier in the day, on the radio, Captain Muller agreed

that the three tanks were no longer needed in Keams Canyon and ordered them to Oraibi, where they had arrived as the sun went down. Corporal Schwabe had talked with one of the tank crews, learning that Muller was surely screwing the superintendent's wife, a luscious piece of ass for a foreigner in spite of her age, which the crew guessed was mid-thirties. Blond hair. Big knockers. Round hips and nice long thighs a man could lose himself in. Like a lot of good German girls, in fact. She was also acting as Muller's "interpreter," and manning the telephone there, handling talks with the Indian Service people in Gallup. She had evidently given them some plausible reason or another for sending a regularly scheduled monthly gasoline truck to Keams Canyon three days earlier than scheduled—it would arrive the day after tomorrow.

Except for the tank crew's earthy description of the superintendent's wife, this all accorded with Muller's own terse report on the radio. Schalberg had no reason for concern about the woman. Women, in Schalberg's view of things, often opened themselves to the fortunes of war, sensibly admiring winners. Certainly he himself had found passionate relief among the admiring women of North Africa, and he saw no reason that Yank women shouldn't find German officers irresistible—even the jugeared captain, Muller, with his irritating laugh. With a tingle in his groin, Schalberg dwelt briefly on his own interlude the night before and tried in his mind's eye to see the face of the young Hopi girl. And tonight . . . tonight duty called. Keams Canyon was secure, and now he stood under the stars and listened for the hum of a Condor's four engines, plunging through the night somewhere to the south, flying low over the terrain like a black angel.

He stood on the rim of the airstrip. Its whitish soil glowed eerily in the starlight, and Schalberg, in an uncharacteristic fit of whimsy, looked this way and that for wolfmen. Hans Schwabe, looking more like a bear than a wolf, was crouched on one knee about twenty yards off, sifting the airstrip's dirt through his meaty hands. Elsewhere, spread out along the rim, forty men and a handful of Hopis waited in the night, old Banyongye among them. The old Hopi had suggested that the signal lights, one at either end of the airstrip, be wood fires, not lanterns. From time to time, he said, Navajos held all-night ceremonies around bonfires—they were called squaw dances. If any American plane flew over, it would look like a Navajo ceremony. Upon questioning, Banyongye could not recall any planes flying over the reservation at night, but Schalberg thought it a reasonable precaution. But what, he asked, if the Navajos were in fact having such a ceremony that very night, creating potentially confusing signals for the pilot. Banyongye said he didn't think they were, he would have heard about it. So the Hopis had gathered ample wood—branches and even trunks of the twisted dwarf trees found here and there on the desert—for both fires to burn for several hours. Soon Schalberg would pass the order for them to be lit, and the second crucial phase of Operation Shatterhand would commence.

The Condor cruised the night at 150 miles per hour, lower than its normal continuous cruising speed, but a necessary precaution. It was loaded beyond normal capacity by four tons, and it had been flying low above unknown terrain for almost an hour now, watching for topographical surprises on the dim screen of its surface search radar.

An hour on a heading of north-northeast had taken the plane and its cargo of men, machines, and fuel to the Mexican–United States border at a place in the state of New Mexico where, according to maps and reports from the Sinarquistas, only a few enormous and mostly empty landholdings given over to cattle were scattered. There, a change of course to roughly a north-northwest direction had taken it over a sparsely populated and mountainous region of the state of Arizona. Then the plane had descended again to four hundred feet and, now headed more nearly north, was at most a half hour from whatever landing strip Schalberg and his troops had provided here in the middle of nowhere. Fritz Bader, the pilot of the much modified Focke-Wolf 200, searched for signal lights on the dark surface of the desert hurtling underneath him.

Bader's missions in these enormous planes now numbered in the hundreds. They had begun on maritime patrols in 1941, when all the Condors had been assigned to Bomber Group 40 stationed in Bordeaux-Merignac, flying great loops from France to Norway and back, seeking out British shipping in the North Sea. Fritz was pleased to have accounted personally—for so he credited such matters—for more than fifty thousand tons of British shipping in the two years before he was reassigned to ferry supplies to the Germans besieged at Stalingrad. One of the few Condor pilots to survive this awful duty, Fritz had then been assigned yet again to what, in his opinion, was his most perilous duty yet, flying men and matériel into the United States of America, of all places, from a crazy Wagnerian German's ranch in Sonora, a place code-named Arabian Nights after all her pretty big-eyed horses, which looked like unicorns without the horns. The whole thing was like an exotic fairy tale, what with the brown-skinned Mexicans with thin mustaches saluting and saying "Heil Hitler" in their funny accent, and the big-breasted Mexican woman Fritz had found in the kitchen, discovering that she liked to do more than cook up enchiladas and tamales. But of course, it was serious business, and now more serious than ever. The United States of America lay below him!

In three years he had been shot at by the British Wildcats screaming up into the air from the escort carrier over the North Sea, and survived. He had been shot down in the snow and the freezing cold near Stalingrad, losing his plane and his crew, and survived that too. But this mission, the first of four scheduled flights over American territory in four successive nights, struck him as the most dangerous of all—and he was exhilarated.

Only minutes before, flying low over the desert, the radar had picked up a huge rocky pinnacle looming ahead of them, and he had strained the plane's metal structure to the maximum veering away from it, missing it by as little as a few hundred feet. Now he had resumed his heading and a cruising speed of 150 miles per hour, searching for telltale lights on the ground, with the adrenaline still pumping his heart rate up.

Behind him were twenty-five German soldiers, five American vehicles called jeeps, armed with Yankee popguns—in Bader's opinion—that had been captured somewhere in Italy, and crate after crate of weapons, ammunition, and supplies of various sorts. The old plane shuddered under its burden as the four engines churned the night. All of the Condor's own weaponry had been stripped away—the forward cannon, the two dorsal machine guns, the machine gun aft in the gondola. They were defenseless. Interior bulkhead, seats, anything that was not designed to strengthen the plane's hull—all were gone. The troops sat where they could among the cargo, freezing their asses off, and no doubt they had rattled around like peas in a whistle when Bader veered away from that damned big finger of rock sticking up out of nowhere.

Under the wings, where Fritz had once carried bombs out over the North Sea, to send them plunging into the hulls of hapless merchant ships, were now detachable tanks filled with fuel. Landing, Bader thought, would be a particular thrill if the landing gear malfunctioned. He had long assumed he would end his days in a grand explosion; many of his friends already had. Except for the navigator, whose eyes were glued to the radar screen, he was alone in his big overweight bird, with only a remembered God to whom he had long since stopped praying on the reasonable assumption that if there were such a being, He had to enjoy war and its explosions and screams since He had countenanced so much of it throughout history. Why, then, if war were one of God's recreations, would He suddenly see fit to intervene and except Fritz Bader from whatever was in store?

Ahead and slightly to the west, Bader saw two lights and banked slightly toward them, throttling down. The lights seemed to dance—fires, not lights—and he banked again, descending a hundred feet. One after the other, about a half mile apart on a precise south-north axis, they slid under the plane, and Fritz put it into a gentle circle, coming again to the lights and again flying over them. Between them, he noted, the ground seemed lighter, and he wondered if Schalberg had somehow limed the airstrip. The big plane seemed fragile under his hand, and he guessed it was the thin air at this elevation—six thousand feet above sea level.

At the end of the second circle he brought her in, holding his breath until the landing gear struck the ground a hundred feet past the first bonfire. The plane bounced slightly and rolled along the smooth ground. Bader brought the plane to a stop about twenty feet from what appeared to be a slight rise, like a rim, in front of him, with a bonfire burning maybe a hundred feet beyond up on a shadowy outcrop. No one, he thought, can land one of these big beautiful cows on the ground with the consummate grace of Fritz Bader. He cut the engines, one after the other, slid the little side window back and leaned his head out into the cool night air, seeing men approach him across the whitish strip.

"Heil Hitler," he said affably. "And up FDR's ass."

It took only forty-five minutes for the soldiers and a few little short Indians to unload the Condor, stowing the supplies and ammunition in two trucks that pulled up to the plane. Bader had made his way back into the plane's cavernous hull, opened the big freight door, let down the ramp and hopped out. The major general, Schalberg, had greeted him warmly, asked about the flight and listened to his report attentively, and gratefully received a sealed envelope Bader had brought from Schalberg's mother. For the rest of the time, Bader had lolled about, smoking one cigarette after another until the plane was empty and it was time to fire her up again. Taking off, the plane feeling light as a feather under him, had been straightforward enough. She had fairly leapt into the night. By the time a yellowish glow appeared a hundred miles or so away on the eastern horizon, the Condor was well over Mexico, flying low above the Sonoran desert and a mere half hour from Arabian Nights. He would be in time for one of those palate-burning, sinus-clearing Mexican breakfasts, maybe a quick roll in the hay with the jolly, round cook, and then sleep. What did they call it? A siesta.

War is hell, Bader thought, grinning.

At about the time Fritz Bader was lifting his great empty bird into the sky southwest of the Hopi mesas, and two trucks—followed by five jeeps—were making their way back across the bumpy ground to Oraibi, Mary Beth Lemmon was lying awake in her now twice defiled bed, sleepless, angry, every nerve end in her body jangling like a million telephones, and her mind racing. In four days the Germans would be gone, clattering off somewhere in their stolen tanks and trucks, she didn't know where or to do what. But they planned to leave in four days. She wondered how valuable the information was. And to whom?

Muller, now asleep and snoring, one of his legs lying proprietarily across one of hers, had leapt upon the information that the agency in Gallup sent a monthly tanker truck of fuel—gasoline—to Keams Canyon, and his face had knotted up with frustration when Mary Beth told him that it was scheduled to come next Thursday. "Too late, too late," he had fumed to himself, as if she wasn't there. She'd had no idea how late Thursday was in the plans of these krauts.

"Maybe I could get 'em to come Wednesday," she had said.

"How?" Muller snapped. "How would you do that?"

"I don't know. Maybe I can think of some excuse, some reason . . ."

Muller shook his head. "No, still too late."

They had sat in the agency office, the air thick and heavy in the midday heat.

"Monday," Muller said. "Could they be persuaded to come Monday?"

"Monday? Gee, that's a lot earlier than their schedule. Three days. They don't like to make any big changes like that. Takes a lot of paperwork and all. Government people don't like anything like that." Mary Beth felt oddly disembodied. She heard her own voice saying these things, but it seemed like it was someone else talking, not her.

Muller paced back and forth in front of the desk. "How much fuel comes?"

"A big truck. Mostly full. I don't know how much it is. A month's supply for the agency here, but it's wartime rations, of course. I don't know what it is in gallons or anything."

Muller kept pacing. In his excitement or frustration or whatever it was, he seemed to be grinning. She had seen a wolf in the zoo in Chicago who did that.

"We need an emergency," he said at last. "An emergency requiring fuel. We are now completely out of fuel here at Keams Canyon, yes? And there is an emergency requiring the heavy use of those two trucks out there. What could such an emergency be? Think."

Mary Beth scrunched up her forehead, frowning to

disguise the excitement she felt from discovering something precise about the Germans' plans. Monday was their last day here before they left . . . for somewhere.

"There's a big old earthen dam a few miles up Wepo Wash," she said after a minute or two had passed in silence. "They built it before the war to catch runoff. Some idea of using the water for irrigation up there or something. It never worked. The irrigation, I mean. Navajos up there weren't interested, just want to run their sheep is all, and a couple of Hopi families up there—well, they're not really Hopis, they're Tewas who talk Hopi and act like 'em—they don't farm that way. Didn't want to learn. It was a dumb idea, like most of the ideas they have here, but there's that dam up there, made out of rocks and dirt."

She fell silent and Muller paced impatiently, finally saying: "What about it, this dam?"

"Suppose it's got a lot of water in it. And it looks like it's about to fall apart. A lot more water than usual. Some freak rain up there or something."

Muller stopped, his grin or whatever it was making his teeth show like a wolf getting wider. "Is it full?"

"I don't know," Mary Beth said. "But they don't know in Gallup either. Those people never come out here. So anyway, it needs to be repaired right away. We got to haul a lot of rock from the quarry back there to fix it before it breaks."

"Perfect, perfect," Muller said, and before long Mary Beth was on the phone talking to one of the men in Gallup who thought it all sounded impossible. Mary Beth stressed that it was a real emergency, the dam was showing signs of blowing, and a bunch of the men including the engineering guy, Bonner, was up there now, and otherwise they would have to evacuate those Hopis up there and a couple of Navajo families, and that would cause an unholy stink, maybe worse than when they shot all the Navajo sheep, and did this guy in Gallup want that on his head? So it was finally agreed that Gallup would send the truck out before dawn Monday. It would arrive Monday morning sometime.

"Very good," Muller had said when Mary Beth hung up the phone. "*Very* good." He stood behind her while she lied to the bureaucrat in Gallup, and now he put his hands on her shoulders, massaging them. Mary Beth cringed inwardly and thought about sticking a knife between *his* shoulders.

Now, lying in bed with his leg weighing heavily on hers, she found herself thinking about a war bond poster she had seen in Winslow a year ago, showing a booted foot crushing three grotesque figures under it—Mussolini, Tojo, and Hitler. The fat-lipped Italian, the buck-toothed Jap, and a wild-eyed Hitler, his face misshapen, his little mustache awry—three evil little gnomes. Whenever she had thought of the enemy, the Axis, she thought of them this way, not real people, but horrid monsters. Diseased.

But this kraut, this Heinie, this Hun bastard with his leg across hers, was not a misshapen gnome. He was a man who, without his uniform, could be from anywhere. It made it all the more disgusting somehow. Her flesh crawled. She thought again about the knife. She knew where it was, an old hunting knife of her husband's, with a thick black blade and a little canal on it he had told her was to let blood out once it was stuck in some animal's flesh. Otherwise, it was hard to pull out. Maybe she should ease her leg out from under the kraut bastard's and get the knife. But maybe, she thought, if she was patient she could find out where the Germans were going Monday night or Tuesday morning after they had filled up their vehicles with U.S. government gasoline. Now that would be really worth knowing. She decided to postpone murdering the German captain. Captain Willie with his stupid laugh.

He murmured and rolled over. She was free. The

knife. The knife. She wondered what it would feel like, plunging it between his shoulder blades, ramming it deep into him, gouging away at his lungs or his heart or whatever it would cut into. Would she be able to do it? Was she strong enough? Yes. She was strong enough, damn sure. But she would wait.

She got up from the bed, pushing her nightgown down around her legs, and crossed over to the window, where she would stand until a bit of light became visible in the sky over Keams Canyon.

It had taken a night and a day for Danny Koots to sober up to the point where he knew where he was—home, in his mother's one-room house a quarter mile outside Keams Canyon and a couple of hundred yards back from the dirt road in the shadow of the canyon wall. He had a vague memory of being yanked out of the Keams Canyon jail by some cop, or was it a soldier, and standing in the dusty road with another one, a big-time cop or whatever. After that, he didn't remember anything else until he woke up with an awful but familiar headache and the feeling that he had been drained of blood—embalmed and thirsty—in the shadowy room that had nothing much in it but a cot and an old woodstove with a stovepipe that no longer reached the hole in the wall he had made for it. There was a spiderweb in the hole, and he looked at that for a while, wondering where the spider was. Gone. Like his mother, who had gone a few years ago. She had died.

Danny wished he had been home when his mother died, but he'd been down at the Morenci mine, getting paid union wages for unearthing copper from the big pit in the ground, helping the war effort, and drinking up most of the wages on his night off just like the other single men there. Then one day he'd quit and come home to find that his mother had died and they'd buried her but nobody knew how to reach him—that's what they said, and he guessed it was so.

He'd hung around awhile and gone back to the mine, but the union wouldn't let him back in, so he'd tried Bisbee. Same story. He guessed he was what they said, an unreliable Indian, though they had less polite ways of explaining it, so he'd got a job in a garage in Bisbee, keeping old Fords and Chevys from dying, and getting into occasional fights with white guys and sometimes Navajos and Pimas.

Now he was home again, back in his mother's house with a hangover, a spiderweb in the hole where the stovepipe used to go, and nothing else to show for two years, or was it three years, of his life. Back among his people, the Hopis, but he didn't feel that much a part of things. He had started to think like a white man, sounded more like a white man. Picked up a lot of the white man's bad habits in the mines and all.

When he was a little kid, his mother had joined one of the mission churches and had learned about Jesus and told him that the katsinas were just superstition, paganism was the word she had used, so he hadn't fit in very well with the other Hopis. Neither did his mother, so they had come over here from First Mesa, built this one-room house out of yellow sandstone, and this was where he had grown up with his bitter old mother until he was old enough to head out. He'd bummed around most of the West, working on road crews, in mines, a month here, two months there, and now he was home again. Danny Koots didn't know what it was that kept him coming back, and he didn't think much about it anymore. He didn't have much to think about anymore—just where he'd go next, not that it made much of a difference. He was just an unreliable Indian.

An unreliable Indian with a bad right leg that ached now. It had been broken when a diesel engine fell on it— just below the knee—and it hadn't knit up right, so it ached a lot, and slowed him down some. Riding a horse didn't make it feel much better—only drinking did, and . . . he sat up suddenly. That horse. How long had he been passed out?

He limped over to the one window and looked out in the corral. The horse was standing there, head down, staring at the water trough. Saddlebags, rifle holster still on it, but he'd gotten the bridle off. Where was his rifle? He spotted it on the floor.

Danny Koots left his house in a hurry, squinting in the sun, and got his horse unsaddled, put the bridle back on, and led it back toward Keams, where there was a windmill that creaked and groaned and usually kept a big tank full of water. He stood by the tank while the horse drank, thinking he'd better get some feed too. From where he stood, just outside a little stand of cottonwoods, he could see the yellow stone buildings of the town. Everything there looked still. Nobody was around.

Parked outside the agency office was an American military vehicle, a half-track, and Danny just couldn't think what a half-track was doing outside the Keams Canyon Indian Agency. He tried to clear the cobwebs out of his head, and his horse raised its head and snorted. Keams Canyon was hardly the kind of place where they'd have a war bond drive. He remembered again the cop pulling him out of jail. It wasn't a cop. It was a soldier. The soldiers had spoken in some other language. Some rough language.

Danny Koots changed his mind about cadging some feed for his horse. You could usually bum something like that from the government people for a day or two before they got irritable with you. He led his horse back to the corral behind his house, noting that it was falling apart, needed work. What didn't around this place? Why was he here? What was that language they had spoken, those two soldiers?

Danny set off over the boulders up a rocky trail that

led up the canyon wall, making his way as quietly as he could with his bad leg, and by the time he got to the top he was huffing and puffing and his headache was worse. He'd lost his hat somewhere along the way these past few days, and the sun was bad in his eyes. He picked his way along the canyon's edge until he got to another trail, the kind of opening you wouldn't notice if you didn't know it was there, and began to descend, this time even more slowly, making sure he didn't make a sound. Below was the agency office itself, and when he got down to the bottom, he stood quietly in the shadow its roof cast, listening. He thought he could hear voices from inside, so he waited a while longer and then slipped around the corner, stood beside the window on the north side of the building and listened. A woman's voice, and then a man's. The woman's voice was familiar—the superintendent's wife, Mary Beth Lemon. The man's voice was clipped, kind of harsh. Not the superintendent who always sounded like he had a bad head cold, sort of whined through his nose.

Slowly, he edged sideways up to the window and quickly glanced in. The Lemon woman was at the desk, and the man was standing next to it, in uniform. In a German uniform! Danny pulled his head back and leaned his head against the stone of the building, breathing through his mouth.

German? What the hell was going on? He listened. They were talking about calling Gallup, saying that there was an emergency, something about the dam up Wepo Wash, needing that fuel truck to come. By Monday. Tuesday would be too late. They'd have to evacuate some Hopis and some Navajos if it didn't come by Monday.

That didn't make any sense to Danny. That dam had fallen down a couple of years ago, last time he was home. And the Hopis up there—Tewas really—they'd left.

Maybe some Navajos had moved in. It didn't make any sense.

So Danny had slipped away, back up the canyon and over to his mother's house, where he had fetched his rifle, saddled up the horse, and rode it west down the dirt road to a place where there usually was some grass. Along the road he saw strange parallel gouges in the dirt, and it dawned on him that they were tank tracks. Tanks. What the hell was going on here? After the horse had eaten enough to be satisfied in Danny's opinion, they had set out north across the desert between Keams Canyon and First Mesa to look into what was going on up Wepo Wash that made a German officer want to get some fuel out here from Gallup by Monday.

Danny Koots wasn't thinking with all of his cylinders yet, he knew that, and it suddenly dawned on him that the dam and all that didn't make any difference. What was important was that there were tank tracks on the road back there and a German officer in the Indian Agency office, and the superintendent's wife was helping him out.

He decided he had better go over to Oraibi and talk to the trader there, Raphael Luna. He was a sensible man. A lot of these Hopis didn't know too much about things like this—like things that didn't happen over and over the same way here on the reservation like they always had. His people got all excited when something new happened, and started arguing, and Danny didn't like to hear all the bickering. And he didn't imagine any of the Navajos around out in the desert would be much help. But the trader—he was a sensible man and he'd know what the hell was going on.

He decided he'd keep on the way he was going, go north around First Mesa and cut across Wepo Wash and on west to Oraibi. Nobody out there but a few Navajo camps. He could get to the trader's by dark if this old gelding didn't die on him. He couldn't remember where he'd gotten the horse. Maybe Holbrook. God damn, that was a hell of a drunk, wasn't it?

By nine o'clock that night, seven hours before the Condor landed out in the desert, Raphael Luna had figured out what Mary Beth Lemon also knew now—that the Germans intended to leave Monday night or Tuesday. Danny Koots had arrived an hour before and, having been fed by Mary Yazzie in the kitchen, sat down with Luna on the rickety porch and explained what he had seen and heard in the Indian Agency office. Then, after Luna explained all the rest of what had been going on, Danny's head finally seemed to clear and he had a whole picture in it.

None of it made any sense at all. A German invasion of the reservation. What the hell were they doing here? The krauts were getting their asses kicked all over Europe—he had heard that on the radio in Bisbee and other places. So what were they doing here?

"Among other things, Danny," Luna said in his phlegmy voice, "that's what we have to find out, isn't it?"

## Part Two
# A GRAND ALLIANCE

To be able to take bad news without pessimism
and reverses without losing our morale
. . . is essential.
—Franklin Delano Roosevelt

# Five

May 13, 1944, and a Saturday for those who attended to such matters, would be the second full day of the invasion of the United States by the 108th Panzer Battalion of the German Wehrmacht. At dawn on May 12, only some forty hours had passed since one prong of the invading force had commandeered the Indian Agency in Keams Canyon while the other main prong arrived in the shadow of the ancient Hopi mesas and announced the "liberation" of the Indians on the reservation from the United States, placing them under the care of the Third Reich. This had been accomplished with but one casualty—a broken jaw—and but one shot fired: a demonstration mortar round that demolished a pinnacle of rock near the village of Oraibi. A landing strip had since been engineered in the desert and successfully used, and various reconnaissance missions were carried out into the surrounding territory, probing the land for routes the Wehrmacht might take when it came time to broaden its mission according to plan. The invading—or perhaps it could by now be called occupying—force had now been swelled by twenty-five German fighting men, five American jeeps, and an additional array of equipment, including ammunition and a modest amount of fuel. So far, the Germans' new allies, the Indians, had proven at best helpful, at worst submissive.

As the sun burst into the sky, as it seems to do every morning in the American Southwest with an eagerness

149

unknown elsewhere, the Germans could content themselves that the invasion had, on the whole, been easier and more successful than they imagined it could be. As the sun came up they anticipated another day of gathering themselves—of organizing, training, exploring, and readying themselves for the events that lay ahead, dramatic events they would instigate in this New World with all the lightning power of surprise, events that would potentially affect the very outcome of the hostilities that raged thousands of miles away on the old continent of Europe.

By dawn in the American Southwest, it was already afternoon in Europe, and German city dwellers again prepared themselves for the rain of bombs that might—or might not—come that night. To the east, the Nazi dream of adding large parts of Russia to the Third Reich had become a nightmare of retreat and confusion. Along the northern shores of Europe, Field Marshal Rommel organized defenses against an imminent invasion by one or another of the armies massing across the English Channel. In Berlin, Adolf Hitler and a select few of his henchmen—their minds long since clouded by mania—pinned some of the Third Reich's diminishing prospects on the effectiveness of a small, highly trained force somewhere in the middle of the American desert. In retrospect it can be said that never in the annals of war had so many depended on so few for so much.

As the sun rose over the Indian lands in northern Arizona on May 11, most members of the 108th Panzer Battalion slept, their officers taking the time available to them—a matter of days only—to change the battalion's waking and sleeping schedule to one more suited for nighttime activity. The Germans were wholly unaware that a change of fortune was imminently at hand. All the Navajos for miles around, emerging from the darkness of their hogans to greet the sun and offer it a pinch of corn pollen and a fervent prayer, knew a change was in store.

Every Hopi, upon setting foot on the dusty ground outside their houses in the villages perched on their three ancestral mesas, knew this day would be significantly different. The change was, specifically, in the air. It was not so much that the sky was cloudless, for that was often the case. Nor was it that the air temperature had not fallen quite so far during the night, nor that the sun's energy was particularly strong in the clarity of this morning. No Navajo or Hopi and no professional meteorologist could have explained exactly what was different, what combination of subtle conditions were at work, but all the locals, all the Indians for miles around, knew it was a day to put blankets over the doors, to seal off their homes as best they could. Hopi farmers and their wives prayed that the modest little windbreaks, placed lovingly around each tender young corn plant in the fields below, would be effective.

For soon enough, once the sun had chased away the cool of the night, the winds would rise, the western horizon would yellow. San Francisco Peaks would vanish from the horizon. The wind, whom the Navajos call Nil'chi'i, and who, in its gentler manifestations, is the breath of life for every living creature, would sweep howling down across the land, dust-laden and angry. Brown, gritty sand would fill the air and abrade the souls of the people, entering every crevice in every home. Whirlwinds would spin into existence, irate eddies whose presence was a sign of the displeasure of the Holy People, and whose touch, Navajos knew, was disfiguring.

As dawn marched from east to west across the Colorado Plateau, all the Indians knew what was in store and began to make the few preparations available to them. Certainly, it was not going to be a day when the katsinas could enjoy a second day dancing, as was usual, so the katsina father sent them off with his blessing and his thanks for their appearance the day before, enjoining them to bring timely rains to the Hopi fields once the winds that were in store ended. Just how long the world would have to stop for the winds, no one knew. One merely had to wait and see. It could be hours, it could be all day. There were many who remembered such late spring winds lasting without letup through two entire days and nights and well into the following day. And so Navajos remained in their family camps, speaking in quiet voices among themselves, speculating to the limits of their knowledge and experience about what this astounding new presence in their country meant, and what these Germans thought they were going to do next. Word had spread among them that it was, for now, a time for waiting, watching, and for keeping the whole thing to themselves. The Hopis, in their more voluble manner, stayed indoors in their villages and told each other stories from their past that might shed light on the present situation, though it did not, since the meanings of the stories tended to be contradictory.

As for the German soldiers, they woke later than the day before and set about the routine chores of an army readying itself for action—maintenance, repairs, planning, eating, soothing raw nerves with coarse humor, some among them even making silent prayers of a kind not officially sanctioned by an atheist regime. By nine o'clock in the morning, the temperature had begun its rapid climb, and some of the Germans, among them Franz Liepzichte, were wondering why no Indians had put in an appearance. And only minutes later, a few weatherwise Germans noticed the gentle wind now blowing from the west and saw the horizon turning an odd yellow. Among them, those who had served in North Africa realized what was coming and sounded the alarm. In minutes the men of the 108th Panzer Battalion had mobilized and frantically begun taking protective measures, covering every orifice they could of every tank, half-track, and other vehicle with whatever piece of canvas or cloth they could find and liberate from its original use, sounding new and even more fervent prayers that the sand and dust would somehow spare the delicate inner working of their machines.

And so the wind reached its full force, thrashing the scrubby plants of the desert into an agonized horizontality, and sending brush, branches, and mountains of dust hurtling at breakneck speeds across the land. Man and beast for miles around hunkered down, faced eastward away from the abrading onslaught, and the world effectively came to a stop. Like a mammoth wave, the dust-bearing front slammed into the great landform called Black Mesa, which sits astride the core of the reservation, a female presence in the minds of the Navajos, and thrashed the mesa's vertical walls, sending updrafts of dust cascading into the air above, only to be rushed eastward again, tearing like tiny diamonds at everything in their path.

Near a modest bend in Oraibi Wash where it descends more steeply on its way across the southwesternmost finger of Black Mesa to bypass the morbid sentinel village of Old Oraibi, there is a place where the banks are higher, rising some fifteen feet above the sandy bottom. Into the eastern bank, Secakuku and Quavehema, the Hopi runners, burrowed like badgers when it became clear they would be unable to run any farther. There, with what was left of their sun-dried mutton jerky and the last few sips of water they carried in canteens, they waited in silence for the noisome fury of the storm to pass. They had, of course, read the terse message received by the ham operator in Medicine Hat, Utah, from the man Hopkins in the White House in Washington, D.C. It made little sense to them beyond the fact that the White House expected more messages to be sent, more information about the German soldiers. They wondered who this man Cameron was who was coming, and where he was coming from, and when he would come, and how he would come. Would he be dropped out of a plane with a parachute like the newsreels they had seen in Winslow? Certainly he would not come until the winds died down, for nothing happened at such times.

So, in a burrow in the lee of Oraibi Wash, the two Hopi runners crouched while their counterparts, two other Hopi runners, crouched similarly in a recently abandoned Navajo hogan amid some piñon and juniper trees near the settlement of Pinon on Black Mesa. These two, freshly outfitted with jerky and water and a new message in the spidery script of the trader Luna, didn't share the Navajos' revulsion at the dead. It didn't bother them at all that someone had died in this hogan, and given the fact that someone had indeed died here, forcing the hogan's abandonment, they were glad it had been recent enough that the hogan's walls were still strong, the mud between its logs still intact. Outside its east-facing entrance, the wind whipped and screamed, tearing pieces from the hogan's mud roof, and the world was yellow.

Mary Yazzie arrived back at Luna's Trading Post that morning after the sun rose but before the wind struck. The trader's mule, which she had borrowed the night before, had a particularly harsh gait, and Mary's backside radiated pain from her thighs up to her shoulders. She was tired from her all-night journey without sleep, and breathless still, not from any physical exertion, but from the bravado with which she had taken certain matters into her own hands, as Navajo women often had to do at certain times. She sat, still as a rock, in a straight-backed wooden chair in the kitchen in Luna's living quarters, trying to keep her heart still, trying not to let her chest heave, trying not to dwell too heavily on her deliberate journey among the powers of the dark.

She, of all people she knew, had suffered from these selfsame powers, her parents gone, her brother struck down by the Holy People while he tended what was left of the Yazzies' herd. She was alone, thanks to the powers of the witch, and whatever glimmer of hope had crept into her life over the past year or so while she tended the strange household of Big Mexican was now gone. It had been necessary to act. But the acts she had found it necessary to perform . . . no longer would she walk the earth in the state of grace that Navajos call *hozho*, or beauty.

It was not the physical act, her stealthy appearance in the Hopi village, creeping among their houses the other night into the lightless room where the German officer slept, and the stormy writhing of their bodies . . . such a bodily performance was neither here nor there in the larger scheme of things in her life as she now measured it. It was the taking of his hair. It was the willful, knowing act of cutting a piece of the German's hair in the dark once he slept again, sodden with exhausted passion, and taking this part of his body, this physical entryway to his very soul with her when she stole back into the night . . . It was the journey the next night on the back of that mule made of wood across Oraibi Wash and out into the desert to the hogan of the witch, a man who had once killed his own brother, who had fathered the son of his own daughter, who had eaten of his brother's corpse and cavorted with his deadly kind in the night on Round Rock, the man whose name she dared not to form even in her mind now . . .

This was the same one who, the medicine man in Pinon said, had visited all Mary's troubles on her, taking her family and making her sick, unable to eat properly for so long that she looked like a stick. The medicine man in Pinon, a star-gazer, had sent her on to another medicine man, and his ceremony had let her eat again, but did not heal the other afflictions that gnawed at her. And, with the help of the trader, there had been yet another ceremony, a squaw dance, but the witch who lived alone in the desert still lived even though a year had long since passed and he was supposed to have died.

So with a perverse flash of insight, she had gone to

him, gone to his hogan in the night with the German's hair—not in any hope that doing so might lift the lingering troubles he had visted on her, but in the brazen determination to put his powers to work in behalf of her people at large, in behalf of the destruction of these Germans. No one else, not even the trader, Big Mexican, had any idea of what Mary Yazzie had now done. Knowing she was now alone more than ever, and without the slightest glimmer of hope, she shuddered while the wind battled the thick walls of Luna's Trading Post and tore the world into tatters. There was nothing now for Mary Yazzie but to wait amid the howling wind for the other storm she had, herself, set loose.

She took some comfort from history. Some years before he had passed on, her grandfather had told her of an incident in the Navajo past when some of the People— over beyond Chilchinbito—came under attack from a large force of Spaniards. Outnumbered, they climbed up into the rocks that had fallen around a great red pinnacle and from there, by use of handholds in the vertical face of the rock, to its top. The Spaniards could not figure out how they had climbed up and decided instead to wait down below. After many days, the Navajos were out of water and out of food and things were desperate. Finally, they turned to their leader and begged him to use the special powers they knew he possessed to rid them of the Spaniards far down below. The leader was reluctant but finally agreed there was no other way. Recognizing the Spaniards' leader from his finery, he focused his powers on him and soon the man was dead. The Spanish soldiers took fright at this and fled, and the Navajos were able to come down from the pinnacle and go about their lives again. Despite the good he had accomplished, their leader was always regretful and never again felt right.

No one remembered the leader's name now, but in such matters, it is the meanings of a story that are important, not individuals, and while it was not often that this story was told, Mary had remembered it. Now, seated in the chair in the trader's kitchen among the familiar, still objects of life, Mary Yazzie closed her eyes, and her shoulders trembled uncontrollably as if the wind were inside her, raging to escape.

Diligently, the wiry man had worked through the night, letting the colored sand fall between his fingers in thin lines on the ground, careful lines made in a prescribed order, creating effigies of a sort, effigies of those among the Holy People he wanted to summon into his presence. The evil ones. By dawn he had finished. His neck ached with tension, and the floor of his hogan was covered with the ugly and distorted painting, a thin veneer of fine-colored sand so carefully crafted in the other colors, the other four colors that no one liked to see. His throat was dry, but he put the idea of a drink out of his mind.

She had brought four hundred dollars and an old but expensive saddle. Good enough.

Once the painting was done, he spread out the *jish* of his craft, the several objects, each in its own little leather bag, that he would use in his ceremony to invite the evil ones into his painting, where he could put them to work. Carefully, he extracted some of the *jish* objects from their bags and placed them with delicate care in the corners of the painting, pointing inward—pathways. Once he was satisfied they were in the right place, he stripped off his clothes and sat naked, his back to the door of the hogan, and chanted, repeating the words over and over again, keeping count in some nether part of his mind. He was dimly aware of the sound of the wind picking up outside, rattling the roof, becoming a low howl with a distant, high-pitched whine as well, and he was pleased to have the wind's angry accompaniment, though it was not something he had invited with his chant.

Abruptly the chant was over. The man stood, walked

around the painting on the ground, and from a shelf he took a rattle in one hand, a small deerskin bag in the other. Seated again with his back to the door, he opened the bag and took a few light brown hairs out, holding them before him in his fingers. He sniffed them. He put them in his mouth and swallowed. Leaning forward, his arms stretched to their greatest extent, he placed the deerskin bag and the remaining hair in the center of the painting, on top of a livid eye. Again, from his *jish*, now all laid out in a circle on the sand, he took four other objects, spat on them, and placed them around the deerskin bag on the eye.

The wind continued to rage outside, rising and falling, while the man shook the rattle in a strange rhythm and began again to chant.

The chant went on as long as the wind, longer, and then in the silence the man stopped again, opened yet another pouch from his *jish* and sprinkled some of its contents on the deerskin bag that sat on the eye in the center of the painting. Corpse dust. In his fingers, he took a pinch of it from the pouch and put it in his mouth and resumed chanting, resumed the deadening rhythm of the rattle.

Before long the eye in the center of the painting began to grow in size, to pulsate and burn, the flames licking at the growing edge of what was becoming a hole in the ground. And into the hole the deerskin bag containing the light brown hair fell. The fire burned higher, drawing the man to the hole, filling him with pain that swelled and screamed until his entire body was on fire as well, and he slipped into the hole in a slow sinuous motion like a snake. In the black of the tunnel now, he looked for the deerskin bag with the hair, seeing only yellow eyes with vertical pupils winking at him, all around him. They came closer, and he slithered away through them, feeling their heat. He sank below into the darker realm of the Monster Women and felt them clawing at him with their gaping, many-toothed vaginas. He screamed, felt blood coursing from the wounds where the Monster Women's sharp teeth tore at his genitals. He slashed at them with a knife, watched the blood explode from them, and slithered on in the endless descent toward a pale light that always went before him. Blinded by his own blood, he fell uncontrollably in the blackness until he confronted the dark one who sat before him, jaws agape: the Beast.

He heard the Beast's challenge somewhere in the depths of his being and, in answer, reached out into its mouth and took the deerskin bag from it, holding it high over his head. As he did so, he felt himself falling again, and screamed and saw the fangs closing behind him, sealing him in . . .

The hogan's entrance cast a long rectangle of light across the sandpainting, and the only sound was the insistent buzz of flies. The witch awoke, sunlit and crumpled on the painting, some of its colored sand leaking meaninglessly from his clenched fists. He was facedown, nostrils clogged. He lay still, waiting for the pain to subside, and watched voracious green flies land in the pool of vomit that had spread around him. The ceremony was complete.

The stench, wafting easterly down the dirt road of Keams Canyon on the morning breezes, had been nauseating. Its tendrils crept invisibly into each of the buildings between the jail and the agency office, finally contaminating even the office as well. A German soldier, a noncommissioned officer named Behrmann, had respectfully asked Captain Wilhelm Muller if he and his men could herd the prisoners out of the one-celled prison for a short period in the air. The application of some air and perhaps some water, the noncom had said, might relieve the jail of its odors, now so unbearable the soldier assigned to bring a bucket of food to the prisoners— a slop of beans along with some soggy jerky—had upchucked on entering the jail that morning, making matters worse.

Captain Muller had promptly ordered that all the prisoners but two be taken outside and kept marching in a lively circle in the dirt road under careful guard while the remaining two cleaned out the latrine and any other source of offense in the jail itself.

Earlier in the morning, Müller had talked—in German—on the radio with the others, saying *ja* a lot. Afterward he had taken out the few maps in the agency's collection and began to pour over them, telling Mary Beth that they would be going for a "pleasant ride into the countryside" later that morning, suggesting with a leer that they might find a way to fit in a bit of pleasure during their reconnaissance. Mary Beth felt the need to control her breathing, thinking that she would no doubt find out something valuable in the bargain.

In the fulfillment of Muller's orders, Sergeant Behrmann singled out the pasty-faced scarecrow, Lemon the superintendent, and the young man with the broken jaw, to remain inside to clean the latrine. Beatty, the man with the broken jaw, was an arrogant son of a bitch, Behrmann thought, snarling through what had to be the pain, and could use the humiliation. Lemon, already humiliated in every fiber of his scrawny body, was the sort of weakling scum who should—in any proper world—be assigned to latrine duty.

So it was that when Mary Beth Lemon looked out the window of the agency office while Captain Muller busied himself with maps, she saw neither her husband nor her onetime lover among the straggling and filthy group of men and two women, walking like ghosts in a tight circle in the dust under the watchful eyes of two German soldiers. For several years now these people, now reduced to this shameful condition, had been the core of her entire world, her society, and she felt a sob rise in her throat. None of them had meant all that much to her—in fact, she had an active distaste for several of them—but even so . . . She swallowed the nascent sob and summoned up her previous resolution: to do anything she could to rid her world of these disgusting, immoral kraut bastards, and in particular the slimy monster at the desk behind her. She turned her head toward him.

"My husband," she said. "He's not there."

"No doubt chosen for latrine duty, along with the other prisoner, Beatty," Muller replied airily. He turned from the map he was smoothing on the desk with both hands. "Does that bother you?" He grinned.

Mary Beth quickly turned back to the scene outside the window. "No," she said, and almost gagged. "It's an awful smell." She tried not to visualize her husband—and her onetime lover, dumb Ollie Beatty—wrestling with the accumulated shit and piss of her entire social world. She hoped that the people shuffling in a circle in the road could not see her. How would they know what she . . . Would they ever understand?

She heard some shouting, like someone barking orders. The circle of prisoners stopped moving and all looked toward the jail, which lay out of Mary Beth's line of vision. She moved over to the agency office's front door, opened it slightly and peered out toward the jail. From that position she could see the jail's front, its door hanging open, discolored water streaming out over the doorsill. Beyond the doorsill was an old hand pump and, under a soldier's guard, Ollie Beatty pumped a weak stream of water into a bucket. Even in the shadow the left side of his face looked dark, discolored, his jaw askew. God, Mary Beth thought, what happened to him?

After some more barking of orders, the circle of people formed a line, at the head of which was one of the two nurses. Ollie lifted the bucket, doused the nurse with the water and set it down under the mouth of the pump. As the nurse turned and walked out of the way, the second prisoner presented himself and Ollie returned to pumping. The procedure continued three more times, and Mary Beth watched these prisoners, barely recognizable and now bedraggled as well as humiliated, shuffle back into the dusty street, where they stood with heads down and were watched carefully by a soldier holding his rifle at the alert.

In the periphery of her vision she saw sudden motion, heard a sharp cry, and looked to see that Ollie Beatty had his guard from behind, an arm locked around his neck and the bucket over his head. The soldier writhed, and the mechanic's lock around his neck tightened. The soldier was still. Ollie yelled something. The German soldier in the street was facing him, his rifle pointed at him. No one moved. Ollie shouted again, but began to crumple even before the electric crack of a single shot rang out and reverberated among the canyon walls. Ollie's arm fell away from the German guard, who spun around crouching as Ollie's body fell forward onto the ground. Even from where she stood, Mary Beth could see the red hole in the back of his head and the blood streaming from it, mixing with the foul waters that still leaked over the jail's doorstep onto the porch and into the street.

She ducked back into the office, letting the door slam behind her, whirled and faced Muller, who was now standing behind the desk.

"What happened?" he barked, his fingers undoing the snap on his shiny black holster.

Mary Beth shook her head, eyes wide, shook her head again and managed to bend forward before she vomited. "Oh God," she wailed, aware that Muller had raced past her and out the door. She went down on her knees. "Oh, God, oh God," she said. There were chunks of food in the yellow mess, recognizable chunks of breakfast, and she vomited again. More came up amid the vile taste of her own bile, and she shook herself violently and froze, like a hunted rabbit.

Outside, Muller's voice barked orders. She looked up

at the desk and the edge of the map. Wiping her mouth with her hand, she crossed to the desk and looked wildly at the map, finding Keams Canyon circled in pencil. Her eyes searched the map for any other marks. In the upper right-hand corner of the map she finally noticed that the word Farmington had been underlined lightly in pencil. Farmington was a town just over the border into New Mexico. The Indian reservation ended around there—yes, she could see the line on the map. She had heard about Farmington, another crummy bordertown like Winslow. She had never been there, didn't know how anyone would get there. There weren't any roads there from here. She wondered what might interest the Germans in Farmington. She wondered as well if the taste of vomit in her mouth would ever go away or if, every time the picture of Ollie Beatty slumping like a rag doll to the wet, sloppy ground full of waste and his own blood came into her mind, the ugly taste would be a part of it.

Later that morning the winds had risen to a fury and driven everyone back inside. Ollie's corpse had been hauled off somewhere and buried and the prisoners reensconced in the jail. About an hour after the winds had finally subsided, Mary Beth watched while another German soldier—one she had never seen—drove down the dirt street of Keams Canyon in what was an American jeep. She watched Captain Muller approach and the two men exchange salutes, and she wondered if the new German was going to be the chauffeur for their little reconnaissance into the countryside, as Muller had put it. If so, everything she had eagerly begun to plan while the winds rattled the buildings of Keams Canyon would be wrecked.

The old mare now hitched to Raphael Luna's buckboard wagon had seen better days. Her once round hips had grown a bit angular along with the rest of her, and she normally held her head low to the ground these days, there being little in her world new enough to capture her attention. Now, with the noon sun overhead, she stood patiently in the traces that Jenkins, the store clerk, had lovingly rigged. Though not a mute, as the Germans had been led to believe in the early moments of the un-planned charade that greeted the "liberators," Jenkins was a taciturn man. He was far more at ease with horses than his fellow man or his fellow man's machinery. Ten years earlier he had married an especially jolly Hopi woman, and they lived, childless, in a lonesome house a half mile west of Oraibi.

Now both Jenkins and the mare stood silently and hip-shot in the sun while Mary Yazzie, followed by Luna himself, climbed into the buckboard, silver with age. The wagon seat's old metal springs creaked painfully as Luna heaved his bulk up into it. Luna picked up the reins, took a deep breath, exhaled, and said, "Thank you, Jenkins. We'll be back in a few hours, certainly before dusk." He was about to slap the reins on the mare's back but paused as he saw the German major general approach, striding briskly ahead of the big bull of a corporal. Luna rested his elbows on his thick knees, and Mary Yazzie looked straight ahead of her, eyes fixed on the horizon. She con-tinued to stare into the distance as Heinrich Schalberg stopped a few feet from the buckboard.

"The wind has quite a personality here, doesn't it, Herr Major General?"

"Indeed," Schalberg said. "Is this your season for such winds?"

Luna smiled. "April. Then we count on the wind. To-day's was a fluke. But then `. . .` this is a fluky part of the world."

Schalberg smiled briefly, then said: "Where are you off to, Senor Luna?"

"A mission of mercy," Luna said. "A man in Bacabi has taken ill. And with the telephone not working, we can't reach the doctor. So we go, to see if there's anything we can do."

"The doctor? Where is he?"

"There's a small clinic in Tuba City," Luna said, lying for the second time in a row. "The Indian Service doctor is there sometimes."

Schalberg crossed his arms and frowned. "The Americans," he said, "they don't provide much for these people, do they? It will be different under a National Socialist regime."

"I devoutly hope so," Luna said. "The family sent a boy to fetch the doctor—if he's there. But Mary and I, as I said, we'll see what we can do for the poor man in the meantime." It occurred to Luna that Schalberg seemed genuinely concerned and, lest he offer to drive him and Mary to Bacabi in one of his vehicles, Luna added: "We've had a few cases of poliomyelitis here in the past few years. I hope it's not that. There's so little anyone can do for it."

Schalberg cleared his throat. "Yes, a terrible scourge. Well, I shouldn't keep you. When you return, I will want to talk to you."

"I'll be back by four, I should think. Is that all right?"

Still frowning, Schalberg nodded briskly and stepped back a pace, and Luna slapped the reins on the mare's back. She seemed to sag briefly and then proceeded in a dignified walk across the open ground surrounding the trading post.

A half hour later Luna brought the buckboard to a creaking halt outside one of the few inhabited houses in Old Oraibi. It was a separate building, a rectangle of yellow stone perched on the edge of the mesa. It faced south, some thirty feet from its nearest neighbors, which themselves were separate from the old and little used houses surrounding the village's plaza. No one passing by Old Oraibi on the wagon track that led to Bacabi and the village beyond that, Hotevilla, would be able to see the buckboard where it was parked.

Luna clambered down and, with Mary Yazzie standing behind him, knocked on the sagging wooden door. He heard a voice from within, opened the door and went inside, followed by the Navajo woman. Inside, two old Hopi men sat facing each other at a table with a yellow and white oilcloth cover. One was the old Bluebird clan leader from Second Mesa, named Nasafti. The other was the host. Both wore white shirts and red bandannas rolled up and tied around their foreheads over graying hair. On one of two cots with bare mattresses against the walls sat the two runners, Secakuku and Quavehema, naked to the waist; on the other, leaning comfortably back against the wall with a lopsided grin, was Danny Koots in a checked shirt, jeans, and a pair of cheap and heavily worn cowboy boots. And, visible only after Mary Yazzie closed the door, the big Navajo Slink stood with his back to the wall, looking uncomfortably at the floor. The two runners scrunched together at one end of their cot to make room for the trader.

Luna moved around the room, ceremoniously shaking hands with everybody present and then sat down on the cot, his hands on his knees. Mary Yazzie stood on the other side of the door from Slink and they murmured a greeting in Navajo.

Luna looked around the room and laughed, a sudden croak in the silence. "There's a first time for everything, yes?"

More silence. Hopi and Navajo eyes flickered around the room and came to rest on the floor, all but Nasafti, who looked severely at the trader.

"Nasafti," the trader murmured. "What have you to tell us?"

The old man spoke in Hopi, his voice high and liquid. After he was finished, Luna looked across the room at the two Navajos and, in English, translated.

"He says that some among the Hopis believe the Germans represent the Pahana. You know of the Pahana?" The two Navajos nodded, and Danny Koots snorted. "Nasafti says that Banyongye was told to produce a sign that this was true. He has not produced the sign, but he has been given another day. Nasafti says that he and the others think it is best to let this pretense go on for another day. He says also that Banyongye's father thought the same thing about the Germans. In the last great war, the Germans wore helmets with spikes on the top, like spear points. Banyongye's father saw photographs of them. He saw a likeness to one of the katsinas."

Danny Koots grinned and shook his head. "My people," he said under his breath. Old Nasafti turned his head slowly and stared. Danny's smile vanished.

"Well, then," Luna said, turning to the two runners. Secakuku, the older by a month or two, held out a manila envelope, and Luna reached out and took it. Opening it, he held a piece of white paper in front of him and read it twice before looking up.

"This message comes from the White House. Where the President lives. It is from a man named Hopkins who speaks for the President. It says that they are sending Ben Cameron here. Do you remember Cameron? The young archeologist?"

Slink looked up from the floor and smiled fleetingly.

"He worked here before the war began. He is now an officer in the army. It says he should be here sometime tonight. It says—Hopkins says the President wishes that the Hopi and the Navajo people will be able to *manage* this invasion for a few days. He uses the word 'manage,' " Luna said, translating the concept once into Hopi and then into Navajo. "He goes on to say that it is important that the rest of the nation not know the Germans are here. Everyone, he says, is busy making war on the Germans and the Japanese, and trying to bring the war to an end soon. He says that Cameron will bring other instructions for us."

Luna folded up the paper.

"That is what the President has to say to his children, yes?" Luna said, and then, as if to himself: "Sometimes people forget that we are not children. Oh, well . . . Hopkins asks that we tell him what the Germans are planning to do here." Luna looked around at the Indians in the room. "And of that we have no idea. We know only that they intend to leave—for somewhere—on Monday or Tuesday." He recounted what Danny Koots had overheard at the agency office in Keams Canyon.

"It seems that the superintendent's wife," Luna went on, "is helping the Germans. Perhaps she has been forced to do so. Perhaps not. Such things have been known to happen in wartime." He shook his head. Across the room Mary Yazzie shook her head slightly from side to side.

"You think not, Mary?"

The Navajo woman shrugged, a nearly imperceptible lifting of shoulders, and said nothing.

"What are we supposed to do?" Danny Koots asked. "Sit around and watch?" Luna was surprised again at how Danny's time away from the reservation had changed his voice. He spoke with a confident drawl and a twang, not the hesitant lilt of Indians speaking English. He spoke very much like an Anglo.

"Perhaps we should find ways to make their leaving difficult," Luna said. "Or late."

"Maybe we should witch the bastards," Danny said with a grin. Luna noticed that Mary, who had glanced up at Danny Koots, now looked down at the floor. A silence fell over the room. Neither Hopis or Navajos, Luna knew, liked to discuss witchcraft except among themselves. And neither ever joked about it.

Luna cleared his throat. He turned toward Danny, turning his entire torso, and glared at the man. Danny shrugged and looked away.

"Maybe," the worldly Hopi said, by way of escaping further punishment, "we can put some sand in them vehicles. Nothin' like some sand in the oil."

"Sugar in the gas tank," Slink said, and everyone looked at him.

"What does that do?" Danny asked.

Slink shrugged. "Don't know. Never did it. Those guys, those Germans, they don't let them vehicles out of their sight. Watch 'em all the time. They got guards on everything. Ammunition, weapons, everything." He lapsed into silence again.

At length, Luna spoke again. "They've been using some of you for guides. On their reconnaissances."

"Old Yellow Tooth," Slink said. "Let 'em run into a wash. They got stuck in there. On their way back from near Coal Canyon."

"We have that one great advantage," Luna said. "Don't we? The land. Where else have they been looking?" Another silence. "Well, then. Perhaps for now the best we can do is keep watching. As Danny here suggested. And meet again to see what we have seen. Tonight? Tomorrow morning? Here?"

After several minutes of discussion, it was agreed that they would meet the next morning before the sun rose, at a house down below in Oraibi, where one of Nasafti's sons now lived, having married a Corn clan woman of Oraibi. As the people in the room stood up and filed out, Slink approached old Nasafti, whose eyes were closed. Luna stopped to watch.

"*Hosteen,*" Slink said, a Navajo word for old man that conveys with it a proper respect for age.

Nasafti opened his eyes and looked up.

"Gonna rain tonight? Out there?" Slink pointed with his lips toward the southwest.

Nasafti said, "We asked the katsinas for rain. They know."

"It'd be real good if it did," Slink said. "Tonight, tomorrow."

The old man looked puzzled. Luna imagined what was in his mind: of course it would be good if it rained out there. That was where the fields were, the corn. This was the time of year when all Hopis prayed for a timely rain.

"Yeah," the old man said and closed his eyes, opening them again to look up at Slink. "You got cornfields?"

Slink shook his head. "I was out there over by Katsina Bluffs. Saw some fields there. Hopi. Near that airstrip they built. It looked real dry out there."

"Maybe it'll rain out there," the old Hopi said. "That's what we're prayin' about."

"That's good," Slink said, and nodded. *"Hosteen,"* he added, and turned to leave.

Old Nasafti giggled, a high-pitched sound. *"Quatsi,"* he said quietly, the Hopi word for friend.

As he walked out behind Slink, Luna raised his eyebrows skyward.

In the wagon, Mary took the reins and clicked the old mare into a walk. Luna settled himself comfortably into the wooden seat and watched a raven fly overhead, headed south toward the Hopi cornfields.

"What do you suppose that was all about, Mary? What Slink was saying to Nasafti?"

Mary raised her shoulders and let them fall. She was, Luna thought, a very beautiful woman. Eyes like obsidian flakes looking out so fiercely on the world from above high, round cheekbones. She smiled, a slight upturn of the corners of her mouth.

"His father was real good at stealing horses," she said, and that was all she said until they arrived back at the trading post and Mary brought the horse and wagon to a halt.

"The German," she said.

"Schalberg?"

She nodded once. "He'll get sick."

"Mary! Did . . . ?"

She looked down in her lap at her hands, which held the reins, and nodded again, one nod.

# Six

In a land so vast, and where the air is so clear as on the Hopi-Navajo reservation, and where the visible pace of life was in these days closer to the pace of the late nineteenth century than the middle of the twentieth, any newcomer got the illusion that nothing much was taking place. In the hinterlands of these hinterlands, one might see an old Navajo woman patiently tending a flock of sheep far off in the lee of some mesa with no one else around for miles. And one could see for miles. For the shepherd herself, the silence would be broken only by the tinkle of the bellwether sheep and perhaps the light scratch of hooves on rock, but from the distance at which a newcomer saw such a cameo, the silence would be total. Time stood still—certainly for the distant sheep and the shepherd—and the newcomer would have an eerie sense that it had stopped for him too.

The silence and the solitude were so great as to be deafening. To people like the Germans, accustomed to the clangor of machines and war, to rapidly moving vehicles and the nearly instant transmission of information by radio, the world was a far quicker place. The mind had to move faster, too fast to see some things. For instance, the notion that information passed from one lonesome Navajo camp in the middle of nowhere to another such camp, not even in sight of the first, would be almost unthinkable. For this new world was motionless, inert.

Even in the shadow of the Hopi villages, where there

172

was always some motion, always someone talking, even
if behind a closed door, and where more often than not
there were children playing intently at one thing or another in the dust outside the old stone houses, life seemed
so unchanged from earlier centuries and so self-absorbed
that it was possible to believe that not much of anything
was taking place . . . and that nothing by way of information was being transmitted from village to village.

And yet, by the end of morning this second full day
since the Germans had arrived, virtually every Indian
within seventy-five miles of the trading post at Oraibi
would know that one of the government people at the
Keams Canyon Agency had been shot. They all would
know that a big black plane had landed in the night,
swelling the German force by some twenty-five soldiers
along with some jeeps.

In the outlying Navajo camps many would have
heard—some for the first time—about the Navajo Marine, returned from the war in the Pacific with a damaged
knee, one of Manuelito's great-grandsons and a big man
from down around Nipple Butte called Slink, who was
emerging as some kind of leader over there where the
Germans were camped. And in those same Navajo
camps, many of the men who had not gone off to war for
one reason or another—because of age or lack of English
maybe—were feeling the long dormant urge of the warrior, the raider, in their blood. In hogans here and there,
old stories were being told. Old rifles, long used only for
game, were being oiled. Old knives, long used only for
slaughtering and skinning sheep, were being honed.

In the Hopi villages, similarly, old stories were being
told, new arguments based on old evidence were being
adduced in support of a wide-ranging array of opinion
about this new presence among them. There were some
whose view of tradition led them to agree with Banyongye, that the Germans indeed represented the Pahana.
There were others—far more—who knew they didn't,

but considered the German presence yet one more inter-
ference brought into their lives from the white man's
world, believing that it too would pass if Hopis tried yet
again to mind their own business. And there were Hopis
who saw that a time had come again when they would be
called upon. These were mostly Hopis from clans whose
task historically had been to see to the frontiers, to the
borders, to discover what the Others—be they Ute,
Navajo, whites—were up to, and to repel them as best
they could, when and if the need arose. And behind the
impenetrable shroud of secrecy that is part of the Hopi
world, these clan members were, similarly, oiling old
weapons, and waiting.

None of this was known, or even could have been
imagined, by Heinrich Schalberg as he sat at a camp
table under a canvas roof erected on poles—his staff
headquarters located some fifty yards from the silent formation of tanks under their nets and brush, and from the
open-sided mess tent where men were lined up for midday rations. But Schalberg had been growing uneasy.
Some soldier's itch told him that something was wrong.
There was nothing he could put his finger on, and he tried
to put the notion aside.

After the wind had died down, the men routinely
turned to policing their machines and their weapons,
scouring out the dust—the eternal task of the desert warrior. Many of them had seen worse winds in North
Africa. Handfuls of Indians reemerged from wherever
they had gone to hide from the wind, and were making
themselves helpful around the encampment. Nothing
seemed awry there either. Schalberg was beginning to
distinguish between them—Navajos from Hopis—mostly
by their physique, the Hopis tending to be shorter and
round-faced, the Navajos taller and more Mongoloid. He
even recognized some by face—the man called Slink, for
example, now standing near the mess tent with another
Navajo, who, Schalberg thought, was Yellow Tooth, the

one who had abandoned his reconnaissance unit the other night, when the unit had to find their way back to camp in the dark.

Schalberg had lost himself for an hour designing some maneuvers for the men to be carried out that night, a mock raid on the airstrip by a fleet of light armor and jeeps, having first weighed the value of such an exercise against the use of precious fuel supplies.

Nothing was awry, nothing to upset his sense of order—the order he was imposing on this strange and alien land—but still he was uneasy.

Sitting at the table in the shade of the canvas overhead, he stared idly at the mess tent. Slink's friend—it *was* that fellow Yellow Tooth—approached the burly corporal who was acting as chef, and gestured over one of the huge pots on the makeshift stove. With a pair of large tongs, the chef plucked a sausage from the pot and held it up before the Indian's face. He took it in his hand, juggled it in both hands and blew on it, and ventured a bite. He stood chewing and smiled.

Schalberg watched, bemused, as Yellow Tooth nodded several times rapidly, almost as if he were bowing obsequiously, turned and ran off to where the Indians had tethered several of their small, bony horses. From a pouch hanging from one of these, Yellow Tooth plucked something and hastened back to the mess tent. There, he held up the sausage he had bitten and the other thing, a sausage of some sort as well, which he offered to the chef. The chef took it gingerly in his hand, smiled and nodded. Yellow Tooth nodded back. The chef looked at this new sausage and then took a bite of it.

Schalberg was pleased at this sharing of food—it rang a bell, an old story, maybe from Karl May and that silly Apache prince. But then the chef bent over and violently heaved, apparently upchucking, throwing the rest of the sausage on the ground, upchucking again. Yellow Tooth and the other Indians assembled by the mess tent were laughing—Schalberg had not seen such quick and jerky motion among the the normally slow-moving and phlegmatic Indians. Some were nearly bent double with mirth. The soldiers around the mess tent, among them Corporal Schwabe, had joined in. Schalberg could hear the belly laughs.

The chef, red-faced, ceased heaving and stood with his hands on his hips and bellowed. Schalberg heard the bellow but couldn't make out the words. The chef picked up a large knife and waved it at Yellow Tooth, and the laughter continued. Even the chef began to join in, and Schalberg saw Corporal Schwabe looking over in his direction. He called him over.

Schwabe arrived, grinning, holding a sausage of his own and chewing volubly.

"What happened over there, Corporal?"

Schwabe swallowed. "Chef gave that Indian Yellow Tooth a sausage. He was hanging around, curious, asking about German food. So he says, 'This looks just like our food,' or something like that, and he goes and gets something from his horse over there. Says it's a Navajo sausage and gives it to the chef. The chef takes a bite, asks what it is."

Schwabe took another bite of his sausage and chewed it noisily.

"It was a sheep's intestine." Schwabe erupted in laughter, and Schalberg couldn't help but join in. For a moment, in all the jollity, his sense of uneasiness vanished.

Suddenly, he felt a sting on the back of his neck.

"Ow!" he yelled, and slapped at it. Maybe some damned hornet. It stung like a hornet. Maybe some spider.

"A hornet? What?" Schwabe said and crossed around behind him. He inspected the major general's neck. He glanced up at the canvas above them.

"I don't see anything. Nothing like a bite mark."

"God, that stings," Schalberg said in a low voice. "Jesus."

"There's nothing there, like a bite," Schwabe said again. "Let me get a hot compress."

"No, no, Corporal. No. It's subsiding. Go on. Join the men." He rubbed his neck some more. "And watch out for Indians bearing gifts." He laughed bravely, and rubbed his neck again. The icy-hot sting remained, bad enough to make him sweat, but it *was* subsiding. He glanced up at the canvas ceiling and returned to his papers and maps.

In the lee of a low rock outcrop where Edgar Flynn of Winslow, Arizona, waited out the cursed wind of the morning, he found what he was looking for: potsherds. The outcrop was little more than a nearly straight line of small boulders and rubble jutting out of the red earth and running for some thirty yards before it disappeared back into the earth. It was like hundreds of others in this large stretch of desert southwest of the Hopi mesas and halfway to the tiny Navajo settlement called Leupp.

Edgar, once a railroad man, always a rancher of sorts, also had a beady eye on the future, even though, by most ways of reckoning these things, he couldn't have much of a future coming to him. In his seventies and a bit hobbled by arthritis, he was hardly at an age to start a new career, but he had been thinking hard about changes coming to the West once the war was over. And soon enough it would be over, what with the Yanks sweeping up through Europe and, as any fool could tell just from listening to the radio, about to invade northern Europe and dump Hitler on his Heinie ass. And how long after that would it be that the combined forces of the Yoonited States, free of the European war, wiped out Tojo and all his buck-toothed little barbarians? And then the world would get back to normal, but it wouldn't really be normal.

Edgar Flynn knew his eyesight might be failing a bit these days, but any fool, he thought, could see that once the world was at peace, there was going to be an invasion of these precincts: tourists. They'd all be coming out here with their little brats in the backseat to see the Grand Canyon, and the old ruins, and Monument Valley—the Wonders of the Western World.

Tourists would be coming with money. Money to spend on hotels, food, and geegaws. And a whole passel of them would have a lot of money to spend on things like Navajo rugs and such. And antiquities. Pots. Old pots. Old bits and pieces of the Indian past.

Edgar Flynn figured he'd get a jump on the future . . . for once in his damned life. So he had taken to pottering—heh, heh—around out in the country south of the Hopi mesas, looking for old ruins, and when no one was looking—which was just about any time at all—he would dig around until he found some whole pots from earlier times and pack them up and cart them back to his home near the old railroad crossing called Hobson. Already he had fifteen perfect pots—had to be five hundred years old—black on white designs, fragile as a bat's wing and dry as dust, sitting there in his house accumulating value. Anasazi pots, they was, left behind when those old people gave up and disappeared, leaving the territory to these Hopis and then the Navajos. Nobody knew where they went, those old people. Just left. Abandoned their big places like Mesa Verde up in Colorado, and those ruins they called Betatikin, places like that, which everyone knew about and where the archeologists had already run off with anything of value and put it in museums. But there were all these little settlements, like outliers, where people had dwelled and farmed a little, and made pots and left them lying around when they left, and the little places got filled in with sand from all the wind that blew, just like this morning.

So, once the infernal damned winds cut off, he had

taken a shovel out of the old Model A he drove out here before sunup and began to dig an east-west trench in the ground under a telltale litter of pot fragments that had risen from the depths like little bubbles of oxygen in an otherwise stagnant pond. Edgar took his time, mindful of the heat, and mindful too that nobody ever got to be his age—never mind his father's age—by rushing around and breathing too hard the way some people did when they were seeking their fortune.

By midday he had a two-foot-deep trench that ran about twenty feet, and no pots. Patient as a spider, he began a series of cross trenches, certain he was onto a good ruin, since he had encountered the top of an old stone wall and an increasing density of potsherds. On his fourth cross trench he looked up from his labors to see what was making a whining sound somewhere to the northeast of him. All around him the land lay flat and colorless. He was on the high point of a slight rise that extended out around him for a mile in all directions, and nothing moved anywhere. But the whine grew louder, and Edgar leaned on his shovel, wiped the sweat off his old brow and listened. Before too many minutes passed, he saw a little plume of dust to the northeast, and he watched it approach. The whine grew louder, and it didn't sound anything like a Model A or one of those trucks they had out here on the reservation. It suddenly occurred to Edgar that what he was doing, digging up old ruins, just might be a tad illegal—he wasn't sure about the laws pertaining to such things, and certainly hadn't asked anyone about them—so he ducked down a bit when he saw the vehicle making the whine pop up over a rise about a mile, mile and a half away. It was a jeep, like the ones he'd seen in the newspaper photographs and the newsreels.

He couldn't imagine what a jeep was doing up here in the Indian reservation. Then he recalled the column of military vehicles—tanks and all—that he had seen coming up here the other day. And recalling that, he also recalled that he hadn't seen any jeeps. So what the hell was going on?

The jeep was now angling more to the west, on a line that would take it about a half mile from where Edgar was, probably illicitly digging up the past. He stepped over to his Model A and fetched a pair of binoculars from the seat, crossed back to the outcrop and trained the glasses on the jeep. It took him a few moments to crank the old binoculars into focus and then to find the jeep, and when he did get it into the narrow and still foggy visual field, he took a deep breath and said, "What the . . . ?"

A machine gun of some sort was mounted in the rear of the jeep, with a soldier sitting next to it. In the front an Indian, a Navajo in one of those big, high-crowned black hats they liked, sat next to the soldier driving. And the two soldiers were wearing gray uniforms, it looked like, open shirts and short pants, and some kind of insignia that didn't look like anything Edgar had seen. Except in news photos and in the newsreels he'd seen a couple of years ago when they showed a bunch of those Germans they'd captured out in North Africa.

Holy shit, Edgar said to himself. Germans. He sat down, lowered the glasses, and thought. Maybe it was some escapees from that prisoner-of-war camp they had down near Phoenix. Word was, they'd caught a whole bunch of those desert troops—Rommel's—in North Africa, and, with the bonehead logic of the military mind at its worst, had stashed them in a big prisoner-of-war camp down near Phoenix right in the damn desert, giving them the kind of place they was already used to. So of course, Edgar reasoned, being desert rats themselves, they could escape more easily. Now why Uncle Sam didn't think to stash those krauts in some inhospitable place like Minnesota, where they had all those lakes, thousands of lakes full of mosquitoes and blackflies and marshlands, or better yet, right in the middle of the Everglades in Florida or something, was beyond him.

So now, it seemed, there was a bunch of desertwise Heinie POWs running around the reservation with the damn Indyinns guiding them—this was bad. Bad.

Edgar looked again at the jeep, now apparently circling north and heading generally toward the Hopi mesas. Soon it was out of sight, merely a plume of dust on the horizon. With no further thought to his destiny as a wealthy purveyor of Anasazi pots, he stowed his shovel, fired up the Model A, and headed for Winslow.

An hour and a half later he pulled on the hand brake and cut off the engine in front of Ruby Phelan's Frontier Saloon, which was situated on a dirt side street a block and half from the Fred Harvey Hotel. Ruby Phelan's Frontier Saloon did not, presumably, have much of a role in the future Edgar foresaw. To begin with, except for a single small window with four grimy panes, it was without light, and that was a blessing since the gloom inside disguised a long and continuing neglect of certain housekeeping details of the sort that postwar touring American families would require. But the locals had no qualms about the grime that Ruby Phelan permitted to accumulate in the corners of her saloon—actually nothing more than a rectangular room with three tables and a bar, which she or her husband tended with a discouraged, even sullen air. Swells—and most women—found the place repellent, which in part was why the Frontier Saloon was popular with those men in Winslow for whom the war effort offered little by way of occupation—and in particular those mostly older gents who wore the armband of the Office of Civil Defense as proudly as they would have worn a deputy sheriff's badge. While the threat of an enemy invasion had long since waned—the latent national hysteria in this regard was mostly a coastal condition, and along with nightly blackouts and fire drills, had died out in 1943—the OCD remained intact in Winslow, giving many of its members an excuse, however shaky, to be abroad from their homes of an afternoon. Indeed, on any afternoon but Sundays, when their wives intervened in the name of the Lord and of decency, a considerable fraction of Winslow's Civil Defense operatives could be found in the Frontier Saloon, nursing beers and memories of wilder and more exciting times, some ranging as far back and as far away as the trenches of World War I. Ruby Phelan's Frontier Saloon was, in fact, the center of a deep-seated but untapped and unfulfilled patriotism in Winslow, Arizona.

When Edgar Flynn opened the door of the Frontier Saloon, permitting a flash of afternoon sun to illuminate its dim interior, seven men in all, wearing the familiar insignia on their arms—a red CD on a white triangle set in a blue circle—sat in cowboy hats and jeans at the bar and at two of Ruby's three tables. They had been there for nearly as long as it had taken Edgar to drive from his newly found ruin, and they had begun therefore to grow sentimental. Brought up short by the announcement of Edgar's shocking intelligence—Germans on the rez—it had occurred to all of them at once that their own moment of destiny was finally at hand.

They discussed the matter with high seriousness, led in their deliberations by Billy Westmoreland, a man in his late fifties who owned the only automobile dealership in town, the war effort having rendered it, and him, largely idle. Billy was a large man with a large potbelly and big, capable hands, a natural leader of men, and it was he who proposed that the men of the OCD form what in earlier days would have been called a posse and get straight up there into Indyinn country and find out what the hell was going on. Sure as hell, it had to be a bunch of escapees from the prison camp down in Phoenix, up to no good at all, what with stolen American vehicles and weaponry, and it was damned important they be rounded up and brought to justice soon as possible. They had best set out later this afternoon, before sunset, and travel through the night for a dawn surprise. All the great wartime triumphs, someone recalled, were launched around four o'clock in the morning. As the heroic possibilities of such a venture dawned on the assembled men, their faces grew taut with high seriousness, their voices dropped an octave, and they spoke with the economy of men at war.

Ruby Phelan, who had been around these men long enough to know that they were perfectly capable of running off pretty much half-cocked, brandishing their rifles and their tattered sense of earlier glory, and wind up getting themselves killed or at least maimed, brought up the alternative notion of calling the authorities at the prisoner-of-war camp to see if any POWs were on the lam, and, if so, turning Edgar Flynn's intelligence report over to them to handle. The suggestion was turned down unanimously, which is what Ruby had expected would happen.

She leaned forward on the bar, allowing her ample old bosom to lean there between the elbows, and said, "Billy, you got old Edgar here says he saw two Germans in short pants riding around in a jeep with a Navajo. Now, are you sure you got enough here to go on?"

Billy, looking truculent, said, "What do you mean, Ruby, enough to go on? There's krauts up there, and we gotta get 'em, dammit."

"Up there where?" Ruby asked. "Somewhere halfway between Leupp and the Hopi mesas, headed sorta northeast."

"Well, I do confess it would've been better if old Edgar here had kept his eye on them longer, maybe tracked 'em some, but we can do that. Track 'em. Right, boys?"

"At night?" Ruby asked, but her caveat was lost in the hubbub, and so it was arranged that the OCD would lead a group of any able-bodied volunteers up into Indyinn country, leaving before sundown, in automobiles—them who had 'em and had enough gasoline—and on horseback. They would follow the Little Colorado up to Bird Springs and then head north along Oraibi Wash. Under cover of dark they'd ferret out just where all these Heinie bastards were and descend on them in the predawn hours. They'd be back in Winslow by afternoon, then they'd call the authorities in Phoenix, tell 'em their escapees were safely in custody in Winslow and the emergency averted.

Ruby asked one more question of a practical nature that afternoon as the boys were parceling out assignments to one other and making logistical lists on the back of the little napkins that said Ruby's Frontier Saloon in one piece of rope turned into script. "What about the sheriff?" she asked. "You gonna take him with you?"

All seven members of the OCD, and Edgar Flynn as well, grumbled and shook their heads, and Billy Westmoreland, after a moment's thought, said, "No, somebody's gotta stay here and mind the public safety." Rebuffed yet again, Ruby Phelan gave in to the patriotic fervor. Bending over, she fetched from under the bar her contribution to this venture in civil defense and placed them, one after the other, on the bar: three one-fifth bottles of rye whiskey.

"God bless you, boys," she said. "And good luck."

Mary Beth Lemon remembered the way the two wagon track/roads separated into forks and then, as if uncertain, changed directions and crossed each other, crossing again and finally going their separate ways across the endless scrub—one winding south to Holbrook and the other eventually straightening out and heading east to Gallup. Both towns were a half day's drive away, Gallup maybe more than that. And only a half mile after the fork, another track led off in serpentine fashion toward one of those strange and abrupt outcrops, a lonely blade of red stone showing layers like a petrified cake, in the shape of which some people—white people in pioneer wagons no doubt—had long ago seen a reminder of some of the river crossings they had made on their journeys to these frontier hinterlands. So they had called it Steamboat as they went by, and the name had stuck. Probably the Navajos who had camps around the outcrop had another name for it, and surely nothing like Steamboat. Mary Beth couldn't imagine how far from here the nearest steamboat might be. They were in the middle of Navajo country now, twenty miles out of Keams Canyon, rattling along in an American jeep, just the two of them.

Captain Wilhelm Muller was in high spirits, no doubt happy to be doing something besides looking at maps and giving orders to the few soldiers under his command. Happy too, perhaps, to be away from the dreary charges of his in the Keams Canyon jail, and the recollection of one of those charges—dumb old Ollie Beatty—with a German bullet in the back of his head, and now buried somewhere. But then, Mary Beth thought, Muller probably didn't think twice about someone being shot. He was at war—some kind of war, anyway—and she supposed that soldiers, German soldiers especially, being rapacious pigs, thrived on blood and noise. She shuddered in the passenger seat, in spite of the heat that poured down from above and the heat that buffeted her face from the engine.

Muller had brought the jeep to a halt, marking the crisscrossing intersection on his map, and had halted again where the track to Steamboat branched away to their right.

"And this goes to . . . ?"

"A place called Steamboat," she said.

"And so," Muller said, looking at the map, "if one went east-northeast from this point, one would reach the place called Washington Pass, and then—"

"Where are you going?" Mary Beth asked. She knew well enough that a road, state road 666, led north from Gallup past Washington Pass and north to Farmington, which someone, presumably Muller, had underlined on the map.

Muller smiled and folded up the map. He looked out to the east and to the north. Nothing lay out there but sagebrush and rolling land stretching to a point where the world evidently fell away. And far beyond on the horizon was the low blue backbone of mountains. Mary Beth didn't know their name or how far off they really were. Muller pointed to them.

"What lies between here and those mountains?"

"Just more of this desert," Mary Beth said, lying. She had never been beyond Steamboat and had no idea what sort of topography lay beyond this point.

"Excellent," Muller said. He smiled at Mary Beth. "And what is Steamboat?" He hit the starter button with his thumb and the jeep roared into life, sending another blast of hot air into Mary Beth's lower torso.

She shrugged. "Just a place. Maybe some Navajos live there."

"Let's go have a look," Muller said, and the jeep bucked across the wagon ruts and onto the track. Within a few minutes he stopped again, idling and perched on the edge of a mini-canyon with vertical dirt sides, a dry wash etched ten feet deep and winding like a snake across the flat land. Far ahead the chunk of red rock rose up.

"Aha," Muller said. "Steamboat. How picturesque." Off to their right, where the land dipped slightly and the mini-canyon was therefore shallower, was a stand of cottonwood trees, looking forlorn in the sunlight. "There. By those trees. We shall have our—what do you call it?—our picnic." Mary Beth glanced over at him warily and then over to the little cottonwood stand.

"Swell," she said, smiling.

Muller was clearly enjoying himself, piloting the open jeep across the bumps. He was dressed in an open-necked, short-sleeved gray shirt, and gray shorts that came down almost to his knees, with gray socks up over his calves, and a pair of tightly laced, ankle-length boots. A black leather shoulder strap crossed his chest and hooked to his black leather belt with its holster hanging on his left hip. On his head he wore a gray, high peaked cloth cap. He handled the jeep expertly, bringing it to a stop beside the trees, and vaulted out. From the rear, under the lethal-looking machine gun mounted there, he took a metal box in both hands and carried it into the shade. As Mary Beth climbed out of the jeep, he opened the box and snatched a cloth out, flapping it with a flourish and letting it float down on the ground. Upon it he placed two large canteens and a smaller metal box, along with two cloth napkins she recognized as coming from her own house. He opened the smaller box and held up a slab of cheese and a loaf of bread with a golden-brown crust. These he set down and, turning to Mary Beth, bowed, saying, "Lunch is served. For the madame."

She had to laugh at his elaborate gestures, and it did occur to her as she sat down on the white cloth that no one had made this kind of fuss over her since she was a little girl and her parents sometimes took it into their heads to pretend she was some sort of princess. So here she was, she thought with an irony that tasted like metal in her mouth, in the middle of nowhere alone with a German officer, a dirty kraut Heinie henchman of Der Fuhrer, an enemy of the United States of America with the gall to invade her country, who had presided over the imprisonment of her people and the shooting of her one-time lover, and he was treating her like a queen.

She sat down, her legs folded underneath her to one side, as Muller held up one of the canteens. "In here is a red wine, the very best that a poor soldier can manage to bring with him three thousand, no, four thousand miles from his homeland, across the ocean, to this place in the shade." He set it down and picked up the other. "In this, water." He shrugged. He knelt down and broke off a piece of the bread, holding it up to her. "A humble feast, yes?"

They ate and drank in silence, and a light breeze arose miraculously, as if generated by the cottonwoods themselves, and rattled the leaves overhead pleasantly. Something, probably the wine, gave Mary Beth a feeling of being detached, as if she were not really sitting inside her skin, not really thinking from inside her skull. She had to admit that Muller was not so bad to look at, especially in these gray shorts and short-sleeved shirt. He had taken off his cap, the leather belt and strap, and could almost be—well, anyone. He seemed completely relaxed. She also had to admit—though she hated this more than she could say—that he was a forceful but patient lover, and it hadn't been as awful, as disgusting, as screwing an enemy pig was supposed to have been. It *was* awful, it *was* disgusting, yes, and she had swallowed her . . . her what? Her everything to put up with it. But it hadn't actually been . . . She shook her head. It *was* disgusting, it was *duty*, a horrible duty.

Muller lay back, his head on his hands, and looked happily upward.

"What are you, um, what are you doing here?" Mary Beth asked.

"Lying in the shade with a beautiful American woman," he replied, reaching a hand out and letting it fall on her knee. Inwardly, she flinched.

"No," she said, putting her hand on top of his. "You Germans." She laughed, and squeezed his hand. "I mean you didn't come all this way just to lock up some guys in Keams Canyon, did you?"

He laughed, the high-pitched laugh that was something like a fingernail scraping a blackboard, and she guided his hand a few inches up her leg to where the hem of her skirt lay. On her other side was her bag, with a hairbrush and a few other items in it that she had brought along. His hand moved yet farther up her thigh, and she felt it tingle even as she shuddered, body and mind engaged in a war of their own. She let go his hand and placed hers on his forehead.

"I mean, you're going somewhere from here, right? After the fuel truck comes. It comes along here, by the way. From Gallup."

"Aha," Muller said with a grin, sitting up. "You're a Mata Hari of the Wild West."

"A Mata Hari? What's that?"

"A spy. Trying to induce me with your charms to tell you the secret plans of the German Army." He was grinning at her still.

"That's funny," she said. "Me. A spy. And when I find out what you guys are doing here, I'm going to build a fire and send smoke signals to President Roosevelt. Anyway, I figure you're going to Farmington."

Muller's eyebrows rose.

"Well, it's underlined on that map you've been looking at. And it's on the other side of Washington Pass and up that road. It's either that or Gallup, south of the pass. Am I right?" She smiled girlishly.

"Why don't you unbutton your shirt, Mary Beth? I want to feast my eyes now. I want to pluck your plums, yes?" He knelt before her. Slowly, she began to unbutton her shirt, from the top down, pulling her shirttails out from her waist and letting it fall around her.

"And the brassiere," Muller said, licking his lips. She obeyed, and Muller's gaze seemed to devour her. "Ah," he said. She felt the breeze on her naked breasts, and again Muller said, "Ah."

He reached out with both hands, and she took his wrists gently.

"What's in Farmington?" she asked. "Willie? I'm curious."

"Oil," he said, still staring at her chest. She let his wrists go. "Oil fields." He bent forward, pushed her gently onto her back. Her skirt fell back around her hips, and Muller said, "The Mata Hari of the frontier has now wheedled from the noble officer all the secrets of state. Now, all the lush secrets of Mata Hari will be lavished on the noble officer, yes? Yes." He unbuttoned his gray shorts, let them drop, and knelt before her, naked below his shirt.

"And now," he said, reaching between her legs and tugging at her underpants, "it is harvest time. Time to pluck the ripe plums," he added, and fell forward on her, a dead weight, crushing the wind from her lungs.

She gasped, gasped again.

What? *What?* There had been a sound, a kind of thunk. And now Muller was lying between her legs with one arm splayed out like a dead man . . . Was this a joke? Some stupid German humor?

"Get up," she said. "Come on, get up."

He didn't move. His head was heavy between her breasts. Jesus, she thought, did he pass out? Heart attack? Here she was, lying half naked on the ground with a passed-out kraut with his pants at half-mast, his naked rear end pointed at the sky . . . "Come on!" she commanded.

Then she noticed the feathers. Black with little stripes of white. Cut to an angle and set in the wooden shaft. An arrow? An arrow sticking up out of . . . *Holy Jesus!* With a surge of strength she shoved the German up off her chest and flung him off to the side. She clutched her shirt and held it up to her chest, looking wildly around. Nothing. Nothing but sagebrush out in the sun beyond the shade of this cottonwood stand. She looked at Muller, lying on his side. A tiny trickle of blood was coming out of one nostril and down to his mouth, where it joined up with another. She went up on her knees and peered over him, seeing the arrow jutting out of his back, and looked wildly around her again. Was she next?

Nothing moved. Someone had to be out there, but nothing moved. There was nothing out there. But there was something out there, some Indian with a bow and arrow. Didn't they give that stuff up a long time ago?

So an arrow had hit the kraut in the back while he was on his knees with his pants down between her legs, and she had been lying . . . there. So it had to have come from . . . She stared out in that direction. Nothing. Sagebrush. And maybe some Indian lying in the sagebrush. And why wouldn't he shoot her too? Her shirt was white. She held it up and waved it. Truce flag. Surrender. Whatever. Then she thought better of it and put it on. This was one terrible mess she was in, out here with an arrow-shot kraut with his pants down and an Indian somewhere out there.

"I better just get out of here," she said to herself. She crawled over to her bag, stuffed her brassiere in it, and crawled over to the jeep, leaving Captain Wilhelm Muller lying dead on the white cloth, his privates hanging down and an arrow sticking out of him, with his gunbelt over beyond. Hey, his gun. Maybe she should get it.

No. Instead she pulled herself up to her feet and climbed in the jeep, hoping that the Indian kept his arrows to himself, and pressed the starter button. The jeep roared and she slammed it into gear, spinning the tires as she swerved out of the shade and spun it around until it was headed down the track back to Keams Canyon and . . .

Keams Canyon? What was she going to do there? Tell those other krauts, those murdering bastards, that she'd been out having a picnic with their big boss, and just after he'd dropped his drawers—for what? Oh, maybe he needed to go to the bathroom—an arrow came out of nowhere and killed him dead, just like in the movies of the Old West with Randolph Scott and all them.

The jeep bounced and rattled over some ruts, and Mary Beth thought for a second she had lost control of it. But it soldiered on, screaming, and she realized it should be in a higher gear. That accomplished, she realized she herself had better get into a different gear. Her mind was running crazy.

Okay. Okay, Mary Beth Lemon, she said to herself. The kraut bastard is dead. Some Indian saved you the trouble, now didn't he? She thought of the hunting knife she had slipped into her bag. The arrow had gone in right where she had planned to stick the hunting knife. So what were you going to do then, after you stuck the knife in his back? Where were you going to go? Who were you going to go to and tell the plan the Germans have to go to Farmington? On Monday night, or Tuesday morning.

She'd have to ditch the jeep. She couldn't go anywhere in it without the dead German, and she couldn't go back and prop him up in the passenger seat and pretend . . . Hold it, hold it. Mind skidding again.

She didn't feature walking miles through the desert, all this scrubland, in her Sears Roebuck saddle shoes, and her blue skirt, and . . . She wished she'd thought to grab one of those canteens, the one with water, and what was left of the cheese. Oh well. That meant she'd have to risk driving this jeep pretty much all the way back to Keams, then ditch it and walk in.

But then what would she say?

Maybe she could go north a ways and get up on Black Mesa. Make her way around to the Hopi villages over on Third Mesa. That trader Luna. Her husband Luther hated the man, said he was always taking the Indians' side, even though he *said* he was just interpreting . . . Raphael Luna. Maybe he'd know what to do with the information that she had so cleverly wheeled and cheated and wormed out of that fucking dead kraut bastard son of a bitch Hun rapist who deserved an arrow in his back . . . Maybe, Mary Beth thought again, she'd get a medal for this, the Mata Hari of the West. Sure deserved one, she thought.

At the place where the two wagon tracks crossed each other like mating snakes before becoming one and heading into Keams Canyon, Mary Beth wrenched the jeep off the track and pointed it north.

Here goes, she said to herself.

It was astonishing—the map. It was one of three on the wall of the windowless cubicle somewhere deep in the innards of the new Pentagon building across the Potomac River from the Jefferson Memorial, the Washington Monument, and those ugly buildings that still housed part of the War Department. The cubicle was where Ben Cameron had reported that morning, accompanied only as far as the door by a tight-lipped and buttoned-down major. The map was of the United States, showing the nation's military camps as of the beginning of the year, 1944. A legend, which Cameron had read while waiting for someone else besides himself to show up in the cubicle of an office said, in part: *To avoid congestion, the recreational areas, camps, colleges, and universities used by the Army and Navy Specialized Training Programs are not shown.* No cities showed on the map either. Nevertheless, it was crowded with type and little dots—hundreds, maybe thousands, of military installations. The cartographer, using the colors pink, lavender, orange, and a brownish-gold, had managed to break the nation up into nine service commands. Elsewhere in the legend, it said: *No questions regarding centers not shown on the map can be answered.*

Naturally enough, Cameron's eyes went to his old stomping grounds, the Southwest, swept around the rest of the map and then back to the Southwest. From Albuquerque, New Mexico, all the way west to Kingman, Arizona, there were no dots on the map, no type. And north from around where Phoenix would be all the way to Salt Lake City in Utah, there were no dots, no type. And nothing much in western Colorado either. An enormous blank region on the map, with its center in the Four Corners, the one place where four states meet. An empty place,

Cameron figured, the size of all of New England, without a single military installation, the largest empty place on this map except for another big blank up in Wyoming and Montana.

After the war, Cameron thought, he would go back to the Southwest, or maybe up into Montana. Someplace that had escaped direct contamination by the military mind and its wondrous, mad logic.

Moments later a side door in the cubicle opened, a tall, dark-haired man with a weary face entered, a brigadier general who introduced himself as the President's military aide, and Ben Cameron became the only captain in the entire United States Army to know that the Jerries had invaded his homeland. Next he learned that the President of the United States, upon considering the news of this invasion, felt as a man might who suddenly had developed a disfiguring boil on his nose—he was pained, even outraged, and wanted it excised.

And embarrassed to be seen in public, Cameron opined to himself.

"We know," the brigadier said, in the course of explaining what the White House had learned from two reports brought out of the reservation by Hopi runners reaching a ham radio operator in Medicine Hat, "that some kind of transport plane brought in yet further supplies in the middle of the night. We don't know where the plane is coming from, but we assume it must be from some place in northern Mexico. Of course, our planes will be up along the border day and night, in case more shipments are coming. The trainees at Fort Bliss are up to that kind of mission. And of course we've raised hell with Mexico City, but there's no hope they'll be able to locate the source of these flights—if they are originating in Mexico. But where else could they come from?

"It's going to take a little more time to get the people at Fort Bliss and Marana Air Base—that's in Tucson—ready for the air strikes."

"Air strikes?" Cameron said.

"Yes. The commandants at those bases say they can get the men and equipment ready for air strikes against the German tank force by sixteen May. That's Tuesday. Eliminate them by air. A minimum of troop movements and all that. We'll send in some ground troops afterward to mop up. In the meantime, your job is to get in there as soon as possible. See if you can organize the Indians into putting up some resistance, maybe just delaying tactics. Try and keep the Germans concentrated in one place. Okay?"

Cameron's mind spun almost out of control. He saw squadrons of light bombers and fighter planes roaring in over the mesa tops, cannons firing—a bunch of trainees on their first combat mission, strafing the thousand-year-old Hopi villages . . . stray shells landing in Navajo camps . . . a calamitous snafu by green troops: Oh, sorry sir, we got the tanks, but some of those old buildings . . . well, you know how it is . . .

"Sir, as I understand it, if the Germans are massed below one of the Hopi villages, air strikes could do a lot of civilian damage."

"Then part of your job is to radio out whatever information you can about the Germans' whereabouts, keep civilian casualties to a minimum. You may need to evacuate the Indians from ground zero. Do your best. The Germans have brought the war to us, Captain. And it is a war. People get hurt in wars. Now, everything we know, which is damned little, is in this briefcase. A plane is leaving Andrews Field in one hour. It'll take you to Kirtland Field in Albuquerque. Time is of the essence, of course. We assume you'll want to parachute in. You know the terrain out there, certainly better than anyone here. You have done that, haven't you? Parachute?"

So it was that a few hours later Cameron was once again headed west, propelled by four droning engines. He put aside any attempts to imagine what on earth a

German battalion thought it was doing on the Hopi-
Navajo reservation. That was something he would find
out when he arrived. Instead he sorted out his memories
of the land, the topography, working out the best place
for him to descend from the sky in a parachute. The main
force of the Germans, they said, was outside Oraibi, with
a smaller group in Keams Canyon.

Cameron would want to get to old Raphael Luna as
soon as possible—he'd know what was going on, if anyone did. But Luna was of course in Oraibi.

"Okay," he said to himself. He knew the place to parachute in. And he knew the best way to get there—if, that
is, an old acquaintance of his in Gallup still had his old
barnstorming plane, that Beechcraft biplane he loved so
much . . . and if it still flew . . . and if the acquaintance
himself still flew. He must be in his late sixties now. And
if . . . well, there sure as hell were a shitload of ifs,
weren't there? So what else was new?

Cameron sat back and closed his eyes and, unbidden,
the sight of a black truck came to mind. It was distantly
making its way across the scrubland, heading for Jeddito
Wash. He was standing above the wash with the big
Navajo, Slink, and three others, watching it approach,
watching it fumble around at the edge of the wash, finally
disgorging two fishmongers. Two fishmongers in the
desert, who then had turned up in the photograph in
the *New Mexican*, part of a bunch of German spies. Was
it possible . . . ?

Cameron smiled.

Anything was possible these days. Anything.

At approximately 1800 hours Saturday evening, the
German noncom named Behrmann radioed his counter-
part in battalion headquarters outside Oraibi to report that
Captain Muller and his American harlot were already
two hours late returning from a "reconnaissance" of the
routes east to Farmington, New Mexico. Over the crackle

of static on the radio, Berhmann heard what sounded like Major General Heinrich Schalberg himself, cursing. Then Behrmann was told to be patient and wait for another hour. At 1900 hours, with the sun nearly down in the west, Berhmann radioed again. Muller was still missing. He was ordered to take one other man in the halftrack and find him.

# Seven

As best the survivors of the events surrounding Operation Shatterhand would later be able to reconstruct them, the hours that saw Saturday, May 13, become Sunday, May 14, comprised the night of the great convergence. It would not be the turning point—that was to come later—but in a single span of six hours, lit for the most part but not only by the myriad stars overhead, new elements arrived into the equation, new information came to light, and the multiple destinies of the participants were, for all intents and purposes, pointed toward a final course.

In retrospect, many of the events that occurred that night would seem coincidental to the point of freakishness, and certainly none more freakish than the appearance against the starlit black velvet of the sky over the desert southwest of Oraibi of a lone rain cloud. At that time of year, such clouds are normally the creatures of the day. But another way of regarding such an odd meteorological phenomenon would be through the eyes of the Hopis. They, of course, had managed to survive by subsistence agriculture in this uncompromising place for a millennium precisely by calling in the spirits who control such things as rain clouds—by saying, in effect, "Look here. Haven't we asked you katsinas into our plazas and provided you with a place to dance, which is something we know you enjoy? Haven't we, at the same time, generously fed you katsinas cornmeal, the spirit food we know you prefer? Haven't we been a rapt audience for your songs? Haven't we done your bidding and tried our best to maintain order and civility among us here on these mesas you told us to settle long ago? Well, that being the case, here now is what we require in return . . ."

Such a direct, even bald reciprocity is not the sort of thing typically featured in the prayers of, say, Christians. Nor certainly is such an ethereal calculus the sort of thing to find its way into modern military histories, but then few modern military histories give much weight either to soldiers' prayers and supplications as factors influencing a battle's outcome. Yet, for all that, deserts are freakish places, the high desertlands of Arizona perhaps more so than most, and there was not a single Hopi nor a single Navajo alive in 1944 who would not have given as much credence to the power of a prayer or a cloud as to a Sherman tank or even a Focke-Wolf 200 Condor.

Of course, it is also true that no Hopi would have been so brazen as to claim any direct responsibility for so freakish an appearance in this theater of war. Nor would any Hopi claim to have known just what sequence of events the appearance of a lone rain cloud could in turn have brought about, as if by some plan . . . Even among the Hopis, with their long practice at such manipulations, the world is not that simple. It is true too that, underneath their well-known internal contentiousness and their even better known tribal certainty about the righteousness of their ways, the Hopis tend to be a modest race.

As night fell on Saturday, the skies over the Mexican border from Yuma, Arizona, all the way to western Texas were aswarm with squadrons of fighter planes—mostly P-39 training planes, to be sure, but reasonably well-armed and, given their general quirkiness, in good enough condition to fly two-hour patrols. They were under orders to see that nothing by way of nocturnal aircraft crossed into the United States, and most of the young pilots, far from imagining they would see their first action of the war, were utterly bewildered. No one, simply no one, not even their buddies in intelligence back at the bases—Fort Bliss, Douglas Field, Yuma—had ever imagined any threat to the United States arising in Mexico, of all places. Dear old backward Mexico had sworn on as an ally, and had even contributed a couple of air squadrons to the war effort. Dear old Mexico had sent thousands of its citizens to the United States to work the fields and lend a hand in factories—a far greater contribution to the defeat of the Axis than their paltry, even laughable air squadrons. Mexico? Mexico was where U.S. servicemen, posted to military installations along the border, crossed over to buy those cheap leather sandals called huaraches, and maybe some colorful toys to send to their kids back home. But orders were orders, and it was pretty exciting being on actual patrol, even if the whole thing sounded like one more demented notion passed on down from the brass.

Flying, as they were, unaided by radar and between five hundred and a thousand feet over the land, they never saw the Condor glide below them like a manta ray hugging the sea bottom, slipping once again into the United States at a point on what is called New Mexico's boot heel. It skimmed between two low mountain ranges—the Peloncillos on the west and the Animas Mountains on the east—up a broad valley, and was noted in passing only by a few members of a herd of some two thousand cattle which enjoyed free run of some of the finest, most unspoiled grassland in the American West, on one of the largest private landholdings in the state of New Mexico.

Once north of what was locally known as the Gray Ranch, the Condor's pilot, Fritz Bader, brought his plane up in altitude in order to cross the mountainous wilderness that lay between New Mexico's boot heel and the empty reservation lands where the jerry-rigged airstrip would again be lit by two fires.

At about the same time, Bob Westmoreland of Winslow, Arizona, unanimously appointed leader of the vigilante force formed from the most active members of Winslow's Office of Civil Defense, decided that they had come far enough. This was a good place, he decided, to make camp. They had come this far, twelve of them, in three Model A Fords with six men on horseback, making their way across the scrublands for six straight hours. Everybody could now grab four hours of shut-eye, and then, around four A.M., they would resume their foray into Indyinn country, continue their reconnaissance, and get to the bottom of things.

Yeah, Bob Westmoreland, decided, there'd be time enough tomorrow for all that. Right now, Bob's ass felt like a bug on a windshield, what with this goddamned Model A rattling over the godforsaken desert in the dark. He came to a stop, and hoped the damn fools in the autos behind looked up and saw him in the starlight and didn't ram him . . . yup. They stopped too.

Westmoreland stepped down onto the ground, massaging his backside. From its place beside the driver's seat, he took out one of the bottles of rye—now half full—that Ruby Phelan had contributed to this mission and had himself a belt, offering it then to Freddy Dunster, his passenger.

Ruby Phelan, of course, had known perfectly well that these men were not going to undertake such a journey without bringing their own booze along, and she knew they would get themselves pretty well tanked up along the way. But she hadn't wanted them to run out before they got really drunk. In that state, she figured, they would likely get lost and eventually turn around and come home, and *that* way they would come to far less harm than if they actually started interfering with the Indians. (Ruby had a low opinion of Indians, arising from the fact that about the only ones she ever saw were falling-down drunks in her own Frontier Saloon.) And of course, if there actually were any German POWs on the rez, they would be more dangerous than a bunch of pissed-off Indians. So she had made her contribution, which Bob Westmoreland and his posse thought of as nothing more or less than an intelligent woman's proper celebration of their willingness to risk life and limb for the public weal and the war effort.

"Now, Bob, that sure is mighty fine whiskey, isn't it?" Freddy said. "How much of it we got left?"

Westmoreland ignored the man and, instead, explained to the rest—now all dismounted—that they would camp here.

"Here?" someone said. "Why here?"

"Where the hell is here?" another said.

"Yeah, Bob, where the hell is this exactly?"

Blood rose in Bob Westmoreland's eyes and he glared at his posse, who, in the minimal light offered by the stars, could see only that he had put his hands on his hips and lowered his head, taking up his angry bull posture.

"We'll camp here because I said so and I'm the leader of this here outfit. Now you men get your bedrolls and—"

"We know how to make camp, Bob."

"Hey, Bob, you think you could help me unroll this here thing?"

"Pass the hootch over here, will you?"

"Yeah, Bob, I be damned if I can figure out this knot."

"Bob? Bob? I gotta go potty."

"How 'bout my good-night kiss, huh, Bob? And hey, Early Biggs, if you take the last swig of that whiskey, I'm gonna cut your earlobes off and mount 'em over the fireplace."

"Shit! Goddamned cactus!"

"Looks like old Early just fell down. Have another drink, Early . . ."

And so it went for another few minutes until the posse got itself bedded down, the whiskey all drunk, and the notion clear in their heads that Bob was going to wake them up before dawn so they could track down the German POWs.

"Yeah. Fricken Huns."

"Fricken Jerries."

"Fricken kraut bastards."

"Yeah."

A brilliant officer named Ralph Bagnold, a major in the British Army, had been much on Heinrich Schalberg's mind ever since he had learned of his responsibility for mounting Operation Shatterhand. Bagnold had been the mastermind of a short-range raiding force of fast-moving armored jeeps that had raised pluperfect hell with the Germans in North Africa and played an important role in the Germans' eventual humiliation there. Of course, all the Afrika Korps knew that if the idiots in the High Command had fulfilled Rommel's repeated requests for adequate supplies of fuel, the war in the desert would certainly have gone the other way. But the Germans had indeed had to evacuate, and Bagnold's rapid strike forces—particularly effective in surprise attacks in the night—had deeply impressed the German tacticians. It was such a force that Heinrich Schalberg envisioned for at least some of his tasks under Operation Shatterhand—or at least a modified, scaled-down version of such a force.

So, at 0130 hours of May 14, he and his second in command, Colonel Franz Liepzichte, stood in a half-track driven by Corporal Hans Schwabe near the eastern rim of the airstrip five miles out on the desert from the village of Oraibi. Four United States Army jeeps were lined up nearby along the rim, each with a German driver and two German gunners manning the 50mm guns mounted in the rear. They were to rehearse the complicated ballet by which four jeeps would *appear* to be at least twice that many. The basic idea, Schalberg had explained and diagrammed earlier, before the sun went down, was to run the edge of the rim, machine guns firing, each jeep making its own circle, then appearing farther down on the rim, firing again. It called for nearly perfect timing, so that two jeeps were on the rim firing at any given time, with the other two emerging somewhere else seconds later, in a repeated, continuing barrage. One of the extreme dangers associated with such a maneuver was that of one jeep shooting up another in the process.

The four jeeps had been through three dry runs under the stars, and Schalberg was satisfied that they had the drill down pat. It had started to rain lightly, then harder, during the final run-through, and Schalberg had pointed out to Colonel Liepzichte that the worsened conditions on the ground and the lowered visibility were all the better. Good practice for whatever lay ahead in the coming days. And then he gave the signal for a fourth rehearsal of the complex dance, in this one the gunners to fire their weapons at an imaginary enemy installation located midway on the airstrip.

The battle commenced. Engines screamed. Jeeps jolted along the rim, spun around, sending sand hurtling into the night. Guns blazed, a violent racket of flame and tracers seething out across the land.

It had not been the sound of engines that woke Bob Westmoreland in his sleeping bag under the stars. It was the feel of rain on his face, a few drops falling lightly, then a heavier rain, finally a minor downpour.

"Shit!" he said, and sat up. "Jesus!" The other men stirred, but evidently even the downpour was insufficient to overcome the whiskey they had drunk. Westmoreland, on the other hand, was a relatively light sleeper to begin with, and a heavy drinker to boot, with a capacity that was legendary in Winslow. Wide-awake now, he cursed the rain again and decided that he might as well get up and sit in the cab of the Model A and plan out some details of the dawn, when the first 50mm tracer went screaming past his head.

He couldn't comprehend it.

He couldn't believe it.

He shook his head, and another round sizzled past him, kicking up dust about thirty yards away. Then a third hit something with a thunk, and Bob Westmoreland realized that someone was shooting at him. *Shooting!* He now actually heard the staccato racket of machine guns. Bullets flew all around him, and the ground was alive.

"Jesus Christ!" he yelled, and scrambled out of his sleeping bag. "Jesus Christ!" he yelled again. "Get up, get up. We're under attack! We're under a goddamn attack!"

He raced around the camp, yanking at the drunken posse one by one, and screamed them into wakefulness. "Get up, dammit, get up!"

As suddenly as it had started, the gunfire ceased. Bob Westmoreland pricked his head up, listening to the silence, and then shushed his men, who were beginning to rise up from the ground groaning and asking what the hell was going on.

"We're under attack," he hissed. "Whole bunch of goddamned machine guns. Now, listen to me. We got to get outta here. You men just leave everything on the damn ground and get on them horses, two of you to each, and get goin'. Don't say nothin', don't make a goddamn sound."

The men began to creep off toward the horses which, miraculously, had paid no attention to the mayhem and stood pretty much where they had been hobbled. Bob Westmoreland kept behind the men, herding them in the right direction, and then the gunfire burst out again, tracers flying overhead, dust kicking up ahead of them. "Run, run, for God's sake," he bellowed over the din.

The men mounted up awkwardly, Westmoreland launching himself at the rear of the last stationary horse, on which Early Biggs had already seated himself, wobbling to one side. Westmoreland reached around Early, took the reins, kicked the horse to a gallop, and took the occasion to utter the first direct prayer to God that he had made in seven years, the last time being when he was waiting for the Ford Motor Company in Detroit to award either him or that oily son of a bitch, Franklyn (Cactus Frank) Graebner, the Ford dealership in Winslow.

By the time the last fusillade sounded over the airstrip, the posse was several hundred yards south of where they had camped, well out of earshot of their attackers and still hell-bent for Winslow.

The posse was too busy clinging to their mounts to notice that the rain had stopped.

Schalberg, along with Liepzichte and Corporal Schwabe, had witnessed the maneuvers with a soldier's exhilaration at seeing crack troops operating perfectly and hearing the satisfying barrage of machine-gun fire pouring forth at the "enemy." Now the rain had stopped. The jeeps were again clearly visible in the starlight.

"Excellent, excellent!" Schalberg was saying as they watched one of the jeeps, the one farthest down the rim, slide over the edge and plummet down the ten feet onto the airstrip itself. The jeep went up on two wheels, nearly tipping over, and one of the gunners in the rear lurched sideways over the side, landing on the ground. Gunning the engine, the driver wrenched too hard at the wheel of the unfamiliar vehicle and it skidded, went into a spin on the airstrip, around and around in slow, graceful circles, sliding as it circled out across the runway like a cow on an ice-covered lake.

Schalberg laughed at the sight and then felt his heart stop. Schwabe leapt from the half-track also realizing the disaster that was about to strike, and ran up the rim and leapt onto the airstrip, his feet slipping and skidding wildly under him.

"The rain," Schalberg barked. "The rain! The airstrip is mud!" He looked at his watch and shrieked out the order for the men at either end of the strip to douse the bonfires that had been lit, by prearrangement, at the cessation of firing. From overhead they heard the sound of the Condor, its four big engines feathering back for its landing.

Out on the airstrip, Schwabe reached the jeep, now stationary and directly in the path of the descending plane. He hurled himself against the vehicle and, with its wheels spinning, spraying white mud up in an enveloping wave, it slewed sideways, got a momentary purchase and skittered to the side of the strip just as the enormous black aircraft, laden with supplies and fuel, a great pod of fuel hanging from each wing, touched down in the muck.

The engines reversed with a throat-rattling roar, and the plane skidded onward, not slowing down, even gaining momentum, tail slewing, white muck flying off its landing gear. It plummeted ahead with a sudden, horrible lurching swoop up the far rim, over it, and into the outcrop called the Giant's Chair with a metal-crushing crash that split the night asunder. The crash left a momentary, gaping silence. Then flames erupted from amidships, followed by a thunderous roar and two more explosions as the wing-tip gas fuel pods erupted. Columns of flames ascended furiously into the night, and the desert was lit for miles around in a ghastly orange light.

Heinrich Schalberg fought off his instinct, which was to avert his face from the awful heat. Instead he faced the towering inferno at the end of the airstrip, the plane a blackened, awkward array of wreckage that rolled and writhed in the updraft. He fought off the despair that

broke like surf over him, and forced himself to compute
. . . to think . . .

He looked down and stared into the agonized face of
his driver, Hans Schwabe, covered in white muck that
now glowed orange, almost red, from the flames consum-
ing the Condor. The plane's cargo of mostly fuel had
now oxidized into nonexistence but for a vast, black,
greasy cloud above the desert. Schwabe's pig eyes
gleamed reddishly. They were wet with pain, shining . . .

"That sure fucks this operation, sir," the corporal said.
"We're fucked."

Schalberg coughed and cleared his throat. He looked
over again at the flames, then back to Schwabe.

"No, Corporal, no. It is a setback. A setback. And we
have work to do here, don't we? Work to do."

He turned to Colonel Liepzichte, whose eyes were on
the flames, transfixed, and began to issue orders to be
passed along to the men.

Had they been looking, people within fifty miles of the
Germans' makeshift airstrip could have seen the column
of orange flame reaching up into the night sky, but few
were awake or abroad at two o'clock in the morning.
Navajos, in the camps sprinkled here and there within
sight of the flames, were in their hogans and houses, out
of the way of witches. Hopis, similarly, though not out of
fear of the night, were asleep in their villages on the three
mesas. Nighttime rehearsals in the kivas for the next appearance of the katsinas would not start for several days.
There could have been an insomniac or two abroad at
that hour, but if that were the case, it is unknown.

On the other hand, Bob Westmoreland's posse did
hear the succession of explosions thundering behind
them, then turned to see the column of horrid orange
flame in the sky. It did little to slow down their flight
back to Winslow; quite the contrary. Their expedition

had become a nightmare, too outlandish to be true—or at least too outlandish to be believed.

At least two other pairs of non-German eyes also saw the conflagration, from its beginning nearly to when it died down to a glow of rubble. One of these belonged to a sixty-seven-year-old, onetime barnstorming pilot, long since retired from those adventurous days, and recently retired as an insurance agent in Gallup, where he had faithfully represented a company in Omaha for twenty-seven years. Just as he had achieved an altitude sufficient, he judged, for a man to parachute from his lovingly maintained two-seater Beechcraft biplane, the flames had erupted below him and about ten miles to his south.

"Fireworks," he shouted, and held out his gloved hand with the thumb up.

The other eyes belonged to Ben Cameron, his face wind-whipped in the seat behind the retired insurance agent, and as he wrenched himself out of the aft cockpit, he fervently hoped that whatever had caused the explosion was distracting anyone on the desert who might otherwise note the passage at one thousand feet of a small aircraft, or to notice a man descending through the night dangling from a parachute.

This, indeed, turned out to be the case. Ben Cameron, feeling something like a piece of bologna in a sandwich, since he was strapped firmly between two canvas packs, one in front, the other in back, landed unseen within five hundred yards of the northernmost side of Katsina Bluffs, his knees bent to take the impact with the ground. The impact threw him into a violent series of somersaults and left him breathless and severely tangled up in the shrouds of his parachute, which lay on the ground like a ghostly beached whale, its edge fluttering in a light breeze.

Despite what Cameron knew would become bruises on his legs and back, he felt a sudden burst of elation, as if a bolt of benign electricity had passed from the ground into his body as he landed. In the dark, in a tangled heap, he grinned at the realization that, after four years in a variety of exotic places doing exotic and wonderfully mysterious military things, he suddenly felt at home again.

A few minutes later, having rolled up the parachute and buried it, then rearranging the heavy canvas packs containing radio equipment so that each hung under one arm suspended by a shoulder strap, he set out across the desert in the starlight on a course he reckoned would take him a bit north of Old Oraibi. He knew it would still be dark when he got there, and from that gloomy perch on the mesa, he could check out the village below and work out a way to make contact with his old friend, Raphael Luna.

There was no way that Mary Beth Lemon could have seen the flames that erupted in the night, though she was well within the fifty-odd-mile radius within which they were visible. From her position east of a long, high mesa that loomed ahead of her like a black ship against the stars, only an orange glow in the sky was visible. But she was not looking up at the time. She was crouched next to a large boulder, one of many that littered the base of the mesa ahead of her, clutching her left ankle with both hands and gritting back the tears that urgently sought to escape from her eyes.

In the fall—she had cracked her shin on one boulder, lost her balance, and tumbled sideways into another much larger boulder—her ankle had twisted violently. It felt sprained. A barrage of pain was shooting through it, up her leg. It had to be sprained.

What did they say? If it's sprained, get up and walk on it? Walk on it? She could barely stand touching it. This was just what she needed. Just what she needed. Oh, Jesus, it hurt.

She stood up and gingerly put a little weight on it.

"Ow!" she said and sat down, and let the tears come.

The image burst into her mind of Wilhelm Muller, for-merly a captain in the German Army and now a corpse, lying in the dirt under those cottonwoods, bare-assed with his pants down and an arrow protruding from his back, probably already half gnawed to pieces by some coyote. He was dead. Killed. With an arrow? Most likely a Navajo. And if so, the German's killer wasn't going to move the body, or bury it, or anything. Those people were terrified of dead people, something about ghosts getting even or something. So the rapist son of a Hun bitch—her lover? Oh God, would He be getting even?—the kraut was probably still lying there, dead. Gnawed. Ugh. And her ankle was exploding—and that jeep. It had sputtered and quit way on the other side of Wepo Wash, and it wouldn't start. Out of gas, she guessed, and just when it was turning dark.

She had tried the starter a few more times, forlorn at-tempts, and then got out and kicked at the jeep in a child-ish fit of pique which got her nothing but some sore toes on her right foot. And then, realizing that she could be tracked—the jeep left pretty obvious marks in the dirt—she heaved and pushed it down an incline until it gained momentum and disappeared into some brushy junk growing in a small ravine. She set out on foot west.

After an hour, the stars came out, and after a long while, picking her way through the scrub and over rocks, she realized that she was off course. The Big Dipper was up there in the sky plain as could be, and she sighted right along its lower lip to the north star and realized that she was heading right for it. Right for Polaris. She was heading north. She had no idea how long she had been going in the wrong direction, probably not the whole time anyway because she had started off in the direction of the sunset. For all she knew, she could be halfway to that Navajo settlement, Pinon.

She walked west for what seemed another two hours, sat down to rest, her back against a large slab of rock at the base of some mesa, and fell asleep. Later she woke up, spent a few minutes rehearsing the day's events in her mind, remembering where she was—in fact, she didn't know exactly where she was, and her feet hurt something awful. She didn't think her shoes would last much longer, and the idea of walking over this awful ground in her socks, or her bare feet—it seemed that she was up against an insuperable set of obstacles. And then she had stumbled on that rock, tumbled over and twisted her ankle, and it was burning her leg up. At least she now was allowing herself the satisfaction of sitting there and crying her eyes out. No more brave Mary Beth Ogden Lemon. No more heroine, toughing it out, swallowing her pride, sacrificing her virtue and maybe her soul to a German pig for a few scraps of information to benefit her nation, which was at war. None of that. She just cried, let the sobs come fast and furious from somewhere down in her diaphragm and erupt into the night, felt the hot tears run in rivulets down her cheeks, and tasted the salt.

Everything ached. Her body was bruised *everywhere* and her ankle wouldn't stop screaming . . .

Presently, she took a deep breath, then another, pushed herself to her feet and limped on. Once she got around this mesa, maybe it would get better, the going easier . . . She did know things. Important things. Didn't she? Yes.

Sometime later, after struggling across the land in the dark for she knew not how long, she came to the edge of an open place and, through eyes that she could barely keep open, she saw the angular form of Luna's Trading Post. She squared her shoulders and limped across the open ground toward it, carefully shoving one foot in front of her, then the other. Her head felt so heavy. In the deepening gloom ahead she thought she could make out a human form, a silhouette, on the porch. A woman? A woman. Oh, my God, a woman. She started to sob again but kept going, one step after another, and began to topple forward . . . but the ground didn't come up and slam her.

Mary Beth Lemon fainted in the arms of Mary Yazzie, who had been standing on the porch these last few hours, sleepless and alone. Mary caught her as she sank toward the ground, and managed to get her up on the porch and into the kitchen, managed to get some water down her throat and get her into a chair, where she wept quietly for several minutes.

When Mary Beth was still, the Navajo woman reached out with two hands, pulled her gently to her feet, and led her out of the kitchen and across a dimly lit hall to a closed wooden door. The Navajo woman knocked faintly on the door with a brown hand, the wrist encircled with a silver bracelet studded with turquoise cabachons like a beautiful beacon. A voice on the other side of the door said, "Come in."

With the Navajo woman's arm around her shoulders, Mary Beth was led into the room beyond. A Coleman lantern sitting on a big desk cast huge shadows on the whitewashed walls. A dark green shade was pulled down over the room's only window. Behind the desk, the trader Luna sat like a huge toad, his eyes wide-open and gleaming. He was clad in a dark maroon bathrobe over light blue pajamas, and his black hair was mussed from sleeping. Before him, on a wooden bench that was like a pew in church, a man in a camouflage uniform sat—an intense-looking young man whom Mary Beth thought she recognized from somewhere. She clung to the Navajo woman and smiled feebly.

She was having trouble thinking, concentrating. Her mind began to wander back to the corpse on the ground under the cottonwood tree, and she wondered if she was in some kind of courtroom or church and people were going to get mad at her for being bad. Then the trader croaked, like he was clearing his throat, and a nice smile appeared on his face. A really friendly smile. Her knees began to give under her again, and the Navajo woman let her down into a wooden chair next to the pew.

"Mrs. Lemon?" the trader rasped, still smiling. "Welcome. You're perfectly safe here. Do you remember Ben Cameron? He used to work out here before the war."

Mary Beth turned her head toward the soldier in camouflage. She looked back at the trader, immense behind his desk, the Coleman lantern on the desk lighting up his face from below, his eyebrows casting shadows on his forehead. Everything ached. She felt again as if she were going to faint.

"You need to sleep," the trader was saying.

"I know . . . ," Mary Beth said.

"Some rest, and a hot bath . . ."

"I know . . . ," Mary Beth repeated.

"Mary here will help you . . ."

"I know where they're going," Mary Beth said. "On Monday," she added, and the light from the Coleman lantern seemed to flicker and go out.

It was nearly midnight when the headlights of the American half-track lit up a man lying on the ground under some trees. The half-track was in the process of backing up away from the edge of a dark crevasse in the ground, and Behrmann barked the order to the driver to stop. The man on the ground lay motionless about fifty yards away. The head was toward them, one arm sprawled out. The short-sleeved shirt was gray. It was Muller. It surely was Captain Muller.

Behrmann sighed, a long sigh, and swore. "It's him," he said. "Muller."

"Shit," the driver said.

Painstakingly, with their orders to find Muller, they had followed the tire marks of the American jeep up the winding road out of Keams Canyon, the headlights picking up the shadows of the treadmarks. Slowly, they had inched along, keeping the treadmarks lit in front of them, along the rutted wagon track, seeing them disappear into the ruts, praying, seeing them emerge farther along in some softer sand . . .

The treadmarks, soon as familiar to their eyes as the blood veins on the back of their hands, had led them on, disappearing and then reappearing, to the place where the wagon track separated into two, one heading toward the northeast, the other to the southeast, only to converge again into one, and then separate again—always the jeep tread coming and going in the path of the headlights, like a dolphin diving under the surface of the sea, only to rise blessedly above it farther along . . .

. . . but disappearing here where the tracks converged another time and the ruts were hard, solid . . .

Behrmann had ordered the driver to proceed—slowly, slowly, no, slower!—in a circle, humping out of the ruts and off into the scrub, crushing the stupid brush under its treads—slower, damn it!—until there! The headlights picked up the familiar treadmark again.

They followed it again until it disappeared once more among some ruts, a different wagon track, it seemed, that went off in a more southerly direction until it came to an end at the lip of a narrow canyonlike crevasse in the ground. Unnecessarily, Behrmann ordered the driver to halt, and stepped down from the half-track to peer into the crevasse and across it. The jeep tracks appeared to stop at the edge, back up and head off to their right, out of the beam of the headlights.

Seconds later the swinging beams picked up the man on the ground fifty yards off.

Motioning the driver to follow, Behrmann now strode through the scrub toward the corpse. Behrmann's shadow loomed large across the ground, stretching far ahead of him. In the shadows in the trees, he thought he saw a pair of eyes glowing, but then—nothing. He stopped, and his nose picked up the sickening sweet-pungent smell of death. Impatiently, he waved the half-track on behind him.

Approaching the corpse—yes, it was Muller—he heard the buzzing of insects, saw them swirling angrily around Muller's face, and saw the shaft of the arrow rising from his back. An arrow? The Indians, the damn savages . . .

Nearer, and he saw the pale skin of a buttock. One buttock.

Nearer, and he saw that the other buttock was gone, just ragged flesh, torn meat . . . and his gorge began to rise.

The damn savages! Killed him and left him to be eaten by . . . by God knows what scavengers dwelled in this godforsaken desert . . . those eyes, glowing.

The woman, the harlot, the bitch . . . where was she? Where was the jeep? He held up a hand to halt the half-track. "Stop! Stop there, you idiot! Jesus! Jesus Christ!"

A scene, a story began to emerge into Behrmann's brain, an explanation based in part but not in detail on the old stories he had read as a boy about the wild American West. A renegade, a band of renegades in horrid face paint. Shot down the white German soldier, snatched up the naked harlot from the ground and carried her off screaming, waving her arms, kicking—dragging her off to be raped by one and all of the band of renegade savages in their barbaric, bloodthirsty . . . a fate she roundly deserved . . .

A deep-seated rage began to rise in Behrmann's throat. Rage at the harlot, Lemon. Rage at the Indians, these so-called allies of the Germans.

Three hours later they were lost.

The remains of Captain Muller, less his identification and his holster and Luger pistol, had been buried in a shallow and hastily dug grave in the desert. They had backed the big vehicle up to the place along the crevasse where the jeep tracks had stopped, and the driver pointed on the ground before them to what appeared to be jeep tracks heading off in the opposite direction, toward the wagon track. Painstakingly and slowly, the Germans had followed it toward Keams Canyon, through the place where the two wagon tracks converged, separated, and finally joined into one. In the beam of the headlights they had seen where the jeep turned abruptly from the wagon track into the scrub, in a northerly direction. And they had followed the jeep track overland, losing it and finding it in the scrub, over and over, coming finally to a place where the track went down a steep incline and into a brushy mess at the bottom of a ravine. Behrmann had sent the driver down into the ravine to be sure that the jeep had met its end there, and to see if there were any sign of the harlot—perhaps her body, mangled in the descent.

The jeep was there, but no sign of the woman. But in minutes they had found her footprints in the sand. They followed them for several miles across sandy desert and patches of rocky ground, then more sand, until the prints disappeared among a clutter of boulders at the bottom of what appeared to be a high mesa.

The two Germans had no idea where they were. Behrmann debated with himself whether it was wise to backtrack, following the half-track's deep gouges in the land, and report to Keams Canyon, radio Major General Schalberg's headquarters with news of Muller's death at the hands of the barbarian Indians . . . or to wait where they were until the sun rose and see if they could pick up the harlot's tracks again. Surely, she would know what had actually happened back there in the copse of trees, and Behrmann would personally, happily, wring it out of her.

In the end they decided to wait for sunrise only some three hours hence, and so, fitfully, in the uncomfortable seats of the half-track, they slept.

Just as first light was showing in the east, Behrmann awoke, his body aching in all its joints from being folded up in so awkward a position. He stepped down from the vehicle, stretched and stepped over to a large boulder among the many that littered the ground. Unbuttoning his fly, he looked up at the mesa, looming above, with other boulders and slabs perched precariously here and there. Above, along the edge of the mesa, were cracked and fluted columns of rock, all in one stage or another of erosion, at some point destined to tumble down the mesa. One of them, Behrmann mused as he enjoyed the sensation of pissing, could fall at any minute. The thought amused him. And as he contemplated such a scene—a loud crack of rock, a slow-motion quiver, a roar as a giant slab fell away and down, crashing on the very spot where he stood, shaking away the last drops of piss in the crisp cool dawn—it was just then that two men, two Indians, bare-chested, bare-legged, wearing only shorts of some kind, appeared around the end of the mesa some fifty or sixty yards off, running his way, legs pumping rhythmically.

Behrmann snatched his Walther pistol from its holster on his belt, dimly aware of the sensation of warm liquid in his pants, and shouted in a high-pitched shriek in his native German:

"Halt! Halt right there, you goddamned savages!"


Victor Talaswaima felt the air cold in his lungs and exhaled. Inhaled, slow and deep. Exhaled. His legs rose and fell, the ground touching his feet, barely touching. He had the sensation he might be flying. He felt good.

He who had been first among the Hopis to see the oncoming battalion of Germans, from high on the mesa near Corn Rocks. He, Victor, who had spotted them just as some ancestor of his almost five hundred years before had spotted the arriving Spaniards and alerted his people. And now he had yet another role to play, a mission—to carry the trader's message to the radio operator in Medicine Hat. The message, written in the trader's spidery script and detailing the German plan, was folded into thirds and then half, safe in the leather pouch tied to his belt. He felt good, running, almost dancing across the ground some ten paces ahead of his companion, the Badger clan boy from Hotevilla, Kasemptewa.

Now there was light in the eastern sky. Dawa the Sun would soon peer over the edge of the land.

Victor ran through the boulders around the point of the mesa and saw the man, saw him spin around, pointing a gun, shrieking something incomprehensible . . . standing with the pistol pointed at him, the man's penis hanging limply out of his pants as he shrieked.

Victor skidded to a stop. The boy behind did the same. Victor clutched at the pouch, dug the paper out and began to chew it it up, violently chewing, as the German with his gun began to run at him. He chewed, chewed, and swallowed the paper, gagging, as the German lumbered up to him, the gun still pointed at him, shouting, "Halt, stop!"

And Victor, thinking with happiness: Too late, too late. It's gone. I swallowed it.

ल ७

# Eight

The stinging pain was back.

Major General Heinrich Schalberg dreamed in the ancient imagery of the Teutonic soul, when the world was ruled by the great god Odin and violent matters were played out every day and night in the shadowy premises of threatening forests, a world of dwarfs and iron forges and odd boreal monsters; where the Valkyries were born, where men could become wolves, and where witches prowled the perimeter of day-to-day life.

Schalberg dreams from a narrow cot in his headquarters, itself nothing more than an open tent in a desertlike land where Indians had long since brooded into being their own panoply of misshapen beings and friendly essences, and where men become wolves, and witches prowl the perimeter of life. Schalberg is dreaming he is answering a knock on his door and stepping across the threshold of his forest house, even though he had been warned not to do so. He has drawn his sword, expecting an enemy to be standing on the stoop, but sees instead the black-cloaked women, the Fylgur, riding down on him from the north on white horses. Not black? Protective spirits, these Fylgur—but also, ambiguously, noxious demons. Which are they now? They fly at him, he is speechless, cannot move, cannot lift his sword. His arms are inert, and the nine dark women are now three—peering at him in his cradle, a candle burning in the dark at each end of the cradle. Two of the women—these must be Norns, the arbiters of destiny, yes?—bestow on him an array of virtues, but suddenly they squabble among themselves. It is incomprehensible to Schalberg lying in his cradle, a mere infant. One is angered—oh, yes, now it becomes clear: she was pushed, elbowed, knocked even to the floor at the cradle side by the other two. She is outraged. In her fury she takes a candle and, screaming, shoves it at him, holds it to his innocent neck . . .

. . . and Schalberg awoke with a lurch, grabbing the nape of his neck where the ice-hot sting had returned. What on earth . . . ? He would have to get Schwabe to have another look.

The sun streamed into his headquarters and filled the desert beyond with a thin, harsh light that promised another day of nerve-wracking heat. He saw again the calamitous events of last night, the columns of fire surging angrily, the blackened wreckage of the Condor writhing in the updraft. He groped his way up and off the cot, over to the mess tent where there was water in a large pot. The men there stood back, wordlessly, as he splashed the water on his face, cupped it in his hands and tried to sluice the pain away from the nape of his neck.

"Sir," one of them said.

Schalberg turned to glare at the man, and went back to his almost desperate ablutions. The stinging subsided ever so slightly, throbbing there, a presence, but one that no longer commanded his entire attention.

"Where is Schwabe? Get him," he barked. "Colonel Liepzichte. Him too." From a pot, he drew coffee, black coffee, into a cup, and from the jury-rigged countertop he snatched up a slab of hard, dried meat. With these he stalked back to his headquarters, where he waved a noncom over to him. The man approached and saluted with precision.

"Find that man Banyongye, the Indian," Schalberg said. "Bring him here. And the trader. Luna. I want those two here in half an hour."

The man saluted again, spun around, and went off at a trot as Schwabe emerged from around one of the tanks and walked briskly in his shoulder-rolling gait toward his commander. Out among the tiers of armor, men who had been idling and making useless comments about the loss of the Condor snapped their cigarette butts into the dirt and made themselves look busy. None of them had failed to note the change in their local climate emanating from their grim-faced commander, just as the early Greeks knew when an irate Zeus was about to raise some hell on earth.

"Sir," Schwabe said. "How is your neck?"

The major general took his hand away from the back of his neck. "My neck is not our problem, Corporal."

"Yes sir, but how is it this morning?"

"It's nothing. Probably some damned insect bite. A bit of water helped. It's fine now."

"May I have a look, sir?"

Schalberg sighed. The peasant would not give up until he had had a look, Schalberg knew. "All right."

Schwabe went around behind him and plucked at the collar of his tunic.

"Sir," he said. "This doesn't look right."

"What do you mean?"

"There's a big red blotch here. Like a burn. It's round. But there isn't any bite mark." He poked gently at it and Schalberg gritted his teeth.

"Leave it," he barked, a bit too loud. "Leave it alone. It isn't anything serious. What is serious is—*Ow!*" Schwabe had touched it again.

"Sir . . . ?"

"Schwabe! It's nothing. I'll put water on it again. Later. Now leave it alone. I don't want the men to—"

Schwabe let go the collar and backed away. "Well, sir, the men know something got you on the neck. Some of 'em are saying maybe it's Indian clap. Sir."

"Goddammit."

"They're proud of you. Look at it their way. Their leader figures out the sideways slit on these exotic Indian broads, gets laid, and has a little mark of Cain to prove it. Clap is like a badge of honor for these guys. They haven't had a piece of ass in weeks, months. Except for the guys that grabbed some down at your mother's place, but—"

"This is no time for this, Corporal," Schalberg said.

"You know that cook, down there? The one with the big knockers, smiled all the time? Let me tell you, she had this . . . "

"Schwabe!"

". . . absolutely amazing thing she could—"

*"Schwabe!"*

"Made a few us feel like conquering heroes, let me tell you, all that soft, brown—"

"Schwabe, I don't want to hear this," the major general said, but smiling now.

"Nothing sideways about that one," the corporal continued, cocking his head. "Maybe all that sideways stuff is bullshit. They're part Indian, aren't they, sir? Those Mexican fur pieces? One night me and Bader, the two of us, that crazy flyboy . . . oh, shit."

Corporal Schwabe stopped, pulled his shoulders back, lowering his chin even farther down onto his neckless chest. "Yeah," he said, "Bader," and fell silent.

Again Schalberg's neck stung. His peasant corporal's pornographic excursion had taken his mind off it, but now it was back.

"Corporal, get me a cold compress of some sort."

"Sir," Schwabe said, and trotted over to the mess tent.

Schalberg tore a piece of the dried meat off with his teeth and chewed thoughtfully, recalling the static-filled conversation with his mother, Frieda, last night over the radio—the radio hookup permitting messages between Arabian Nights and this godforsaken place—calls limited to those that were utterly essential lest the signal be picked up by American snoopers. Schalberg smiled inwardly. Why shouldn't Americans snoop? It was their country, wasn't it? And Schalberg was here—the 108th Panzer Battalion was here to . . . something had to come of this mission. Had to. But now, of course, they were alone, this fraction of a battalion, these twenty tanks, five jeeps . . . Schalberg ran over the numbers in his head yet again. That was it. There would be no more. It had been the last radio contact with Arabian Nights.

"My God, Heinrich . . ." his mother's voice had said over the static. He told her to get rid of all the rest of the equipment there, the supplies, the ammunition waiting there for the Condor that would not return.

"But Heinrich—"

It was essential, he said in a clipped voice, to be heard over the static and to emphasize the official nature of this communication to the adoring civilian who was his mother, that nothing of the German presence be discovered there. It could, he pointed out coldly, lead to the further discovery of the forces of Operation Shatterhand.

"But—"

"Do as I say," he said, and then: "That is all," and the static had ceased. Later, raising one of the soldiers in Keams Canyon on the radio, Schalberg learned that Corporal Behrmann was yet to report back. He was still out there somewhere seeking Captain Muller and the American woman. This had been at 0400 hours. The same had proven true two hours later: Behrmann was still out there somewhere. Who, then, would man the telephone in case a call came in later from the Americans at the Indian Agency in Gallup? The soldier thought that they wouldn't call, it being Sunday and the Americans not working on Sundays, but nevertheless he had cut the line; it would seem to anyone calling to be out of order again. Schalberg had congratulated the soldier.

Where, then, was Muller, still absent now at 0800 hours? What in hell had happened? Another damned fuck-up, he thought, feeling the sting on his neck and sensing a great opacity closing in around him in this alien land with its peculiar inhabitants—people, he thought, that lived in some insubstantial medieval world of their own. He fought off the sensation of claustrophobia and noted that the trader was now in sight, walking toward the mess tent in the measured, careful pace of the overweight, the world always being a bit uphill for such people. And farther off, rounding some boulders at the base of the mesa, the little Indian, Banyongye, was picking his way toward the mess tent, followed by the two almost identical Indians who seemed to be perpetually attached to him, never speaking. The old Hopi was looking down at the ground as he approached, studying the ground before his feet as if he were looking for something he had lost.

Raphael Luna said, "Thank you very much, I will," when Schalberg offered him one of the camp chairs under the canvas roof. He eased his torso into the narrow chair and added that it would be another hot day today but not, thank God, one that would bring with it any more wind. The trader's eyes gleamed with their usual brightness. Banyongye by now had reached the tent and stepped under the canvas, his two subalterns pausing outside. Colonel Liepzichte stood in the shade to the side, his thin lips grimly compressed, and Major General Schalberg sat one haunch on the camp desk, a polished boot swinging back and forth before him. A wet, gray cloth was wrapped around the back of his neck. Corporal Schwabe stood about twenty feet away, his back turned, but those in the headquarters tent could see that he was oiling a blue-metal Luger pistol that gleamed with lethality in the sun. Schalberg pointed to the other camp chair and looked at Banyongye. The old man nodded, smiling briefly, and sat down, his old eyes looking out across the ground to the rows of tanks.

"You no doubt have heard that the plane went down last night," Schalberg said abruptly. "With it, we have lost men, weapons, and fuel supplies. The men cannot be replaced. The fuel must be. Today you will tell me about the fuel reserves on this reservation." He looked from Banyongye to the trader. Banyongye was looking absently at him, as if he had heard someone speaking in a foreign tongue. The trader was expressionless, his gleaming, nearly black eyes unreadable.

Schalberg looked again at Banyongye. "You do understand? It is important that you have your people bring us all the fuel here that exists."

"If I may, Herr Major General . . . ," the trader said.

He spoke the syllables of rank with elaborate precision, and Schalberg couldn't tell if it was done with just a hint of derision. He nodded.

"Sources of fuel here are limited, greatly limited. The Hopis have none to speak of, none at all in fact. None of them have any vehicles, you see. Only a handful of Navajos possess such equipment, which are scattered here and there"—he gestured widely around him—"out there. A few old Model Ts." He shrugged. "And mostly immobilized. The war." He leaned farther back in the delicate camp chair. "I have barely enough for my trucks for a run to Winslow. We usually go in mid-month to stock the trading post with canned goods, that sort of thing. Otherwise, there's Keams Canyon, the Indian Agency there . . . but I presume your people have made their own assessment. And then there is Tuba City." He gestured to the northwest. "There's another trading post there, not much else. The man who runs it is not terribly reliable. An old man now. That's up beyond Coal Canyon, quite a long way. Sixty miles if we were ravens, but more like ninety once you've made your way around all the obstacles."

Schalberg said nothing.

"I doubt the old man has enough fuel to make the trip

worthwhile. Indeed, fetching it would be a net loss, I suspect. Worthwhile if you're headed that way, of course." The trader looked out across the desert.

Still probing, this trader is, Schalberg thought.

"I'm afraid there is no way to make any substantial additions to your supply," the trader said. "You will, of course, take what I have left."

Colonel Liepzichte shifted his weight from one leg to another and snorted.

"It is amazing but true," the trader resumed. "In my experience here since I was a boy—in my experience, no one from the outside has ever underestimated the supply here of what we think of as modern goods." He let the thought sink in, a rueful smile on his face.

Schalberg turned to face out across the array of armor to the desert beyond. He took note again of the distant windmill, and briefly watched a dark bird, its wings in a shallow V, dipping this way and that far across the land.

"I have noticed," Schalberg said, his back to the people in the tent, "that there are very few young men here among these Indians. Men of, say, eighteen to thirty. Why is that?" He turned to look at the trader, who looked back at him, not unlike the way a frog or a toad observes one from the edge of a pond.

"Poliomyelitis," the trader said after a long pause. "There has been a scourge here. A most horrible disease. And it has affected the youth in a way that is disproportionate. Young men—and women." He shook his head. "No one has explained why that is so." He shook his head again. "But not just the youth. That old man I went off to see the other day? He died. Tragic." The trader looked at the ground.

Banyongye shook himself, as if waking up. He looked at the trader. "Uh . . ."

Luna turned to him and stared. "Banyongye here," he said, speaking to Schalberg but keeping his eyes fixed on the old Indian, "lost several members of his family to the scourge. Seven, as I recall. Right, Banyongye? It was as if the whole world had turned on his family." He looked back at Schalberg, and Banyongye looked down at the ground, head bent.

"Before the turn of the century here," the trader said, "it was smallpox. Decimated the people. Now this ... Nothing, Herr Major General, nothing the white man has done to these people, has been as cruel as the disease he has brought with him, however inadvertently."

The sound of an engine broke the silence, a heavy vehicle grinding through the village behind them. They turned to watch it appear between two yellow stone buildings as a small pack of dogs scuttled out of its path. Schalberg recognized the man in the seat next to the driver: Behrmann, whom he had ordered into the desert to find Captain Muller. There was no Captain Muller visible in the half-track, no woman either. Just Behrmann and the driver. Schalberg strode out of the tent, ducking under the edge of the canvas roof, and motioned the half-track toward him. It turned slowly, like a huge predator from some earlier age, approached within ten feet of the tent and stopped. Behrmann stepped down from the beast and saluted crisply.

"Report, Corporal." Schalberg swallowed his impatience and the fury boiling inside him. The stinging was back, burning his neck. He snatched the compress off and let it drop to the ground. The driver alit and turned to the back of the half-track, climbing up into it.

"Sir," Behrmann barked. "We found Captain Muller, sir. Last night at about midnight. He was dead, sir. Killed by an arrow in his back. A single arrow. This was fifteen kilometers east of Keams Canyon, sir, off a wagon track leading east. Of course we buried the captain. His effects are"—he turned back to the half-track—"in there. We tracked his vehicle back this way, then north. The woman, sir. Somewhere out there it went off a cliff of some kind, into a canyon. The woman wasn't in it. We tracked her for several miles and lost the track in some rocky place. Captain Muller, sir. It must have been an Indian, some Indian, a renegade . . ."

"I'll take your report, Corporal," Schalberg said gently. "Later you can give me your opinions." He felt this world closing in on him again. In some removed part of his brain he was saying "Shit" and repeating it over and over.

"Sir!" Corporal Behrmann said. "This morning, sir, at dawn, before we started in this direction to report, we intercepted two Indians. They were running. Came right at us. I told them to halt." Behind them, the driver had hauled two Indians from the back of the half-track. They were naked except for some sort of loincloth and moccasins. Young men, Schalberg thought, who had somehow escaped the scourge of poliomyelitis. "It seemed suspicious, sir, these Indians running like that. So I brought them here. They won't talk. Maybe they don't speak, uh, English."

"Bring them here."

The driver pushed the two youths toward the tent. Their hands were bound behind their backs, and the rope lashed them both together tightly enough that they had to scuffle forward as if they had but three legs between them. Schalberg stared at them and said in a loud voice, "So, Mr. Luna, what have we here?"

The trader cleared his throat, a loud phlegmy croak, and spat on the ground.

"This is Talaswaima from Second Mesa. The one on your right, Herr Major General. The other boy is Kasemptewa. From Hotevilla."

"Do they speak?" Schalberg asked, still facing them.

"Only Hopi," Luna said.

"Ah. Only Hopi. And what were they doing running out there at dawn?"

"One of them, sir," Behrmann interjected. "That one on the right put something in his mouth and swallowed it before I could get to him." Behrmann, his face red, looked as if he was about to strike out at the Indian.

"All right, Corporal. We'll get to the bottom of all this. What," he said again, "were they doing out there?"

Behind Schalberg's back the trader pushed himself out of the little camp chair and looked pointedly down at Banyongye, who glanced up at the big man and then down at the ground.

"Practice," Luna said. "A rehearsal."

"Yes?"

"For a ceremony that takes place later this summer. It's called the Soyalsum," he said, manufacturing Hopi tradition from thin air. "Soyalsum means—among other things—the great journey. A journey like a migration. It recalls the great migrations that brought the Hopi here, and part of it, you see, part of it calls for young Hopi men to run more than a hundred miles—fifty miles out to a shrine and back. They bring back some salt the Hopis believe is sacred. These boys here, they were chosen for the run, so they have to practice, to get the muscles, the lungs—"

"It is fortunate, isn't it," Schalberg said, turning to the trader, "that they have been spared by your scourge of poliomyelitis."

The trader shrugged. "Indeed."

"So what was he chewing, this pilgrim?"

Luna said something in another language, and the young man, Talaswaima, looked down at his pouch and uttered a word or two in the same language.

"Jerky," the trader said, translating. "Dried mutton. They take only that and some water. It's an ordeal. You'll find the jerky in the deerskin pouch."

"Behrmann?"

The corporal reached over and fumbled with the pouch, stuck his big hand in, and held up some brown flakes with a look of disgust.

"Jerky," the trader said, and sat down again in the little

camp chair. He glanced over at Banyongye, and back to Schalberg. "Soyalsum is held in late July most years, isn't it, Banyongye?"

Banyongye looked up and nodded.

"Will your village be taking part this year?" the trader asked. "Or is it at Hotevilla only?"

The old man muttered something.

"Yes," the trader said, beaming. "Just at Hotevilla. It's quite an honor for Talaswaima here to be asked to run. He's a Second Mesa boy, as I said, and the people from the two mesas often don't see eye-to-eye on these things. It's such a complex place."

Schalberg's eyes rested on the trader, watching him settle back into the little chair.

"Where, then," Schalberg asked, "do you suppose the woman went, this Lemon woman?"

"That would be hard to say, of course," the trader began. "Do your men know exactly where they were when they lost her tracks?"

Schalberg snapped his fingers. "The map." Colonel Liepzichte picked a map up from the makeshift desk and took it to him. Schalberg gave it to Berhmann, who bent his head, blinked, and drew on it with a finger.

"We went out there," he said. "Then back to about here, then north. I don't know, sir, maybe about here?"

"What lies between here and this place called Pinon?" Schalberg asked. "They were there."

"Good God," the trader said, shaking his head. "There's nothing out there. Just mesas, rock, stretches of scrubland. A person could be lost out there for days. It was a few years back. Before the war. A young missionary, a Baptist as I remember it. He and his wife . . ."

Corporal Schwabe had long since finished tending to his Luger and now was simply standing with his arms folded across his round chest, listening to the conversation in the headquarters tent. He had watched a number of Indian men materializing here and there among the crews and armor, and watched as one of them, the big Navajo called Slink, approached, chewing on a thin stick like a toothpick and limping with his straight, bad leg. He was hatless today, the high-crowned, wide-brimmed black hat having been left behind somewhere, and Schwabe noticed that his shiny black hair was drawn back into a bun tied with white string behind his neck. Slink glanced up as he approached, then looked somewhere past Schwabe, limped to a halt beside him and stood silently, his arms similarly folded across his chest. Schwabe carefully looked away too, and in another direction from the Indian's gaze.

Neither man spoke for several moments, and the sound of the trader's voice droned on in its throaty rasp. Schwabe smiled inwardly, accustomed to the odd rituals of peasant men.

"That guy," Slink said presently, removing the stick from his lips and replacing it on the other side of his mouth. "That missionary."

Schwabe waited.

"We called him Slippery Hands."

Schwabe continued to wait in silence, but with the beginning of a smile tugging at the corners of his mouth.

"Touching the girls all the time," Slink said. "The young ones. You know . . ." He put one hand out, palm down, about four and a half feet off the ground.

Schwabe sniffed loudly. "What do you do about that?" he asked. "Cut off his balls?"

Slink chewed on his stick, grinning briefly. "I guess they didn't think of that," he said, and fell silent.

After a moment Slink said: "Those tanks. I guess they use a lot of gas, huh."

Schwabe looked at him.

"Hard to get these days," the Navajo continued. "Need them ration coupons. You forget to bring your ration book?" He laughed at his joke, and Schwabe smiled along. Slink removed the stick from his mouth and pointed southwest with a little rise of his chin. "Hosteen Jasper," he said. "Down near Leupp. Over there near Flagstaff, that way. Hosteen Jasper got two gas pumps down there. Big sign, says 'Out of gas.' "

Corporal Schwabe waited, then said, "But . . ."

"The old man been keepin' some back since—" Slink looked up skyward. "—let's see, maybe six years now, before the war anyway. Must have two hundred gallons in there."

"Near Loop, you say?"

"Yeah. Leupp. There's just Hosteen Jasper's place and a few camps down there. School there, it closed. White teachers, they joined the army. Went off to fight the Germans." Slink glanced over at the corporal, who nodded.

"You didn't," Schwabe said after a moment.

"Bad knee," Slink said. "Broke. Anyway, the army didn't want us Indyinns. We're too lazy." After a thoughtful pause, he added, "Us Indyinns don't feel real comfortable in them white man's uniforms. Lazy people with these long memories."

Schwabe permitted himself a sympathetic chuckle. The Navajo dropped his well-chewed stick on the ground and looked to his left, then to his right.

"Well, I gotta get goin'," he said.

Schwabe nodded as the Indian turned, and said: "What *did* they do to that missionary?"

Slink stopped. "Oh yeah. Some of those men, they told me the women took off his clothes one day. Everything but that little white collar around his neck. Painted his thing with sugar and water and tied him on a red anthill. That's when he and his wife—after she found him and got him untied—that's when they ran off. They got lost for a while, like the trader was sayin'. I don't know where they went after that. Someplace they don't have any Indyinns, be my guess."

Slink hobbled off a few paces and stopped. "Hosteen

Jasper," he said. "He's been hoardin' all that gas, other stuff. Got enough to run one of these tanks awhile, huh." He limped away toward a group of Navajos loitering a few feet from the mess tent.

When Mary Beth Lemon awoke, an earthy, smoky aroma filled her head, and she heard voices, quiet voices of women talking with the peculiar lilt of Indian women speaking English. It was not the sort of thing Mary Beth would have analyzed, but it is a lilt arising mostly from a speaker putting the same emphasis on each and every syllable of the unfamiliar words. There is something extremely reassuring about it, this lilt, and this was something that Mary Beth felt without any analysis. She opened her eyes and found that she was looking up at a ceiling made of a few heavy logs that held up thin branches and what looked like straw or hay. On the whitewashed wall beside her, over her head by about three feet, a small katsina doll, carved out of wood and brightly painted, hung from a nail.

A Hopi house.

She let her eyes stray to the side, across the small room. A woman in a long skirt—purple, velvet—stood with her back turned. She was stirring something on a stove made out of some sort of oil drum. She wore a blue velvet shirt and her shiny black hair was tied up in a knot behind her neck. A Navajo. Next to the stove a round little woman in a cotton print dress and an apron sat at a table. A Hopi.

A Navajo woman stirring something in a Hopi house. She closed her eyes and decided she was dreaming. She opened her eyes again, to the same scene, and said, "Hello?" Her voice was little more than a croak.

The two women turned toward her. The Hopi woman smiled, and the Navajo woman just glanced at her and looked back to the stove.

"You're awake," the Hopi said.

"Yeah, sort of. I—"

"This Hopi stew is almost ready," the Hopi said. "You were real tired, huh?"

"Yeah."

"Uh-huh." The Hopi woman put her chin in her hand, elbow on the table, and watched the Navajo stirring at the stove.

"This is Mary, here. You know, Mary Yazzie, she takes care of the trader."

"Oh," Mary Beth said. "She . . . you . . ."

"She caught you when you fainted."

Mary Beth still had no idea where she was. Maybe it *was* a dream.

"Yeah, you were fallin' down then, and she caught you. You know Jenkins, at the trader's? He's real tall, real skinny." She giggled, a high-pitched sound. "He lives here. This is my place."

"I'm very—"

"I guess you're hungry, huh?"

Mary Beth sat up and put her hands on the edge of the cot. Every part of her from the hips down cried out in pain. She looked down at her bare feet on the floor and hardly recognized them, they were so swollen. Misshapen. She wondered if they'd ever look the same again. She was dizzy.

The Navajo woman, Mary Yazzie, spooned some stew into a white-enameled metal bowl and brought it over to her. She was beautiful, Mary Beth thought, with Oriental-looking eyes and high cheekbones. A full-lipped mouth. Her skin looked like velvet too. Regal, sort of.

"Here," the Navajo said tonelessly. "And here's a spoon. It's stew. It's Hopi, but you can eat it."

The Hopi woman giggled again. "These Navajo peoples," she said. "They make these ugly pots and their stew is real thin. All runny."

Mary Yazzie said something that sounded like "Fsshht," and smiled. "Here." Mary Beth took the bowl and the spoon gratefully and, blowing unceremoniously on each spoonful, ate what was there.

"More?" the Navajo asked, having returned to the stove, where she now stood, arms crossed. Mary Beth nodded.

"See?" the Hopi said. "*Noquivi.* Real good."

Mary Beth shifted on the cot, smiled and said, "Uh, can you . . . I don't know where I am exactly."

The Hopi woman giggled again. She had a round face, open and friendly. "Well, this is my house. It's in Oraibi, outside, you know. Not in the village. The trader said you should stay here. Those Germans, he said they wouldn't look for you here. He said—" She giggled again. "—they'll be lookin' for you over near Pinon. You know, where you got lost."

Mary Yazzie brought another bowl of stew across the room.

"Well," Mary Beth said. "I wasn't really lost out there. Not really."

"The trader told 'em lots of people get lost out there," the Hopi woman said. "You're safe, you know. Here."

"What's going to happen?" Mary Beth asked.

"The men are gonna have a council. Some of them." She said something Mary Beth couldn't make out, something in Hopi. Evidently a name. "She's the Bear clan lady in Old Oraibi. Our village leaders, they're always from the Bear clan. And the Bear clan lady said they should have a council about these Germans. So the men, and some of these Navajos too, they're going to meet."

Mary Yazzie nodded, smiling to herself. She was accustomed to the way the Hopis always took the credit for things.

"This morning sometime," the Hopi woman added. "And that *pahana* man, Cameron. He came last night too. He's in the army."

Mary Beth remembered him now, the man in military camouflage in the trader's office. Years ago she had seen him around Keams when he'd been doing some archeological work with the Indians. He looked so much older now. He'd been just a kid then. And last night—this morning, whenever—he listened intently when she told the trader what had happened back there at Keams. How she pretended to be helping so she could find out . . . how the Germans wanted to go to Farmington next, to get oil. The oil fields. She hadn't told them about . . . or had she? She wondered if they knew, if these women here knew what she had really done, what she'd had to do. She looked up at the Navajo woman, so beautiful, standing with her arms folded across her breast.

"Men," the Navajo woman said presently. "They have councils, do the fightin'. But sometimes they don't know what the women do so they can win." She shrugged and turned to the Hopi woman. "You Hopis put too much hominy in this stew. Someday I'll show you . . ."

Mary Beth's mind tuned out.

So these women knew, she guessed. They were so different—the regal Navajo, taller, her gestures so deliberate; her features, her expression, so slow to change. And the Hopi, her round face so quick to crinkle up into a smile, her hands moving busily. And both so sympathetic.

She thought she would just lie down again for a minute, maybe get a few minutes more sleep.

On the other side of the wall from Mary Beth Lemon's cot, in a room reached by a separate entrance to the house where the trader's clerk, Jenkins, lived with his Hopi wife, Ben Cameron woke up when a patch of sunlight inching down the wall above him lit up his face. He opened his eyes, glanced around the room, and closed them, feeling content. For four years now he had felt many things about whatever circumstances the war had put him in, but contentment had never been one of them.

As an intelligence officer, he had seen little combat, though he'd been in a number of scrapes. The most awful had occurred in a forward command post in North Africa, serving as American liaison officer for Montgomery's command. He had stepped out into the moonlight over the eerie sands outside of El Alamein when a Heinie shell out of nowhere hit the ground on the other side of tent, exploding in a sheet of orange, metal hunks flying past him along with what he realized were pieces of his British comrades . . . then, as now, perceived in a ghastly slow-motion, although the explosion and its aftermath had taken only an instant.

From the horror of death to the satisfaction of performing creatively in the bizarre world of military intelligence, Cameron had experienced many sensations, yes . . . but now, for an odd moment, lying on this thin mattress no doubt visited by bedbugs in a stone house on the outskirts of Oraibi, he felt content. So much everywhere else he'd been had changed—indeed, the world changed daily before his eyes—but here time had stopped. Raphael Luna looked the same—four years hadn't registered on his large frame, hadn't etched another line in his wide face. How could that be? From what little he had glimpsed—in the trading post and the village, which they snuck through before the first light of dawn—nothing had changed here on the reservation.

Of course, there was a German armored battalion improbably perched right outside the village: that certainly was something new under the sun. A German battalion, here, while the war itself was being waged toward its inexorable conclusion thousands of miles east of this place. And west, of course, in the Pacific. Seven or eight *hours* east of here, as time was reckoned by the turning of the earth under the sun. It was afternoon in Europe. And what kind of war was being waged here—here, where even the presence of a German battalion seemed to have so little effect on how things looked, how things were done? Or was that an illusion?

The trader had told him that the big Navajo, Slink, was

here, back from the islands and atolls of the Pacific with a knee that would never work right again. The trader said Slink had emerged, in the quiet and unspecified way of the Navajos, as what might be thought of as war leader. War leader? What kind of war was being waged here?

The trader told him that the Hopis had allowed the Germans to believe that Banyongye, the so-called traditionalist, spoke for all Hopis—as well as Navajos—who were all pleased to have been liberated from the American yoke by the Third Reich. The Hopis had been "discussing" all this among themselves, the trader said, and had now for the most part concluded that this was not a visitation that would simply go away if ignored. The old men of Hotevilla and Second Mesa had concluded that action would be needed. Of course, they were yet to invest anyone among the younger Hopi men with a leadership role. The trader hoped that he would be able to hasten such decisions, and that Cameron's presence here would have the same effect.

Matters were certainly coming to a head—whatever those matters in fact were—since the supply plane of the Germans had crashed, limiting the German force to its present configuration: some twenty tanks, a few half-tracks, some trucks, and five jeeps. Perhaps 125 men. Some rough estimates were available about the extent of the Germans' fuel supplies, but no one here, until Cameron arrived, was capable of computing how far that would take these tanks and half-tracks. Slink and the other few Indian vets had served in the Pacific, where tank warfare was almost nonexistent.

Some of the German armored contingent—if not all of it—was evidently scheduled to leave on Monday, or Tuesday morning, after a fuel truck arrived from Gallup. And that contingent evidently planned to proceed to Farmington and its new oil fields—but for what purpose?

The war in Europe having now reached what everyone knew would be a lengthy and bloody endgame, but an endgame nonetheless—what possible good for the German cause could a ragtag battalion in the American desert do?

It was madness, sheer madness, Cameron thought. Hitler was a nut, a raving maniac, and everyone knew that. Even his generals knew that. But Hitler was the nut in charge over there. God knows what he had in mind for this battalion here. A diversion? Diverting the Allies from scouring up the Germans and wiping their asses across northern Europe was about as likely now as diverting a Sherman tank with a . . . with a what? A bow and arrow.

But that, in a sense, was just what Cameron had in mind. They were going to kill this excrescence, the brigadier general had said. Send in the air corps. Maybe the Indians could put up a little resistance, keep the krauts concentrated in one place. Make it easier for the air corps. Can you—can you and those Indians—do that?

"Yes sir," Cameron had said without blinking an eye. There had been something a bit . . . what? a bit patronizing about the brigadier, and Cameron's back had gone up. "Those Indians," he had said. Fucking snob.

"Yes sir," he'd said to the brigadier, and held his tongue.

Now Cameron got up from the cot, stretched luxuriously, opened the wooden door and stood looking, sniffing. Outside, the desert was lit up with sunlight. The smell of Hopi stew was in the air, along with the pungent smoke of piñon logs. The air was cool, as pure as water in a mountain stream, and Captain Ben Cameron was as content as a man can be with orders to oversee the solution to a problem that seems more of a dream than anything that could really happen in the world. But then this was Indian country—home to the Hopis and the Navajos—where nothing much ever seemed to happen and nothing happened the way most people would expect, and where such things as dreams and visions often appeared to be at the core of the world. And there was, after all, a bunch of tanks and Germans out there not even a mile away from where he stood.

He looked down at the baggy homespun trousers Raphael Luna had given him, and the old boots. They were cracked, their toes turned up, but with a little wear they would fit—more or less. He placed the wide-brimmed black hat on his head—another gift from Luna, who had pointed out to him, unnecessarily, that at nearly six feet, he had a better chance passing as a Navajo than a Hopi. Feeling a bit ridiculous, Cameron followed his nose to the other door of this lonesome house on the outskirts of Oraibi and to the pot of Hopi stew he knew was simmering inside. Had there ever been a time within human memory in these parts when, whatever else was going on, Hopi stew was not simmering inside?

## Nine

"We better do something about this," Corporal Schwabe said. "It's a boil, sir. Something like a boil, right in the middle." He stepped around in front of his commanding officer, a lugubrious expression on his face, his big hands hanging at his sides.

"Good God, Schwabe," Heinrich Schalberg said. "You look like the doctor telling the patient he's dying. So what do you propose that we do before the patient dies, eh?" He bravely attempted to speak with a bit of humor, but the pain from this boil, or whatever it was, this horrid reservoir of poison on the back of his neck, was driving him crazy. It was an insistent, unrelieved burning, much too tender to touch. It felt like it would explode—he wished it would explode. Schwabe had described it as an angry nipplelike growth, a hard, dark purple nipple rising from the center of the round red patch, which itself was deepening in color, the skin turning in texture into something like rough, flaky cardboard. No doubt it was responsible for the fever that now had overtaken him. His forehead sweated, alternately hot and then cold. He felt a bit nauseous as well. And all of this, he knew, was affecting his ability to think, to concentrate on the matters at hand—and there were so many matters at hand, all of them calling for decision so that order could again be imposed.

Order.

It is the mark of a natural born battle commander to

perceive in the chaos that erupts during war an emerging
pattern of events and, by force of understanding and will,
force that pattern into conformity with the overall goal.
Schalberg had observed—from afar, to be sure—the
master of this, Erwin Rommel, exert his indominable will
over actions in the desert, making lightning-quick decisions from his mobile command post, shaping the raw
material of unpredicted events as they occurred, forging
from momentary chaos a desired outcome.

Now Schalberg was faced with the same need amid a
cascade of unpredicted and unpredictable events: the loss
of the Condor, and the implications of that for this mission—an undersupplied mission in the best of circumstances, and now . . . The murder of Captain Muller, with
the concomitant confusion over the whereabouts of his
American harlot-consort—he should, he realized, have
put a stop to that early on; God knows what she knew,
God knew where she was. The ambiguous state of loyalty on the part of the Indians, or some of the Indians—
someone had shot that fatal arrow into Muller, after all.
Was it a singular event, or part of an emerging pattern?
Were the Hopi runners part of a ceremony, as the trader
said, or part of an insidious intelligence operation?
Schalberg had the unfamiliar and unpleasant experience
of watching his normally orderly mind reel even as he
sought, one by one, to make sense of the matters at
hand—sense being the first prerequisite for the imposi-
tion of order.

Yes, he had told Corporal Behrmann, the noncom who
had found Wilhelm Muller's body last night and then had
caught the two Hopi runners early this morning.
Behrmann was among those who listened to the trader's
explanation—the ceremony that entailed running and all
that. Schalberg had, of course, noticed the noncom's
hard-faced suspicion, his volcanic silence until the trader
hauled himself up out of the camp chair and made his la-
borious way back into the village, followed by the Hopis.

"Sir?" Behrmann had said when they were out of earshot. "What if that's a lot of shit? Excuse me, a lot of lies."

"The thought crossed my mind," Schalberg said. He himself had begun to entertain the idea that what these Indians—and the trader—were allowing him to see was only part of themselves. And, of course, why wouldn't that be so? Even as a child in Mexico on his mother's hacienda, the Mexican peasants who worked for her had much in their lives that they kept locked away from others. Schalberg had no illusions about that. And, ever the rationalist, he was well aware that such unrelated events as the crash of the Condor and the murder of Wilhelm Muller probably had nothing whatsoever to do with yet other matters that gnawed quietly on the edges of his mind.

There was Banyongye, for instance, the Hopi leader who welcomed the Germans as representatives of their long-lost mythical white brother. His presence was hardly felt. It was the trader, Luna, who had done all the talking, while Banyongye sat nodding like some ancient Buddhist idol. Perhaps Hopi leaders typically let others do the talking, but . . . In any event, Banyongye hardly seemed to be exercizing anything even remotely akin to Schalberg's notion of leadership.

It was all murky. And what had ever happened to his night visitor? Schalberg had wondered several times in the midst of his more military considerations. Unseen in the pitch-black of that Hopi storeroom, she simply vanished like a wraith. Were it not for the purple welt on his neck where she had affixed her mouth while she squirmed underneath him, he might well have believed the entire escapade a soldier's dream. Good God, he thought, could the welt she had bestowed on the front of his neck have anything to do with this current excrescence on the back of his neck? A poisonous . . . ? Impossible. But who was she, and where was she? More murk. And to Schalberg, his mind rattled by the ever-present stinging, the presence of any murk was increasingly ominous. He shook his head back into the present.

"If they're messengers," Behrmann had continued, "they'll go again. Wherever they were going."

"You don't trust our allies here, these Indians?"

"No sir, I don't. I wouldn't trust any of these savages. Shifty scum is what I think."

The pain screamed out again in Schalberg's neck and he looked desperately around. "Schwabe!" he called.

The corporal rolled up, looking concerned. Schalberg explained what Behrmann had said. "What, then, do you think, Corporal? You seem to have developed a kind of rapport with these people."

Schwabe pondered this for a moment, his beefy arms across his chest. "I agree. If they were running a message, then they'll run it again."

"Can't they be forbidden?" Behrmann suggested. Schalberg's head swam. Sweat poured from his forehead. Forbidden? What, lock them up?

"If it was me," Schwabe continued, "I'd go back."

"Go back where?"

"Sir," Corporal Schwabe said. "This morning you ordered a detail back to Keams Canyon. They're getting ready to go. If Behrmann here goes back too, that would look normal enough. But then he could double back to where he found those runners. Wait for them."

This seemed to make sense, and Major General Schalberg took Schwabe's advice, ordering the noncom Behrmann to do just that—to take one of the jeeps scheduled for deployment in Keams Canyon and make his way to a point where he could observe the movements of the runners, if they in fact chose to resume their mission—if, indeed, they had a mission as opposed to a ceremonial role.

With that matter resolved, Schalberg had asked his loyal driver, the neckless Schwabe, to have another look at the back of *his* neck, and Schwabe recommended that he try to lance the angry, nipplelike boil or growth that was now the centerpiece of this awful efflorescence, which in turn was surely the root cause of the major general's feverish condition and the sense of doubt that now plagued him.

"Go ahead then, Corporal," Schalberg said, and ordered the sides of the tent facing the rest of the encampment be lowered. It would not do, Schalberg believed, for the men to see their commander being stuck like an ailing pig.

With his commander stripped to the waist and seated resolutely in the rickety camp chair, Hans Schwabe busied himself with preparations. He had ordered a soldier to fetch two pots of water, cold and hot, from the mess tent some fifty yards away, and shooed the men off when they lingered curiously. He had, himself, collected twisted roots and branches from the scrubby sagebrush plants and, in a hastily dug shallow pit, made a little fire. Carefully, in the pot of hot water, he washed his hands, scrubbing himself up to the elbows, and put the pot on his little fire, crackling now quite gaily, fine tendrils of smoke rising up and disappearing in the arid air. On the table before the major general he placed the pot of cold water and dropped into it one of the towels from a little pile. Another towel he dropped into the pot of hot water over the fire. Then, from a leather holster on his belt, he pulled his knife with its shiny black five-inch blade of steel. This he held in the flames for a moment and, from the rear, approached the major general.

"Now?" Heinrich Schalberg said.

"Yes, sir, now."

Schwabe bent over, peering at the angry purple nipple. It looked like it would burst at any minute, even without the knife. But, of course, it wouldn't, Schwabe knew. He put his left hand on the major general's shoulder—clammy with sweat—and Schalberg jumped.

Quickly, Schwabe brought the point of the knife up to the boil and, with a sudden turn of the wrist, slashed through it.

The major general jumped again, the cords of his neck popping outward, and a spurt of slime erupted from the boil. Schwabe jumped backward involuntarily. The slime—the pus—was greenish-yellow, streaked with red: horrid stuff, and Schwabe almost gagged. He turned, grabbed the towel from the pot of hot water, and as he was about to cover his commander's neck with it, saw something move. He looked more closely. Something shiny, wet, brown—something was moving under the torn skin of the boil—pulsing. Schwabe looked on in horror, and the major general emitted a low moan.

"Christ! What the . . . ?" Schwabe said, watching the brownish thing emerge, like a grub or a worm, but it seemed to have two pairs of short, dark brown legs that groped at the world. Horrified, he watched it curl up and roll down the flesh of the major general's neck and fall to the dusty ground. Instinctively, he crushed it under his boot.

"God, Schwabe," Schalberg said through gritted teeth. "What—"

"Something was in there," he said between breaths. "I don't know what the hell it was. Like a worm." He put the hot towel over the wounded neck and rested, one hand leaning on the camp chair. "Christ, sir . . ."

"Probably not, Schwabe," the major general said. He too was breathing heavily. "Probably not. Where is it?"

"I crushed it. On the ground." He peered at the ground, couldn't find the slimy thing in the sand where his boot had pressed the dirt down. He shuddered at the thought of it, the sight of it pulsing, groping its way into the light. And he shuddered again, this time at the thought that suddenly occurred to him: Maybe it wasn't the only one in there.

He stood erect, breathed deeply, and removed the

compress. The cut flesh now looked yellow, a small insignificant wound against the round, flaky field of red. He couldn't see much else.

"Sir?"

"The stinging is gone, Hans. Thank you."

"Yes sir. Maybe you'll just want to sit here for a minute. I'll be right back." He replaced the hot towel with a cold one and left the tent, walking in rapid strides toward the boulders ten yards away, where he threw up.

"Ya-ta-hey," Ben Cameron said. "Hey, Slink!" He watched the big Navajo limping toward him across the room. They were in another Hopi house in Oraibi, a handful of men crowded in the small space. Slink's face had broken into an uncharacteristically wide grin, turning his Mongol eyes into the merest slits.

"Ya-ta-hey," he said and put out a hand, giving Cameron a characteristically limp Navajo handshake and quickly withdrawing it. "How you been?"

"Good, good. What happened to your leg? You were in the Marines, they say. In the Pacific."

"Yeah. They had me out there. Doin' my warrior stuff. Then I got hit. I been back here since—" He looked up at the ceiling. "—I guess it's been about January. Been polishing my Purple Heart medal. I been thinkin' I could pawn it with Big Mexican." He laughed.

Cameron couldn't remember Slink saying so many words all at once. They stood facing each other, smiling.

"So the President sent you, huh," Slink said.

"Well, not exactly. I'm here to help."

"Yeah. I remember you were real good at digging." He laughed again. "Showed us Navajos how to unbury the dead with a spoon." He laughed again.

Cameron noticed that the room had fallen silent, men seated and standing against the wall all watching the old comrades in the middle of the room.

"That's Yellow Tooth Yazzie," Slink said, pointing

with his lips to a Navajo leaning against a wall. "And over there, that Hopi is Danny Koots. I don't know the old Hopis' names, those old guys sittin' next to him. Hosteen Begay, he's the one in the corner. Medicine man."

"So we're waiting for Raphael?"

"Yeah."

"I hope he comes before all you people start arguing."

Slink laughed again, quietly. He found a place on one on the cots, and Ben Cameron squatted on his heels nearby.

One of the Hopis put out a hand. "Danny Koots," he said.

"Ben Cameron. Glad to meet you."

"You're from the White House. The Great White Father." The Hopi was smiling.

"Not exactly," Cameron said, smiling back. This Hopi spoke more like an Anglo.

"Oh, no? So maybe that guy Collier sent you. Indyinn Affairs?"

"The army sent me. To help."

"Oh," Danny Koots said. "That's good. That guy Collier is one big asshole. You a colonel? General?"

"Captain."

The Hopi nodded thoughtfully as two raps came and the door opened, letting in a shaft of bright sunlight. It opened farther and the bulk of Raphael Luna filled the doorway. His face was expressionless as he doffed his hat and went around the room, ceremoniously shaking— or touching—the proffered hands, speaking each name quietly. A chair was produced next to the kitchen table, and he sat down with a grunt. He looked around the room and his eyes rested on the old Navajo medicine man.

The old man cleared his throat of phlegm and opened his mouth to speak when two more raps were heard.

"Come," Luna said. The door opened and Mary Yazzie entered, her eyes on the floor. She closed the door and stood leaning against it. The men in the room glanced at her and then at each other. It was not usual for a woman to attend such a council. No doubt it had been the trader's idea, and by their silence the men acceded to this strange break with custom, as they had at the earlier meeting the day before.

The old Navajo, Hosteen Begay, opened his mouth again and began to speak—in Navajo. When he was finished, Luna translated.

"Hosteen Begay says the Navajo and the Hopis have a lot of arguing to do but that now is a time when both people will have to tolerate each other and work together. He wonders what the President says. What does the President ask the Navajos and Hopis to do? He says that should be known before the Indian people decide." Luna glanced over at Cameron and then his eyes fell on an old Hopi man, the Bluebird clan leader from Hotevilla, who began speaking—in Hopi.

When he was finished, Luna again translated. "He says that the Bear clan leaders have met and asked him to tell us what they have thought. He says the Bear clan leaders are the fathers of the villages, the spiritual fathers of the people, responsible for all of their children's spiritual well-being. As such, they cannot be concerned with the matters we are discussing here, the presence of the Germans and what is to be done about them. As is the tradition, they appoint someone among the Hopis to act on their behalf. They too know this is a time when the Hopis and the Navajos may have to put aside their differences for the duration and work together. They have therefore appointed Danny Koots to represent the Hopis in this council. They say he has been abroad, away from Hopi many times, and is more familiar with the ways of white men."

All eyes turned to Koots, then away. Cameron wondered who this Anglo-speaking Hopi was. For a time, no one spoke.

"Captain?" It was Danny Koots.

"Ben," Cameron said. "Ben."

"What does the President say?"

Cameron cleared his throat. He had been dreading this moment. His orders were one thing—have the Indians watch, delay maybe, before the army killed it. But the Indians were patriots, made good soldiers, fought like devils against the enemies of America in both theaters. Even so, Cameron recalled enough from his earlier days to know that here, on this reservation, among these ancient people with the ancient baggage they each carried, nothing was that simple.

"The President hopes that the Navajos and the Hopis will be able to deal with this German invasion." He stopped and looked around the room.

"The President wants the Hopi and Navajo citizens of the United States not to let the Germans leave the reservation." Again he paused.

An old Hopi, sitting next to the Bluebird clan man, snorted, and spoke in English. "He put these Navajos here on Hopi land a long time ago. Didn't ask us Hopis. Now he's puttin' these Germans here?"

"No," Cameron said, suppressing a smile. "That's not it."

"Where they gonna stay?" the old man said.

"The President doesn't want them here either," Cameron said. He paused to let this sink in.

Hosteen Begay spoke, also in English. "FDR, he's a good man. He said we have to fight this war. So we sent our young men away to fight for him. Maybe he should send some of his young men here, help us with these Germans." He looked at Cameron. "Did you ask him that?"

Cameron shifted uneasily on his heels, and sat down on the floor with his legs crossed.

"Uh, no, I didn't. The President—well, the President says it would be a bad thing if the rest of the country heard about this. Germans here and all. It would confuse everybody. He says the Americans are about to invade Germany and bring the war in Europe to an end. He wants us to handle these Germans here."

There was another silence.

The old Hopi began to speak again. "FDR is a good man. He sent you here to help us. To help us with these Germans, huh? So maybe you should go and talk to them. Tell them to go back where they came from."

Hosteen Begay nodded.

"Well, sir, I'm afraid—"

The old Hopi went on, not to be interrupted by an answer. "Maybe they'd do that, go away. But not if any more Navajos shoot them. They say that one of those Germans got killed over near Steamboat. Killed with an arrow." He shook his head, and Hosteen Begay's mouth popped open, then his eyes narrowed and his mouth closed.

The trader spoke. "These are very good questions the elders here ask. And this is a very complicated situation we have confronting us. Captain Cameron is here with us now. He has been in the army for four years, an intelligence officer. He has seen much of this war himself, has fought against Germans himself. And Slink here, he's a Marine." Luna smiled at Slink. "Once a Marine, always a Marine, I've heard them say."

Slink merely raised his eyebrows as the trader continued. "He has fought the other enemy, the Japanese. And the Bear clan has asked Danny Koots to represent them in this council. There are many things to be thought about, discussed. Many details. Perhaps we should ask these men to come up with a plan to present to the elders."

Heads nodded assent.

"We do know something now that we didn't know before," Luna continued. "The superintendent's wife, Mrs. Lemon, was able to find out some of the Germans' plan before she escaped. They plan to leave here and go somewhere by Tuesday. That's two days from now. I sent two runners out with this message to the President. They were stopped by the Germans and brought back to Oraibi. I told the Germans they were part of a ceremony"—he smiled ruefully—"and have sent them out again. We think that some of the Germans will go toward Farmington. Others may go toward Flagstaff. Is that right, Slink?"

Slink pulled the brow of his black hat a little lower on his forehead. "I told that corporal, the one who's always around the general? I told him that a guy was hoarding gas down at Leupp."

"Is he?" Danny Koots asked.

Slink shrugged. "He might be, if he was real."

Koots laughed. "Think they'll go for it?"

Slink shrugged. "They don't have a lot of fuel for them tanks," he said.

"So," Luna said. "Perhaps we should let these elders go now, and come up with a plan we can discuss . . . when? Tonight? Here?"

There was general assent, and the older Indian men rose and left without another word, their dignity intact. When they had gone, Danny Koots turned to Cameron and said, "Those old people—it sounds like they still wish the whole thing would just go away. You know, like the Spanish did once us Hopis killed that priest."

Cameron sighed. Even this Hopi, Danny Koots, with his Anglo accent and his non-Hopi demeanor, had to talk about history. The Hopis had rebelled against the Spanish by hauling the one Spaniard at Hopi—a Franciscan friar—out of his house in Old Oraibi and killing him in the plaza. They threw his body over the edge of the mesa and burned down the church he had made them build, and that was that, as far as the Hopis were concerned. That had been in the year 1680. Cameron wondered how long it had taken those old Bear clan leaders, and their appointed war chiefs, to decide to kill the priest. Then, a while later, a priest did come back, was welcomed into a village called Awatobi, where the people took up Christianity again. Finally, the other Hopis swept down one night on Awatobi and killed all the men there. The village was now a ruin where nobody went . . . and here am I, Cameron thought, rehearsing Hopi history too. He shook his head. There was a lot to do. And if the Germans were planning to leave in two days, Cameron thought . . .

Corporal Friedrich Behrmann had twice been elevated to the rank of sergeant and twice busted back to corporal, in each case for outrageously and flagrantly beating a lower ranking soldier to the point where he was no longer useful to the German Wehrmacht and, once out of the hospital, had to be sent home a cripple, perhaps to assist the war effort in some factory or another. Before the war began in 1939 with the invasion of Poland, Behrmann had been a member of the Hitler Youth, distinguishing himself less as a good and obedient future soldier than as an accomplished street thug. There were many like him, of course, and he had taken great pleasure in roaming the streets of Berlin with like-minded comrades, brutalizing Jews and any others he saw fit. Not surprisingly, he had come to the attention of recruiters for Göring's Geheime Staatspolizei, known otherwise as the Gestapo, but had been passed over as too independent, too unstable even for that grim service. Mildly chastened by this rejection, Behrmann joined the general army, rising rapidly to the rank of sergeant until his temper, bottled up for so long, erupted and a young soldier who had whispered "pig" at the wrong moment was permanently maimed.

Demoted the first time, Behrmann served admirably in France and then in North Africa, rising again to sergeant, until another eruption of rage put him back to corporal, and a new campaign, this one in Russia, kept him busy just surviving. Apparently reformed—he was a highly effective soldier, after all—he was chosen for Operation Shatterhand and assigned to Captain Wilhelm Muller's squad, and now felt his natural bile in every pore of his body, along with the sweat that poured forth and evaporated almost immediately, the result of his exertions climbing to the top of a mesa in this godforsaken country peopled by these execrable subhuman Indians. By way of rationalization this time for his rising fury, it had been an Indian arrow—an *arrow*, for God's sake—that had done in his officer, and a noncommissioned officer owed absolute loyalty to his officer, just as an officer owed his life and honor to the Fuhrer. And so Behrmann, his natural brutality now justified by military protocol and focused on Indians in general, was on a quest for revenge—a matter of honor.

He was alone now, which was how he liked it. The driver of the American jeep was down below and a mile back, he and the jeep secreted in the shadows among the slabs and boulders at the mesa's eastern end, and out of the way. If the runners happened on the driver, he was to immobilize them and summon Behrmann by firing his pistol two times. But Behrmann was certain the runners would arrive from the west, where their degraded villages lay, and from his perch Behrmann could see for several miles.

He looked out across the stretches of empty scrubland, broken by other mesas, immobile slabs of rock lying supine on the land—a hopeless place, unsuitable for human habitation. He was seated on a flat rock, peering over the edge of two others that formed a kind of natural blind some two hundred feet above the desert. Except for a raven croaking as it swooped by and disappeared over the side, the world was stone silent. Nothing moved anywhere under the early afternoon sun. It was as if the world had stopped altogether.

Behrmann sat equally still, his Luger warm in his

hand. Patience, he thought, enjoying the stillness and the sense that all this land below him, all the land he could see stretching away for miles, was his domain now.

Motion. Something moved in the periphery of his vision. He turned his head, and in the dirt saw a lizard only some two inches long, a tiny gray-brown thing now perched motionless and alert in the shadow of a rock. Slowly, he moved his hand, pointing the barrel of his pistol at it, and it darted out of sight as quickly as an electric spark. Behrmann laughed inwardly and turned back to surveying his empty world.

I am, he thought, the German eagle.

The final preparations a military force makes before proceeding into combat may not differ even in detail from the routine rehearsals of battle-readiness that have gone before. But they are obvious to anyone, no matter how unschooled he or she may be in the ways of mechanized, modern warfare. The clatter and click of magazines being affixed to automatic weapons has a different sound—a sound of finality. The bodies of men are differently tensed; the gaits of even the lowest in rank take on a new authority and self-absorption. The simplest manual drills associated with the care and feeding of large machines like tanks have an ominously crisp choreography. Light armored vehicles move about with an angry abruptness, and orders that have been heard for days over the hum and even the roar of war machines have to them a new and metallic sense of urgency.

By noon of Sunday, May 14, these and other signs were easily read by Indian observers of the 108th Panzer Battalion of the German Wehrmacht. It came as no surprise to any of them when a small detail of five tanks fired up in the early afternoon and headed east out of the encampment near Oraibi. They were accompanied by two half-tracks, a pair of lumbering trucks, and one jeep. Two other jeeps along with a half-track had already gone in that direction earlier. Simple arithmetic showed that the main force remained in the desert outside of the village. But it was clear a major movement was imminent.

The Germans were positioning themselves for something, and speculation was rife among the Indians in the neighborhood, who otherwise seemed to go about their normal affairs. Some men and a few boys loitered on the periphery of the encampment, as they had before. The occasional Navajo appeared in the distance and rode slowly past the war machines to the trading post, only to ride back later to camps somewhere beyond the horizon. Hopi women moved between houses, fetching firewood, carrying loaves of bread. They tended outdoor ovens, and hissed at children when their play grew too unruly. Old men sat in the shade of old stone houses, as they had for a thousand years, watching the world pass by through cloudy eyes.

Only the most acute observer of the ways of the Hopis and the Navajos, perhaps someone who had made a study of gesture and the subtle meaning of bodily movement, would have noticed any new tension, any new alertness, among the Indians near Oraibi that afternoon. It was apparent in little else but a slightly more rapid movement of dark brown eyes as they scanned their world. Otherwise, the murmur of life appeared unchanged.

And it had been just that—this consistent and evidently unchangeable murmur of daily life—that had unnerved some of the men in the 108th Panzer Battalion over the past few days. They had been accepted by the Indians, even welcomed, if in a most undemonstrative way. Some of them had worked side by side with Indians, unloading trucks, moving equipment, touching up the ground of the airstrip. Some among the German soldiers had even engaged in harmless pranks with the Indians, and in the raw humor of men at arms. But for the most part the Indians had gone on with their own lives in spite of the massive presence of the Wehrmacht. Soldiers tend, and rightfully so, to find their own presence to be of overweening importance in any region they occupy. That their presence here in this wasteland of a desert among these Indians had made so little apparent impression, much less disruption, left many of them feeling a bit uneasy. They had thrust a metaphorical fist into what they expected to be a cushion, and had found instead that it was somehow as insubstantial as a cloud.

If a bit bewildered and made uneasy by what they had seen of the American Indian, many of the Germans took refuge in a soldierly contempt. Even though Major General Schalberg and his second in command, the stiff-necked Colonel Liepzichte, had repeatedly reminded them that the Indians were their allies, they had few illusions. When it came time for Operation Shatterhand to move on to its more perilous phase—whatever that was to be—these Indians would be of little if any help. Even those Germans whose education had ended in the elementary grades had learned from their schoolmasters the fundamental dictum of northern European sociality, *familiarity breeds contempt*, and they had now met the real thing here, not some storybook version of Indians. The Indians, indeed, probably were a lost tribe of Israel which, in its unimaginable wanderings, had become even more degraded than the Jews of Germany. After all, it was universally known in the ranks by Sunday, May 14, that Indians ate the entire intestinal contents of sheep— that is, shit.

At the same time, tensing for whatever was imminent, and a bit uneasy about the Indians in general, they were to a man aware also that their commanding officer had contracted some kind of mysterious Indian disease, perhaps some desert-borne plague. All of them felt pinpricks erupt here and there on their bodies, like the momentary bites of insects, only to find nothing alien there upon inspection. None of them mentioned these pinpricks to each other, this unconscious recoiling of the flesh, but it did nothing to assuage a generalized irritation of the soul that was upon them.

And none of the German soldiers except Corporal Hans Schwabe and Colonel Liepzichte knew the extent of the suspicion with which their commanding officer was beginning to regard these confounding Indians.

Schalberg's suspicion was in part a kind of paranoia brought on by his own ill health—and Schalberg himself was aware that this might be the case. While the disgusting creature had been expelled from its horrid lair in his neck, the fever lingered and he felt moments of dizziness, moments where his mind seemed still a bit addled. But part of his suspicion was fueled by the actual unraveling of events, of the order he had believed he was imposing on this narrow world where he and his few men and machines represented the purpose and the grandeur of Adolf Hitler's Third Reich. So Major General Heinrich Schalberg was ready for a decisive stroke—some action that would restore his sense of discipline and his unchallenged control of events.

The opportunity for such a decisive stroke presented itself later that afternoon, when the sun was almost imperceptibly producing its first tentative glow of pink on the clouds far off in the western sky.

A jeep driven by Corporal Friedrich Behrmann at a dangerous rate of speed bounced and careened over the rough, sagebrush-covered land south of Oraibi, its engine and transmission whining angrily at the strain. In the passenger seat, the onetime driver sat with a pistol trained on one of the men in the back, a Hopi. The other man in the back, also a Hopi, lay as if unconscious, his legs twisted and his head rattling against the jeep's metal side.

The jeep came to a dusty stop twenty yards from the commanding officer's headquarters, the tent now with all four of its canvas sides rolled up. Major General Schalberg was alone under the tent, and pretended to read a list he had written earlier while the jeep made its clamorous approach. He looked up as Behrmann stepped out of the jeep, took his sidearm from the holster on his belt, and barked something at the soldier in the passenger seat. Schalberg watched as the soldier stepped out, beckoning the seated Hopi out and to one side. Then the soldier reached into the back of the jeep and picked up the cumbersome body of the other, unconscious Hopi. He approached the tent and, at an order from Behrmann, dropped the Hopi onto the ground, where he lay in an ugly heap.

From the distance of some ten yards, Schalberg could see the red and purple marks on the coppery Hopi flesh. The side of the face he could see was purple and misshapen. The arms, the chest, the abdomen—all had the unmistakable signs of a brutal beating—welts, open tears—and one arm protruded oddly, as if it had two elbows. The white bone of one of these elbows protruded from reddened skin. Schalberg could also see that the Hopi lying crumpled on the dusty ground no longer breathed.

Corporal Behrmann approached, walking behind the other Hopi. Schalberg stood up from his makeshift desk and said, "Report."

Behrmann's chin receded self-importantly into his neck. "Just like we thought, sir, we caught these men running out there. Pretty much the same place as this morning. This one here swallowed something again, sir. Just as I jumped them. Chewed it up and swallowed it before I could get there. I told him to spit it out, stuck my finger down his throat. Nothing. But he swallowed something, sir, and it wasn't no goddamn mutton.

"And this one, sir"—he gestured at the corpse with a contemptuous flick of his Walther—"started to run. I grabbed him, knocked him down. He resisted. I told him to stop. But he kept on. I had no choice here, sir, he was flailing like a banshee."

Schalberg nodded. "Go on, Corporal."

"I tried to interrogate this one, sir. Nothing. He wouldn't talk. Told him he'd get the same as his buddy here, but he wouldn't say nothing."

Schalberg looked at the Hopi. He stared from black eyes straight ahead. His body seemed to have slumped, but his chin was raised in apparent defiance.

"You!" Schalberg barked. "Your name!"

The Hopi said nothing, moved nothing.

Schalberg turned to his right. Colonel Liepzichte had come up from the tanks along with some other men, including Hans Schwabe.

"Schwabe," Schalberg ordered. "Have one of those men get the trader. Bring him here at once."

As a soldier set off at a run toward the village, Schalberg watched with satisfaction as other soldiers began to move in small groups toward the headquarters tent. From the village, also, Indians began to appear and move tentatively in his direction: women, old men. Navajos, their long hair up in knots and some wearing the characteristic wide-brimmed black hats, approached silently. Before long, silent clumps of people had formed around the tent and the jeep and the two German soldiers with their weapons trained on the Hopi who was still standing. For several minutes not a word was spoken. Schalberg waited, his eyes from time to time meeting those of Corporal Behrmann, the uniformed onetime street thug who took to looking hungrily up and down the five-foot frame of the Hopi youth standing slumped but defiant before him.

Presently, a small group of people made its way past the outlying stone houses of Oraibi toward the ring of people. In the lead was the trader, Raphael Luna, walking with his head down and with an urgency that forced him into a purposeful waddle. Behind him loomed the lanky frame of his clerk, Jenkins. Two Hopi women struggled along behind the clerk, and behind them strode a taller woman in purple, the housekeeper, Mary Yazzie. Behind her, at a more casual stride, came the German soldier, looking satisfied.

This new clump of people emerged through the ring, and Luna came to a stop, his hands partly raised before him.

"My God!" he shouted, his voice breaking the murmur of the people like a rifle shot. "What have you people done?"

In a loud voice, clipped and menacing in its intensity, Heinrich Schalberg spoke so that all could hear him.

"There has been a betrayal here. A betrayal of the trust I have placed in you people. That Germany has placed in you people. These messengers were captured—"

"They are *not* messengers," Luna barked. "They are part of a ceremony—"

"They are messengers," Schalberg said, "and we shall prove it. Luna, tell this man to talk, to answer my questions."

"He won't do that."

"He would rather die, then, like this other one?"

"This is vicious, Schalberg, vicious, barbaric—"

"We are at war, Mr. Luna, we are not playing some peasant game with bureaucrats. Will that man speak?"

"He is a boy, for God's sake. A boy, not a man. And this one you've savaged here, even younger."

"Will he speak?" Schalberg insisted.

The trader said nothing. Schalberg stepped up to the Hopi.

"Look at me!" The Hopi, Victor Talaswaima, looked away to the north.

"*Look at me!*" Schalberg shouted. He grabbed the youth's face and wrenched it around to the front. "You are a messenger. Yes? Who sent you? Where were you going?"

The questions came out like rapid gunfire.

"Who sent you? What was the message? *Speak!*"

The Hopi said nothing. His eyes stared defiantly past the German officer in his face.

Schalberg stepped back. "He is a messenger, and there is still a way to prove it. The human digestion does not work overly fast."

"You can't!" Luna shouted, lunging a step forward, but he was held back by the German soldier. "God almighty!"

"Behrmann," Schalberg barked, and in a swift, untrackable gesture, a knife with a black blade some five inches long appeared in the corporal's hand. He stepped in front of the Hopi and held the knife point against his stomach.

"Jesus! No!" Luna shouted.

"Shoot him first, Behrmann," Schalberg ordered. "We're not savages," he said.

The sound of the pistol exploded into every ear, and Victor Talaswaima, the first Hopi to see the oncoming dust cloud of Operation Shatterhand, lurched back a step, then another, and stood staring vacantly past Behrmann's face, then fell like a curtain of water to the ground. For a moment the world stood still, immobile and soundless but for the continuing echo of the single gunshot.

Raphael Luna lurched forward, screaming. Before he had taken two steps, Behrmann swung around, a form leapt toward him, and he fired again, and again. The form—the lanky body of Jenkins—fell to the ground like a broken piece of furniture, a bleeding hole in his chest, another larger hole ripped jaggedly across his back. The trader, spattered with his clerk's blood and with a hole flowering in his chest, toppled, stopped momentarily and gasped, and then fell.

Schalberg's sidearm was in his hand, and he noticed weapons in the hands of the soldiers around him, now bent intensely toward the center of the ring. A woman in a long purple skirt silently fell on the body of the trader, her head buried, her fingers pulling at his shirt.

"This is the German Army," Schalberg shouted. "This is the 108th Panzer Battalion of the German Wehrmacht. I am Major General Heinrich Schalberg. I wear the Iron Cross, the highest military award the Third Reich can bestow on a soldier. There shall be no more betrayals! Do you all hear? Do you all *understand*? *Ja? Ja?* Now go back. All of you. Go back to your slovenly homes. Take your dead. Bury them. Pray for them. And remember the price you will pay for betraying me."

The people stood in awe. Presently, some of them began to move, to shuffle forward to the two fallen Hopis and the two others lying on the ground.

Talaswaima of Shipaulovi village on Second Mesa.

Kasemptewa of Hotevilla village on Third Mesa.

Jenkins, of Oraibi, a *billeganna*, with an Indian wife, a Hopi.

And Raphael Luna, Big Mexican.

Hopi men and two Navajos, one of them with a pronounced limp, leaned down, and raised the fallen onto their shoulders, and carried them back to the village of Oraibi, followed by the rest of the people. Schalberg turned to his second in command, Colonel Liepzichte, and told him to carry on. He, Schalberg, needed to sit down for a while and run through in his mind one more time the plans for the next day.

Later that night, long after the sun had set, but while the Germans were still occupied with their endlessly fussy preparations, the Indians vanished.

It would be hard to say how they vanished so quickly. It went unobserved. Except for a few old Hopi people too frail to travel far, and a number of children who could care for the old people for a time and be cared for by them, the village of Oraibi emptied of people. Those few Hopis who still clung to a life in Old Oraibi on the mesa above—they too vanished into the night. For miles around, in the lonely hogans at the end of long dirt tracks, snugged up against the steep walls of mesas, the only humans present were old women and young children, perfectly capable of tending the sheep that were also left behind.

In their swift and silent evacuation, the Indians had paused only to bury the three dead men and to heap the bulky body of Big Mexican into the bed of a wagon, where, on a mattress and propped up by pillows, he had regained consciousness and was puzzled by the great pain he felt, the most urgent part of which emanated from his side below his chest. He was greatly confused and he couldn't believe what Mary Yazzie, hovering over him, was telling him—that he had been shot—as the wagon, its metal wheels freshly lubricated, rolled silently away from the Hopi mesas under the weak light of a handful of stars.

# Part Three
# ENDGAME

And there's one thing you'll be able to say
when you do go home. When you're sitting
around your fireside, with your brat on your knee,
and he asks you what you did in the great
World War II,
you won't have to say you shoveled shit in
Louisiana.

—GENERAL GEORGE S. PATTON, JR.

# Ten

No one to this day knows what year it was, but what took place sometime before 1680 in the plaza of the then bustling village of Oraibi, up on the mesa, had a profound effect on the psychology of the Hopi tribe and on the way it thenceforth looked upon any intruder into its affairs. The event occurred after a peaceable enough period in which the Hopis helped a Franciscan friar erect a mission church south of the village on the mesa, and attended the friar's services with a minimum of grumbling. Some accepted the new rites eagerly, in fact, and among these was one Juan Cuna, who, in due course, became a trusted acolyte. On one occasion, the friar had something else to do and asked Juan to lead the service that day, which he was evidently happy to do. But then, for some reason, the friar returned before the service was complete, and found that Juan's service differed from his own: the assembled worshipers were laughing. In the mission church itself. During the sacred service.

This was sacrilegious, so sacrilegious indeed that the friar hauled Juan Cuna out of the mission and gave him a public beating. Unsatisfied that the Lord's wrath at such an insult had been appeased, the friar then proceeded to pour turpentine over the still-conscious Juan Cuna and set him afire.

Such scenes as Juan Cuna's immolation do not vanish from the memory of such people as the Hopis, never mind inane homilies about the healing power of time.

Indeed, they tend to grow more vivid with the very passage of time.

The fate of Juan Cuna three centuries earlier inevitably sprang to the minds of the Hopis on May 14, 1944, when they watched the Nazis shoot down Victor Talaswaima and saw him join his fellow messenger in death. Also, Juan Cuna's name was much on the lips of the Hopis, and the Navajos—who do attend to such stories, even if they are not Navajo in origin—who assembled that night in a labyrinthine canyon formed by the high, irregular walls of Katsina Bluffs west of the Hopi mesas.

Never had there been so many Indians of any kind in the immediate neighborhood of Katsina Bluffs, much less secreted among its serpentine folds of red sandstone. Not even in the days around Juan Cuna's brutal murder and the sanctions the Franciscan placed on pagan Hopi dances, forcing them to invite the katsinas to perform clandestinely in this very spot out on the desert. But of course the Hopis present now were not equipped with cornmeal for feeding katsinas. They were armed with whatever weapons—mostly hunting rifles—they could muster. Nor had there been so great an association of armed Navajos in one place anywhere since their failed attempt to take Fort Defiance from the United States Cavalry almost eighty years earlier. And certainly there had never been in history or prehistory so large a group of both Hopis and Navajos in one place without hostilities breaking out among them.

Moving among them, clumps of men and women barely visible in the shadows cast by starlight and rock, and with conversation kept to a low murmur, Ben Cameron tried to clear his mind of all but military strategy. In a place where the walls separated enough to form a fairly wide oval of bare sandy ground, he spotted the big Navajo, Slink, standing next to the shorter but almost as broad Hopi, Danny Koots, both men seen only in silhouette, each resting a bad leg. How odd, Cameron thought, that the two tribal war leaders should both be a bit crippled. Cameron stopped a few yards off and heard the Hopi, Koots, say, "They tell me it was you that found that airstrip for the krauts." Cameron saw the shorter man pointing southward with his lips. "Pretty good. Pretty good," Koots said. "That white caliche's real firm until it rains, huh?"

"Yeah," Slink said.

"So how'd you know it'd rain there?"

Slink laughed quietly. "I didn't. Left that up to you Hopis. That's what you're supposed to be good at. You and them katsinas."

"Hey," Koots said. "Here's Cap'n Cameron, the intelligence man. You gonna talk to us about how to kill these Germans?"

"Well," Cameron said, "I've got some things, some information, that may help. We know something about the commanding officer, Schalberg. And how he probably thinks. And what he'll probably do."

"He think different than other white men?" Koots asked.

"A little."

"Well, let's have a listen, then."

A few minutes later the wide place in the innards of Katsina Bluffs was filled with men and women, all pressed together, and the voluble Danny Koots had explained who Cameron was, though by then everybody already knew and was prepared to listen to what the white soldier from FDR's army had to say before they made their plans. Some among them were, like Slink, returned veterans, mostly bearing old wounds from the war against the Japanese, and were accustomed to awarding officers their due respect. Others—the older ones in their thirties and forties—were new to warfare of any kind but for occasional shoving matches in bordertown bars. They all listened carefully while Cameron, having shed his large Navajo hat, stood bare-headed among them in the darkness.

"Yesterday," Cameron began, "I was in Washington, D.C., where the President lives. He sends his best personal wishes to all the Indian people here, Hopis and Navajos. He wants to thank you for sending so many of your men to join the armed services and fight the country's enemies in faraway places. Europe and the Pacific."

He cleared his throat in the silence.

"And now he hopes you will see fit to help him again. The President is very upset to hear that these Germans are here. The U.S. and its allies are taking the war to the Germans now. Allied soldiers are pushing the Germans back, and they hope to end the war in Europe before too many months from now. But these Germans here—it would make people here at home, in America, very upset, even scared, to know the Germans were right here in America.

"The President wants to get rid of them, to stop them right here on the reservation before . . . well, right away. Some of the President's advisers told him he should send in some troops, some war planes, from El Paso, Tucson, Kirtland Air Base over in Albuquerque."

There was a rustling of bodies, a murmur of voices.

"FDR," a voice said. "He's a good man. Our people have gone to fight for him. But we don't want no soldiers comin' here. Those advisers he got don't know nothin'."

"Them government peoples," another voice said. "Last time they come, they killed all our sheep. Call it 'livestock reduction.'"

Cameron waited while others spoke, each voice recalling other incidents when the presence of United States government agents in their midst or, much worse, United States troops had wrought havoc among the Indians. The Hopis dwelled on the time at the turn of the century when troops came to the villages to haul children off to boarding schools. The Navajos spoke darkly of the Long Walk, when the U.S. Army marched thousands of Navajos from their lands in the 1860s across New Mexico to a concentration camp called Bosque Redondo. As the voices droned on, Cameron marveled at the irony: the Indians were fiercely patriotic—especially in time of war—but had virtually nothing good to say about the government and in particular its army. Where did this patriotism come from? He couldn't imagine. Maybe they just missed being warriors. He was counting on that.

"Some others of the President's advisers," Cameron lied, "said they thought that the Navajos and Hopis might be able to take care of the Jerries. The Germans. Get rid of them. I said I thought you could do that. I told them I thought it would be a bad idea to send a lot of soldiers and tanks and planes in here. Everybody outside the reservation would hear about it, and there'd be a lot of panic. I tried to explain what a mess it would make here."

Again a murmuring broke out, and Cameron waited for it to subside before resuming his cock and bull version of presidential deliberations. "So the President decided. He told me to come here and ask you to get rid of the Germans. But he said he'd get soldiers ready, troops from El Paso and those places, get them ready to come in here after three days and fight the Germans if we haven't killed them or captured them."

More murmurs arose, and a voice said, "What's he want? Killed or captured?"

Cameron cleared his throat again. "Killed. That would be the best."

"And we got three days. From when?"

"From yesterday."

"So we got two days."

"Yes."

"Before the American soldiers come."

"Right," Cameron said, and went on to explain that the German officer, Heinrich Schalberg, had served in another desert under a wily German general named

Rommel, who commanded the German tank corps. Schalberg, he went on, probably had learned to think a lot like this general everybody called the Desert Fox.

At this, there was some long-winded conversation about the shrewdness of various animals found in this desert, to which Cameron listened intently, and when it died down, he resumed, explaining first some of the background of the German and British war in North Africa.

"This man Rommel's secret of success in the desert was like this. First, he would engage his enemy in open battle, all his tanks out there arrayed against theirs, firing away from a distance. This way he hoped to weaken the enemy some, maybe get some of them to bunch up a little here and there along the line. Then suddenly, like lightning, some German tanks would break away from where they were and join another group. Suddenly there would be this concentrated bunch of German tanks, working together, and they'd encircle some of the enemy—on three sides or all the way around. By acting suddenly, real fast, he'd surround a bunch of British tanks and kill them. Then he could go on to another bunch."

There were murmurs of understanding as the Indians visualized this in their minds, and a few said: "Yeah, that's real good. Real good."

Someone asked, "How come he lost?"

Cameron laughed. "Good question. For a long time he didn't. Kept winning and winning. But then the British were able to get a lot more tanks, and outnumbered him. Finally, the British simply had too many tanks, too many guns. And also, he couldn't get enough fuel there at the end."

"Well, we don't have no tanks," a voice said. "All we got is horses."

"Right," Cameron said. "But we know—or think we know—the two main places he'll be going. Toward Farmington, and probably toward Leupp. Right, Slink?"

Slink explained about his imaginary hoarder at Leupp. There were a few quiet titters. "Sounds like a Navajo," one Hopi said.

"Probably he cuts it with water," another said.

"Maybe those Germans'll believe all that," Slink interrupted. "Maybe not. We'll just have to watch 'em."

"Right," Cameron said. "And we'll get to that. But we know something else—probably. We know how he's going to be thinking. Like Rommel. If we confront him, he'll want to spread us out first, then try some of those quick, encircling punches, and then kill us. Then encircle some more, kill them. So what we've got to do is think one step ahead of him, maybe two. Make him think we don't know what he's going to do, and be ready for these quick strikes. And there is something else we've got besides horses. We know the territory better than him."

"We got something else," a voice said. It was the Hopi, Danny Koots. "This man here, Lomakema, he says he's got some dynamite. Kept it from when they were doin' that work over near Wepo Wash. He says he got six sticks of dynamite, and the caps and fuses. All that stuff."

"That's swell," Cameron said. "Anybody got anything else like that?"

Silence.

"We can make a few secret weapons too," Cameron said. "Let me tell you about Molotov cocktails. Some people have been using them against the Germans in Europe . . ."

The council at Katsina Bluffs went on for several hours. In the course of it, groups of Indians left—at first, mostly women—heading in various directions, fanning out across the land. Two hours before the sun rose, the Indians were all hastening across the desert on horseback or on foot to take up positions among the arroyos and on the mesas of the reservation. Every one of them had a task, a mission, some more arduous and perilous than others, but none unimportant. A small group remained at

Katsina Bluffs, which, of course, is not only a prominent landform, but by its nature an excellent vantage point from which to watch a large portion of the lands west of the Hopi mesas.

It was a strange, even desperate strategy hatched that night at Katsina Bluffs. It pitted what at best could be thought of as cavalry and infantry *versus* tanks and light armor. More accurately, it pitted a few seasoned—but mostly disabled—veterans among a small host of amateurs, armed for the most part with hunting rifles or less, *versus* a smaller but highly trained, battlewise force armed with cannon, mortars, and machine guns.

If sheer numbers were on the side of the Indians, the odds—as might be computed from any known military experience—certainly were not.

The almost total absence of Indians in the vicinity of Oraibi was noticed not so much by their actual absence, but by the presence of something highly unusual, something quite alarming that the Germans saw when the sun was still below the eastern horizon but casting a thin glow in the sky: smoke. All around in the distance, from countless landforms, thin, wispy columns of smoke arose, vanishing into the cool morning air.

From the sheer numbers of separate fires burning out there, it was deduced that the Indians were gone—and up to something, presumably no good. And their total absence, but for a handful of old men and women and a few children, from Oraibi and the village above, was soon confirmed. Major General Schalberg immediately ordered three jeeps with three men in each to proceed with all haste to the nearest three fires—those burning from the mesa tops to the east. The jeep in the command of Corporal Friedrich Behrmann was the first to return.

"Only a fire up there, sir. No Indians. But they were there."

"Of course they were there, you moron. Someone started the fire."

"Yes sir," Behrmann said, crestfallen. "There were tracks of people up there, all around. But there wasn't anyone in sight. When we got up there, we saw another fire start, way off the east. I decided not to pursue them."

"Very good, Corporal. Dismissed."

Schalberg sat down to think. There were how many?—dozens of fires burning on the horizon. All around. Everywhere. Meaning what? Were they taunting him? Challenging him? Challenging a German tank battalion? Impossible. Luring him on to some confrontation? But luring him which way? And what difference did this all make to his plans? To his orders?

Yes, his orders. God, how long since he had received his orders.

Operation Shatterhand.

Hitler had loved that, the reference to those old books. So, at least, Schalberg had been told. The great man had hugged himself and laughed at the appropriateness of the code name.

And his orders had come down, passed directly from the Fuhrer to the trusted, owl-faced Heinrich Himmler, chief of the SS, to Schalberg:

With—or without—the help of the Indian population, to create the maximum amount of havoc, embarrass, and otherwise occupy the attention of the United States, while the Wehrmacht prepared the defenses of northern Europe and fought off whatever forces were amassing in Great Britain with a view to the defeat of the fatherland.

An attempt to buy time?

Utter madness?

Perhaps one of several such missions that, unbeknownst to Schalberg, were going forward simultaneously—an outburst of diversions?

Or a lone mission?

A lone suicide mission?

It made no difference, then, did it? Operation Shatter-hand was, in fact, born of the original Schalberg Plan, and he was its very father and now its commanding officer, seeing to its execution. An exalted role. Exalted perhaps in all of modern military history. He would carry it out. His orders came direct from the Fuhrer himself, the very fountainhead of Germany's greatness, the personification of the Third Reich.

No group of ragtag Indians with their stupid fires could stand in the way of Schalberg's mission, Schalberg's very brainchild. He summoned to his headquarters the officers and noncommissioned officers in his command. He explained that the mission—the two prongs of the mission—would go forward as now planned, moving out at 0900 hours.

Schalberg dwelt momentarily on the original scheme—a three-pronged mission, one force to proceed to the city of Flagstaff, as now. The main force, it had originally been planned, was to drive to the east. From it a highly mobile force, mostly of jeeps and light armor, was to reach the town of Holbrook in the early evening after dark and create a few hours of havoc before racing for Gallup, there to do the same. Meanwhile, the main tank force was to drive across the reservation northeastward and blow up the oil fields in Farmington, and continue to create as much chaos as it could in that populated area as long as it could. Now, of course, with the wreck of the Condor, the mission was necessarily truncated. But, Schalberg was determined, it would still create plenty of havoc right in the very midst of the Americans.

He explained to his men that the Indians, ranged around the horizon, might well try to encircle them in a pathetic attempt to divert them, or slow them down. They should, in such a case, be careful of their flanks and rear and, using the minimum amount of ammunition, kill any savages who came within range of their weapons. No doubt, he said, they would scatter in panic at the first out-

burst of German fire. Contrary to the hopes the Third
Reich had held for these people, Schalberg said, the Indians were after all a degraded lot—contemptible and
unworthy. Operation Shatterhand, he announced, would
now proceed—and all the better for it without the
Indians.

By the time the morning sun was halfway up the eastern sky, the force dubbed Shatterhand West rolled in the
direction of the old volcano, San Francisco Peaks,
against which the city of Flagstaff nestles a hundred
miles southwest of the Hopi villages. The volcano, now
eroded into several separate mountain peaks ringed
around the remains of a fir-covered crater, was blue on
the horizon and capped with the last of the year's snow.
For anyone inching across the Painted Desert toward it, it
seems to recede, rather than draw near. It is an illusion,
of course, and one to which travelers in the West have always had to accustom themselves, rather than give up
hope. But to newcomers it can be a mystifying if not irritating experience, sometimes giving people a diminished
faith in what their senses tell them.

There was little, in fact, about the landscape that did
not irritate Colonel Franz Liepzichte, even now after the
three and a half days he had dwelt in it. The vast and
empty distances made this son of a Hanover fisherman
uneasy: there was nothing oceanic about them, nothing
of the calm, flat certainty of the sea and its blue horizon.
Here the horizon was jagged and bleak, interrupted by
ominous lumps and spikes lurking under an unrelievedly
blue sky, the air so dry that his hands were cracked and
sore, and his lungs under assault.

Liepzichte rode in a jeep at the head of his armored
column, clattering and lurching along the rutted wagon
tracks headed southwest. The nervous anticipation with
which he confronted the task ahead of him and his men
was made all the more electric and unsettling by his dis-

taste for the physical world around him. Behind him three more jeeps, two half-tracks, and five tanks thundered along below an immense dust cloud that rose up and strung out behind them, a sunlit pennant that pinpointed his position for all of the damned Indians he knew were watching him from every godforsaken mesa top on the horizon.

To the right of the armored column and about a half mile away were clumps of trees eking out a living in the dry bed of Oraibi Wash. Beyond that loomed the red sandstone walls of what Liepzichte took to be another mesa but which in fact was Katsina Bluffs, from which his progress was carefully observed by two groups of Indian women who also tended the signal fires burning atop the bluffs, one at each end, sending a thin column of smoke into the blue air.

Ahead of Liepzichte stretched mile after mile of unbroken, featureless scrubland, through which progress could be measured only by the increasing thinness of the scrubby vegetation on the reddish soil, and the shift in color of the soil from dull brick-red to deeper red, to lighter red, to stripes of near white, brown, mauve, near blue—the odd face of the Painted Desert. From time to time a pair of ruts veered off to one side or the other, leading across the wasteland and out of sight, or to a desolate and distant lone building and fenced corral—an Indian camp. Peering this way and that way in disgust at the alien world through which he and his force made their way at a steady fifteen miles an hour, neither Liepzichte nor any of the men he had singled out to keep an eye out for Indians noticed the occasional rhythmic flashes of sunbeams cast by handheld mirrors on Katsina Bluffs, alerting another group of women on the edge of a low mesa some twenty miles off that the German column was headed straight for its first challenge, one that would take place on the sandy banks of Oraibi Wash not far from the settlement of Leupp.

\* \* \*

At about the same time, far to the east of where Liepzichte and his brave armored column proceeded across the desert toward Leupp and its ultimate destination, Flagstaff, Yellow Tooth Yazzie and a group of four other Navajos dismounted at the base of a yellow sandstone cliff along the wagon track out of Keams Canyon where it begins to descend toward Jeddito Wash. Each of the Indians, upon dismounting, opened up their saddlebags and those on two packhorses on leads and inspected the contents to see that none of the empty bottles they carried had broken. It was an odd array of bottles, many shapes and sizes, most of which had been filled and refilled many times with moonshine over the years, but which included a handful with the familiar shape and light green glass of Coca-Cola.

Yellow Tooth's strangely equipped detail was some four miles to the east and south of Keams Canyon. Back there, among the orderly stone buildings of the Indian Agency, a small group of Germans and their armor awaited the main detail from Oraibi under the command of Major General Schalberg.

Here on the high ground above Jeddito Wash, Yellow Tooth and the other four Navajos had a view of the desert stretching many miles ahead, and soon enough their particular quarry appeared, a thin column of dust on the horizon ahead of them and coming their way. They watched it in silence as it crept across the land, resolving itself, as they expected, into a fuel truck, the long round tank painted white to reflect away the sun's heat. When it was halfway between the far rise and the wash below, the Navajos mounted their horses and began to make their way down to the crossing, a wide place in the wash where the banks were especially low—only a matter of two or three feet.

Appearing to be merely a group of Navajos on some innocent mission like a hunt, the five horsemen sat casually on their mounts on the near side of Jeddito Wash, watching the big fuel truck as it paused on the far side. The driver opened his door, climbed down into the sand, and waved.

"Ya-ta-hey!" he said.

The Navajos nodded a greeting.

"Ya-ta-hey," Yellow Tooth said. He recognized the *billeganna* driver, a man named Clyde who worked for the Indian Agency and showed up in Keams Canyon every now and then, driving one or another supply truck. Clyde was a short, round man with, Yellow Tooth knew, a balding head under his straw cowboy hat. The story on Clyde, which most of the Navajos who lived in the vicinity knew, was that if you got him a little drunk, he would bet on anything. It was said that when he was still a miner of some kind over near Gallup before the war, he had bet and lost two thousand dollars in one afternoon of horse racing the Navajos had held at Steamboat. That had been Clyde's entire life savings, and hearing about it, his wife had kicked him out in the street. In hopes of getting back into her good graces, he'd taken a steady job with the Indian Service as a driver. That had been five years ago, and it hadn't worked. It was said his wife had taken their kid, a girl, and gone to live someplace up in Colorado.

"Hey," Clyde said affably. "You fellows wanta wait while I cross the wash? If I get stuck I'll give you five dollars to help me out."

Yellow Tooth grinned widely and nodded.

Clyde climbed back in the truck and started the engine. He backed up twenty feet and began a rapid approach, descending the shallow bank with a lurch, engine roaring, gaining speed for the run across the wash. When he looked up, two of the mounted Navajos were in front of him, signaling him to stop. He plunged on, but the horsemen didn't move. Swearing, he hit the brakes, shut off the engine, and stormed out of the cab. Now all five of the Navajos were ringed around the front of his truck, and he said, "What is this? You sons of bitches know if I stop in this goddamned wash—"

He stopped, mouth agape, as each of the five Navajos pulled a rifle from his scabbard and pointed it at him.

"Hey, what the . . . ?" Clyde said.

"We need some of your gas," Yellow Tooth said calmly, smiling his wide grin, which revealed his four front teeth. "Gonna make our cocktails." The Navajos smiled.

"Cocktails? What're you talking about. Look here—"

Yellow Tooth motioned to his rear. "Go on up on there."

"Well, shit!" Clyde said, his voice nearly an octave higher than normal. He scrambled up the bank and turned.

Two of the Indians had their rifles leveled at him. "Keep goin'," Yellow Tooth said. "Go on."

"Well, shit," Clyde said again, and set out at a wad-dling walk up the rise along the wagon track. Nothing like this had ever happened. A holdup, a robbery. The In-dians stealing a truckful of gas? He swore to himself, an-gry but aware of his helplessness, and kept walking, turning every now and then to grab a look at the thieves busying themselves around the truck, now all dis-mounted from their horses. About two hundred yards away, sweating profusely in the midday sun that poured down on him, he turned and stopped to watch. One of the Navajos looked up at him from the wash and sighted his rifle at him. Clyde turned and bustled upward again, panting and swearing to himself.

From the top of the rise he looked back at the Navajos, now miniature in the distance. They were stuffing their saddlebags. It didn't make any sense. Stuffing them with what? Frigging savages. Now they were mounting up, riding east. They were leaving his truck in the wash. He would go back after they were out of sight, over that rise, and get it. He watched them ride up the far bank of the wash, five abreast, and proceed east up the track. Then one of them stopped—the guy with the bad teeth—while the others continued. The one with the bad teeth turned his horse. He was lighting something. He threw something back toward the truck and spun around and took off at a gallop after the others.

Next, Clyde saw an orange flash, a sudden sheet of orange flame spreading out under his truck, lifting it up and then dropping it, and after that a tremendous outburst of flame—red, orange—and the roar of the explosion reached him, deafening him, just as the hot shock wave struck him, pushing him back and nearly off his feet. His truck! His truck! The big white tank, the whole back of the truck, was no more. The cab, the place where he sat in his truck, and where he had the Kodak of his little girl, was a blackened shell in a writhing, seething, rising column of flame and black, greasy smoke, billowing up, carrying shreds of metal up . . . They'd blown up his truck! Blown it up! Blown it sky high, those fucking Indians. His truck. And his Kodak of his kid, little Jessica in her pinafore and shiny black shoes. His angel. Jesus Christ!

The sun was nearly overhead, bleaching all color from the low rolling scrubland, when the lead vehicle of the force called Shatterhand West—a half-track with Franz Liepzichte standing Rommel-like in the front—came into sight of the banks of Oraibi Wash. Liepzichte saw low ragged clumps of trees that marked the wash, saw that they curved toward the south. Off in the distance in several directions, wisps of smoke drifted up into the sky—the damned Indians, watching.

Liepzichte signaled the armored column to a halt while he surveyed the ground before him and compared it to the poor map he had, even more barren of features than the land before him. He reckoned he was about ten miles from the place called Leupp, where Schalberg had told him he might find some additional fuel. Distantly, beyond the wash, the land was broken here and there by long, low ledges of red rock. They looked low enough to be no impediment to the armored column, but high enough for a man to hide behind. Dust began to settle on him out of the motionless, windless, silent air—dust from their own plume. He was about to motion his driver and the column behind onward when a sound sang horribly in his ears and ceased.

A bullet! Now he heard the crack of the rifle, and ahead, from the edge of the wash, saw the tiny puff of smoke. Then another. He ducked, looked around. The only fire came from ahead. Indians with their popguns were in the wash ahead. He turned and barked an order to the men in the back of the half-track, and turned back to watch. He heard the thump and swoosh of the mortar behind him and watched as the sand on the wash erupted, saw the flame, heard the explosion. Listened for screams.

Nothing.

He signaled the column forward and followed the ruts of the wagon tracks toward the wash, pausing on its shallow bank. Flat sand lay ahead, white in the glare, beyond which was the shallow bank on the other side. Midway across, a hole about ten feet in diameter broke the flat sand, featureless but for the wagon ruts that crossed and crisscrossed in a crazy geometry. The Indians had evidently fled. He barked another order, and one of the men in the rear of the half-track vaulted out and walked down into the wash, pausing to probe at the sand with a rifle butt. Presently the soldier gestured, thumbs up, and Liepzichte waved the column forward.

A hundred yards away, among a small group of cottonwoods and willows, a Hopi turned his wrist, and sun glinted from a small fragment of mirror in his hand. Another hundred yards upstream, near the mouth of a narrower tributary wash, another mirror flashed. Catching this flash of sunlight, two Hopis standing at the base of a circular earthen dam a hundred yards up the small tributary set fire to the end of a yellow fuse that curled along the sandy bottom to the base of the ten-foot-high, smoothly curved wall of packed earth. Satisfied that the spark was leaping satisfactorily along the fuse, the two Hopis scampered up the dry banks and disappeared over the side.

Downstream from the tributary, Liepzichte's half-track made its way up the shallow bank of Oraibi Wash and pulled off to the side while the rest of his column followed him across the sandy bottom—another half-track, two jeeps, and two tanks. The other three tanks were making their way rapidly across the sand, with two jeeps still waiting on the far bank, when the sound of an explosion, a dense roar, was heard.

Upstream, over a slight rise, Liepzichte saw an eruption of sand rising like a cloud, white in the glare of the sun. Turning back to his column, he waved furiously for them to speed up. Whatever that was, he didn't want his column in the midst of crossing this infernal wash when whatever happened next . . . Then he heard the roar, a different sound altogether, a continuous low roar, and he saw a wall of water crash into the curve upstream, roiling, gathering upon itself, a wall of water as tall as a man boiling down the wash toward them, lowering as the banks widened but plummeting ahead, some tortured pieces of silver wood rising and thrashing in the current. Liepzichte watched helplessly as the wall of water crashed into the three tanks still in the wash, sending foam spraying high above them. He heard the tanks' engines roaring, saw one of the jeeps on the far bank, its wheels spinning, trying to back up as the water raced past it, tearing at the bank under its front wheels. He watched in speechless fascination as the jeep suddenly fell nose forward into the water and three men leapt out into the torrent, watched still as the three tanks appeared to sink lower into the water in the middle of the wash.

As suddenly as it had arrived, the flood passed, leaving a few rivulets in the sandy bottom, and wet sand glinting in the sunlight. In horror, Liepzichte saw that little more than the upper half of the three tanks were above the sand. They were half buried. The firm bottom of the wash had turned to quicksand in the sudden torrent. He had never heard of such a thing. His column—his armored force—was decimated. The crews were now climbing out, standing on the tanks' metal backs, peering at the sand below. It was as if they had suddenly been transported to an ocean, turning up marooned on three tiny islands. It made no sense at all. On the opposite side of the wash, the men in the jeep on the bank were yelling, but Liepzichte couldn't hear the words. The other jeep was nose down in the sand, its hood buried, and only one of its three occupants was in sight, a hundred yards down the wash, lying like a rag doll among some twisted silver branches.

Liepzichte waited for his body to resume breathing.

Two thousand miles away in an office in the basement of the White House in Washington, D.C., the President's military attaché was on the phone, his face red with anger.

"No, Mr. Hopkins ... No, we haven't heard from Cameron, not a word ... No sir, we don't know *exactly* what's going on out there. His parachute could have ... A lot can go wrong on a mission like that, as I told you ... Yes sir. The Army Air Corps is ... Yes sir. Tuesday at dawn ... Well, sir, they'll find them. They've been trained for this, they fly target practice over desertland every day ... Right. Their first real mission, but the squadron leaders have been in combat. I'm sure they're up to it. Yes sir ... I know the President is deeply concerned about this."

The brigadier looked furiously into the phone and hung it up. "Christ," he said to himself. "Civilians."

## Eleven

Thanks largely to the topographic peculiarities of the lands beyond Keams Canyon, the sound of the explosion that demolished the fuel truck in Jeddito Wash was not heard by the German force making its way in that direction. Instead the sound waves reverberated back and forth between the great rises on either side of Jeddito Wash in a chorus of derisive echoes. But the plume of black oily smoke rose high in the windless sky and was perceived by Major General Heinrich Schalberg as his column moved south and east. Clearly this was something altogether different from the infernal wisps of smoke from the strange and, as far as Schalberg could imagine, pointless fires the Indians had set at various points ahead and to the sides—and behind. What, then, was this huge fire?

When they crested the rise, it was all too apparent. The charred remains of a truck lay between the banks of Jeddito Wash, wreckage that would make their crossing all the more arduous, and wreckage that signaled another loss, another amputation of the hopes pinned on Operation Shatterhand. The fuel truck that Captain Muller and that woman had arranged to come early, the one they expected to rendezvous with: the goddamned Indians had blown it up.

Schalberg signaled Corporal Schwabe, driving the half-track at the head of the column, to stop. Behind them the rest of the column ground to a halt, none of it in a position to see over the rise and learn the cause of the oily plume of smoke. The two men in the lead half-track sat without speaking, watching the smoke curl and rise from the wreckage.

"Shit," Schwabe said eventually.

"It doesn't change our plans, Hans. We can still make Farmington."

"No sir, but it's going to make crossing that wash down there a problem." He took a half-empty pack of Lucky Strikes from his shirt pocket. "Smoke, sir?"

Schalberg laughed bitterly. "There's too much smoke already, Hans. What do you suppose those other fires are?"

The big round-shouldered corporal squinted in several directions, looking again at the thin wisps of smoke here and there. He tapped a cigarette out of the pack and lit it.

"My guess is the Indians are telling us how many Indians there are. Watching us. And my guess is they're lying."

"And they think we're going to fall for that?"

"I doubt it."

"Then why would they do it?" Schalberg asked.

"We don't know how many *are* out there, do we?" Schwabe said. "Do we, sir?"

Schalberg laughed again. "Nerve-wracking, isn't it?" he said. "Maybe Indians here, maybe Indians there. Maybe watching us, maybe not. But none to be seen."

"I don't think these people are stupid," Schwabe said.

"Who said they were?"

"You did, sir. Back there in Oraibi. If you don't mind me playing Sancho Panza again."

"Who the fuck is Sancho Panza, Hans?" Schalberg said. "Let's go. We have a long way to go."

Far to the west, Corporal Friedrich Behrmann had watched the floodwaters of Oraibi Wash surge past, watched the jeep ahead of him slowly topple over the bank, watched the men sucked under the torrent as it swept by. Now he saw the tanks hopelessly sunk in the sand in the wash, silvery with the water saturating it. He leapt out of his jeep, ordering the driver to shut up, and stood on the bank, waving uselessly at his commanding officer on the other side. He watched as the men on the opposite bank began to fan out, returning with branches and brush which they began throwing into the wash. There was nothing he could do from here, Behrmann reasoned, and he got back into the jeep, gesturing the driver to go downstream. Upstream, some of these damned savages were lurking, the ones who had been shooting, who had blown the dam or whatever it was. There had to be another crossing downstream. He looked around at the land to his left, noting the low ridges of red rock, high enough to hide a man. He held his Walther firmly and ordered the gunner in the rear to keep an eye peeled.

The jeep lurched over the desertland, and to their right the banks of the wash steepened. Behrmann felt the first pinpricks of anxiety. The jeep's gears strained, the engine complained, and Behrmann didn't hear the shot, but something, a soldier's sixth sense perhaps, made him turn in his seat in time to see the helmeted gunner lurch backward, his hand to his bleeding face. He saw another wound appear on the man's chest as he fell from the jeep.

Screaming, "Drive! *Drive!*" at the man at the wheel, Behrmann fired his sidearm three times to their left, where the shots had come from, and leapt into the rear of the jeep, taking command of the mounted machine gun. He spewed a burst of bullets over the land as the jeep hurtled forward, spumes of dust rising from its wheels.

Two hundreds yards farther, Berhmann directed the driver in a wide circle through the desert, and his eyes raked the teritory where there should have been at least one, and more probably two, Indian attackers, but he saw nothing. No one. In Berhmann's mind the wide circle should have brought them back to the edge of the wash a hundred yards below where the column had crossed and been hit by the flood, but when they reached the bank, nothing lay before them but a white sandy bottom five feet below and the desert lying beyond the opposite bank. Somehow in this wasteland, they had gotten lost.

He wasn't ready for this. Prowling the streets and alleys of Cologne and Berlin for prey had not prepared Behrmann, the accomplished street thug, for the illusory nature of this particular landscape. Not even his brief stint in the grim landscape of North Africa had taught him how to find his way in a place where ambiguous landforms—landmarks of a sort—simply disappeared. Skin prickling with the heat, drying sweat, and the soldier's most faithful and often useful companion—fear— the two men in the jeep headed south, looking for a place to cross the wash. In the distance, from three places on the horizon—on the east, north, and west—thin smudges of smoke rose into the air. And about two miles to their south on a low, gentle rise bleached of color by the sun overhead, a lone horseman appeared as if from nowhere and stood watching, as motionless as the enormous sky overhead.

In low gear, the jeep bucked slowly over a patch of rock that had emerged from the sandy red soil, then crawled down a low incline and up the other side. Ahead was the low, gentle rise on the horizon, but the Indian on the horse was gone.

Ten minutes later the jeep pulled up on the bank of a large, wider wash that was in fact the Little Colorado River, dry as a bone, for all its width and nomenclature, with long swirls of dead white salt marking its sides. From the low bank to the other side a hundred yards away and beyond, Behrmann could see open land sparsely dotted with colorless scrubby plants. To his left and his right, the low empty riverbed stretched away, flat and inert. From just beyond a slight rise on the other side of the riverbed, the black struts of an old windmill were etched against the sky, the circular windmill itself hanging off at an odd angle, like a man with a broken neck. The sight of the riverbed filled Behrmann with hope. All around, there was no sign of life. He ordered the driver to cross, and the jeep dipped down and crawled across the hard sand.

They labored over the far bank and up the incline—steeper than it had seemed from the other side—and came out on a high table of the same sparsely vegetated land of red dirt. Ahead, the broken windmill presided over the ruin of an old stone building, now merely three roofless walls, and the collapsed remains of what might have been a barn or horse shed of some kind, now little more than silver tatters of wood. Some two hundred yards beyond was a structure of some sort Behrmann could not figure out—thick timbers rising against the sky. They stopped to survey the ruin from afar, and Behrmann felt the touch of a breeze on his cheek. He spoke in low tones to the driver, and the jeep lurched forward, moving slowly in low gear toward the ruin, its machine gun trained on the near wall.

When the jeep had come within fifty yards of the ruin, it suddenly accelerated and skidded into a left turn, as Behrmann leapt from the back, running low and fast to the right. He pulled up in the dust and hurled a grenade, ducking back into his crouching run. What was left of the old stone walls burst outward in the explosion, and dust flew into the air, raining pebbles and larger rocks on the ground around. The jeep spun in a circle, raced back toward Behrmann and slowed while he vaulted into the back. He fired three bursts of machine-gun fire into the tattered old shed, and its boards shivered and sagged under the onslaught. Then there was silence except for the sound of the jeep's engine idling.

The indecipherable structure of timbers now had taken on the shape of a bridge, a trestle bridge, which made no sense to Behrmann whatsoever—a bridge in the middle of flat desertland—but as they crawled toward it, they saw the chasm it crossed, a steep gorge with sides of red earth—perhaps twenty feet deep—that extended like a new wound across the land.

Behrmann signaled the driver to halt, and eyed the timbers of the bridge. They looked sound. Whoever had lived in the ruin behind them had built this bridge, at least, to last. He couldn't imagine who might have lived here, or what they might have done with themselves. But the bridge did look sound. The planks across seemed intact, solid enough, though a few were visibly loose. Gingerly, with his sidearm drawn, he stepped onto the bridge and jumped in place. He took a few more steps and jumped again. Solid. He turned, motioned the jeep forward, and walked across. As he reached the last few planks, he heard a loud crack and spun around to see the bed of the bridge giving way beneath the jeep, its rear end sinking.

"Faster, faster!" he shouted, gesticulating. The jeep's rear wheels spun against the planks as each in turn cracked and fell, and Behrmann watched the driver's face turn white—his mouth a round black hole—as the vehicle dropped out of sight with an awful scream of tractionless spinning wheels and the crunch of breaking wood. Behrmann leapt backward off the planks, knelt and peered down into the crevasse. The jeep was on its back, twenty feet below, its wheels still turning slowly. It looked obscenely exposed, naked. The driver's arm protruded from under it, lying limp in the dark red earth.

"Shit!" Behrmann snarled, and stood up. He trotted away from the chasm, wanting some distance between it and himself when and if the jeep blew. All around him was silence. Not even the small breeze on his cheek made the slightest sound. Only his footsteps in the sand, and his breathing.

\* \* \*

Yellow Tooth Yazzie was delighted, and he repeated the story yet again, complete with gestures and sound effects that issued from his mouth. "Boom!" he said, his eyes sparkling and his four yellow teeth exposed to the gums. He held his hands palms down before him, and raised them slightly. "Like this," he said. Then, in a grand gesture, he opened his arms wide and again said, *"Boom!"* Reaching down nearly to the ground, he brought his hands up and out, his fingers spreading in a fine imitation of a billowing column of smoke and fire. There were flecks of spit in the corners of his mouth. "Real good," he said. "These cocktails work real good!"

Yellow Tooth Yazzie had never seen anything quite so beautiful, had never felt so great a surge of personal power, had never believed that he could bring about so great an event. He was the wrong age to have served in either of the United States government's world wars and thus prove himself a warrior deserving of respect. He was rumored by those in his tribe who knew him—or knew of him—to be a witch, thus earning instead of respect a kind of ostracism: an always courteous avoidance based on fear. But Yellow Tooth Yazzie had now found his métier.

"Who's this guy Mollytoff?" he asked, still grinning. "A real good man, huh?" He was standing beside his horse, which rested on three legs now, oblivious to the excitement around it and the lethal cargo in its saddlebags.

Some of the Navajos standing around for this second iteration of the great explosion glanced over at Cameron, who was standing next to his borrowed mount, a short-legged, compact paint horse that was doing its best to bite him. Cameron tugged sideways at the reins. "Chico! Knock it off," he said. "A Russian."

Yellow Tooth's smile faded, giving way to a look of confusion.

"Rushin'?" he said.

"A guy from Russia. People in some of the Russian

cities used these to fight tanks. They named 'em for this guy Molotov."

Yellow Tooth shrugged. It meant nothing to him. He smiled again, his teeth all the more horrible in the crooked orifice. "They got those other trucks," he said. "More gas."

"Two," Cameron said. "But it's not gonna be as easy the next time."

Yellow Tooth continued to grin. "Smoke?" he said, a hand out. Without thinking, Cameron plucked a cigarette pack from his shirt pocket, shook a cigarette halfway out and extended it to the Navajo. Yellow Tooth put the cigarette in the corner of his mouth and pulled a wooden match with a blue head from his pants.

He was about to scratch it across the seat of his pants when Cameron shouted, "Not here! Jesus!" and grabbed Yellow Tooth's wrist. The other Navajos smiled.

"Scared you," Yellow Tooth said, and stepped away to light his cigarette. "Boom," he said, drunk with power, and, with the graceful gesture of a ballet dancer, his hand described a billowing column of smoke in the air. "Real good boom."

Cameron and a group of Navajo horsemen were gathered in the shade cast by Balakai Mesa, several miles north of Steamboat, where Captain Wilhelm Muller had been brought down by an arrow in the back two days before. One of the Navajos present claimed responsibility for this first assault on the German war machine, and had explained how the German officer, his trousers around his knees and his pale-faced ass sticking out, had collapsed between the legs of the *billeganna* woman. The vision of this had brought forth some highly vocal merriment among the assembled warriors, and it too had to be retold several times, complete with gesture and ribald reenactment. To begin with, few things in the world are more amusing to an Indian than the notion of a white man caught with his pants at half mast. Add to this the well-placed arrow, the collapse of the dead man before his own arrow could see action, the ultimate in coitus interruptus indeed, and then the perplexed thrashing of the half-naked *billeganna* woman trying to escape from underneath . . . not even the dread with which Navajos contemplate a dead body had been enough to stem the mirth.

None among the Navajos had enjoyed the story more, it seemed, than the two women among the horsemen whom Cameron now turned to. In Navajo fashion he pointed with his lips and a lift of his chin toward the high point, a buttelike remnant atop the ocher rock of Balakai Mesa. The women nodded and set off on horseback and in single file up through the boulders at the mesa's base. Once there, they would start yet another of the fires it had been decided would haunt the Germans, dogging their every move through the day. And from there, the lookouts could see which way the German contingent chose to go in their march on Farmington, and signal the horsemen located here and there in the nooks and crannies of the empty land.

East from Keams Canyon and the large, brooding land mass called Black Mesa, of which Balakai Mesa was a finger, lay a vast area of upland desert, mesa, dry wash, and canyon that would have to be crossed. But this vast area was hemmed in on the east by a mountain range running north-south like an enormous exposed backbone. These were called the Chuska Mountains though they had other names the farther north one went—Lukachukai, Carrizo. The desertland gave way relatively abruptly in the foothills to a nearly alpine region of pine and, higher up, spruce forest where bears and elk made summertime livings and where a few remote summer herding camps were the only Navajo presence except for unseen Holy People. Beyond this verdant backbone, to the east, lay another vast stretch of arid lowlands and a north-south paved road, state road 666, that ran monotonously from Gallup straight to Farmington.

Cameron and the others had determined that the Germans, leaving Keams Canyon, would almost certainly follow the old wagon road east as far as Steamboat, rather than try to knife northward into the rugged hem of Black Mesa's skirt. At Steamboat they could take a southerly route across the highland desert, a place of rolling rises and low mesas, which would lead them toward Washington Pass through the Chuska Mountains. Or they could take a more northerly route that would take them across flatter desertland but with far more dry washes to ford, toward a more northerly and more difficult pass farther up where the mountains are called the Lukachukais.

Cameron had no idea how detailed the Germans' maps of the area were—how well those fishmongers had done their job eons ago, for instance—or what choice the Germans would make. But he was counting to some degree on the two German columns having radio contact, and counting on the German column to the west having had a bad experience crossing Oraibi Wash . . . perhaps this main force would seek to avoid too many more perilous wash crossings. In fact, Cameron wasn't counting on these things at all, just holding them up as possibilities. This was all a new kind of warfare for him, to be sure. If it succeeded, he thought, maybe the War College would ask him to give a lecture someday. "Desert Triumph: Super-Flexible Guerrilla Warfare and the Indian Horse."

He smiled, yanked at Chico's reins again as the paint horse made another sideways swipe at his hip, and said, "Okay. Let's ride." He swung his leg up over Chico's back, trying to remember the title of the movie where John Wayne had said just that. They'd shown it in Cairo, and everybody had cheered as the U.S. Cavalry rode down a bunch of wild Indians wearing the warbonnets of the plains, even though the battle took place in Monument Valley.

Or maybe it had been Randolph Scott.

\* \* \*

The midday sun was no use to Friedrich Behrmann as a navigational tool, and it beat down unmercifully on his neck and shoulders. He sweated profusely in the heat, and his sweat evaporated at such a rate in the superarid air as to give him occasional chills as well. He had no idea how far he had come since the jeep had toppled into the chasm—and with it, the supply of water, except for what he had in the canteen banging against his hip. Not much. It sloshed audibly in the metal container.

Ahead of him the silvery remains of a fence protruded, curved and canted on an angle, from the red, sandy dirt. It made no sense, this onetime fence in the middle of nowhere. Nothing in the landscape made much sense to Friedrich Behrmann. His tongue was growing, filling up the dry cavity of his mouth. He passed the fence, stopped and looked back at his tracks, a straight line there at least, leading down from the top of the rise, past the fence, and now headed . . . where? Straight ahead. Don't make any turns, Behrmann said to himself. You've got to come out somewhere that way. No turns. Another gentle rise of reddish dirt and the occasional scrabbly bush lay ahead, and, one foot after the other, he ascended it. From the top he looked ahead, seeing more of the same, except for a low ledge of red rock, almost like a stone wall that had become partly buried in the sand, over to his right. Along the base of this ledge he saw a dark stripe of shade. He veered off his straight path, drawn by the thought of the shade—a few moments to rest and get his parboiled neck out of the infernal sun.

Minutes later he stood before the ledge, here about four feet high, descending to the right and left into the sand. He looked with dismay at the narrowing band of shade it cast, now thinner than a man. But it was better than nothing, and he sat down, his back to the rock, and imagined a stripe of coolness on his shoulders. He reached down and unhitched the canteen, shaking it. A sip or two? For a time he debated with himself, then opened it and put the warm metal mouth to his.

He let the warm water lap against his oversized tongue, held it there, and pushed it back into the canteen. Glancing upward, the canteen still at his lips, he spotted a dark speck in the sky. He followed it as it made a wide circle high up where the sky seemed almost blue-black. He watched the speck—a bird of some sort, perhaps an eagle. He thought of the eagle insignia sewn on the front of his cap, the German eagle, resplendent, defiant, talons spread.

What if the speck was a vulture?

He thought again of his own eagle, and thought of taking off his cap to look at it, to be reassured by it out here in this wasteland. He put his hand up, grasped the visor, and looked up to see to his right the wide brim of a straw hat, a round copper-colored face, a grin—white teeth gleaming in a neat row . . . squinting Oriental eyes, looking at him from two feet away. He looked to his left. Another face.

They were peering at him, on the ledge above him. His hand dropped the canteen while the other groped for his pistol in its leather holster, the flap now caught, and he felt hot metal against his cheek.

"Bad idea," one of the faces said in a quiet voice. "Real bad idea." Another gun barrel prodded his other cheek. Another quiet voice said, "You put your hands out real wide." He did so. "Now," the second voice said, "you get on your knees. Like you're prayin'." He did this too, and was aware of two men vaulting off the ledge to stand behind him.

One of the Indians came around to stand before him. He was wearing a red bandanna of some sort rolled up and wrapped around his forehead. Black hair hung neatly down below the ears, cut off there. He had a dun-colored shirt, streaked with brick-red smudges. Behrmann now noticed that he had a thick stripe of reddish-brown running vertically down each cheek, as if he had smeared red clay on his face with a thumb. At the top of each reddish stripe was a horizontal stripe of black. The eyes glittered from behind the ledges of blackened cheekbones.

"You lost?" the Indian said. "Get lost out here?" He held a small rifle of some kind in his left hand, holding it like a revolver pointed at Berhmann's groin. "Stand up." Behrmann got to his feet and stood still, arms hanging limply at his sides.

From behind him the other Indian said, "Maybe he's a messenger. Got lost bringin' his message."

"Yeah, that must be it," said the man in front of him. The Indian reached around behind his back, and his hand reappeared holding a hunting knife.

"Maybe this messenger ate the message," he said. "Chewed it up."

"Wonder what it said," said the voice from behind.

"Oh, no," Behrmann erupted. "Oh, no."

"Oh," said the man with the knife. "Says he isn't a messenger. You believe him?"

"Believe a white man?" came the voice from behind, and Behrmann watched in horror as the knife plunged forward into his stomach. The pain was unspeakable, and he watched as some blood came out of the great gash in his pants, along with the blade, and followed by a snake—a wet pink snake? Oh God, no, not a snake. Him. His guts.

Behrmann sank on his knees, stared up at the face above with its glittering brown eyes.

"Please," he said, his tongue sticking to the roof of his mouth. "God, please!" He closed his eyes, pleading silently, and heard the welcome explosion in his ear . . .

∽ ∾

# Twelve

What might have become known as the Battle of
Canyon Diablo, had military history been permitted to
extend a curious tentacle into the old and little known
lands of the Hopi-Navajo reservation, took place in mid-
afternoon of Monday, May 15, 1944.

Canyon Diablo is one of many canyons that lace the
countryside east of Flagstaff, Arizona. The others have
less ominous names—Young, Padre, Mormon, Grape-
vine—suggesting that they never played much of a role,
and never formed much of an impediment to settlers in
the early history of the place. Canyon Diablo, on the
other hand, presented a problem to one of the first white
men to encounter it, a Lieutenant Amiel Whipple, who,
in the course of his survey of the thirty-fifth parallel in
1853, was surprised to come across so precipitous a
gorge in this area. Whipple guessed the canyon to be a
hundred feet deep, and noted a tiny trickle of water—
it was December—in its innards. In fact, where he
encountered it, the canyon is 250 feet deep, a steep
chasm etched into magnesian limestone 300 feet across
at the top.

Among its serpentine cliffs, golden eagles have nested
far longer than humans have known this country, and the
canyon has lain within the sacred eagle-gathering land of
the Hopi Spider clan for longer than anyone can remember. Thus there are small shrines in certain secret places
along Canyon Diablo where the Hopi priests make small

301

offerings—usually in the form of chunks of sky-blue turquoise—to thank the mother eagles in advance for making their young available to the Hopis so they, the eaglets, may act as messengers to the rain spirits. Here and there along the bottom of Canyon Diablo are other treasures as well for the sharp of eye, heavy pieces of shiny metal, both iron and nickel—the shards of a meteorite that plunged into the earth some ten miles to the east about 25,000 years ago, when there were no people on the continent, no religious practices, no hostilities.

In any event, Lieutenant Amiel Whipple must have been at the end of his rope, or nearly so, when he came upon the chasm of Canyon Diablo and gave it its name. It did cause him to turn and go north some twenty-five miles to cross it so that he could get on with his survey of the thirty-fifth parallel, but such a simple diversion—perhaps a day's ride for a heavily outfitted scientific expedition—hardly seems severe enough a disruption of federal business to attribute to so malevolent an agent as the devil himself. But Canyon Diablo it was named.

North, where Lieutenant Whipple finally could resume his eastward trajectory, the canyon is hardly worthy of the name canyon, much less devil, being nothing more than a wide, low area opening out onto the desert plain on which sits the bleak and remote settlement called Leupp. There the federal government in the 1920s had caused to be built an elementary school for both Hopi and Navajo children, dragging the children away from their families for an immersion in the English language and Christian civilization, and it consisted of a half-dozen one-story sandstone buildings—classrooms, dormitories, and the like—that clung to the windswept earth in lonely solitude. The only other buildings in Leupp were a half mile away from the school, an Indian Agency office or two and a garage for two agency vehicles. The buildings of Leupp were all the more lonely since being closed during the war, the teachers and agents having mostly chosen to escape this awful place by enlisting in the armed services. The garage had begun to sag, and its single gas pump now stood like a forlorn and long-forgotten sentinel, staring from a blank face at an empty neighborhood in the midst of a wasteland.

So it was essentially a ghost town of recent vintage that confronted what remained of the armored column dubbed Shatterhand West as it rolled along the rarely used ruts of an old wagon track and successfully crossed the Little Colorado River, now dry as dust and hard-packed under the relentless white sun. The armored column consisted now of one jeep, two half-tracks, and two tanks, and men numbering twenty-five, including the commanding officer, Franz Liepzichte. Two jeeps and three tanks had met their end in the quicksand of Oraibi Wash, along with three soldiers. The whereabouts of one jeep and three men including Corporal Friedrich Behrmann were unknown. They had last been seen moving southward along the far bank of the wash before turning rapidly and plunging back in the direction from which the column had originally come.

Now San Francisco Peaks loomed high on the western horizon, visibly clad in green, a commanding presence that somehow made the outpost of Leupp seem all the more forlorn. The settlement's depressing buildings looked abandoned to the eyes of Colonel Liepzichte, but he knew that they represented a hazard. He halted the column and ordered the half-track to circle them, then search them. Within a half hour the Germans established that the school and the other buildings of Leupp were empty of people of any kind, much less Indians, that the old gas pump had long since fallen into disuse, and that there was no sign of the old Navajo Hosteen Jasper or of his hoard of gasoline. Of course, Liepzichte reflected, the Indians had been lying about this.

Liepzichte was not the sort of soldier to question the orders passed down to him by a superior, but from the very beginning, he had not considered these Indians reliable, as Major General Schalberg had. Most of them—the Navajos—would not even look people in the eye as they talked, and their very mode of walking across the ground, while not expected to be military, of course, seemed somehow defiant in its very suppleness. That they would be relatively useless as allies on this mission had not surprised Liepzichte, but he hadn't expected them to become outright enemies, initiating hostilities, rearguard guerrilla attacks. And now, here he was, his armor reduced to less than half its original force, with sufficient fuel to move forward to Flagstaff, yes, but not much farther than that, under orders to shoot up the town and cause as great a disturbance as he could.

Earlier, from the bank of Oraibi Wash, he had radioed the eastward-moving column under Schalberg's command to report his losses, and Schalberg had instructed him to proceed nonetheless, to continue west to Flagstaff. He refused to question these orders, but the notion had been growing unbidden like a tumor in his mind that an attack on Flagstaff or any other place here in the United States was nothing more than the dream of madmen, and probably a suicidal nightmare for him. But . . . once committed to the greater organism of the military, he reflected, one's pride and purpose can only be served by carrying out one's orders. The armored column, now greatly diminished and with three more tank crews than tanks, would rest here until nightfall and attack Flagstaff under cover of dark.

Liepzichte noticed that the fires that had sent smoke into the air on every quarter during their march across the desert to this godforsaken outpost now could be seen only behind them—to the east, south, and north. How transparent, he thought, are the minds of these savages, thinking they can lull a German soldier into thinking the path is clear to the west. Certainly, there would be another confrontation, Liepzichte knew, but this time on dry ground.

Liepzichte's assessment would prove in part accurate. The confrontation did come on dry ground. The vigilant driver of the half-track was first to spot the presence of the Indians—or at least one Indian. He was standing about three hundred yards away to the west, visible from the waist up, apparently emerging from the ground itself. The driver blinked, stared, and signaled his commander. When Liepzichte looked in the same direction, there were three Indians, standing partly exposed, immobile, watching them. They were arrayed ten yards apart. Then some distance to their right, others appeared—and to their left. Along a rise bare of all but bunches of grass sparsely scattered on the ground, yet other Indians appeared. In a matter of seconds some forty Indians stood arrayed to the west, equidistant from one another, a long thin line against the backdrop of the looming mountain far off beyond them. They were all armed with rifles, which they held at their version of parade rest, and they stood staring, an eerie and silent presence. A bit crazily, Liepzichte's mind filled with the image of seagulls all perched equidistant from one another on the peak of a roof—his father's roof on the shore of the North Sea. As a boy, Liepzichte had enjoyed tossing rocks at the gulls, seeing them scatter in nervous and raucous irritation.

Quietly, his eye still moving back and forth along the row of Indians, Liepzichte gave an order to the gunner behind him and heard the familiar thump and whoosh of a mortar round. He waited, seeing the plume of reddish dust rise before he heard the explosion, stunning violence in the silence and inertness. As the dust settled onto the ground, he saw that nothing had changed. No Indian had moved, no breach made in their foolish, defenseless thin line.

Liepzichte ordered his column to move. Engines

rumbled into life, emitting exhaust like great dragons, and with the two tanks in the lead, began to rumble west toward the center of the Indian line. After they had proceeded a hundred yards, there was still no motion whatsoever among the Indians, but Liepzichte could now see that they all wore red bandannas around their foreheads and their faces were streaked with red.

War paint, for God's sake.

He gestured the column onward and watched as the Indians began a slow retreat, the entire line of them moving backward a step at a time in some bizarre choreography. As the tanks closed more closely, the center of the line began shifting perceptibly to the left as the Indians retreated more hastily, some of them turning to run. Some paused in their retreat to fire, inane gestures, Liepzichte thought scornfully. In a few seconds the entire line had bunched together more closely and was in full retreat, the Indians loping off to the left.

Like clockwork, the tanks spread out, gaining speed, racing toward the flanks of the retreating Indians, with the two half-tracks and the single jeep forming the middle of the arc of armor, a widening claw of steel that would soon snap shut. The Indians, now in a totally disorganized rout, ran farther to the left, stumbling over one another in their panic, heading for some lower ground, and the tanks pressed onward, boiling over the dusty ground at twenty miles an hour, closing on the ragtag band.

To the sides of the pincer the land was now rising slightly, and the Indians were in full flight ahead. The tanks gained on the mob but suddenly began to lose ground. Liepzichte shrieked for more speed and gesticulated. The pincer pressed onward, the tanks now bucking over more rocky ground. Liepzichte called to his gunner behind, and the machine gun clattered. He saw two Indians fall, the rest leaping and racing ahead between the two bluffs rising on either side. Ahead of the Indians the bluff on the left seemed to fall away, and the mob raced on, veering away to follow it, the armor in increasingly close pursuit.

Clutching the door as the half-track lurched over the rocky soil, Liepzichte watched the tank on the left, then the one to the right curve between the two bluffs, closing slightly on the stream of Indians, soon to squeeze . . .

But the walls of the two bluffs had now steepened. It was the walls that were squeezing—both the retreat of the Indians and the onslaught of the German armor. The leftward curve of the open ground continued, and the Indians scrambled on, now in their grasp. Liepzichte called for more fire and the machine gun clattered overhead. He saw the cannons mounted on the tanks blasting, saw smoke and rock erupt from canyon walls, and the curve ahead tightened yet more, the tank on the left disappearing now around it.

When Liepzichte's half-track came around the curve, he saw the right-hand tank slowing. Before it rose a high wall of yellowish rock. To his left, the other tank had already slowed among some ragged rock that lay at the base of yet another steep wall. The bluffs through which they had charged had now become the steep walls of a canyon which turned sharply to the left at nearly a right angle, and into this dark gorge the Indians were making their way, evidently near exhaustion.

Liepzichte saw one of them rise up and shake like a rag doll caught in the wind, then fall to the earth. He waved the column forward, and the pincer again gained ground on its prey, closer, closer . . . and then, like a school of fish exploding in panic in the silvery light, the mob of escaping Indians suddenly broke to pieces, scattering in all directions, some even turning to run at the half-track, *past* it! The machine gun behind Liepzichte clattered, and he heard the accompanying fire from the other half-track and the jeep, saw the ground around him erupt into plumes of dust and smoke. The tanks ground to a halt, and the canyon was alive with darting Indians, disappearing Indians . . . The canyon! Liepzichte spun, firing at the back of an Indian who scampered around a boulder and disappeared. Then he saw the rocks begin to move, boulders and slabs of rock separating from the walls above, tumbling down behind the column, and he watched in horror as they crashed down behind them, sliding into the canyon floor amid a rising cloud of yellowish dust that filled the air. He screamed the order for the column to turn around, to retreat amid the cascading rocks and thickening dust, blocking retreat, and saw his driver slump over toward him, a ragged place on the top of his skull. Bone splinters cut Liepzichte's face like shrapnel. He reached for the door handle, wrenched it open, and before he could leap from the half-track onto the rocky ground beneath him, he was briefly aware of an unbearable pain in his neck, and, with a profound sadness, he saw the boulder on the ground rise up to meet him in the enveloping black.

Danny Koots peered down into Canyon Diablo, looking for any sign of life among the smoke and dust. It had been maybe a half hour since any German returned the fire from the canyon rim. What was it the white men said? Like shooting fish in a barrel. Danny felt a little sick. He'd felt a little sick even before it was over—once it was clear that the Germans below didn't have a chance. The salty tang of vengeance had then given way to a sour feeling: an ugly job to be finished.

While something of a loner, a drifter, maybe even a bit of an outcast from his tribal ways, Danny was still enough of a Hopi to be haunted by the analogues of the Hopi past. He was reminded, inevitably, of Awatobi, now a ruin off to the east near Jeddito Wash. The Hopis there had welcomed the priest back, and the others waited until one night when all the worshipers were down in the kiva, and swept down on the village and killed all the Awatobi men. No one ever bragged about it. Probably, Danny Koots thought, that was partly because it had been something like shooting fish in a barrel. The salt of vengeance wears off long before the job is done.

Danny turned to the Hopi nearest him on the rim of Canyon Diablo, a man from the Tobacco clan. Dust and soot now covered the red streaks on the man's cheeks.

"I guess that's it, huh," Danny said.

"I guess so," the Tobacco clan man said.

"We got to go down there, bury them."

"The Germans too."

"Yeah," Danny said. "Them too." He heard a distant cry. "Hey, hear that? There it is." He pointed down the canyon with his lips. A dark brown eagle swooped below the canyon rim, headed their way. It suddenly pulled up with its talons out and landed on a ledge a couple of hundred yards distant, on the opposite wall. Below the ledge, the rocks were stained white with droppings. In a few weeks some old men would come back here to Canyon Diablo to collect the young eagle that was in the nest on that ledge. The eaglet would grow to adulthood in a Hopi village, and then, later in the summer, its spirit would soar home to tell the deities known as the Chiefs of the Four Corners if the Hopis had been doing things right. If so, the rains would come.

Danny Koots smiled and said to himself, *That eagle's gonna have one hell of a tale to tell.*

"Well," he said to the Tobacco clan man, "we better get on down there." He stepped back from the canyon rim and began to limp on his bad leg toward the trailhead that led down to the bottom. "I wonder," he said, "how them Navajos are doin' with the Germans that went the other way."

≈ ≈

# Thirteen

Slink had tried to talk him out of it, but it was too good to be true.

Yellow Tooth Yazzie had used a graphic Navajo term more often applied to livestock than to people to describe the sight they had come upon. They had watched the main German column under the command of Major General Schalberg rumble eastward across the land below them, a quarter mile away, making its way between two low mesas to where more open desert scrubland began, when it had paused. Backtracking through the rocks, the Navajos—in all ten of them—reached a vantage point from which they could see the rear of the German column—two tanks and the two fuel trucks.

Each truck was closely linked to a tank by a black hose, and Slink had smiled when Yellow Tooth suggested they were mating. The four vehicles sat motionless, the tanks like patient toads, their evil-looking proboscises pointing east and slightly skyward, as if in a kind of ecstasy as the trucks sat beside them and rearward, servicing them. Each coupling was presided over by a lone, armed soldier, each of whom—from where the Navajos some two hundred yards away watched—could be seen scanning the surrounding rocks nervously. The rest of the column, now bunched relatively closely together, lay about a quarter of a mile ahead, as if providing the two couples some privacy for this intimate act, though one of the tanks had wheeled around and sat, engine idling, its cannon facing back toward the refueling.

Yellow Tooth explained what he had in mind and Slink shook his head. There was no way, he said, they could get close enough before the soldiers saw them and alerted the rest. There was no way to get down there and back. The tank up ahead, with its cannon pointed back at the four vehicles, would blow them away if the others below didn't. But Yellow Tooth was in a state of excitement, a state nearing euphoria. His jet-black pupils were huge in his brown eyes, and while Slink explained why they would have to wait for a more opportune moment, Yellow Tooth swayed in his saddle.

Suddenly, like an arrow, he was plummeting down the slope, elbows flying, headed straight for the two trucks linked to their mates. He was well down the slope, flying over the loose rock, when the soldiers looked up and saw him skid to a stop, his horse's hindquarters nearly on the ground, a cloud of dust enveloping him. From where he watched, Slink could see the flame—saw Yellow Tooth apply it to the two rags, saw them burst into flame, saw Yellow Tooth wheel on his horse and charge down the slope, trailing smoke from each outstretched hand, clinging with his legs to the horse underneath him.

Slink saw the soldiers train their rifles at the oncoming horseman galloping wildly at them, veering, nearly crashing into a large boulder, leaping over another, the flames orange in his hands. He saw the smoke from the carbines as the soldiers fired, saw Yellow Tooth come to another sliding halt and heave his flaming missiles, one after the other, at the trucks. He saw Yellow Tooth's horse jerk its head up and career sideways, saw Yellow Tooth seeming to leap out from under it, only to crumple and fall to the ground, just as two huge orange flames erupted, one after the other, enveloping the trucks and with them the two soldiers, and then the two tanks in two separate sheets of flame which joined, mated, into one seething, roiling column that seemed to be screaming as it rose into the sky in a spreading cloud of black smoke.

Slink looked down the rocky slope and saw Yellow Tooth's horse struggling to its feet. Yellow Tooth lay amid the rocks, his legs at awkward angles. The horse finally scrambled to its feet and took a tentative step, only to lurch forward, its right shoulder down nearly to the ground. Again it recovered its footing, again fell forward, and again regained its footing. It stood on three legs, skin quivering on its body, its head jerking sideways while the melee of flames roared beyond it.

Slink got the horse's rolling eye in his sights and squeezed the trigger. He watched the horse stop, as if momentarily distracted, and then fall to the ground ten feet from the body of Yellow Tooth Yazzie. Muttering something he had heard his mother say when he was a little boy, something she'd said over and over again one day when there was terrible trouble—trouble he couldn't understand at the time, being so small—Slink retreated behind some rocks and made his way back to the others. He pointed east with his lips, and the nine horsemen set off at an easy lope across the mesa top.

They had only another ten miles to go before joining up with Cameron and the others, waiting now on the far side of a gentle open place in the land that Navajos call Beautiful Valley—a place the Germans would be crossing on their way to Washington Pass in the Chuska Mountains.

In the high desert country of northeastern Arizona, the late afternoon sun in late spring takes on a special ferocity even as the dry air is showing signs of cooling down. Its light, now beginning its shift into the red end of the spectrum, seems to burn more deeply, as if the sun, knowing it will soon be forced to go to bed against its will, is gearing up for a tantrum. It burned now on the back of Major General Heinrich Schalberg's neck, needles of painful heat that probed mercilessly at the site of his disgusting visitation, making him wonder if Schwabe's surgery had left some vestige, some other creature, burrowing there. Schalberg shuddered at the thought but resolutely put it aside, as he had tried with occasional success to put aside the cascade of troubles that had plagued his column since it rolled out of Keams Canyon that morning bristling with determination.

First the fuel truck from Gallup—up in smoke. Then his own fuel trucks—and two tanks and two tank crews, also up in smoke. Eight men. And only one casualty on the other side—the crazed Indian plummeting down the hill with his Molotov cocktails.

Yes, the other side. The enemy. He had to reckon with that—knew since dawn he'd have to reckon with that.

Radio contact with Liepzichte and the column proceeding to Flagstaff had ended at 1300 hours. Silence. God knew what had happened there.

Schalberg tried again to put such thoughts out of his mind. Ahead of him the land stretched down and out, a wide-open valley that was almost inviting after the rough transit so far through bizarre mesas and lonely rocky landforms. Two miles out into this shallow valley where the land flattened out, he could see a single house, what he knew to be a Navajo camp. It looked abandoned. He could see no sheep in its corral. Way off from the camp, perhaps a quarter of a mile, a lonely windmill stood, motionless now. Where he stood, there was the slightest breeze playing over his face, but down there, below, it was insufficient to stir the windmill.

The armored vehicles behind him cast long shadows out over the land. Beyond the low valley, the blue-green backbone of the mountains he would cross rose up distantly. Out there, in that open land, there was little cover to speak of, nothing to hide the movement of the column, but more important, nothing much to hide the Indians who, he knew, were watching.

Schalberg stood beside the half-track, stretching his legs, his back, and feeling the sun burning his neck. He looked back at his column, now much reduced from the brave squadron that had set forth from Keams Canyon, the main force of Operation Shatterhand. He snorted a bit ruefully now at the irony. Operation Shatterhand. The code name based on a romantic folly, a folly he had done nothing to dispel back in the High Command's basement office how many years ago—seven? eight?—when a young major he hardly remembered now had seen a partnership between the valiant and victorious Third Reich and the descendants of an imaginary figment named Winnetou.

So here was all that was left of Operation Shatterhand, perched now on the edge of a valley that would soon be shrouded in shadow as the desert sun moved lower in the sky in this desolate place. Ten tanks and one half-track, all American. Two tanks lost to fire. Three more drained of their remaining fuel so that the rest could proceed. A mission cannibalizing itself, eating itself, so that it could live. A depressing thought.

Thousands of miles from here the sun had already gone down. It was night in Germany, nearly midnight. He had heard nothing of Germany, nothing of the Third Reich, for days now. Five days was it, six? Since the grand sunlit moment when the 108th Panzer Battalion had rolled across Route 66 into the reservation lands, the unknown.

The events of the early days of the invasion flitted through his mind, sunlit days of gold and promise, yes? In these alien lands among these odd people in this dreamlike slow-motion world. Never mind. He had been then—as he was now—alone, hadn't he? He was then— as now—for all practical purposes *the* Third Reich. Here, embodied in himself, a soldier, by God, was the Third Reich. The vision of a woman's face slipped into his mind, a tearstained face, tears of pride. Smiling through tears of pride at what her blood, her very loins, had brought into the world to give luster to . . . to glorify . . .

Schalberg closed his eyes. The breeze fluttered on his face. He opened his eyes, looked over at Corporal Schwabe sitting in the driver's seat of the half-track, unconcernedly blowing a column of blue smoke out in front of him, squinting at it from his little eyes.

"Schwabe."

"Sir."

"Do your people have anything to say at times like these?"

"You mean pig farmers, sir?"

Schalberg shrugged.

"No," Schwabe said. "When there's shit to be shoveled, they just shovel it." He flipped his cigarette over the windshield, and Schalberg watched it arc through the air and land in a gray-green shrub.

"So," Schalberg said. He climbed into the half-track and sat with his arms folded across his chest. "Well, Schwabe?" he said, and pointed at the mountains.

Ben Cameron sat comfortably on his horse, the paint called Chico, watching another group of Navajos coming toward the ledge on the western edge of Beautiful Valley. Lit bronze in the late afternoon sunlight, they looked for all the world like a band of Mongols, and he played with the idea for a moment, wondering how people might have felt in some earlier century in some far eastern European outpost, watching band after band of expressionless Mongol warriors mounted on their wiry horses assembling on the horizon. Probably, Cameron thought, they felt lousy.

Of course, the assembling Mongol horde probably numbered in the thousands, and here there were only some fifty Navajos. And, Cameron could see from where he sat, those were of course tanks coming across the valley a few miles off—ten tanks and a half-track—not a bunch of foot soldiers and horsemen armed with cross-bows or whatever they were armed with in those medieval times. Centuries ago. Aside from that, though, what else was new? Men fighting men. Same old story. What had ever happened to peace in our time, and the war to end all wars or to make democracy safe forever, or to bring Roman civilization to the barbarians of Europe?

Enlightenment.

Cameron looked again at the oncoming horsemen. Slink was in the front, loping along as if his ass had grown out of the horse, just one creature now, though his right leg with the busted knee stuck out thanks to some Japanese shrapnel. How many guys had fought both the Nips and the Jerries? The horsemen were now about thirty yards away, and Cameron scanned them for familiar faces besides Slink's.

Whoa, here was something new in modern warfare—probably something new in the old wars against the Mongols too. One of the Navajos was a woman. It was that housekeeper at Raphael Luna's—Mary. Mary Yazzie. Dressed like the others. Her eyes were slits now, like all the rest, dark slits behind those high cheekbones—grim. Man alive, these people could look grim.

He flipped his hand in a quick salute as the Navajos pulled up a few feet away. The horses ducked their heads, lifted them, twisted them against the bits—nervous. A lot of hooves pawing the ground. Slink's horse danced sideways over to Cameron.

"Ready?" the big Navajo said.

"Yeah, we're all set."

Slink nodded, looked out across the valley. From here and there on the far horizon, a few tendrils of smoke still rose into the air, lit gold now.

Cameron pointed with his chin toward the woman Mary Yazzie, whose horse was nervously jerking its head up and down.

"She said Big Mexican was okay," Slink said. "They

got him in a house over at Hotevilla. Flesh wound. She said she was comin' with us."

"That's okay?" Cameron asked.

"She said she was comin' with us," Slink explained again. He smiled. "Didn't they teach you in anthropology school? Out here, this is a matriarchy. Nobody argues with a woman."

Slink turned in his saddle and looked back at the Navajos. He nodded once toward the valley, and they nudged their horses into a walk which, in a few paces, merged into lope, soon a gentle thunder descending into Beautiful Valley.

Major General Schalberg saw them come over the rise about two miles off, a large group of horsemen, no telling how many. His column was moving across the scrub at fifteen miles an hour, five tanks to either side of the half-track in a tight formation. He watched as the band of horsemen began to spread apart, steadily approaching. He could see now there were about fifty, forming a line across the desert, maybe thirty feet between each horseman, riding down at them. He gave a hand signal that sent the tanks rumbling alongside him into a slightly wider formation. The horsemen were still coming, a slow, deliberate loping.

Another hand signal, and the tanks bucked as their big cannons roared, ten shells hurtling across the distance, ten explosions of smoke and dust rising among the Indians—three horses wheeling, dropping. An old image flew into Schalberg's mind, a grainy black-and-white image of white horses, big eyes walling white, necks and heads writhing like giant snakes before the onslaught of iron. Poland, 1939. September.

The line of horsemen kept coming, the implacable, stupid single line, spread out, but now the spaces narrowing between horsemen, loping toward them.

Another hand signal, another thunderous roar of cannon,

more explosions of smoke and fire and dust, two more horsemen down, and the line drawing together, filling the spaces, riding at them, implacable, stupid . . .

Like clockwork, the half-track slowed, the tanks spread out, forming an arc, racing across the open land toward the horsemen, the tanks on the far flanks gaining speed—the arc becoming a huge mobile pincer . . . but then the horsemen wheeled, all of them, wheeled to the left and were galloping sideways across the arm of the pincer, then turned farther, racing away in retreat. Without a signal from Schalberg, the armor on his right wheeled in pursuit. The horsemen, now at full gallop, rode wildly ahead, gaining ground. Schalberg signaled again, and again the cannons fired, earth erupting amid the fleeing Indians. The ground racing past beneath them, clattering—no desert. Flat rocky ground, flat rock. Closing in, the great arms of the pincer racing forward, the backsides of the Indians and their horses now becoming individual things in Schalberg's vision, the distance narrowing, maybe fifty yards to close before the flanks could pinch in . . . what was this?

The horses, wheeling, hooves skidding, horses racing sideways. One falling. More horses racing across the tanks, across . . . out of the arms of . . . was that a woman rider . . . thrashing her horse along the edge . . . the *edge*!

Now they could see it, now it was too late and they could see it, the void opening up, the vast chasm—invisible from . . . Brakes, screaming of brakes, mechanical screams. Schalberg saw the tanks on the far flanks topple over the side, then the next . . . and the next, toppling, plummeting, disappearing . . . Schwabe shrieking, stiff arms on the wheel, feet jammed. He jammed his own feet against the floorboards, the half-track slewing, veering on the rock, red rock—*Stop!*—near tanks slowing with them, no, too late, toppling forward, vanishing, goddammit, *stop* goddammit . . .

He was alone. He had always been alone. The canyon

opened hugely, slowly, before him, a mile wide, without bottom yet, no bottom to it yet, and the half-track's wheels dropped, thunk, over the side, the body scraping, and he could see down, way down now, the canyon opening up, swirling red walls out there, green down below, beautiful green there, miniature trees and a miniature river winding, way down. It was all happening so slowly, straight down, sailing down, and there! There was a rocky promontory, something to break their fall, yes, he would hit it nose first just so, and it would break the fall ... was he going to hurtle beyond it? No, no, it would break his fall and everything would be ... he saw the white horses writhing, couldn't hear them scream, but he heard the crying, saw the tears streaming down her face, tears of pride, yes, surely this would end ...

Above Slink's head, on the rimrock, horses wheeled and clattered, men shouted. Warriors triumphant. He could almost see them through the blood. Below, his knee was screaming at him, broke again. Again. Damn. Hold on. He was holding on to the gnarled arm of a cedar, good cedar, just stay there, cedar, don't move. He didn't think he could move, but he was going to have to. He was going to have to get his other arm loose, out from under him, and get another hold on that cedar—good cedar.

Slowly he inched his arm out, heard pebbles rattle away down over the side. He didn't want to look down over the side. He wiped his face, wiped the blood out of his eyes, told his knee to stop screaming at him, reached for the branch and got it. That was easy. Easy. Easy now. Up over the side. He pulled, and the good cedar didn't give. He pulled some more, scraped his body on the rock. It was a long way down, maybe a thousand feet, to the bottom of Canyon de Chelly. Beautiful place.

He reached up with his left hand, felt his fingers grasp

the side of a fissure in the rock. He pulled himself up, got his chest over the side. There.

Now he was sitting, sitting on warm rock. Somewhere over there above him, he could hear the horses' hooves on the rimrock, men yelling, whooping. Big triumph. He wiped his eyes again.

That's a lot of blood coming, he thought, and wiped it again. He was on a shelf, maybe five, six feet below the rim of the canyon, still holding the cedar with one hand. Someone was there on the shelf, lying there, looking at him. It was that German, the big guy, the corporal. Schwabe. Was he dead? No, he was looking at him.

Slink reached down to his side and pulled out the big Colt. He wiped his eyes again, got the blood off, pointed his Colt at Schwabe.

Schwabe was up on one elbow, looking at him. Bleeding, too. His other arm looked crazy, bent that way. He was sitting up. He was saying something. Slink listened carefully.

"In another time," Schwabe was saying. "In another place." He was sitting up now, the German. One of his arms was crazy. Broken.

"You shouldn't've killed those runners," Slink said. "The messengers."

Schwabe's face went blank. "The messengers?"

"You shouldn't have killed them."

"But they were . . . they were Hopis. You're Navajo."

Slink was tired. His knee was screaming. "Indyinns. We're Indyinns. You're a white man."

Schwabe was moving his good arm. "But we're Germans. Not the Americans. We could—"

"We're Americans. You guys didn't know that?"

Schwabe's arm was still moving. Slink watched it.

"So, if we hadn't killed the runners, you wouldn't have fought us?"

I'm really tired, Slink thought. I need to lie down real bad. Go to sleep.

"Yes?" Schwabe said.

"No." The Colt leapt with the explosion, almost jumped out of his hand.

The German's face was mostly a big hole now, just pieces, and Slink watched it as it slid and bounced once and went over the ledge, followed by the man's empty hand, a big hand, red, its fingers cupped like they might have been holding something.

At 8:32 A.M. Eastern Time on May 16, 1944, the brigadier general who was military attaché to the President of the United States hung up the telephone in his tiny office in the basement of the White House, stood up, and tucked his shirttail deeper down inside his pants. He looked down at the words he had written on his yellow legal pad, the words of a telegram received five hours earlier in the new Pentagon building across the Potomac:

CALL OFF THE JUNIOR BIRDMEN STOP JERRY IS DEAD
STOP SIGNED CAMERON

The brigadier shook his head, tore the sheet from his pad and walked out of his office and down the hall to the elevator. A few moments later he stood at attention in the Oval Office before the desk of Franklin Delano Roosevelt. The great man looked tired, more so than usual, and the brigadier wondered again, as so many were wondering these days, if the President were seriously ill. Panicky rumors fluttered around the White House like heat lightning.

Sick or not, the President seemed massive enough, seated behind the desk, while the gaunt-faced Harry Hopkins, standing behind him, looked to be the fragile one of the two.

"At ease," the President said, summoning up his irresistible smile. "What have you got there? Good news, I hope."

The brigadier put the sheet of paper down on the desk. "This telegram arrived before dawn in the Pentagon, sir. From Holbrook, Arizona."

The President studied the message briefly and looked up, puzzled. "And . . . ?"

"It's over, sir. The Germans in Arizona. That lunatic invasion. It seems the Indians split the krauts and destroyed them. All of them. Evidently the Hopis took on one group, and the Navajos took the other."

"Really?" the President said, his smile broadening. Even his deeply shadowed eyes crinkled. "How extraordinary." He leaned back in his chair. "How marvelous! Eh, Harry? Thank heavens that's over."

"Maybe it isn't," Hopkins said.

"What do you mean, Harry?"

"There are about fifty thousand people out there, sir. Hopis and Navajos. They don't usually get along, they tell me. But now the two tribes cooperated on this . . . this triumph. Without any help from us."

"Yes," the President said. "Isn't that splendid? Pulling together for the war effort. Putting aside old grievances. Burying the hatchet." The President laughed, a booming sound. "Actually burying the hatchet! How marvelous!"

"What if that's not all?" Hopkins said. "They're successful. They're armed. And we're in their debt."

"Good God," the President said, his eyes widening. "What do you suppose . . . ?"

"If I were in their shoes," Hopkins said, "I'd be thinking about land."

"Land?" the President repeated.

"Arizona, for example."

"*What?* The state of Arizona? Harry, that's unthinkable!"

"I thought of it, Mr. President. Why wouldn't they?"

# ✎ FREE DRINKS ✎

Take the Del Rey® survey and get a free newsletter! Answer the questions below and we will send you complimentary copies of the DRINK (Del Rey® Ink) newsletter free for one year. Here's where you will find out all about upcoming books, read articles by top authors, artists, and editors, and get the inside scoop on your favorite books.

Age _____    Sex ❑ M ❑ F

Highest education level: ❑ high school ❑ college ❑ graduate degree

Annual income: ❑ $0-30,000 ❑ $30,001-60,000 ❑ over $60,000

Number of books you read per month: ❑ 0-2 ❑ 3-5 ❑ 6 or more

Preference: ❑ fantasy ❑ science fiction ❑ horror ❑ other fiction ❑ nonfiction

I buy books in hardcover: ❑ frequently ❑ sometimes ❑ rarely

I buy books at: ❑ superstores ❑ mall bookstores ❑ independent bookstores
❑ mail order

I read books by new authors: ❑ frequently ❑ sometimes ❑ rarely

I read comic books: ❑ frequently ❑ sometimes ❑ rarely

I watch the Sci-Fi cable TV channel: ❑ frequently ❑ sometimes ❑ rarely

I am interested in collector editions (signed by the author or illustrated):
❑ yes ❑ no ❑ maybe

I read Star Wars novels: ❑ frequently ❑ sometimes ❑ rarely

I read Star Trek novels: ❑ frequently ❑ sometimes ❑ rarely

I read the following newspapers and magazines:
| | | |
|---|---|---|
| ❑ *Analog* | ❑ *Locus* | ❑ *Popular Science* |
| ❑ *Asimov* | ❑ *Wired* | ❑ *USA Today* |
| ❑ *SF Universe* | ❑ *Realms of Fantasy* | ❑ *The New York Times* |

Check the box if you do not want your name and address shared with qualified vendors ❑

Name _____

Address _____

City/State/Zip _____

E-mail _____

page/operation shatterhand

**PLEASE SEND TO: DEL REY®/The DRINK**
**201 EAST 50TH STREET  NEW YORK  NY  10022**

# DEL REY ONLINE!

### The Del Rey Internet Newsletter...

A monthly electronic publication, posted on the Internet, GEnie, CompuServe, BIX, various BBSs, and the Panix gopher (gopher.panix.com). It features hype-free descriptions of books that are new in the stores, a list of our upcoming books, special announcements, a signing/reading/convention-attendance schedule for Del Rey authors, "In Depth" essays in which professionals in the field (authors, artists, designers, sales people, etc.) talk about their jobs in science fiction, a question-and-answer section, behind-the-scenes looks at sf publishing, and more!

**Online editorial presence**: Many of the Del Rey editors are online, on the Internet, GEnie, CompuServe, America Online, and Delphi. There is a Del Rey topic on GEnie and a Del Rey folder on America Online.

**Our official e-mail address** for Del Rey Books is delrey@randomhouse.com

### Internet information source!

A lot of Del Rey material is available to the Internet on a gopher server: all back issues and the current issue of the Del Rey Internet Newsletter, a description of the DRIN and summaries of all the issues' contents, sample chapters of upcoming or current books (readable or downloadable for free), submission requirements, mail-order information, and much more. We will be adding more items of all sorts (mostly new DRINs and sample chapters) regularly. The address of the gopher is gopher.panix.com

**Why?** We at Del Rey realize that the networks are the medium of the future. That's where you'll find us promoting our books, socializing with others in the sf field, and—most importantly—making contact and sharing information with sf readers.

**For more information, e-mail** delrey@randomhouse.com

Return to Shannara...
with the newest Terry Brooks novel—

now available in hardcover!

# FIRST KING
# OF SHANNARA

Horrified by the misuse of Magic they had
witnessed during the First War of the Races,
the Druids at Paranor devoted themselves to
the study of the old sciences, from the period
before the collapse of civilization a thousand
years earlier.

Only the Druid Bremen and a few trusted
associates still studied the arcane arts. And for
his persistence, Bremen found himself an outcast, avoided by all but the few freethinkers
among the Druids.

But Bremen soon learned that dark forces were
on the move. To defeat them, Bremen would
need a weapon, something so powerful that
the evil Magic of Brona, the Warlock Lord,
would fail its might.

FIRST KING OF SHANNARA
A Prelude to *The Sword of Shannara*
by Terry Brooks
Published by Del Rey® Books
Available in your local bookstore.